hushed HARMONY

KAYLENE WINTER

Sensitivity Statement

Dear Readers,

This story explores difficult themes with care and respect. For a complete list of content warnings, please visit my website.

Kaylene Winter

LIAM

Prologue - Present Day

I shouldn't have come.

This was the conversation I had with myself on the flight.

And again, when the taxi crossed river Liffey and the Dublin skyline came into view.

I've never been here. This is a city I've spent years avoiding. Until a few months ago, my band Fireball had never played in Ireland at all. I made sure of it. Always found a reason to avoid it.

Too many ghosts.

Too much history I wasn't ready to deal with.

A few days ago, Linus messaged.

Simple. Polite.

Linus: If you're passing through
Dublin when you're done with the
European tour, maybe let's talk.

Fuck.

I've spent what seems like a million years chasing the rockstar dream with my twin brother Padraig. Living out of vans. Crashing on floors. Putting out music. Bleeding for every gig. He should've walked years ago to follow the girl he loved. He didn't because I needed him to stay.

I live with the guilt every fucking day.

Our once-close family is a mess. After a car accident, Da turned into a bitter, misogynistic drunk. Gambled the family money. Drove the business into the ground.

Oh, and he nearly killed me.

Apparently, none of this was bad enough for my ma to leave him.

My oldest brother Connor gave up everything when the old man went down. Quit college. Took over the business. Raised the rest of my brothers like a second father. Now he's the bass player in Less Than Zero, the biggest band in the world.

This summer, he gave Fireball a much-needed boost by giving us the opening time slot on their European tour. We were able to fill in the gaps with a slew of festival gigs.

We killed it, but in true Fireball form our lead singer quit and now we're back to the fucking drawing board.

Once again, the band is teetering. Padraig won't say the words, but I see it in his eyes. He's almost out.

He's always followed my lead, trusting my determination to make us a success even when he's wanted something else. Now, we're back to square one, and he may not have it in him to continue.

I don't blame him. Without a stable front person, we're probably chasing something already dead.

The thing is, I've poured my entire life into this band and can't give up on us yet. Abandoning the only steady thing I've ever had isn't an option.

I understand loss. I've fucked my way around the world to try to quell the grief. Men. Women. Whatever would help me forget the only person I've ever given my heart to.

Linus O'Donnell.

My college love. He managed the band. Believed in us and the music when few others did. We were working our way up when his visa expired and he returned home to Ireland. I didn't ask him to stay. Fight for him when it counted.

At the time, I convinced myself I didn't deserve to have love when my brother gave up his.

I've purposely stayed away as both penance and punishment.

Until now.

Goddammit.

He's gonna break me all over again.

I'm a self-destructive motherfucker.

It's the end of the business day. I'm sitting in a café in the heart of the city, I pretend the coffee in front of me is worth drinking. The place is quiet, warm, and full of people typing or reading or staring at their phones. My leg won't stop bouncing.

The door opens.

Linus steps in, shakes off the drizzle, looks around and spots me instantly.

He glides through the room like temptation in human form. Button-down snug across his chest, sleeves rolled barely enough to expose the tattooed edges of his forearms. Slacks hug his hips like they are a custom fit. His dark hair is longer now and a thick beard covers his square jaw.

He doesn't try to be hot. He just is. My cock stiffens the second I see him.

Always has. Always will.

When he catches my eye and smiles, tentative and crooked, my stomach lurches.

I'm done for.

He walks over, calm as ever, and I stand without thinking.

"Liam."

"Hey."

He slides into the seat across from me and sets his phone face down on the table. No handshake. No small talk. Unflappable fucking composure, considering.

For an impossibly long moment, neither of us speaks.

Two grown men pretending we don't remember how it felt to share air like this. To frot our cocks together, desperate and leaking. To love each other so fiercely it nearly destroyed both of us.

He breaks first. "You look tired, so you do."

"Tour ended yesterday." I lean back and cross my arms protectively over my chest.

"Youse headin' home soon?"

"A few days." I relax a bit. "Padraig's up at Connor's new Belfast estate. Helpin' him get it ready for his famous girlfriend."

He nods. "Wow. An estate in Belfast. Sounds like a true rockstar move."

"Aye." I look out the window. It's challenging to maintain eye contact with the one man who owns you.

Silence again.

I glance at his hands. Strong. Capable. Once they explored every part of my body. "Congratulations, by the way. Seems like you're livin' the dream. Isis Management's a big deal."

"Thank you, it's doing well. Movin' operations to LA soon." He doesn't take his goddamn eyes off me. We both know we're not here to talk business.

"Avonna seems to be the magic sauce." I don't mean to bring up his client and I certainly don't mean for it to come out so sexual. Like I'm already thinking about her mouth on my cock.

But hell. I am who I am.

The woman is a fucking knockout. Voice like velvet and razorblades. The deep pain behind her eyes makes you wanna fuck her and protect her in the same breath. She played a few of the same festivals with us this summer. Lit the place on fire and walked off stage like it was routine.

She's unreal. Exactly my type.

"She is." He smirks. He knows exactly what I'm thinking. "One of the best voices I've ever heard."

"I agree." I nod too enthusiastically. "She's special."

"Aye. Special," he repeats, eyes fixed on me. "You like her."

It isn't a question.

I shift in my seat. "Well sure, she's talented."

"Not what I meant." He leans forward slightly, studying my face.

I stare into my cup. "You want honesty?"

"Always."

"Yeah. I'm attracted to her. Probably too much. We had some good chats on the road." I think back to the handful of times she and I had an opportunity to visit in between our sets.

What I don't say is, other than the man in front of me, she's the only other person I've instantly connected with on an otherworldly level.

"Do you wanna fuck her?" The words hit like a punch.

I choke on the air in my throat. "Jesus, *Linus.*"

"Do you?" His gaze doesn't waver.

I drag a hand through my hair. "Fer fuck's sake. You manage her. She's magnetic. Gorgeous. I can't be the only one."

"There's a lot more to Avonna than what men want from her." He clasps his fingers together and leans forward.

Instantly, I feel like a dick. "Uh...I know. I, uh, didn't mean..."

"Why'd you come here, Liam?" He stares into my eyes.

I hold his gaze, heart pounding. "You asked."

Emotions flicker across his face. Surprise. Relief. Pain.

I exhale. "We saw each other a few times this summer. You barely spoke to me. When you texted, I couldn't ignore it this time."

"Liam. I've reached out *dozens* of times over the years." He winces, finally showing his emotional cards. "You ignored every outreach."

"I know." I scrub my chin with my fist and cast my eyes down.

His jaw wobbles. "I thought we meant somethin'."

"We meant everything."

"You broke me." He shakes his head, more weary than angry.

The words land heavy. I don't try to deny them. "I broke me too."

The quiet between us strains with everything unsaid. Dozens of people bustle past the window. Somewhere behind the counter, an espresso machine hisses.

I meet his eyes. "I'm sorry."

"For which part?" Linus leans back and folds his arms.

"All of it."

He shakes his head. "Do you think saying sorry fixes it?"

"No."

"Then why bother?"

"It's true."

He studies me for a long time, like he's trying to find the man he used to love inside the one sitting across from him. Maybe he regrets inviting me to Dublin. Maybe he hopes I'll walk out the door and never look back.

Maybe he's daring me to stay.

"I hated you for givin' up on us," he says finally.

"I know."

He swallows. "Still do, some days."

"I deserve it."

He nods. "Aye. You do."

We sit there for another prolonged silence. Two ghosts in a city filled with history and war and heartbreak far worse than ours. I don't know what I thought this would be. Closure? Forgiveness? Maybe I wanted proof he and I were once real.

When he finally speaks again, his voice is softer. "You didn't have to come."

"I did," I insist. "You invited me."

"Curiosity isn't the same as closure." He bites his lip, probably to avoid saying more.

I call his bluff. "Well, then, why did you text?"

He holds my gaze for a long time, something shifts behind his expression.

Hurt. Longing. Restraint.

"I wanted to see if there's anything left."

"And?" My blood pressure spikes.

He arches an eyebrow. "Still figurin' it out."

We both laugh under our breath. It's not funny, but it's real.

"I've missed this," I admit.

He looks down. "Which part?"

"All of it."

This earns me the faintest smile. Gone before I can memorize it.

Outside, the rain gets heavier. Inside, it feels like we're both teetering at the edge of something we never finished. Neither of us moves to leave. Neither of us asks for more coffee.

We sit here in a buffalo stance. Two versions of the same wound.

I shouldn't have come.

But, realistically, I never had a choice

Linus thankfully changes the subject. "So. How's Padraig?"

I glance out the window. "Same. One foot in, one foot gone. He swears he's quittin' every six months, but he never does."

"Still loyal."

"Still pissed."

"At you?"

I shake my head. "At himself."

Linus watches me, unreadable. I go on. "He had everything once. A great love. Someone to grow old with. Now he's only got me and a rockstar dream he never wanted."

"Not true. He always intended on doing this with you." He nearly reaches for my hand, but visibly restrains himself.

"It's complicated," I concede. "He loves makin' music with me but doesn't enjoy the rest of it. The grind. The instability. We've lost three singers. Koko was the best of them. She lasted the longest."

Linus tilts his head. "So, it's true? Is she really gone?"

"Yep. Left after the last show." I wince. "Got a solo deal."

"Timing is terrible. You're finally on the mainstream charts." Linus furrows his brow.

"Yeah, well, she wants her own thing. Said the band didn't feel sustainable."

"Is it?"

I let out a bitter laugh. "Depends who you ask. To me, Fireball is all I've dreamed of. To Padraig, it's all he's got. Truthfully, we're taking a short break to regroup."

Linus nods slowly. "Wow. Heavy."

"Yeah."

"Will he walk away?"

"Ach, no. Probably not on his own accord." I keep my eyes fixed on Linus' strong hands before I flick my eyes up to his. "Maybe I should let him."

He doesn't answer. He doesn't have to.

Then he says, carefully, "So you're in Dublin to patch holes."

I exhale. "Aye. I suppose I am."

The shift is subtle, but I feel it. The weight of everything unsaid pulls the air tighter between us.

Things we didn't finish. Lingering feelings.

I remember the last time I touched him. Boarding pass in his hand. My heart clogged with grief. The frantic way he kissed me. Held me so tightly like he never wanted to let go.

Now we're here. The past bleeding forward, asking if we still matter.

We do.

God, we do.

I feel the tether between us. Tenser than it has any right to be.

He finishes his coffee and leans back. "I'm a few blocks away."

I nod.

He doesn't say come over. He stands, trusting I'll follow.

I do.

We walk without touching. Like our bodies are afraid of remembering too fast.

By the time we get to his building, I don't know if I want to kiss him or punch him.

Maybe both.

He opens the door, steps aside to let me in.

I cross the threshold and feel it. The weight of the years. Breath catching before something breaks.

I turn toward him.

Neither of us speaks.

It's not awkward.

It's inevitable.

One

Twelve Years Prior (Age 19)

I DIDN'T EXPECT HIM to fall asleep here.

Waking up next to a warm body beside me in my childhood bedroom wasn't on my bingo card.

Panic hits fast.

What's the guy's name? Curtis? Maybe Callum. Fuck. I wasn't paying attention.

Tall, lean, naked. Close to my age. When I saw him at the party, his eyes pinned me as though he'd already decided how the night would end. My cock agreed. I brought him home, not because it made sense.

Probably because it didn't.

My life is complicated. I've got three wee brothers in their early teens, Padraig, my twin who knows me too well, and

Connor, our older brother who stepped in when Da spiraled into pain-killer and alcohol addiction after a car accident. Ma's busy taking care of him, so all of the family activities we used to enjoy have fallen by the wayside.

Truth be told, Connor's held the whole family together for the past couple years. He gave up his own college dreams to make sure all of us finished school. He's financing me and Padraig's college education. Yet, somehow, it always feels like we're on the edge of disaster.

Fuck. I don't know what I was thinking bringing my sex life into this house. I'm smarter than this. I've gotta get this bloke outta here before Da wakes up. It's tough to know how he'll react if he realizes I enjoy cock on occasion.

Nah, it'd blow his addicted mind.

Anyway, sure enough, my phone buzzes with a new text from Padraig. He's downstairs making breakfast for Seamus, Cillian, and Brennan. Fuck.

"You gotta go." I pull on a pair of sweats. "The family's awake."

I scrub a hand over my face and type fast to my twin.

```
        Me: WTF? Can you cover for me?
```

Padraig replies before I can blink.

```
    Padraig: All good. Coast's clear if you
    take the front stairs.
```

I nod at Curtis-Callum, who's mostly dressed. He doesn't say much, which is preferable. He was good with his hands and generous with his mouth. Better than I usually get in the small bum-fuck town where I go to college. I slip on my T-shirt as we leave the room. I motion toward the front stairs. "This way."

We step into the hall. The floorboards creak so fucking loud I swear they're trying to sell me out. I wince and hurry him forward.

Curtis-Callum tries to slip on his hoodie, then freezes at a drunken voice behind us.

"Who the fuck's are youse?"

My da's voice slices through the air like a rusted knife. Slurred. Furious. Full of whiskey before it's even breakfast.

I close my eyes. *Shit.* "Leave it, Da. It's my business."

I hear the scraping of his plastic knee brace dragging across the floor. Curtis-Callum stiffens behind me, hoodie half-on, shrinking toward the staircase like he could disappear if he moves slow enough.

I step forward, planting myself in front of him. Protecting him? Or baiting Da?

I don't even fucking know.

"This is my feckin' house, you wee bastard," Da bellows. "Your business is my business. Who is he?"

Curtis-Callum retreats a step. I stand taller.

"Leave him be. Let's go."

He starts to descend.

"Jesus, Mary, and feckin' Joseph, my son's a feckin' poof."

I bite back bile.

Curtis-Callum leaps down the stairs two at a time and bolts out the front door, squawking, "Jesus, is your dad homophobic?!"

No time to answer. Da's hand hits my shoulder. Clamps down like a trap.

I lock up. Since the accident, every bottle turns him mean. His Irish lilt is full of venom, scarily prejudicial. I swear to fuck he wants to purge me from his bloodline.

No matter how much I try to ignore him, his words hit bone every time. No lead-up. No signal. Only impact.

"You dirty wee pansy," he hisses into my ear. "Is this what you are now, a faggot? Bringin' men into my house? Under your ma's roof? Corrupting your wee brothers?"

Yup. His words eviscerate me more than his fists ever could. But I don't flinch.

I won't.

Instead I give it back to the bastard. "Go back to your room and pass out, you useless cunt."

He moves fast. Reeking of whiskey, sweat, and rot. His eyes are yellowed. Wild.

"You fuckin' shame me," he snarls. "I break my back for this family, and you're in my house suckin' cock like it's a badge of pride?!"

Suddenly I see a flash of movement behind me.

"Stop." Padraig's climbing the stairs. "Let him leave. You're drunk. You don't mean it."

Da turns. His gaze locks on Padraig. His rage deepens.

"Don't you feckin' defend him."

"I'm not—"

The sound of the slap is louder than the shout. I see Padraig's head whip sideways. I move, but not fast enough.

"*Padraig*!" Seamus's voice pierces the chaos.

Everything spins.

Da isn't finished. He swings again. Misses. This time, it's meant for me.

"You gonna hit me too, Da?" I spit, full of venom. "Try it."

"You're not my son."

Then his fist flies.

It's not a punch. It's a fucking wrecking ball.

I don't remember the moment it lands. Only the fall. The sound of it. My body slamming down the stairs. Each thump another betrayal. Boots scraping. Elbow cracking. Skull bouncing.

The world blinks out.

I hear voices. Distant. Warped.

"Liam," someone says. "Hey. Look at me."

Padraig.

Nothing. I'm floating.

A grunt rips out of me. My throat's raw.

My eyes fight me, but I open them.

Everything is haze.

"There," someone breathes—Cillian? "He's okay, right?"

"I don't know," Padraig says. "Dar. Can you move your arms? Legs?"

I try.

Fingers twitch. Ankles flex. I groan. "*Fuck.*"

"You scared the shit out of us." Padraig squats next to me.

"I feel like I got tackled by one of Connor's football teammates," I mumble. "Help me up."

"Not yet," Seamus warns, panicked. "You're not supposed to—"

"I'm fine," I lie. My voice is hoarse. Broken.

Padraig slides an arm behind me. Cillian's on the other side.

"Careful," he murmurs. "Tell me if it hurts too much."

It *all* fucking hurts so I say nothing. I let them lift me. *Excruciating.* I lean against my twin, body sagging like it forgot how to hold weight.

"Let's get downstairs, lads." Padraig gestures to the younger brothers.

Thank fuck. The basement is our rehearsal space. Dank concrete floor, sagging ceiling, rugs and egg cartons slapped up to kill the echo. Cables everywhere. Padraig's kit in the corner. Mic and guitar stands against the walls.

The only place in this goddamn house where I can be myself.

We make it down step by step. Brennan ushers Seamus ahead. Padraig and Cillian lower me onto the beat-up couch. I clench my teeth in agony. Seamus brings a towel and an ice pack. Doesn't speak. Padraig presses it to my temple. I wince.

"Fuck. *Hurts*."

Seamus curls in the corner. Brennan vanishes behind his laptop. Cillian stares at the wall.

Padraig's face is wracked with guilt. "I'm sorry."

I arch an eyebrow. "For what?"

"Not getting there sooner."

"You tried."

Padraig's the only one who knows me. The real me. Even he doesn't know how deep this goes.

"He looked at me like I was filth," I whisper so the wee lads can't hear. "I told you he fucking hates me for being into guys."

"You're not filth." Padraig shakes his head.

"He thinks I am," I correct him. "Part of me understands. I want to be with women. I want to be with men. How am I supposed to choose? How will I ever have what you and Stevie have?"

Padraig doesn't answer right away. Stevie is his soulmate. He's loved her since he was a kid.

"Da doesn't get to have an opinion about you." He slumps down to the floor. "Not ever again. You're allowed to be yourself without worrying about him."

I close my eyes. Let the cold bite of the ice numb the pain.

Thankfully, we don't talk. Not for a while.

Eventually, I sit up. Arms crossed, body aching. "Fuck this mopey bullshit. I wanna play."

"No. You're concussed." Seamus pops up and tries to keep me from picking up my guitar.

"Ah, I'm grand, wee one." I muss Seamus's hair and push to my feet.

The amp crackles. Strings tremble beneath my fingers. One chord. Two.

Then I fall into it.

Padraig gets behind his kit, counts us in with his sticks.

My face might be a mess and my ribs might ache like a motherfucker, but my guitar is home.

We play until the walls forget what happened.

It's the only way I know I'm still alive.

Two

Six Months Later (Age 15)

THE CHAPEL IS COLDER than usual.

Even with the spring dusk curling in, the stone floor feels like it's storing winter deep in its bones. My fingers are still buzzing from the last hymn as I slide my guitar into the cupboard behind the pulpit, careful not to let the latch click too loud. The cloth covering it smells faintly of must. I always tuck it here, as if hiding it might keep the instrument mine a little longer.

As far as I know, no one's still here but me.

The rest of the children filed out after service, heads bowed, arms full of shawls and dish pails and younger siblings. I linger like I always do, enjoying the only moment of peace and silence I'll have today.

I should go. Mother will be watching the horizon, waiting for me to bring water, start the fire, wash the basins. My youngest sister has obedience recitations to learn, and I'm expected to correct her.

Moving through the side corridor toward the exit, I count the steps. My feet know the rhythm of the stones. Left. Left. Right. Avoid the loose creaky board. Pass the old baptismal closet—

I freeze.

Three low voices. Male. Familiar. One sends a chill straight through me.

Master Prophet.

The door is ajar. Not wide. But enough.

Light spills out, pooling across the hallway stones like something alive. I don't move a muscle. I have no desire to eavesdrop but if they catch me, a beating will follow.

I have no choice but to hide.

Dropping to the ground, I crouch behind the door.

"She's getting too old," says one voice, an Elder. "Should've been matched last year. She's fifteen now. Should've borne a child by now."

"She sings like she wants to be coveted," says another Elder. "She's dangerous."

"The girl is too free," a third voice rings out. Master Prophet. Calm. Measured. "The Lord gave her beauty and melody. He did not create her for accolades. A girl who draws attention to herself is a girl in danger of believing she deserves it."

Everything about their tone turns my stomach.

They're talking about me.

There's no mistaking it.

"She has too much freedom," says the first voice. "She lingers after service. Wanders the yard without supervision when she thinks no one is watching."

"She's not promised," the second man says, as if it's an accusation. "The girls her age are already settled."

Master Prophet responds, "Her spirit is expanding too far. The Lord is clear: A woman's shape is not her own. It must be molded. Declared. Taught how to serve."

Cold slithers through me. Ice water under my ribs.

"She's a beautiful girl," one of them says. "Untouched. Best to get her under control before the rebellion becomes intolerable."

"I fear we're too late. She'll resist what we have planned."

Master Prophet's voice is absolute. "She won't have a choice."

Then silence. A pause long enough to make my heart stutter.

"Brother Gideon has petitioned."

It's all I can do not to shriek.

"He's faithful," says another. "Obedient. Strong."

"His contributions entitle him to a young wife," adds the Prophet. "The Lord makes provisions for a faithful devout like Brother Gideon."

"He's been waiting for a few years," someone murmurs. "His other wives are now barren."

"All flowers begin with man's seed," Master Prophet continues. "They don't flourish until they're planted. She'll bloom in his hands."

Laughter follows. Dry. Knowing.

My knees want to give out. I lean against the wall, heart slamming.

I don't know exactly what they're implying, but I know this.

They do not consider me a person.

I'm being traded.

They speak of obedience, dowry, lineage, his home near the western edge of the compound. Close to the boundary wall, where no girl wants to live. Too isolated. Too far from the chapel. Too close to the men's bunkhouse.

"She's not yet broken," one of the men says. "She still walks with too much pep."

"Brother Gideon will drive it out of her," Master Prophet assures him. "As the Lord desires."

I nearly throw up.

One of them asks, "Will her parents agree?"

"It isn't up to them. They'll be brought into alignment," Master Prophet replies. "Brother Gideon has made an offering large enough to ensure their cooperation."

"And the girl?"

"She'll be guided," he says. "There will be prayers. A laying on of hands. She will be made to see this is her role. Her salvation."

A pause.

"On her birthday she'll be betrothed," he commands. "She's clever. Not clever enough to outrun purpose."

Without giving it another thought, I back away from the door. My legs feel wrong. I'm not sure how I move, but I know I need to get out. *Now.* I need air. I need to run. The chapel doors swing wide. I stumble into the dusk, the world bathed in lavender shadows and ash-colored dust.

The compound looks the same. But it isn't.

Every outline is sharper now. The fences. The smoke curling from chimneys. The goats bleating in the distance. I see the tin roofs for what they are. Cages. I see the path back to my family's home. A funnel to hell.

I have nowhere else to go, though. Women walk past me, arms full of laundry or babies or bread pans. No one looks up. No one ever does.

Inside my family's home, it's too warm. My sisters argue over a piece of dried fruit. Mother slices onions with mechanical focus. My father hasn't returned from the barn. I curl up on my sleeping mat like a child, face to the wall. My breath shudders unevenly.

I think about Master Prophet's words.

She will bloom in his hands.

All flowers begin with man's seed.

My stomach heaves. I shove my fist into my mouth to keep the sound in. I don't understand what's coming. Not fully. Enough to know my name has been offered, my body is not my own, and I have no say.

I lie there long after Mother whispers evening prayers and my sisters drift into soft, safe dreams. I replay their voices.

A girl who draws attention to herself is a girl in danger of believing she deserves it.

She will be made to see this is her role.

She'll understand her purpose.

Brother Gideon is old and strange with empty and claw-like hands. He's always watching me when I sing at Sunday service.

My body curls into itself, muscles aching from holding it all in.

No one asked if I wanted this.

No one ever will.

Three

LINUS

Six Months Later (Age 19)

THE SUN DIPPED THREE hours ago.

I'm still sweating.

Everywhere's too hot. The tiled walkway under my sandals, the back of my neck, the inside of my chest.

"Go for a swim." Da shooed me out of our caravan. Told me I've no reason to be irritable.

He hasn't a clue. I've been holding my breath for three days straight for an opportunity like this. I cut left through the garden path behind the main lodge, pretending I'm taking a walk to clear my head.

Really, I'm hunting.

I saw him again today. Ripped. Blond. Tank top stretched over his chest like sin itself. A jawline sharp enough to cut glass. He's been here with his family since Monday, same as us. I clocked him straightaway.

In the dining room, his eyes follow mine. Lips quirk into a smirk every time we're at the pool.

He *knows*. He's patient. Waits for me get the courage to find him.

Now's my chance and every part of me is on fire.

This morning, my parents ambushed me over breakfast. Instead of enjoying my juice, croissant and tea, I had to endure a whole lotta shit. Mum pulled out the pamphlet Niamh gave her of a wedding venue she loves in County Clare. Seaside views. Seating for two hundred.

"You'll be twenty in a year," Da reminded me like I'd forgotten. "It's time to think seriously about your future. Niamh's a great wee girl. Lock her down, son."

They didn't take the news well when I told them I've been accepted into the hospitality program at Washington State University and my plan is to leave in the fall.

Mum gasped like I'd slapped her. "You applied without telling us?"

Da didn't raise his voice, not in public. His silence was worse. Thin-lipped fury.

"Why would you go to America?" he shouted once we made it back to the caravan. "You've a good job in Dublin. You've a future here. Niamh's father lined up a proper path for you."

I reminded them I've worked for Brian Callahan's booking agency, Tri-Color Tours, for two years already and done every job he's thrown at me. Booking, logistics, artist relations. Every music festival in Ireland, every goddamn late night. Every grunt job possible.

It's not enough for me. Brian's way of doing business isn't sustainable. I won't have a future there unless it ends with a house in Dun Laoghaire and a ring on Niamh's finger.

No one in my life knows I've been questioning everything about myself.

I can't marry a woman when I have dreams about different hands on my skin. Rougher. Broader. Stronger.

Guess I'm about to find out if there's something to them.

Alone in the dark, sweat under my collar, I'm half-hard as I nervously edge through the resort garden like some fucked-up fairytale. I should turn back.

I don't.

Around the bend, I see him. Leaning against the stone wall near the gym, one foot propped on the wall. His body glows silver in the moonlight.

"You lost?" His lips curl into a smile when he sees me.

My throat's dry. "No."

"Good." He flicks the cigarette to the ground. "Been watchin' you watch me."

"Didn't think you noticed." My cock's rigid as steel.

He shakes out his hair. "Took you long enough to come find me."

I glance back toward the resort. Stupid instinct. No one's around.

"Am I blowing you or are you just gonna stand there?" He whips off his T-shirt.

His chest catches the light, smooth and sculpted. Sublime. I want to put my mouth on him. Taste the heat on his skin. Trace every line with my tongue to memorize it before he disappears.

He comes forward and cups my face like we've done this before. No hesitation. His mouth crashes into mine, hot and assertive. My back hits the wall before I can breathe.

It's not like kissing Niamh. She's soft, familiar. He's stubble and danger.

My cock is fully on board.

His hand slides to my chest. Then my stomach. Then my belt.

I tense. "Wait."

"I want to suck your cock. Tell me to wait again and I'm outta here." His mouth finds my ear.

I shut the fuck up. He undoes my belt, pushes my shorts down with a quiet authority. There's no room for shame. My head lolls back, dizzy with want.

"I've never—" I start.

He drops to his knees like it's nothing. Like kneeling for me is natural. "First time?"

I shake my head.

"By a bloke?" He licks his lips. When I barely nod, he grips my base. "Don't worry. I'll make it good."

I freeze. Not from fear, from impact. Every part of me lights up. A hit straight to the chest. This is something I've needed and buried. He stares up at me with parted lips and steady hands.

When his mouth takes me in, no hesitation, I fucking break.

I rasp before I mean to. Can't stop it. Won't try.

His tongue traces the underside of my cock like he's reading me. Like he *knows*.

Of course he does. He's built like me. Niahm's no slouch in the blowjob department, but this isn't about comparison. It's addition. This guy is showing me how a man uses his mouth on another man.

A different kind of pleasure.

My hands scramble for something. His shoulders, the wall, I don't know. I'm off-balance, overstimulated. Not in control. I don't want to be.

His tongue swirls around my crown. One hand steadies me at the hip, the other cradles and rolls my balls like he already knows what'll make me beg. Without warning he engulfs my entire cock and lets me slide down his throat.

"*Nnnnnghhhh,*" I gasp.

He groans low, allowing the vibration to shoot through me. My hips jerk. He takes all of it. Every stifled part of me.

I've gone my whole life pretending I could live without this. I can't. Not now. Not ever. This man fucks me with his mouth like he means to undo me.

I let him.

The roar tears out of me when I come. My orgasm hits like a fault line splitting open. Shaking, I spill into his mouth. My, heart pounds like thunder, drowning out the sound of my breath.

I don't know if I've fallen or if he's still holding me up.

He swallows. Licks his lips. Stands.

"See?" he says. "Easy. Gotta go."

He kisses me on the lips. I taste myself. Then he disappears into the dark. I'm left half-dressed, stunned. Cock still leaking. My heart rattles like a snare drum.

Holy fuck.

I pull my shorts back up and stumble toward the path. Everything's different. I sit on a bench by the pool, head in my hands, letting the night breeze cool down my sweat.

I've cheated on my girlfriend. Not emotionally. Not with love. I was exploring a truth I've never dared say out loud.

A truth no one will ever understand.

Certainly not my parents.

God help me, I love the way Niamh feels under me. Her curves. Her scent. The way her mouth goes slack when she comes. I love her. Love fucking her. I've never faked it. Never needed to.

She doesn't have all of me, though. Especially not the part of me I've spent years trying to ignore. The part dreaming of a man fucking me. Of me doing the same to him.

For years I tried to convince myself it was a phase. A kink. A thing to push down.

It never went away.

Tonight, I finally gave in. Let it happen. I needed to know if the wanting was real or if it was some idea I'd built up in my head.

Now I know. It wasn't a fluke. It wasn't a mistake.

It was right.

I shouldn't have done it without breaking it off with Niamh, though. I can't continue to lie to someone who trusts me with her whole heart. I love her. I do.

My family won't understand. Neither will hers.

It's best I leave. Take space to figure out who I am when I stop pretending.

Somewhere I can explore my sexuality without guilt bleeding into every touch.

I'm going to America.

Where I can finally stop hiding.

Four

LIAM

Two Weeks Later

SOMETHING ABOUT A LONG span of highway is calming for me.

The way distance builds between your actual life and the possibility of something better. Especially when the light is strange, caught between day and night.

I guess I like it when things feel temporary. No one expects anything from me, which is good.

I don't have much to give.

Padraig drives, both hands on the wheel. Calm. Steady.

He's always steady. My opposite twin.

Wind whooshes through the half-open window, whipping my hair into my mouth. I tap my foot against the floorboard, chasing a rhythm in my head. Something fast. Angry. A beat to keep me from thinking too much.

"She texted yet?" I ask about his girlfriend, Stevie, who's back home in Seattle for the summer. I don't like it when Padraig's sad and he never likes to be separated from her, even for a minute.

"Aye." He doesn't look at me. "Said her mom nearly cried when she walked in. She'll check on Ma and the wee lads tomorrow."

"How long's she staying?"

"A few weeks."

I stare at the road ahead, trying not to seem elated. "So it's the two of us for a while?"

"Aye."

Our eyes meet for half a breath. Then he looks back at the road.

I try again. "Dar, I'm glad we have some time. It's been years, you realize."

He doesn't answer.

"All I'm saying is there isn't any part of us she isn't part of anymore." The words come out sharper than I mean.

Truth always sounds like an accusation when it's been festering.

He shifts in his seat. "You're not being fair."

"No? Tell me. Why exactly are we checking this singer out if you're gonna choose Stevie over me and the band in the long run?"

"What the fuck?" He turns, confused. "Do you have something you need to say?"

I might as well get it off my chest. "Stevie isn't into the band stuff for the long haul. Do you not listen to her?"

His mouth sets in a thin line. I'm right, and he knows it. Even if he doesn't want to believe it.

I don't hate Stevie. I never could. She's sunshine in human form. Our next-door neighbor and childhood friend turned twin's lover. She's believed in our band from the beginning.

On the other hand, she's Padraig's gravity. I'm watching him orbit further away from me every day and I already have plans.

Big plans.

"I don't wanna create music with anyone else, Dar," I tell him. "I'm gonna do it no matter what. With or without you."

He gives me a look. Part hurt, part pity. "Jesus fuckin' Christ. What's gotten into you?"

"You don't even notice I haven't been around much," I mutter. "At least you haven't said anything."

He stiffens. Guilt flickers behind his eyes, but he doesn't apologize.

"See," I say. "She's the most important thing to you. Not school. Not me. Not Fireball."

Padraig grips the wheel. "Stevie doesn't take me from you. She fills something else."

"No, you fill her. Ten times a day. Trust me. I'm in the next bed. Can't fuckin' wait to get out of the dorm room."

His voice sharpens. "Don't be a dick. She's one of your best friends. She's the woman I love. I won't continue this conversation if you disrespect my relationship."

"Fer fuck's sake," I mutter. "I didn't mean it as a shot. I'm not pissed. I'm realistic."

Padraig keeps his eyes on the road for a while. Like if he stares long enough, he won't have to continue the conversation.

"Look, I noticed," he says finally. "I figured you needed space."

I laugh bitterly. "Yeah. Well…"

"You could've said something."

"Say what, Dar?" I look out the window. The sky's bleeding into a gray space where day turns useless. "I fucking detest being an extra body you keep around."

"C'mon. You're actin' a maggot."

"No, it's true. You and Stevie are so close, I'm starting to feel like a shadow in my own fucking space. Every night I'm in the corner trying not to choke on it."

Padraig doesn't flinch.

"I want what you have," I admit. "But, it's never gonna happen for me. I've spent the last couple of years trying to figure it all out. I've tried fucking the shame out. Campus, clubs, whoever will have me. It doesn't answer any questions."

The words are sharp in my mouth, but I don't pull back. "I don't know how to build anything lasting. I don't trust myself to stay faithful."

I look at him. He's quiet. Listening carefully.

"You and Stevie make it look easy. I'm not saying it's perfect, I know it's not. It's close, though. I see the way you look at her like she's home. I see the way she lets you in..." I pause. "But, she's not going to tour with us. You hope she'll change her mind. She won't. It's going to hurt. I'm scared you don't see how much."

Padraig's fingers flex on the wheel. "She loves me. She's not going anywhere."

"I hope you're right."

We sit in silence, which I can't stand.

"Fuck, I'm not jealous," I blurt. "I'm *lonely*. I watch you build something and all I can think about is how I don't even know how to start."

"You start by being honest."

"I'm trying." I slouch down in the seat. "It's tough when everything you want feels wrong."

"You're not broken." He palms my shoulder.

"I don't want to be the one always leaving. I want to stop feeling like a mistake." I look down at the floor.

Padraig slides his hand up to the back of my neck, warm and steady. "No matter what happens, Dar. I've always got you."

I don't know what to say. I don't know if I believe him.

He sighs. "I promise, you've got me."

"Not all of you." The words slide out before I can stop them. I look out the window, the fading light unfolding across the hood of the truck. "Don't you think you're too serious? I heard you and her whispering about fuckin' marriage. You're twenty, for God's sake."

"Not for a few years. Jesus." He rolls his eyes.

I laugh under my breath. "Don't feckin' lie to me or yourself."

He doesn't argue. He doesn't have to.

I can see it written across his face. The way he looks when she texts. How he melts into goo when he says her name. He's already gone and I can't let him leave.

I need the band.

Fireball is the only thing keeping me going anymore.

Padraig flips on the headlights as the sky deepens to indigo.

"Would you choose her if she gave you an ultimatum? I deserve to know."

"I don't want to choose," he says.

I turn away. "Well, I guess we'll see."

We've arrived in Spokane. The Big Dipper's neon flickers ahead. We park in the lot and reality sets in.

Inside, it's either a new start. Or another disaster. Probably both

We've got no lead singer. No time to find one and be ready for the new school year. We're here following some rumor from a stage tech about a girl with a voice so special the sound isn't coming from her, but through her.

Inside the venue, the floor's tacky with old beer and other unrecognizable fluids. Bad lighting. Musty smells. Patrons don't look up. Until she walks on stage.

She doesn't even have to say her name.

Felicity.

I feel her presence like a blade against my ribs.

She takes the mic like it's a secret only she knows. Her eyes catch the light, and I swear she notices me immediately. Not Padraig. Not the crowd.

Me.

When her mouth falls open, the room doesn't fall silent, it leans in. Every man gapes. Every woman stares.

I forget everything I was brooding about.

The band behind her fades into wallpaper. The tech was right, her voice is the only thing worth paying attention to. Smoky, jagged, sweet with teeth. She could pour gasoline on a torch and still make it sound like a lullaby.

I'm already picturing her on stage singing our songs. I imagine pulling her backstage, my fingers wound around her hair as I bend her over an amp and fuck her. No foreplay. No questions. Heat and sweat and beautiful, broken cries when my cock bottoms out over and over again.

She'll hate me for it. Then beg for more.

I don't even pretend it won't ruin everything. I can already see Padraig's face. Tight-lipped, disappointed. He's probably picturing how her voice blends with ours, how she'll look on a poster. Her and Stevie getting facials together.

Me? I know better. This woman isn't made for spa treatments.

She's going to ruin us and we'll let her.

It'll be worth it.

I want the chaos. The destruction. I want to bleed for something to make me feel again. She's it. Her voice, her body, the way her eyes slice through the crowd and pin me to the wall. This is what I've been chasing for years.

She's also what Fireball is missing.

Felicity finishes the song.

Padraig leans in, whispering something about tone and control and how perfect she is.

He's right.

We're going to bring her into the band.
I'm going to fuck her.
It's all going to burn.

Five

AVONNA

One Month Later

MASTER PROPHET'S CARRIAGE ROLLS through the compound on a windless afternoon.

The dust doesn't rise, it hangs in the air like judgment suspended.

Everyone stops to watch, even those who pretend not to. A bucket clangs against a well stone. A baby starts to cry and is shushed. No one speaks or moves unless they're spoken to.

He steps out first. White robes, dark boots, the weight of his authority carved into every movement.

Brother Gideon follows.

His bones creak. His beard is long and uneven. He limps from an old knee injury, but stands tall when he spots our door.

Everyone in our village knows what they're here for.

Me.

After Mother tidied the house this morning, she laid a new blue dress across my sleeping mat. The only new piece of clothing I've ever worn. When she braided my hair, my sisters all watched with wide eyes. She didn't speak to me at all, let alone tell me what was happening.

Why would she? In my religion, a woman's life is not her own.

They're here to assert ownership over me. I huddle behind the curtain separating the front room from the kitchen and watch as my father opens the front door. The Elders enter and chairs scrape as they sit down.

"Thank you for welcoming us into your home." Master Prophet's tone is commanding. "We've come to confirm what has been ordained. Brother Gideon has chosen your eldest."

I close my eyes, trembling. I knew it was true, but hearing the actual words is devastating.

Mother shoves me from behind the curtain, "Go on now."

I stumble into the room.

The blue dress hangs awkwardly on my frame, too snug in the shoulders, too short at the ankles. My shoes are scuffed. My hands won't stop shaking.

"Turn," demands Master Prophet, not gently.

I obey.

The group of men circle me like I'm a calf being weaned.

"She's small," Gideon says. "But not too small."

"She'll grow into the role," Master Prophet answers. "Her voice will soften with obedience. Her inner light is strong, but unshaped. This is the husband's duty."

Gideon's eyes move down my arms, to my hands.

"She's a worker," he speaks to the other men as though I'm not there. "Good hips. Hands like a farmer's daughter. She'll carry."

My skin goes cold. I fix my gaze on the wall above the Prophet's head, willing myself not to cry.

"Any signs of rebellion?" Master Prophet narrows his eyes.

My father answers, "She sings too freely. Questions too much."

"She won't once I'm done with her." Gideon smiles wickedly. "Silence and obedience are virtues."

He touches my chin. Tilts it upward.

"She's got a pretty face. Shame to see her prideful."

Mother says nothing.

I meet his yellowing eyes and hold his gaze for a second. Then I look away.

It's over. I'm done for.

When they leave, the house falls silent except for a wind rattling the windows like the bones of something long buried.

"I won't marry him," I vow.

No one looks at me.

"You've been chosen." Mother begins to busy herself with house chores.

"I don't care."

My father stands forebodingly. "You'll do what you're told."

"No." My throat closes. "He's old."

"Daughter." Mother grips my arm. "You don't have the luxury of preference."

"I don't belong to him."

"You don't belong to yourself," Father says.

The words split me open.

"I don't want to be property," I whisper.

The slap knocks the air from my lungs. My head snaps sideways. My cheek burns. I blink to find the room tilting.

"Enough." Father raises his hand to strike again. "You *shame* us."

"I won't do it," I say again.

He grabs my arm. Mother doesn't intervene. He drags me toward the pantry room.

I fight, but I'm not strong enough. The door slams shut behind me. A bolt locks into place.

Darkness.

The air is thick with the smell of onions, stored grain, and old soap. I scream. Shriek until my throat shreds.

No one comes.

I pound on the door with both fists. "Let me out!"

I claw at the wood. I sob. I beg.

I yelp again. Until I can't.

Time passes differently in the dark. There's no light except a sliver under the door. Sometimes I hear footsteps. A cup of water appears once. Then a heel of bread. Then nothing.

I think about Master Prophet's voice and become determined.

They will not shape me.

Over the next few days, the dark becomes familiar. I begin to count breaths. Sing to myself in a whisper, notes and melodies flow through my body. I feel them in my chest, in my bones.

My name becomes a prayer. I press my hands together and promise:

I will not belong to them.

I will not marry Gideon.

I will get out.

When the door finally opens however many days later, my eyes sting as they adjust to the light.

Mother stands there. Pale. Empty. "Have you calmed?"

I nod.

She thinks my acknowledgement means surrender.

It doesn't. Inside me, something sharp has taken root. Something permanent.
Not rage. Not fear.
Resolve.
They want me quiet so I'll be quiet.
Careful.
They want me small, so I'll be smaller than a speck of dirt.
Invisible.
One night soon...I will disappear.

Six

LINUS

Two Weeks Later

THE GIG WRAPS LATE.

The lads in the band are already half-pissed when we lock up the venue, tossing thank-yous like confetti as they disappear into the neon-soaked streets of Galway.

Niamh and I handle the settlement ourselves. Her on invoices. Me on gear logistics. It's our dynamic. Has been since we were sixteen. She handles the front of house, I take care of the backstage chaos.

Her da says we're the perfect pair.

No. I'm a fraud. Living someone else's life.

We walk back to the hotel in silence, her fingers curled into the crook of my elbow. There's nothing wrong on the surface.

The gig went off without a hitch, the band is thrilled, her da will be pleased with the money they made.

My stomach is in perpetual knots.

Inside the hotel room, the lights are soft. Niamh kicks off her boots and flops onto the bed. I watch her slide down her leggings and undo the top button of her blouse, lips parted, pupils dilated. She's still buzzing from the high of a good show, and a couple of gin and tonics.

"You've been weird all night." She shrugs off her top and undoes her bra. Plumps up her tits and rolls her brown nipples into points.

"I'm tired." I avert my eyes and shrug off my jacket.

"Linus." She narrows her eyes. "Don't lie to me."

I undress down to my boxer briefs and sit beside her. She leans over and kisses me. Her tongue traces the inside of my mouth like she's done a million times before. My hands find her waist by muscle memory. Her body is familiar, comforting. I've loved her for years.

She grabs between my legs. I'm flaccid.

"Seriously?" She pulls back. "We haven't fucked since you got back from holiday two months ago. You talked a big game at the merch table this afternoon."

"I know. I said I was tired."

"Is it me?"

"No. Fuck, Niamh. It's not."

Determined to prove something, I cup her breasts. She arches into my touch. Gasps when I pinch her nipple. I trail kisses down her stomach, tongue flicking over her navel as I nudge her thighs apart.

She's already wet.

Pulling Niamh's panties to the side, I go down on her. She writhes and clutches at my hair. I know every inch of her. Exactly how she likes her pussy licked. This is the least I can do. Her legs shake when she comes.

When she tugs me up and slides her hand into my boxers, she discovers I'm still only half-hard. Not even.

"Jesus, Linus."

"I'm sorry."

Her hand works me, lips brushing my ear. "Do you want me?"

"Aye."

"Prove it."

I nod, mouth dry. She pushes me onto my back, swings a leg over, and kisses down my chest. Her mouth is warm and soft. She yanks down my briefs to my knees, takes me down her throat. No hesitation. No gag.

It does the trick. My cock springs to life.

When she climbs on top of me and sinks down, my erection lasts maybe a minute before I start to go soft inside her. Her brow furrows.

"What the fuck," she snaps, climbing off. "You're not even trying."

"I *am* trying."

"Then what is it?"

I sit up, heart thudding. I've been carrying this for weeks. Swallowed it like glass and let it shred my insides. Now my secret is pushing its way out, jagged and burning.

"There was someone else."

Silence. Niamh's shoulders go still. She scrambles off me. "You *cheated* on me?"

I nod.

Niamh opens her mouth like she's going to speak, then stops.

Thinks on it then blurts, "Was it a girl?"

Her question takes me by surprise.

I shake my head.

She stares at me. No yelling. No confusion. No collapse.

Her face stays still, but there's something in her eyes. Sharp. Unreadable.

"Jesus fucking *Christ.*"

In this moment, I realize she must have suspected long before I ever admitted it to myself. I never lied to her about how I felt. I love her. I still do. I can't help it if there's something inside me I don't fully understand. Buried too deep to touch without setting off alarms.

Part of me wonders if she's been waiting for this moment to ask questions she doesn't want answers to. Not to punish me. Maybe to punish herself.

I take her hand. "I didn't plan it."

"Oh, well. Makes the news so much better." She sniffs, "When?"

"On holiday—"

She holds up a hand. "Oh, so you fucked a guy in Greece? Well, that explains it."

I nod again.

"I knew you were acting off when you came home." Niamh pulls her hand away.

"Well, we didn't fuck, though. He gave me a blowjob," I explain. "It was only the once."

"Oh, brilliant. No big deal."

I wince. "It didn't mean anything."

"Linus." She shakes her head. "*So. Much. Worse.*" Niamh paces now. Her chest heaves with hurt and anger. "So you're *gay?*"

"No," I answer too quickly. "I'm not. I'm attracted to women too. Obviously."

"*Obviously?* Linus. One wee blowjob from a random bloke has killed your sex drive for me. Are you fuckin' serious?"

My silence doesn't help.

She shakes her head, tears forming in her eyes. "I thought we were solid."

"I'm sorry."

"Are you sure you still want me?" Niamh's voice is vulnerable. Sad.

"Yes."

"Then prove it."

Niamh charges forward and pushes me back onto the bed. Climbs over me, wrapping her hand around my cock. Strokes me fast. Rough. Once I get the beginnings of an erection, she straddles me again, riding me like she's trying to erase everything I told her.

I grip her hips. Watch her tits bounce as she fucks me. To stay with it, I fantasize about the man. The way his lips worked my cock. How he knew what I needed before I did.

Niamh comes. I manage to ejaculate too, not sure if it's from her or the memory of the guy's mouth on me. Either way, it proves...something.

She collapses beside me. Neither of us says anything for a while.

After a long silence, she strokes my chest. "I forgive you."

I stare at the ceiling.

"I don't know if I want to be forgiven."

"If you're not gay," she pulls the covers around us, "we can move forward."

"I don't know what I am."

"I love you."

"I love you too."

It's true. Unfortunately, it's not enough. There's more I haven't told her yet and when I do, she'll withdraw her forgiveness.

When she falls asleep, I scroll to the new email on my phone. Washington State. My welcome package.

I turn the screen face down.

Even if I'm too much of a coward to tell her tonight.

I already know I'm leaving.

Seven

LIAM

Four Months Later

I LOCK THE DOOR before I even kick off my boots.

Slide the bolt. No hesitation. Wedge the chair under the knob. My routine for the past couple months.

You get burned enough times, you stop touching the fucking stove.

Everything with Felicity has moved fast. Padraig and I found the rental house at the start of summer. Off campus, close enough to the bars where we play, far enough to make noise without the cops showing up. When we brought Felicity into the band, he and I invited her to move into the spare room across the hall from me.

Stevie came back a couple weeks later. She and Padraig share the master on the other side of the house.

At first, Felicity was a pretty easy roommate.

Until we crossed the line as I knew we would. Her being across the hall from me made the sex easier. She rode me like she had something to prove, and I let her. We both got off and she curled up next to me like we were something.

Then she came back the next night. And the night after. Slid her hand into my boxers while I was half-asleep and got me off before I said a word.

I didn't say no until I'd had enough. She seemed to take it well. I thought we both knew what this thing was.

Unfortunately, Felicity doesn't respect boundaries. Not when she's bored. Or horny. There's no aspect of her life where she thinks rules apply to her.

It's got to stop. I don't want her living in the house, but we're stuck. At the very least, I want her gone from my bed and personal space. She lingers like smoke. Always watching. Singing in the kitchen like the house belongs to her. Acting like she's the reason Fireball finally has traction.

She's not.

The band is me and Padraig, busting our asses to make something stick. Writing constantly. Rehearsing until our voices go raw. She has a great voice and is a good performer, but she's not the engine. She's the window dressing.

Padraig and Stevie haven't caught on yet. Ideally, I don't want them to. Which means Felicity's holding a card I don't want her to play. She hasn't used it yet. But she will. Eventually. Probably the second I say no in a way she can't twist.

I stare at the chair braced under the knob. This is madness. I walk across the room and pull it away.

She'll knock. Or she won't.

Either way, tonight, I'm not hiding.

Sure enough, I hear a soft shuffle. Bare feet on the hallway runner. I know it's her.

I sit on the edge of the bed, staring at the floor, palms sweating. I wipe them on my jeans. Stand. Sit again. My stomach's a knot, but I'm done hiding. Pretending like my situation isn't going to catch up with me.

I cross the room and rest my hand on the doorknob. Breathe.

Open it before she knocks.

Felicity wears an oversized sweatshirt and no makeup, which somehow feels more calculated than the full glam she rarely goes without. She looks soft, undone, like a young, innocent girl.

"Thought I'd have to beg tonight." She bats her eyes at me. "You've kept me out for a while."

"You still might." I turn and sit back down on my bed. "Not for what you think."

She smiles like she's already halfway to getting her way and slips inside, closing and locking the door behind her. She moves toward me like she's measuring the space between the bed and the gap between us. I sit on the edge of the mattress, elbows on my knees, waiting.

"So...I've been thinking." She scoots next to me. "You and I didn't give it a real shot. I think we can be something."

"No, we can't." I shake my head. "This was never going to be anything other than a couple of fucks."

Her expression is intense. "Are you seriously saying, I was a *mistake*?"

"No. You were a choice I made." I peer up at her. "We agreed we'd get the sexual tension out of the way so we could move forward in the band."

"I didn't mean it," she pouts, sliding her hand up my thigh. "Not when you fucked me so good. Don't you remember how hard I made you come?"

I place my hand on top of hers to keep it from moving. "Well, I *did* mean it. I liked fucking you and now I'm done."

She flinches. Good. We're through pretending.

I stand up and move toward the window to put some distance between us.

"Felicity, let's focus on the band. You can sing circles around anyone else. I want you there. I want Fireball to blow up. It's not gonna happen if we're dragging personal shit into every set."

She crosses her arms. "So you got what you want and I'm supposed to pretend nothing happened?"

"No. I don't want to pretend." I meet her eyes. "I want you to be clear about it not happening anymore. Like I'm being now."

"You sure Padraig would appreciate your version of clear?" She crosses her arms.

There it is. I don't react. I've been waiting for this moment.

"I know you haven't told him yet," I admit. "You will. Eventually. When you think it'll sting more. I think you're the kinda girl who'll take great delight in watching it land."

She lifts her chin but doesn't deny it.

"He'll be pissed," I continue. "He'll have every right to be. I fucked up. I should've thought about the band and what it would mean if this went south because of my cock."

She watches me like she's trying to find where I'll break.

"Get this straight, you stupid cunt," I continue. "I'm gonna tell him myself. You won't stop me from making this right. I won't fuck you again. I don't play games and I won't let you try to convince yourself this was something it never was."

Felicity rolls her eyes. "You're outta control."

"No. I think I'm finally in control." I walk to the door.

She steps closer. Runs a finger along the hem of my shirt. Soft, teasing.

"C'mon, Liam," she purrs.

"No." I take a step back. "Please leave. Now, I'm bored."

Her voice drops to a whisper. "Liar. You still get stiff when you think about me."

"I get hard when the wind blows," I deadpan. "Nothing to do with you, specifically."

She scowls. "Fuck you, Liam."

"You keep trying, but no thank you." I gesture for her to leave.

"You think you're the only one who's scared of losing something? I didn't join Fireball to fall for you. I wanted to be in the band. I wanted to matter. But you—" She chokes on her words. No tears fall. It's not grief. It's fury. "You think Padraig's the only thing I can burn," she snaps.

I nod. "If you start lighting matches, we all go down. You included."

She fucking hates me for saying it out loud.

"Don't make me your enemy, Felicity. Don't ruin your, our shot over something we both agreed wasn't going to last."

She gulps. "I don't want to be your enemy. I want you to want me."

"I did." I meet her eye. "Then I didn't. I'm being honest."

She stares at the door. Doesn't move.

"For what it's worth, I didn't lie to you," I add. "I didn't handle it right either. I'm sorry for hurting you."

She storms out.

When she's gone, I lock the door. Sit down. Dig the heels of my hands into my eyes.

I've never lied to my twin. I'm going to correct my error immediately.

No more hiding.

No more running.

Fireball is my life.

I'm done setting fires I don't know how to put out.

Eight

AVONNA

One Month Later

Today is my sixteenth birthday.

It's also my wedding day.

To a sixty-two-year-old man, with four other wives. I heard there was a fifth, but no one's seen her in years. My sister also found out he didn't want me at first. Said sixteen was too old. I was too mouthy.

Apparently, the Elders promised him a seat on the Counsel and gave him free rein to take charge of my penance. It makes me shudder to think about it.

Marriage in our sect isn't about love. It's ownership, obedience, purification.

I wake on my wedding day. An ivory dress showed up in my room sometime in the night.

If things don't go exactly to plan, my goose is cooked.

Today, Master Prophet will declare me chosen. I'm supposed to be sweet and smile while Brother Gideon stands at the chapel altar, lays his hand on my head and forces me to repeat vows to him, binding us forever.

What Master Prophet, Brother Gideon, and my family don't realize is, today is when I leave this place forever.

I've been meticulously planning my escape ever since I found out my fate. Every errand, trip to the well, walk around the grounds, I've plotted. Figured out my route. Back-up plans. There's a hole in the fence behind the tool shed. It's small, rusted through and hidden behind a brush pile no one's cleared in years. It leads into a barren field where nothing grows except dust and snake grass.

I have to make it to the gravel road I saw on the map in the chapel office. The mental picture is burned into my brain. It leads to a main highway, and from there I'm gonna take my chances.

Master Prophet says the outside world is a pit of filth. Asserts no woman could survive alone.

I say, we'll see.

At eight, Mother comes into the room and helps me into the wedding dress. I hadn't noticed it's yellowing under the arms, which means I'm not the only one who's worn it. I try not to think about who came before me as she sews a ribbon into my hair and warns me not to cry.

She needn't have said a word. There's no time for emotion today. My hands don't shake. My voice doesn't crack. I'm counting down the minutes.

My life depends on it.

Father waits by the door. He advises me not to disgrace him.

I smile. Promise to play nice.

Inside, I'm already a million miles away.

The service is at noon. They lead me to the prayer hut where I'm to wait for them to bring me to the chapel.

At precisely 10:14, I slip out and gather the thing I've stashed behind the old meal barrel. It's not much. A cloth pouch holding a compass, some clothes and forty dollars I stole from chapel donations.

Quickly, I change out of the disgusting dress into the men's work trousers, a heavy coat, and boots I swiped from the laundry shed. Shove my hair under a hat and I'm ready.

For a moment I stare at the guitar. Contemplate. Decide.

I sling it across my back and start running.

The hole in the fence is smaller than I remember. I'm forced to crawl on my belly through dry thorns and barbed grass. My arm snags, tearing the sleeve of the coat.

I don't stop. I can't afford to.

Once I'm through, the air feels different. Lighter. Dirtier. Real.

The field expands in every direction. For a minute, I can't remember which way to go. Taking a deep breath to center myself, I get my bearings and start walking.

Hours later, my legs are cramping, but I'm too scared to rest. I'm surprised no one has come after me. Then again, they probably think I'm hiding. No one would ever believe meek little me would fly the coop on her wedding day.

Eventually, the road finally appears, two ruts in dry gravel, old tire tracks seemingly running toward nothing. I follow it. By dusk, I reach a huge, paved highway. I've never seen anything like it. Cars fly past. Bright, loud. I crouch by the guardrail as the sky turns dark.

My boots are soaked. I'm freezing. My stomach threatens to eat itself.

There's some sort of small building up ahead. Led by flickering lights, I decide to see if there's any food there. No such luck. Only a soda machine with glass bottles and a man yelling into a phone behind the counter.

I slip into the bathroom. It smells like bleach and rust. After I do my business, I wash my hands and notice a piece of paper on the floor. I pick it up and stare at it. It's a list of printed numbers with a person's name at the top: *Avonna Parilla.*

Avonna Parilla.

What a beautiful name. I stuff the paper into my pocket and start back on my way. Luckily, no one sees me and I'm able to travel adjacent to the big, scary road until night swallows everything.

It's freezing, but the sky is full of stars. It seems like each one is sparkling for me.

When I can go no farther, I curl up under a tree cradling my guitar. I dream of nothing.

It takes me five days to reach Pullman. I walk when I can, hitch rides from farmhands, stay invisible as much as possible. I eat granola bars from machines. Drink water from hoses. Sing quietly under my breath to remember I still exist.

I arrive to the town grubby. Hollow-eyed. Wearing the same torn trousers and a jacket two sizes too big.

Still, no one notices me. Which is exactly what I want.

I walk past a store filled with washing machines. Inside, there's a woman with four kids. A man asleep in a chair. A girl a little older than me arguing with someone on her phone. She angrily pushes through the front door past me and enters the cafe next door.

Slipping inside, I watch her dryer until it stops. She's still in the cafe so I walk over, unload the warm clothes into a bag I brought with me. I score jeans, T-shirts, two clean hoodies. Socks. A beanie. A red bra.

I take them all. I have no choice. Tonight I'm going to pray for forgiveness, but I can't look back. What's done is done.

With my stolen clothes in hand, I head to the abandoned shop I scouted earlier. It's a building with the windows boarded and the doors padlocked. A crooked "For Lease" sign hangs in the window. Locating the loose board in the alley I found when I was scoping, I squeeze through. Inside isn't too bad. Clean enough. Broken tile, abandoned office furniture and a dented freezer.

Nicer than most homes on the compound.

I climb the stairs, past more plywood nailed over windows, to a crawlspace. The floor's dry and the vents from below miraculously push enough warm air to keep both me and the pipes from freezing.

I curl up against the wall with my guitar cradled to my body and use the red hoodie as a pillow.

This will do.

A tiny piece of nothing.

It's more than enough for now.

<h1 style="text-align:center">Nine</h1>

LINUS

<h2 style="text-align:center">Two Months Later</h2>

WINTER IN PULLMAN SETTLES into bones no matter how many layers I wear.

I've been here long enough to recognize the routines. Late-afternoon sunsets. Students shuffling across icy walkways. The way everyone's breath fogs in a shared cloud at bus stops. Enough time to build a life, at least on paper.

Not long enough for the loneliness to quiet.

Classes. Dorm. A job at the student union. A set of new acquaintances who think my accent is charming and my shyness is deliberate rather than reflexive.

I've put on a good facade. Pretend the guilt of cheating on Niamh doesn't follow me from lecture to lecture. Delude myself into believing the quick, clumsy blowjob is the only real confirmation of the part of myself I've tried to keep buried.

Pretend I'm not tracking Liam McGloughlin everywhere he goes.

It's not intentional. I'm not a stalker. At least, that's what I tell myself.

The Wazzu campus isn't big and Liam's the big man on campus, though he doesn't seem to give a fuck. His band, Fireball is building a following, and both he and his twin brother stand out without trying.

Liam's hair always looks like he ran from bed to class without checking a mirror. He wears the same beat-up black boots every day. Girls orbit him. Guys too. He moves with an easy confidence I can't look away from.

I don't want to stare.

Always do.

He's captivated me. No two ways about it.

Doesn't matter if he's strumming his guitar on the cold concrete steps outside the Communication building or laughing with his brother in the dining hall, his energy is impossible to ignore.

Each time I'm near him, the yearning is deep and inconvenient. It isn't lust, not entirely. It's something sharper.

Recognition, maybe.

He moves through the world with a freedom I've never allowed myself to imagine.

I haven't spoken to him yet. I want to.

Probably too much.

Tonight, there's a party on the far side of campus. I don't usually go out. I hate cheap beer and small talk. I pull on my coat anyway, because there's a good chance Liam will be there, and I promised myself I'd say an actual word to him next time I had an opportunity.

The cold hits my face the second I step outside. The air smells like snow, even though none is falling. Shoving my hands in my pockets, I walk fast, boots crunching on leftover ice. Music spills from the house before I reach it. Bass vibrates through the porch boards.

Inside, it's too warm. Bodies are packed shoulder to shoulder. Lights flashing inconsistently, like someone wired the house badly or wants to induce seizures. Conversations overlap into a single crowded hum.

I scan the room before I realize I'm doing it.

There he is.

Liam.

Back against the far wall, hands tucked into the pockets of his dark jeans, silver chain glinting at his throat. His hair sticks up in all directions, darker under the dim lights. He's talking to someone. A girl with a high ponytail and dramatic eyeliner. He looks alive, bright, carved out of something fiercer than everyone around him.

He holds a bottle of sparkling water, tapping it against his palm with restless rhythm. His eyes sweep the room, cataloguing faces. When they pass over me, something in me jolts.

I push off the counter before I lose courage. The girl he was talking to drifts toward the hallway and a space opens at the arm of the couch.

A chance.

I take it.

He notices me instantly.

"Hey." He sits on the cushion next to me. His voice is deeper than I expect. Rough, warm, carrying the faintest trace of a Belfast accent. He studies me briefly, curiosity sparking in his eyes. "Don't think I've seen you before."

I manage a half smile. "Hey yourself."

"You're new," he says, like it's a fact he's been turning over in his mind.

"I've been here a few months."

He studies me without apology, then nods. "I'm Liam."

"I know."

The second it leaves my mouth, I regret it. Too eager.

He laughs once, soft and quick. "Right. And you are…?"

"Linus."

His eyes spark when I say it. "Irish?"

"Dublin."

"Aye." He leans forward slightly, elbows resting on his knees. "My folks are from Belfast. Makes my lilt come and go, or so I've been told."

I relax before I mean to. "I hear it. It suits you."

"So, Linus." His smile is small but real. "Why are you in Pullman?"

"To study entertainment and hospitality."

He nods like it's important. "You into music?"

"Sure. I worked for a talent booking company in Dublin. Logistics mostly."

His eyebrows rise. "You serious? Proper gigs and everything?"

"Depends on your definition of proper."

My chest loosens when he laughs.

"So you already know about Fireball." He pushes loose hair off his face.

"*Everyone* knows Fireball."

He looks pleased when I mention his band, like he isn't used to hearing praise yet but wants to be. "We're still figurin' things out. Got a new singer who's a pain in the ass, but it's my dream."

"You're good," I say before I can chicken out. "I've heard you."

His eyes sharpen. "Where?"

"On the radio. Saw you at a house party…" I trail off, mortified.

He grins wider. "You've been doing recon."

"No, I—"

"It's fine." He palms my thigh. "I'd watch me too."

I choke on a laugh.

He shifts slightly so his knee brushes mine. The contact is small, fleeting. Enough to jolt something low in my stomach.

"You seein' anyone?" He leans closer.

"No," I answer, too quickly.

"You want to be?"

I swallow. "Maybe."

His smile fades into something softer. Careful. Curious. "Who? Lotsa pretty girls around."

This feels like a cliff I've been inching toward for months. Adrenaline pumping, I force myself to look him in the eyes.

"Aye, but I came tonight hoping you'd be here."

His gaze lowers, not to my mouth. To the space between us, like he's imagining it gone.

"That so?" His thumb strokes my thigh.

I nod. "Yeah."

He shifts closer, and when he speaks next, the lilt in his voice is unmistakable. "You don't flirt much, do you?"

"No," I breathe. "I was in a relationship for three years. We broke up when I moved here. I don't really know how."

"You're doing grand." Liam's eyes bore into mine, warm enough to pool heat low in my stomach.

His face inches closer until I feel the warmth of his breath against my cheek. He isn't cocky now. Not teasing. Something in his eyes looks almost shy. Careful.

"You're not like anyone I've ever met," he murmurs. "I'm glad I came over here."

I exhale shakily. "Me too. I've wanted to talk to you for weeks."

"So let's talk."

The whole party blurs at the edges. The noise, the lights, the cold wind pushing in every time the door opens. All of it fades.

There's only him.

The way he patiently gives me all the time I need to choose the next moment.

The pull between us is unmistakable, undeniable. For the first time in my life, wanting a man doesn't feel like a secret I need to hide.

Tonight feels like a beginning.

A terrifying, beautiful beginning.

I think he might be into me too.

Whatever this is.

Whatever it could be.

Ten

LIAM

A Few Weeks Later

IT STARTS WITH A dare.

Linus O'Donnell leans against the fridge, cup in hand, claiming the air around him. I met him at party a couple months ago. We've been hovering around each other ever since. Haven't fucked yet, which is a first for me, but I kinda like where this is going.

No matter where we run into each other, we always seem to gravitate into conversation and low-level flirting.

I know he's into me, which is why I haven't gone there. Everything in my entire being tells me this could be something real. Not a body for the night.

Not another secret.

The problem is, Linus is a relationship guy, and I don't do commitment. No time for it. Padraig has practically been married off to Stevie, since he was sixteen. It's stupid. We have our whole lives ahead of us.

Besides, I can't tie myself to any one person.

Music's where my heart is. Fireball's become the piece of me I salvaged from the wreckage of my family. It's kept me alive. Gave me somewhere to put the rage, the hurt. Even with the Felicity drama, I'd be nothing but scars and silence without it.

Linus is unexpected. Unsettling. I haven't figured him out yet, but he's under my skin. Sharp eyes. Calm voice. Broad shoulders, thick forearms. His beard is neat and tidy. Fuck me, he's handsome with full lips I like to imagine around my cock.

I want to fuck him. This much, I know. Whether there's more to it? I'm not sure.

Linus watches me as my mind cycles through all the reasons this is a bad idea. He doesn't say much. He observes. Listens. Dissects situations internally before offering his thoughts. When he does speak, his Dublin accent is smooth and low. Confident. His laugh is joyous. Free. It stirs something I haven't let myself name.

I keep looking at those lips. My cock thickens under my jeans.

Backing down from sexual tension isn't in my nature.

I *do* want him. Fuck, I do.

We're at a party off campus. Another rundown house with sagging floors and overpriced thrift-shop rugs. A few people pretend to care about a pretty, raggedy-ass girl in the corner playing insipid cover tunes on a beat-up acoustic. Linus leans next to me against the chipped tile counter, sipping warm beer from a Solo cup like it might become something better if he wills it to be true.

"I can't feckin' stand Justin Timberlake," he grumbles, barely audible over the latest offering from the songstress.

I glance sideways. "Finally. Someone with taste."

"Aye." His lips twitch. "Manufactured talent. The girl has a decent voice, though."

I lift my cup, filled with water, toward him. "Music scene isn't what it used to be."

He quirks a brow. Licks those luscious lips. He knows my band is killin' it right now.

The air shifts.

His shoulder brushes mine. He doesn't move away.

The dare's in his eyes before it hits his mouth.

A silent one.

If I lean in, will you?

"I live off campus," I say. Casual, like I haven't been thinking about this for months. "Not far. Place I share with my twin, Padraig, his girl Stevie, and our singer."

He tips his cup in acknowledgment. "You bring many lads home then?"

"No." I try to sound nonchalant. "Keep my sex life outta the house usually."

Linus steps toward me. "Why?"

There's a moment. Long enough to choose if I'll lie.

"My da was in a car accident when we were seventeen." I don't look at him, my eyes are fixed on the sticky tile where my boots are planted. "Didn't heal right. He couldn't work. Got hooked on pills, then whiskey."

Linus doesn't speak. His shoulder brushes mine.

"Summer after first year, I brought a lad home." My eyes burn. I've never uttered a word about this outside our family, and we avoid the topic like the plague. "He caught us in the hallway. Lost his mind. Said some things…"

It takes a minute for me to continue.

"Padraig stepped between us first. Took a punch to the face. I got shoved down the stairs. Split my head open. Out cold. It all happened in front of my three wee brothers."

Linus doesn't move or flinch.

"My older brother pays for college. Padraig and I are here at Wazzu so I'm not in danger." I press my palm flat against the wall beside me, grounding myself. "So I don't have to hide who I am."

Linus speaks low and steady. "You don't have to be afraid with me."

I nod once. Doesn't undo anything. I don't know this guy, really. Yet his words, somehow, settle something inside me "I'm fluid. Bisexual. Pansexual. Hell, I don't know. I like fucking who I want. Not the judgment from others."

"Aye." He exhales through his nose. "Sounds familiar."

"Yeah?"

"My da's a politician," he says quietly. "Mum's on the school board. Church every Sunday. Before I came here, I broke up with my long-time girlfriend. I cheated on her. Let a guy blow me on a family vacation. I couldn't tell my parents or my siblings why. None of them would understand."

I laugh bitterly. "Catholic guilt'll kill us all."

"Not if we fuck it to death first." He flashes a grin. Licks his lips. Fixes me with those eyes.

The heat between us shifts.

A dare.

Could we be something?

His hand grazes mine where it rests against the counter. I flip mine over, let our fingers link.

He watches me. "Do you want to kiss me as much as I want to kiss you?"

I don't say yes. I pull him toward me. He cups my face. No hesitation. His mouth crashes into mine, hot and assertive.

We leave the party with a buzz, and not from alcohol.

Linus walks beside me, hands stuffed into the pockets of his jacket, shoulders hunched against the late-night chill. I match his pace, each step syncing closer to his, like I'm already memorizing the rhythm. He doesn't say much. Doesn't have to.

I *feel* him.

We cut through the side alley skirting the cracked pavement near the dumpsters. My rental house glows dimly ahead, porch light flickering. There's something charged in the quiet between us now. Anticipation.

He hesitates when we reach the steps. "This your place?"

"Aye." I twist the knob and push open the front door into the warm air.

In the low hallway light Felicity is standing in front of my room wearing a see-through top and a hoodie knotted around her waist. She freezes when she sees me with Linus. Her eyes rake over him, with his hand on my back and our bodies brushing in a deliberate way.

The air turns icy.

"How interesting..." Acid drips from her tongue. "Guess I'm not your type after all."

Linus pauses beside me.

I don't flinch. "You never were."

Her nostrils flare. "Funny, you weren't complaining last time we fucked."

Linus shifts his weight but doesn't step away.

"Ages ago." I meet her gaze, unbothered. "As I told you, doesn't mean I want more."

Her laugh scrapes like glass. "You're nothing but a sad little fraud who'll fuck anything to feel something."

The words land like shrapnel. Sharp, targeted. I freeze.

Her bedroom door slams shut before I can recover sufficiently to reply.

Linus waits until the echo fades. "You're in a band with *her*?"

"Gotta love the drama." I try to ignore my urge to punch a wall and instead lead him into my room. "Full disclosure, we hooked up a couple times. Her idea. Got possessive. Now, I have no choice but to ignore her."

He glances over at her room. "Is it working?"

"No, unfortunately."

I kick the door closed with my heel. The click reverberates in my chest.

"She's the reason I haven't brought anyone here," I confess like it's a sin.

Linus steps between my legs. "Yet, here I am. So, you're into me?"

I don't answer.

He tilts my chin up with two fingers. "No?"

"You're... different."

Linus doesn't ask how. Doesn't need to. He kisses me, unhurried, mouth parted, tongue tracing the edge of mine. His hands cup my jaw, then slide through my hair. I grip his hips, drag him close.

When we part, we're both out of breath.

He pulls off his hoodie, then the shirt beneath. His chest is solid, dusted with dark hair, tattoos inked across his biceps and ribs. Designs I plan to trace with my tongue. His belt clicks open. He strips down to briefs and waits, watching.

I undress methodically to let him take me in. His eyes roam my body like he's cataloging every inch. I'm as rigid as a steel pole.

He's hard, too. Impressively so.

We move at the same time.

His mouth finds mine again, more urgent now, all heat and want. I push him onto the bed, climb over him. His thighs part for me without hesitation. I kiss his throat, the hollow of his collarbone, the line of muscle down his chest. I drag my tongue over his nipple, then bite lightly.

"*Fuck*—Liam." He fists the sheets.

I look up. "You good?"

"Aye." His hand threads through my hair. "Don't stop."

I quirk a brow then drag my mouth lower, lave him through the fabric of his boxer briefs until he's panting. I hook my fingers in the waistband and pull them down. His phenomenal cock springs free. Thick, long. Dark at the head. I wrap my hand around the base, stroke once, then lick a line up the underside.

HIs deep, guttural grown reverberates through my bedroom.

I take him in my mouth, inch by inch, until my nose brushes the hair at his base. I hold there, swallowing around him.

His whole body tenses. "Christ."

I set a rhythm. One hand stroking what I can't fit, the other sliding up his torso, feeling every breath. His hands roam my back, then grip my ass, pulling me closer.

"Wanna taste me on you," he wheezes hoarsely.

I ease off him with a wet pop and crawl up his body. He flips me without warning, straddles me, mouth crashing to mine. His hips grind against me, causing our cocks to rub together. He licks into my mouth like he owns it. Like he's marking territory. Within moments, we're a jumble of sweat and hunger, hips grinding in sync.

Linus curls his fist around both our cocks, knuckles grazing my stomach with every stroke. There's no lube. Only my spit and our pre-come making it lubricated enough to slide. Messy enough to make me lose my mind.

The friction's perfect. Rough and real. Skin dragging over skin. He frots us faster, hand working us like he knows the edge and wants us teetering on it together.

"Fuck," I wheeze "I'm gonna—"

"Come with me." He nibbles my chin.

We do. One brutal, blinding second and we're both spilling into his fist, our come mixing, hot and thick, smearing over each other's skin.

It's lascivious. Intimate. *Ours.*

Linus keeps stroking us through it, softening the pressure.

It's the most intimate experience of my life. He slumps against me, chest heaving, hand still wrapped around both our cocks like he's reluctant to let go.

I don't want him to. I reach down and cover his hand with mine so we're both gripping our softening shafts. Eventually, our hands loosen, leaving a smear of drying come across our bellies. I should be embarrassed by how fast it happened, by how badly I wanted this, but I'm not.

I've never felt more wanted. More seen.

Linus shifts, pulling his arm under my neck again, settling in like he belongs there.

"That was..." I start, but there's no word strong enough.

"Yeah." His thumb brushes my jawline.

"I've had sex." I keep my eyes averted from his. "A lot of it. Never felt so fuckin' good."

He doesn't tease. Doesn't smirk. "Same. Aside from the resort, this is my first time doin' it with a guy, though."

I'm floored. He chose me. I'm gonna make this so good for him.

I turn toward him, nuzzle into the slope of his shoulder, and let my eyes close. For the first time in ages, I don't feel the need to guard anything. Not my voice. Not my skin.

I want this to mean something. "Stay. Let's keep going."

"I wasn't plannin' on leaving." Linus shifts closer and wraps both arms around me. Kisses the side of my throat.

His leg slides between mine. My chest rises against his. There's nothing rushed or desperate left in either of us. I'm struck by a strange kind of ease I've never felt after sex. My body aches in all the right places. Muscles coiled, lips tender, nerves still humming. Something deeper settles low in my chest.

He doesn't feel temporary.

Linus curls around me like he's supposed to be here. A quiet certainty. A sense of home.

I breathe in and let the thought settle like an anchor.

I fall asleep. Wrapped in Linus.

For the first time in forever, I don't feel alone.

Eleven

AVONNA

That Same Night

THE BULLETIN BOARD IN the student union promised a hundred dollars.

For three hours of singing, if you could imagine.

I lied when I called. Said I'd played dozens of times and here I am.

To say I'm terrified is an understatement. If I didn't need the money so bad, there's no way I'd have the courage to follow through with it.

Desperation wins, I guess.

My stomach's so upset with nerves and hunger, I feel like I'm gonna throw up. It's the first time I've ever played in front of people and the first time I've ever played pop songs. Over the past six days, I've holed up in a room at the library and taught myself as many hits as possible. Now all I can do is pray...

No. I can't think this way.

I've left my old life behind.

I take my place on the cracked stool, wrap my arms around my guitar and tune it by ear, humming to check the sound against memory and instinct. It's probably twice as old as me. Beat up, wood dulled, strings changed who knows when.

Eight weeks ago I escaped the place I grew up in. It feels like a lifetime.

Truthfully, this outside world scrapes against my skin like raw wind. It's loud, fast and too full of color and noise. Lights burn all night. No one prays before touching merchandise on store shelves. For the past two months, I've been walking through a foreign land, desperately trying to learn the language without giving myself away.

Now I'm in this strange house. The air is thick with sweat, cigarette smoke, and something sweet and rotting underneath. People shout over each other, drink from bottles I've only seen in whispered warnings and grind their bodies together like animals.

It's chaos. Senseless, wild chaos.

Every flash of bare thigh feels indecent. Also, dazzling. Back home, a woman showing her ankle would be caned. Here, women compete over who can wear less clothes. They laugh with their mouths open wide. Kiss men openly. Laugh with their heads thrown back.

My prior self screams *you shouldn't be here.*

The sinful part of me thinks maybe I belong.

The only thing I know for sure is I won't go back.

Even if they find me.

I'd sooner die first.

"Hey, are you the singer?" A baby-faced boy is suddenly in front of me. "You can start any time. Find me after and I'll pay you."

He's off without another word. With his directive to start, I need to do as he says. I don't want to lose any of this money. My life depends on it.

On the first song, a ballad by a singer named Justin Timberlake, my voice shakes, but my fingers somehow remember the chords. As I continue, to block out the dark cloud, I squeeze my eyes shut.

My set is filled with other people's hit music. To me they're brand new. When I sing, I pay attention to the words and pour myself into it. Try to exorcise pain I've hauled around since long before I tore my name off like old skin and started fresh with the one I found on a gas station receipt.

Avonna Parilla.

It's beautiful. Close enough to who I was, but far enough from who they're still looking for.

After about an hour, I open my eyes to realize nobody at this party is really listening to me. Not the guy with the broken glasses sprawled on the couch. Or the girl pouring something into a red plastic cup. Certainly not the boy in the corner sketching tattoos on his arm.

I'm background noise. Which is fine by me. The less conspicuous the better.

It's comforting, actually. None of these people know my name's not real or I'm only sixteen. They probably assume I'm a student enrolled at the college trying to pay tuition.

It's no one's business if I'm sleeping in a storage loft above an abandoned mechanic's shop with a backpack full of clothes I stole from a laundromat.

Besides, I'm used to being ignored and fading into the background. Considering my circumstances, it's probably for the best.

By the time I play the last few songs, my fingers smart and I'm ready to leave. I long for the solitude and quiet of my own space, where I can carefully plan my next move.

Then my eyes are drawn to the kitchen.

Two boys who don't interact like the others. They're not loud or obnoxious. Both move in tandem. There's a quiet tension between their bodies like an invisible thread pulls them together, the rugged one carries unleashed emotion like scripture, his dark curls brush his shoulder.

He has secrets too, of this I'm certain.

The other guy is solid and grounded, confident in his own skin. Capable. Kind.

I can't help but stare at the way they lean together. How their feet mirror one another's stance. I feel their energy from here, across the entire room. Something deeper than attraction. A closeness I've never witnessed in real life. Intimacy never spoken of where I come from.

I notice the way the one says something and the other boy laughs, head bowing for a breath. It's gentle. Beautiful. They don't even touch, but my whole body lights up. Like an awakening, of sorts.

I've never seen two men together like this. Where I come from, love only counts between a man and a woman. Anything else is wicked. Unnatural.

A stain on the soul.

The kind one leans into the boy with secrets and the air bends around them, thick with something warm and sacred. They kiss. Right there in the kitchen like it means something.

I nearly stop singing, I'm so shocked.

This doesn't look like sin, it looks like truth. Like they never have to hide anything from anyone. When their lips part, both of then smile. I see it. Desire, real and holy.

Exactly what I want.

I feel it, so far inside I almost miss it.

The first crack in everything I was ever told about sex.

Boys like them were beaten and sent away. Master Prophet preached how they were broken. Touched wrong. Possessed. Sinners who could infect the rest of us, like mold on bread.

But the way the two of them lit up? It didn't look sinful. Didn't look wrong. It looked like something I want but never thought I'd have.

I manage to keep singing, but my voice's gone strange in my throat. I'm not jealous. I'm not sure what I am. Except maybe even more unsure of everything. What else did my people lie about?

After the set, I pack and get my money. I walk home fast before someone asks too many questions, keeping to the shadows with my hands in my sleeves to try to stay warm.

When I reach the shop, I climb the broken stairs past the plywood still nailed across the windows. I sleep with my stolen coat on. Breathe fog when I wake. Count the days since I ran.

Figure out how much more I need to save to get to Seattle. Or Portland. I'm too close to Idaho to feel safe.

As I fall asleep, I remember the way the boys looked at each other like their love wasn't forbidden. They weren't afraid to be judged for loving each other.

I'm still frightened beyond belief.

Of being found.

Moreso, what I might do if I stop hiding.

Tonight gave me something I didn't expect.

Hope.

I'm not safe—

Maybe someday, I will be.

Until then, I need to unlearn everything I thought I knew.

Twelve

LINUS

Three Weeks Later

LIAM'S LEGS ARE HOOKED over my shoulders.

His eyes are half-closed.

I focus on his gorgeous, thick cock. Watch it bounce on his belly as I thrust deep and unrelenting. Pre-come oozes out of his crown.

"Fuck, Linus." His fingers curl around the edge of the mattress, knuckles white.

He's close. I brace one hand beside his head and wrap the other around the base of his cock. "You're takin' it so good for me, love. So fuckin' good."

His hips lift to meet every push, greedy and desperate. We're coated with lube. The wet sounds of us fill the room.

Sex with him is divine. Perfect.

His ass seizes my cock and I feel it all the way through my spine. "I'm gonna—fuck, I'm gonna—"

I don't let him finish.

Pumping him in time to my thrusts, I make sure to twist my wrist at the head the way he likes it. A few passes in and he breaks apart beneath me. Thick, hot cream spills over my knuckles.

"*Ahhhhhhhh*...." I drive in deep one last time, filling him until I feel it leak down between us.

Liam pulls me close and I drop against his chest, still buried inside him, both of us breathless. His lips find my temple. He never speaks right away after. Doesn't need to.

Minutes pass, maybe more.

When I finally pull out, he whines.

"You're insatiable." I kiss the corner of his mouth.

He grins. "You love it."

I do. God help me, I do.

I settle in beside him, one arm behind my head, the other resting on his belly. He traces a circle around my nipple with a blunt fingertip. His whole body glows. We've been fucking all weekend, so he's satiated. As am I.

This is something more, though. I feel in my bones when he touches me like this.

The corner of Liam's mouth curves. "So. Was fuckin' me a long con to get into the band?"

I huff a quiet laugh, dragging my knuckles across his ribs. "Aye. You caught me. Knew if I sucked you off enough times, you'd let me manage the band."

Truth is, I didn't plan to get involved. It was somewhat foisted upon me. The morning after Liam and I first had sex, I'd barely had time to button my jeans before Padraig and his girlfriend, Stevie caught us making out in the kitchen.

Felicity sauntered in right after, sizing me up like I was the biggest piece of shite on the planet.

The next thing I knew, Stevie tearfully owned up to missing an email costing Fireball a headlining slot. Regret written all over her. She wasn't careless, only stretched too thin.

I spoke before I thought. Offered to help. Didn't do it to impress anyone. Certainly not to wedge myself into their world through Liam.

I don't regret it, though. I love what they're building. The music. The chaos. The energy of it all.

Fireball's got something rare. If I can help hold it together, even as a fill-in, I'm happy to.

"Good on ya'." He nuzzles my neck. "You're a pro, after all."

"I didn't mean to overstep, you know. Thought I was bein' polite. Helpful." I don't want Liam to think I'm opportunistic. Not when I dig what we have going on so much.

"You offered to fix a fire." He shakes his head. "We've got a lot of fires. She's been runnin' herself ragged to keep Padraig happy. Stevie never wanted to manage us and she's all we ever had."

"I'm not tryin' to replace her."

"I know." There's a pause. Comfortable, but heavy. "Maybe you should, though."

My eyes widen. "Let's give it a beat. Let Stevie or Padraig make it their idea."

"Aye." His response is immediate, almost too quick. "She likes you. You've got your shit together. It probably won't take long. Only if you want to, though."

I contemplate, then add, "It's in my wheelhouse. I've seen you play many times now. If I were your manager, I'd tell you Felicity's gonna be a problem."

This gets his attention. His eyes cut to mine. He arches an eyebrow. Waits.

"No, not because you fucked her. Truthfully, she's got talent," I offer. "Her ego is gonna explode, though. She's not right for Fireball. Not long-term. I think she knows it."

Liam exhales, then rakes a hand through his hair. "Yeah. Don't I fuckin' know."

"She's not the type to bow out gracefully."

"No," he says bitterly. "Take it from me. She's not."

We lie there for a beat, the weight of their sexual history flickering between us.

"So I'm not purely a hot fuck with a color-coded spreadsheet?" I try to shift the mood back to where we were a few minutes ago.

He squeezes my ass. "Nope."

"High praise."

He groans and flops back into the pillow. "Fuck off. You know I love it."

Oh, I know it. I can feel it in the way he touches me, the way he lets me see under all the bravado. I've been around musical egos before. Entire rosters full of them. But Liam?

He's different.

I want to stay long enough to see where it goes

"You're stayin' tonight, yeah?" he asks, as if it's still a question.

"I practically live here now, don't I?" Most of my stuff has migrated into Liam's bedroom. "We can walk to class tomorrow."

He laughs. "Yeah, but you've got the Dublin guilt. Thought maybe you'd slink back to your place to pray or whatever."

"I'm not prayin' for forgiveness, love."

His smile falters.

Silence thickens between us, not uncomfortable, but charged.

"I haven't told them I'm movin' in," I admit.

He doesn't pretend not to know who I mean. "Your parents."

"They're payin' for my flat near campus. Think I've been focusin' on school and workin' in the lab. It'd be impossible to tell them I'm shackin' up with the bloke I'm shaggin' every night," I say to the air above me.

I call things as they are, so I do.

His hand stills on my chest. "You think they'd care more about us or the degree?"

"Us, probably. I'm hopin' as long as I do somethin' with a suit and a salary I'll be able to come clean about you."

Liam tilts his head. "Tell me more about the work you did at the..."

"Booking agency," I finish. "Started when I was sixteen. Niamh's da ran the place. He gave me a foot in."

His gaze sharpens. "Niamh...your ex."

"Aye." I nod. "We were together five years.."

"She's the one you cheated on?"

"Aye." I shift uncomfortably. "I told her the truth before I left. She broke it off. Didn't like the idea of me cheating with a guy, which I regret to this day. Both of our families' hopes of marriage were dashed."

Liam looks at me quizzically. "So, she didn't take it well."

"No." I swallow. "I get it. I made her feel small. Like she wasn't enough. I tried to explain, but..."

Liam's eyes squeeze shut. He gets it.

"Look, what I did was wrong. I wouldn't ever do it again. She wanted to brush it under the rug and keep goin." I wince at the memory of the girl I spent so much time with. "I broke it off by comin' here.."

"Her da?"

"Dunno. I begged her not to tell him." I internally recoil at how desperate I felt in the moment. "Mostly, I was worried he'd tell my folks."

Liam's fingers cover mine.

"She's not cruel," I add. "But she's hurt. And hurt people can be dangerous. I'd like to be able to control my own narrative, ya know, but it's outta my hands."

Silence sits between us for a beat.

"Aye. I know." He bites his lip, likely in memory of his da's violence. He hasn't talked about it much since he confided in me, but I can tell it weighs on him.

"I wasn't lyin' to her when I said I loved her," I confess. "She was real to me. But there's a part of me she never touched. Not 'cause I didn't want her to. I didn't know how to tell her I was bisexual. I never want to be in a relationship without full transparency again."

Liam watches me. No judgment, no distance. Only understanding. "Tell me about the guy."

"Summer holiday with my folks."

He goes quiet, letting me fill the space on my own terms. "There was this lad at the resort. Ripped. Blond. He caught me starin' and smiled like he knew what I was after. On our last night, I decided to take a walk around the hotel grounds. Hoped I'd see him. Sure enough, he was waiting. I followed him into a dark corner. He dropped to his knees."

Liam strokes my chest, listening.

"I let him. I needed it. Wasn't even thinkin'. Burned for it."

"You finish?" He smiles.

I nod. "In his mouth."

Liam whistles.

"I felt sick after." I bite my lower lip. "Not 'cause of what we did. 'Cause I liked it too much. Spent the whole flight home tryin' not to cry at how I'd betrayed her."

"You knew you were bi then?" His eyes searched mine.

I kiss his forehead. "Being with him made it real. Tell me about your first time."

Liam brushes his fingers along my thigh. "You really wanna know?"

I nod, already half-mast. All this talk about sex has me ready to go again.

"Happened right after I turned seventeen, a few months before Da's accident. I'd been fucking girls for years. Easy, fun, nothing deep. I'd been noticin' guys since my dick started gettin' hard. Never said it out loud. Never acted on it. Only Padraig knew." He shifts beside me, eyes on the ceiling, remembering. "Anyway, there was this older guy who worked at a vintage record store on Capitol Hill. Always flirted when I came in. One night he invited me upstairs to his loft. It was quintessential Seattle. Velvet couches, incense and candles."

He glances over at me. "I was nervous, but horny as hell. He offered me a beer, which I declined, and sat beside me so close our legs touched. When he kissed me, I didn't hesitate. I let him push me back onto the couch."

"He didn't fuck me." Liam's voice lowers. "I thought he would. I wanted him to. He could tell I was tense. Inexperienced. Said he'd ease me in."

Picturing the scene is so goddamn hot.

"He undressed me. Lubed my ass and fingered me. One, then two. Scissored them. When he hit my prostate, my whole body lit up. You know what I mean. He blew my fuckin' mind and I forgot to be afraid."

Liam notices my dick standing at attention and fists it, stroking me as he speaks. "When he took my cock in his mouth, I came so violently, I thought I'd blacked out."

A beat of silence.

"I walked home sore. Shaky. Smiling the whole fuckin' way." Liam's lips lift, barely. "It's how I knew I want both."

Liam's lips quirk when he feels my cock twitch in his hand.

I shift toward him. Rest my forehead against his, our breaths tangling. His palm works miracles. He draws something out of me I've never had the courage to embrace.

"I've never told anyone before," he murmurs, so close I feel the words on my lips.

I kiss him. Not soft. Not sweet. Open-mouthed and hungry, like we've already lived a hundred lives and wasted most of them not doing this.

"This isn't about fucking, is it?" Liam pulls away for a second.

I shake my head.

"I used to think it was about preference. Now I think it's about energy." Liam hesitates. "I don't do relationships because I know I won't stop wantin' what I don't have."

He climbs on top of me, thighs straddling mine. Our cocks slide together, heat meeting heat. He grinds against me, rhythm building, dragging pleasure up my spine with every push of his hips. I buck under him, hands gripping his waist, anchoring him there.

"You're not the only one who wants both," I breathe shakily. "You're the first person who's ever seen all of me."

His mouth is on my neck now, biting enough to make me gasp.

"Say it again," he rasps. "Tell me I see you."

"You do." I arch up. "More than anyone."

Liam braces a hand beside my head and shifts. Slides lower until his mouth finds my chest. He kisses down, slow as sin, until I'm shuddering beneath him. My hand threads through his hair, anchoring myself to the moment.

Liam lifts his eyes, mouth trailing lower. "You good?"

I nod.

He doesn't break eye contact as he takes me into his mouth.

It's not a rough, fast blowjob. This is deeper. Focused. He watches me as he sucks me down, inch by inch, his tongue mapping every vein, like he's memorizing the shape of what we are.

I can't look away.

I clutch the sheets, my hips lurching once, twice before I manage to hold still. I want to make this last. For him to know I trust him enough to let go like this.

"*Unghhhhhh.*" Liam's sexy vibrations around my cock drag a curse from my throat.

I thread my fingers through his hair again, trying to hold on to anything. My thighs tense. I'm right on the edge when he pulls back, breathing heavy, lips swollen. He crawls back up my body, grinding against me again until we're both insane with need.

He lines us up, and fists us together, stroking in tandem. Our skin slides. Hot. Thick. Intense.

"Come with me," he demands against my mouth.

His words do something to me. Everything coils then explodes. Floods through me. I cry out his name when I spurt into our fists. He follows, our release catching between us, messy and beautiful.

Liam grabs a towel from the floor and we silently clean up. Then we lie coiled together in the quiet.

His head on my shoulder. My heart in his hands.

I don't say it out loud, not yet.

But it's already true.

I'm in.

Whatever this is.

<h1 style="text-align:center">Thirteen</h1>

<h2 style="text-align:center">Four Months</h2>

THE RESTAURANT SMELLS LIKE cardamom and rain-soaked pavement.

A tiny bell over the door rings when we step inside, half-drowned out by sitar music floating from a decrepit old speaker hanging from a tenuous wire. It's the only place still open this late, an Indian café tucked between a pawn shop and a tattoo parlor.

After three weeks on tour, it feels almost civilized.

Linus orders a mango lassi. I get water. Neither of us touches them.

We've been sitting here for fifteen minutes, and I can feel him studying me. Not judging. Watching. He's good at observing me until I crack.

"You can stop lookin' at me like I murdered someone." I lean back in the booth, shoulders aching from load-in.

His mouth twitches. "You've been broodin' since soundcheck. Don't tell me it's nothin'."

"Could be the four hours of sleep or the fact we've spent three weeks living on crisps and gas-station coffee."

Linus folds his arms. "It's Felicity, isn't it?"

I freeze. "What about her?"

"Come on." His Dublin lilt wraps around the words, low and steady. "She's snappin' at the crew, changin' setlists mid-show, and glarin' daggers at Padraig every time he opens his mouth, so she is. You can't tell me nothin's going on."

My stomach turns. He's not wrong. He never is.

"She's being herself," I say finally, a poor attempt at dismissal. "She wants control. Always has."

"She's got it." Linus's gaze is sharp. "Over you, at least."

I bark out a bitter laugh. "Jesus. You don't miss a thing."

He doesn't blink. "Wanna tell me what's up?"

The question lands like a punch. I glance at the table, at the tiny cracks in the wood, at my own reflection in the thick varnish. I want to lie. I really do.

Linus deserves better.

I exhale sheepishly. "Padraig doesn't know I fucked her."

His breath catches, barely. No shock, just quiet resignation. "You never told him?"

"I planned on it." I'm mortified. My twin and I have never kept secrets. "Then it went too long. Now it's weird and shouldn't matter, but she's tryin' to use it to her advantage."

He waits.

"She's been danglin' it over me ever since," I admit. "She hates Stevie. She knows how much it'll destroy Padraig if he finds out I messed anything up with her, and she knows it. It's diabolical, isn't it? She smiles and sings and makes me feel like filth in my own band."

Linus nods once, the way he does when he's processing. "Can you tell Padraig?"

"I've meant to for ages. He's already on edge." I pinch the bridge of my nose. "Christ. No. I can't tell him. Not with Stevie gone on her internship. He's barely holdin' it together."

"Maybe you underestimate him."

"Maybe you don't know him like I do."

He leans forward, elbows on the table. "You're carryin' all of it, Liam. The guilt, the band, your brother's heartbreak. You'll snap if you keep it bottled."

"Wouldn't be the first time." I force a half smile. "You saw tonight. I nearly lost it when she tried to rewrite the bridge mid-set."

"She's poison." His voice softens. "You know it."

"Yeah." I stare at the condensation trailing down my glass. "I thought with my dick and not my head. Jokes on me."

The waiter drops off our food—saag paneer, naan, two plates we don't touch. I pick at a corner of bread, tearing it into pieces I never eat.

"How's Padraig really doing?" Linus asks after a while. "With Stevie away for so long?"

I huff out a breath. "How do you think? He hides it well, but he's gutted. She's in fuckin' Switzerland livin' her dream and he's stuck here with me, playin' small clubs and pretendin' he's fine."

"He loves her."

"He does." I nod. "He can't seem to see she's chasin' something for herself. He wants to hold on for dear life."

Linus studies me. "You're scared he'll leave the band."

"Wouldn't you be?" I meet his eyes. "He's my twin. My anchor. Without him, I don't know who I am."

He doesn't answer. He doesn't have to. The silence says enough.

For a while, we eat. Conversation around us blurs into white noise. Outside, the streetlights smear across the wet glass. I catch our reflection in the window. My sharp, unshaven cheekbones. His thick beard and brown, knowing eyes.

Two men who look far older than we are.

Linus clears his throat. "You know, you're doin' good work. With the band, I mean."

I snort. "We're hanging on by a thread."

"Maybe. It's not pure luck you've still got fans showin' up, radio play, sold-out college shows."

I glance up. "You really think so?"

He smiles, a little crooked. "Aye. You've got something special. It's messy, sure, but it's real. You need to believe in it again."

Something inside me softens. He doesn't know what it means, hearing someone I care about give me encouragement.

"You've saved our arses more times than I can count." I smile over at him. "You're a bloody miracle, Linus."

He laughs quietly. "I'm a manager, not a saint."

"You're both."

My comment earns a shy, faint grin. "Careful. I'll start thinkin' you fancy me."

I tilt my head, watching him. "What makes you think I don't?"

His eyes darken. The air shifts, dense and charged.

We sit in silence again. This thing between us looming.

Finally I break the tension. "We need to talk about us, don't we?"

"Probably."

"Your visa runs out when school's over. You goin' back to Dublin?"

"Unless someone offers to marry me," he jokes, then winces when he sees my face. "Sorry."

"Don't apologize. I don't want to think about losin' you."

He traces a finger around the rim of his glass. "What do you want, Liam?"

The question lingers. I stare at my hands, calloused and raw from the guitar. Try to find the words.

"I want Fireball to make it. I want Padraig happy. I want my family whole again." My voice drops. "I want you."

His lips part. "You have me."

"For now." I look up, meeting his gaze head-on. "Be honest. How long can we last? You'll finish school, go home, build a life. I'll still be chasing gigs in shitty bars. I'll still want things I can't have."

He frowns. "Such as?"

"Sex. Connection." I drag in a breath. "I love men. I love women. I've tried to choose, but I can't. I don't think I'm meant to."

He's quiet. The candle between us flickers, throwing light across his face.

"I don't want to cheat on you," I say. "I also don't know if I can be the man who stays faithful to one person forever. It's not about you. It's about whatever's broken in me."

"Maybe nothin's broken," he murmurs. "Maybe we both want more."

I huff out a laugh. "More doesn't exist. Not in the world we live in. People don't get to love two at once. Have you ever seen it in real life?"

"Polygamy?" He extends his hand across the table, fingertips brushing mine. "You ever think maybe there's someone out there who could love all of you? And all of me?"

"Someone like who?"

"Maybe we'll find her together someday."

I shake my head, half laughing. "You're mad."

"Probably." He squeezes my hand. "But it's possible."

His optimism does something to me. Something dangerous. I want to believe the world could be wide enough for an unconventional kind of love.

We fall quiet again, the background noise of the restaurant fading into white noise. He eats a few bites, finally drinking the lassi. I sip my water and let the moment settle.

"I don't know if I'm courageous enough."

Linus's fingers trace my knuckles. "You're not a coward, Liam. You're the bravest man I know."

The words affect me more than I expect. I swallow around the lump in my throat. "You shouldn't make me feel things in public."

He laughs softly. "Then finish your food before I make a scene."

I grin despite myself, tearing off another piece of naan. "Bossy."

"Manager," he corrects.

We eat in companionable silence until the plates are nearly empty. Outside, the sky's bruised purple. The rain's stopped. When we step out, the air is cool and clean. It almost smells like a new beginning.

We walk side by side down the wet pavement, our shoulders brushing. Past neon signs, the rattle of a passing bus. He slips his hand into mine without hesitation. I don't let go.

At the corner, he stops. "You still ashamed of what happened with her?"

"With Felicity?" I ask.

He nods.

"Every day." I run a hand through my hair. "I wanted to feel something. *Anything*. I hate myself for it."

He squeezes my hand. "Now you need to stop beatin' yourself up. You made a mistake. Own it, learn, move forward."

"You make it sound easy."

"It's not, trust me. I do think it's worth trying."

I look at him then, really look, and realize how much I need him. His steadiness. His quiet faith in me when I've got none left for myself.

He steps closer. "We'll figure it out, yeah?"

"Yeah." My voice is rough. "We will."

We stand there for a long moment, the city lights glinting off puddles, his breath mingling with mine. Then he leans in and kisses me, tasting of mango and promise.

When we finally pull apart, I whisper against his lips, "You're gonna ruin me."

He smiles, forehead resting against mine. "Maybe. But I'll make it worth your while."

For the first time in weeks, the noise in my head quiets.

Whatever comes next. Tour, chaos, heartbreak, I know tonight will stay with me.

The moment when I believe something will last forever.

Even if it won't.

Fourteen

AVONNA

One Month Later

I'M NOT SUPPOSED TO be here.

This thought follows me everywhere. All the time. Every minute.

Clings like the grease film on my diner apron. Lingers like the Lysol stench in the communal shower. It's embedded in my bones when I scour mildew from strangers' baseboards on a cleaning job. The air in my lungs when I call three hundred numbers a night to sell some insurance policy I'll never use.

Life on the outside is more grueling than I ever imagined.

I wasn't raised for this. I was meant to be someone's wife. A vessel to bear children. A helper. A silent shadow behind a hallowed man.

Instead, I'm in Tacoma with no car, no family, no future. A pay-as-you-go cell phone I don't know how to use properly, three jobs, and a body I don't recognize as mine.

I'm not sure how to crawl out of this hole.

It's difficult to break ingrained patterns. I still fold my clothes like they'll be inspected. I pray without thinking. Out loud, sometimes. Quiet little words under my breath when the anxiety turns to static. People around me look at me like I'm a ghost.

Maybe I am.

The house I live in is probably not even legal. Me and eleven other women. Six rooms. Bunk beds with scratchy sheets and sparse furnishings. The bathroom doors don't lock right.

Still nicer than the house I grew up in.

I keep my guitar and other things in a plastic tote under my bed. The same clothes I stole months ago. Plus, a new hoodie from my diner job.

My roommates don't ask where I'm from. I'm too weird. I don't smoke. I don't party. I don't wear makeup.

I haven't sung in almost a year. Not since I ran out of places willing to pay me to play. There's nowhere to sing here anyway. Gigs require a network, transportation, belief in your own worth.

I don't possess any of those things. Even if I did, I'm scared of what might happen if I let myself feel too much. Music still lives under my skin, but now it terrifies me.

As for the money I do earn, I wear it strapped to my body. I don't trust banks and there's no way I'd leave it at home. I've nearly saved enough for a decent car. Then I'm leaving Washington. Moving somewhere where I can start fresh. As to where, I haven't figured it out yet.

In any case, there's no point in worrying about it now. Moving is months away and my shift at the diner starts at six a.m.

I walk to work in the dark. Forty minutes down back roads, past boarded-up gas stations through rough neighborhoods. I used to keep a rock in my coat pocket. Now I carry a kitchen knife in my boot. I don't think I'll need to use it, but it makes me feel less helpless.

The work isn't bad. I pour coffee. Wipe counters. Memorize breakfast orders and pretend diner's small talk doesn't make my stomach tie up in knots. Sometimes they leave good tips. Sometimes they don't. It all evens out in the end.

The regulars call me "quiet girl" or "baby doll." I don't mind the nicknames, sometimes it's the only part of my day I feel like anyone notices me. My boss and workmates are nice enough, but we're from different worlds.

Marcy, one of the waitresses, is blonde and sharp and perpetually wears bright-red lipstick. She offered me a vape once, then laughed when I held it like a crucifix.

"You ever think about stripping?" she asked me two days ago while stirring powdered creamer into her coffee like it wasn't the most jarring sentence I'd heard in my life.

Speechless, all I could manage was to shake my head.

She shrugged. "You've got the face and body for it. So much mystery. Your quiet-church-girl thing? Men go wild. You'd make an absolute fortune. Let me know if you change your mind."

I went home and vomited in the toilet. Then I cried for an hour, curled around the idea of being touched. Watched. Desired. The idea of taking off my clothes in front of strangers made my skin crawl.

Worse, it made something inside me spark. Like a match I was never allowed to strike.

The spark scared me most. Not the disgust.

The curiosity.

Later, I prayed harder than I ever have since leaving. Cried from shame and confusion. It wasn't the first time I thought about going back to my old life. Most nights, I've wondered if they'd take me back. Marriage to Brother Gideon would at least be predictable, if it was still on the table. Maybe I could repent, do penance, earn back my place.

The truth is, I know what would actually happen.

They'd punish me. Beat me within an inch of my life. Disfigure me. Probably sterilize me too. Anything to make me permanently undesirable. Strip me of any chance at a future. I'd never be allowed to marry. Never be allowed children. I'd be a cautionary tale brought before the congregation during sermons.

A living, breathing example to keep the rest of the women in line.

There's no going back and, truthfully, even in the most challenging moments I don't want to.

I've made my bed, so to speak.

For now, I'm suspended. Hollowed out and waiting for my life to begin.

Today, the diner is quiet. A few booths full of truckers scarf down huge breakfasts and a couple old men read actual newspapers. I move through my section without thinking, hands robotic, lips stitched in a polite smile as I refill coffee.

I notice a woman at the far corner booth. She's been coming in every morning the past couple of weeks. Mid-forties, short brown hair streaked with silver. Wears a thick flannel jacket over a white T-shirt and jeans. Her eyes track me gently, not in a creepy way. More like she's studying something she remembers.

She tips twenty on a six-dollar bill.

When I thank her, she asks, "Could you meet me outside for a moment when your shift's over?"

Panic flares. My first instinct is to flee. Is she from the compound? I don't recognize her. Will she try to bring me back?

When I take a breath, something about her kind smile calms me. It's not threatening. It's...knowing.

I finish my shift a couple hours later. Clock out. Pull on my hoodie. My hands shake a little when I push the door open and step into the overcast gray. I doubt the woman would wait this long.

Sure enough, though, she's leaning against a blue sedan. Smiles when she sees me.

"Sorry if this is weird." She wrinkles her nose. "When I came in a couple weeks ago, something about you brought back some memories for me."

I nod, unsure how to respond.

"I used to be where you are," she adds. "Staring into space. Robotic politeness. Deep, bone-chilling terror. I see it in your eyes."

I glance down at the gravel. This conversation is making me extremely uncomfortable.

"Forgive me for being blunt. Have you escaped from somewhere fundamentally religious?"

I freeze. I don't recognize the term, but I understand intrinsically what she's asking.

She whispers, "Yeah. I thought so. Me too."

A long silence settles. The wind kicks up. I hug my arms around myself.

"You don't have to say anything, sweetheart." She crouches down to catch my gaze. "I only want you to know you're not crazy. You're not alone. What you're feeling? The shame. The confusion. The fear. It's valid. It'll get better."

I look up at her, tears sting my eyes.

"I couldn't live a normal life for years without crying," she confesses. "I couldn't date. I felt out of place. Like I was a demon in disguise."

Tears spill before I can stop them.

She reaches into her coat pocket and pulls out a business card.

"There's a group here in Tacoma. Therapy for people recovering from purity culture. All of the counselors are survivors themselves. It helped me. Saved me, really."

I take the card.

Her name is Megan Malloy. She gives me her personal number.

"Please don't go back." She takes my hand. "Whatever they told you, shame isn't salvation. Silence isn't virtue. You deserve your own voice. Call the number any time, you're not alone."

With a quick wave, she gets in her car and drives away.

I stare at the card in my hand until my fingers go numb.

Black ink on soft cream paper. No cross. No scripture. A name, a phone number, and a small, hand-drawn spiral. The walk home feels longer today with the card in my coat pocket. Every few blocks, I touch it again. As if it might vanish if I don't keep checking.

My mind whirls around the concept of help.

I have no idea what to think.

Back home, help meant confession. Kneeling in the prayer tent for hours. Fasting until the world tilted. Chanting until your soul felt scraped raw.

Help meant silence. Obedience. Suffering. Earned pain was proof you were worthy of salvation.

This? A stranger with caring eyes and a business card? I don't know how to trust it.

I do know something in my chest is shifting. There's a stir I don't understand.

At the house, no one's around. My bunkmate's probably still at work. The bathroom's empty. I lock the door, just in case. Sit on the toilet lid and take out the card again.

I read the name over and over.

Tacoma Healing Collective
Trauma Recovery & Therapy | Sliding Scale
Specialists in Religious Harm & Purity Culture
(253) 555-0012

My thumb rubs the edge until it starts to fray. A year ago, I wouldn't have dared to think about therapy. But now, I'm already so far from who I was a year ago.

I tap the number into my phone. My finger hovers over the call button.

Then I hit save instead.

Small steps.

Fifteen

Five Days Later

I'M BUZZING FROM THE sheer joy of it all.

Fireball's final show of the West Coast run.

Seattle didn't just show up, they roared. I felt every beat of it. From the crowd and stage and everywhere in between.

I'm good at my job. Coordinating all the details.

Load-in at noon, backline tuned and techs briefed by four, security swept by six. I scheduled the interviews, wrangled Felicity a makeup artist when she threw a fit. Chased down Liam's replacement guitar strings when his high E snapped in soundcheck. I even stopped a drunk house tech from knocking over Padraig's kick pedal mid-set.

Every fire handled, every cue hit. They don't see it, not really. If I'm doing my job correctly, they won't need to.

God, I feel it.

Something bigger. The prospect of this band becoming a movement.

Fireball's not perfect. They're messy, chaotic, too scattered at times. But they've got it. The "thing."

Liam. Jesus. Watching him play tonight, something inside me cracked open.

His fingers blurred across the fretboard, curls plastered to his forehead, black shirt clinging to his spine. He tipped his chin up during the final chorus of *Tír na nÓg*, sweat gleaming under the lights, and for a second, he wasn't playing, he was flying.

I swear he levitated during the bridge, caught in the gravity of the crowd.

No one could look away.

Including me.

I linger near the stage door long enough to make sure the house staff's wrapping up the VIPs, then duck backstage and head for the green room. I'm exhausted. Elated. Wired.

When I push the door open, the McGloughlin twins are already inside. Drenched in sweat, adrenaline still leaking from their pores. Their older brother Connor's there too, slouched into the busted loveseat with a root beer, looking like he's right where he belongs.

I clock him instantly. Same brown eyes as Liam. Bigger. Taller. A few more lines in his brow. He's young, yeah, but there's weight behind his gaze. A weariness.

I stiffen slightly, caught off-guard. Liam never said his brother would be here. Or maybe he did and I missed it in the rush.

"Linus, there you are." Liam nods at me from where he's pacing. "Connor, this is our manager."

Manager.

Not boyfriend. Not partner.

Not the man Liam kissed three hours ago behind the amps, gripping the back of my neck like he couldn't get close enough.

Not the man he bent over right in this fucking dressing room after sound check.

Just...*manager.*

The word cracks something in me, even though I knew it was coming.

We agreed to keep it quiet in our families. Until we figure out how to make it work without blowing up the band. So, I get it. I do.

Hearing me reduced to a title burns. The distance in his voice, like none of us ever happened. Like I'm here to carry gear and cut checks.

I stay quiet. Swallow it. The truth is, I'd do anything for him. For all of them. Even if it means pretending I'm not the one who gets to see the real Liam when the lights go down.

Connor stands, offers his hand. "Heard good things. Cheers."

I take it. "Pleasure. Congrats on joining the encore."

Connor shrugs like it's nothing, but there's pride in his posture. He looks from me to Liam and back again, eyes narrowing like he's connecting dots I'm not sure he wants laid bare.

Before I can say more, the door swings open again and Felicity breezes in, all eyes and attitude.

Her dress clings in ways beyond comprehension. Navy satin draped low on her back, lips painted the color of bruises. She heads straight for the mirror and blots her lipstick with practiced disdain.

"C'mon," she coos. "Can't we splurge on champagne for the last night of tour?"

She's not talking to me. She never talks to me when there's someone more important in the room.

Padraig doesn't flinch. "Felicity. If you want to get fucked up, we have the next few weeks off. Do it on your own time."

"For Christ's sake," she scoffs. "For a bunch of Irish guys, you're no fun. Too fucking wholesome."

Connor raises his eyebrows. Liam's silent.

I sense it before it hits. The shift in energy.

Connor gives her a polite nod. "Hey, love, mind giving us a minute, yeah? Family stuff."

"Me?" She blinks at him in mock confusion. "Oh, don't worry about me. I *belong* here. Go about your business."

Her eyes flick over me, lingering a fraction too long.

Liam growls, "Jesus Christ. Take a fuckin' hint."

His words give her the opening she's been waiting for.

She straightens intentionally, every motion rehearsed. "For the record. This is *my* band too. I've been part of every show. Every mile on the road. Every song. I'm sick of being treated like an outsider."

I see it then. The crack in her mask. Not hurt—calculation.

Padraig tries to soften it. "Felicity, c'mon. We haven't seen our brother in over a year. This isn't band shit, its family, okay?"

She scoffs. Grabs her bag. Flips her hair.

Exits, stage left.

The door clicks shut. Silence falls.

Liam collapses into the chair across from Connor. Padraig rubs his temples. Connor leans in, ready to talk shop.

I retreat, giving them space. My job's done in here. I most certainly am not family.

Outside the dressing room, I lean against the wall, head tipped back, trying to quell my thoughts. The inevitable fallout with Felicity. Me leaving eventually.

"Manager, huh?" I whisper to no one.

I'm not naive. Unless something changes, we have an end date. One I try not to think about. I know I'm not merely their manager. I'm the man he wakes up beside every morning.

I know how he likes his coffee and how his breath stutters before he comes.

Still. The scene in the dressing room twists something deep in my gut. What if I'm not with them one day?

I don't get long to dwell. Felicity storms over, heels clacking like gunfire. I instinctively step back, but she sees me.

Of course she does.

"Oh." Her voice is syrupy with venom. "The shadow emerges."

I don't rise to it. "Rough night?"

"Don't start with me." She stalks past, then doubles back. "Actually, no. Let's do this."

I blink. "Do what, exactly?"

"This." She throws her arms wide. "This little silent war everyone's pretending isn't happening. You think you're so fucking clever, managing the band, playing nice with the twins. I see through you. You're not special."

I meet her gaze. "I'm here to keep the band on track. Nothing more."

She laughs, bitter and broken. "Oh please. You're in love with Liam. You don't think I hear you guys fucking every goddamn night?"

I stay silent.

Her voice drops. "You don't even realize you're another notch on his belt."

My spine straightens. I'm aware of Liam's fuck-boy past, but hearing it from her point of view is raw. Real.

"How many times do you think he fucked me? Twice? Three times?" She leans in, breath hot. "Try nine."

My stomach turns.

"Every time he was bored. Or lonely. Or drunk on the high of the crowd." She smirks. "You think you're different? Nah. You're the clean-up crew. A fuck-buddy until he decides to move on again."

I exhale in defeat. "You're angry. I get it. Whatever's happenin' between Liam and me isn't your business."

"Oh, it is," she snaps. "I've been pushed aside. Replaced."

"You're not being replaced. You're choosing not to be part of the team." My tone is intentionally callous. "You're talented, Felicity. But you treat everyone like they're beneath you."

For a split second, I see something underneath the bravado. Pain.

Then she shoves it down.

"You'll see," she says softly. "He doesn't stay. He never stays."

She walks away.

Back in the dressing room, the energy's calmer. Liam's laughing at something Padraig says, head tipped back, eyes crinkled with joy. He looks younger when he's happy. Lighter.

He sees me and waves me in, eyes sparkling.

"Everything sorted?" he asks.

I nod. "Venue's happy. Merch sold out. Tour's a wrap."

He gives me a quick grin, all teeth.

Later, when I fall asleep next to him, he pulls me closer than usual. Like he's afraid I'll disappear.

We still have months before we have to cross that bridge.

For now, I'll take whatever he has to give.

Sixteen

LIAM

Nine Months Lataer

PADRAIG'S IN THE LIVING room when I get home.

No surprise. It's Sunday, early afternoon, where else would he be?

He's curled up in the corner of the couch, one arm hooked behind his head, eyes closed. Not asleep. Motionless. He does this a lot lately. As if moving might make something else fall apart.

I toe off my boots by the door and drop my jacket on the hook. "You miss church or did you finally renounce God for rock and roll?"

His lips twitch, barely. "Don't need church when you live with a judgmental bastard."

"Fair."

I flop into the armchair across from him, legs wide. There's a mug on the coffee table. Half-drunk tea, probably cold by now. A stack of spiral notebooks, none of them mine. One of my cracked picks sits on top as a useless paperweight.

He still hasn't looked at me.

"Stevie made it to New York okay?" I ask, even though I already know. I watched her Instagram story this morning. She posted a sunrise over the Hudson with the caption: *New chapter begins.*

Padraig nods. "She landed last night. Her mom went with her."

No mention of how he wishes he'd gone with her. No mention of the shattered look on his face when her name came up at the show last night. For weeks until she left, he'd been pacing the house like he's looking for something he can't name.

My brother's got a heart the size of Ireland and doesn't know what to do when it cracks.

I lean forward, elbows on knees. "You talk to her?"

He opens his eyes, finally. They're bloodshot. "Texted a bit."

"Good." I pause. "I know this is brutal, Dar."

"No, you really don't." His voice is rough, not unkind.

Fair enough. I don't exactly know...*yet.*

He sits up straighter, rubbing his palms together, trying to generate friction against something he can't name. "You think it's a good thing, don't you?" he mutters. "Her leavin'. For you it's a win."

The way he says "win" hits me in the sternum.

Doesn't mean I'm going to react. "Well, if you mean by "win," I think it's good she's chasin' her dream, then yes. Same way you should feel."

He stares at me. "What the fuck do you mean?"

"It means you've been playin' house since you were seventeen. Her getting' the job in New York could free you up to remember who you were before she made you her everything."

He jolts. "She didn't make me do anything."

"Didn't say she did. I love Stevie, you know I do. In my opinion, though, you've forgotten how to want somethin' for yourself."

"Huh. Seems rich comin' from you."

I tilt my head. "What do you mean?"

"You and Linus, always off whisperin' about the band. Pretending it's all strategy, when really it's an excuse to be together." He jabs the air. "I've never hidden how much I love Stevie. You hide behind Fireball, so you don't have to admit how much you love him."

His comment cuts deeper than I expect.

"I can admit it." I shift in my seat. "I'm not ashamed."

"Could've fooled me. You barely look at him when we're out."

I tense. "Our relationship is no one's fuckin' business."

"Exactly." His voice drops. "No one's business but the people who give a shit. What are we doin,' Dar? Linus is someone who sees you, backs you, would burn the world down for you, and you treat him like he's disposable."

Ugh. His words land like a clean strike to my gut.

I blow out a breath, trying to keep my hands from shaking. "Can't go all in on my relationship when I'm tryin' to keep the band from fallin' apart."

He shakes his head. Not angry. Sad. "I get it, Dar. I do. But Stevie's gone. She's *actually* gone. I can't pretend I'm not wrecked. Can you give me a fuckin' break?"

His voice fractures. I hate for him to hurt this bad. I can't fix it and I'm the reason we're here circling each other like strangers instead of the only constants we've ever had.

"I never hid how much I love her." He squeezes his eyes shut. "I never made her feel small for being part of my world, I wanted her to be *immersed* in my world. It hurts she didn't want the same thing. You have someone who'll do anything for you—for Fireball. You treat him like he's leavin' and he's not even gone yet." His eyes flash open. "Make it make sense?"

I rub my eyes. This conversation is spiraling into territory I'm not comfortable acknowledging myself, let alone discussing it with anyone else. Besides, I haven't even broached what I came here to say.

"About the band." I let out a heavy sigh. "We need to talk about what's happenin'."

He scoffs. "Here we go."

"I'm serious."

"So am I. You want me to promise I won't follow her, right?"

I flinch. "No. Well, yeah, kind of. Fireball won't continue if you're not with me."

"I'm *here*," he snaps. "I chose Fireball. I didn't fuckin' go to New York."

"You're half here. I need you all the way in."

"I'm not a machine."

I stand and pace. My hands are fists at my sides. "Do you remember what this band means to me? To us? Do you even fuckin' recall the sacrifices Connor made for us to have this shot?"

He blinks. "Of course I do."

"No." I turn to face him. "I don't think you ever really did. You've been distracted by Stevie for years. God, my ears used to bleed at the sound of you two fuckin' like rabbits in our dorm room."

He doesn't answer.

"For me." I gesture around the room. "Music's the only thing to ever make sense. The only thing I had when Da threw me down the stairs. Something you and I create together."

Padraig flinches. Of course he knows. He's the one who stood between us and took a shot in the face trying to stop it from happening.

In the hovering silence, I might as well say my piece.

"You think I don't want to let myself love Linus the way you love Stevie? I do. *Jesus*, I do. But what's the point? His visa's up soon. He's not stayin.' Why open my fuckin' heart up any more than I have when I know he's goin' to leave? Both of us know it'll be fuckin' impossible for us to have a long-term, committed relationship with each other. Neither of us want to be in a monogamous gay relationship."

I rake my hand through my hair, restless. Raw.

"I have to focus on the only thing I've ever been good at. I pour my pain into the songs. Into the stage. Into you. Fireball and you are the only two things I have that don't make me feel like my life is a mistake."

Padraig's expression flickers. Concern etches his brow. I'm not saying this to manipulate him, I'm bleeding out the cold, honest truth I've been afraid to admit.

"I'm alive because of this band," I finish. "Knowin' we'd be doing this together...we can be great. Make a difference. Not only for us. For Connor."

Padraig lets out a bitter breath. "If I ever lose you, I won't be able to bear it."

I pause, taken off guard.

He steps closer, voice low but shaking. "I've chosen you for years, Liam. The band. The dream. Every time Stevie needed support, I was focused on the next gig. Every time she talked about us raisin' a family together someday, I blew her off like it wasn't a priority. When it comes down to it, I didn't give her any hope she could have a happily ever after with me. She's always known you and the band are my priority. I'm tryin' to come to terms with my choice, Liam. Can you please give me the space to process?"

"Padraig—"

"No. You don't get to act like I've been half-in. You don't get to question my loyalty when I've been bleedin' for Fireball right alongside you."

My throat goes dry. He's not yelling. He doesn't need to. The hurt in his voice says everything. I've asked him for too much and he's given it. I'm a fucking asshole. "I know. I'm sorry I made you feel otherwise."

"Are you?" His voice cracks. "Most times, it feels like none of it counts. Like I'm never enough."

"Can we both dial it back for a second?" I beg. "We've got a real fuckin' shot and we have to make a decision. You and me. Linus sees it too, and I know you trust his opinion. Felicity's dead weight. We can't take her with us if we want Fireball to work."

Padraig shakes his head, exhausted.

"I want to dump Felicity," I state plainly. "Then rerecord the EP with a new vocalist. Someone who actually wants to be in the band, not create drama for the sake of it."

He crosses his arms. "Are you fuckin' serious? We've done too much with her. Rehearsals. Studio time—"

"So what. Now's a good time to cut our losses and start fresh. She's not the right fit."

"She's good."

"She's poison," I shoot back. "In the past year, she turns every rehearsal into a power struggle. The woman terrorizes Linus with her demands. And stop pretendin' she's not trying to get in your pants. It's so fuckin' obvious she's turned her obsession with me to you."

His jaw sets. "She hasn't—"

"She has," I snap. "She's been givin' you the ooey-gooey, honey-bear treatment to get you on her side. You think I don't see it? *Everyone* does."

Padraig looks away, color high in his cheeks.

I carry on. "Dar, you're loyal to a fault, but this isn't about loyalty. It's about purpose. About buildin' something lastin' so the sacrifices we've made are worth it."

"Truthfully, I don't have it in me right now to make a change." He exhales. "I don't see how you do."

"A toxic dynamic isn't getting us anywhere. If we don't dump her, what do we do? Tell me."

He can't.

"You've said more than once," I suppress my fervor for a second, "I'm your anchor. The truth is, you're mine, Dar. I *need* us."

His eyes flick up. "You could have Linus if you wanted."

I close the distance, drop onto the coffee table in front of him. "I love Linus. I really do. But, our time is almost up."

Padraig frowns. "You don't know..."

"I do."

"Really?"

"I think..." I scrub a hand down my face. "I think I don't want to be tied down. I want to fuck who I want. Love who I want. Build a career no one can take from me."

He shakes his head. "I don't believe you. You'd take fuckin' around over Linus?"

"Yes."

"*Bullshit.*"

I meet his gaze and double down. "Believe me. I want this to be you and me. You *beside* me. Not behind me. No distractions. We started this together. It's the only thing we have."

"I miss her." His shoulders slump.

"I know."

He buries his head in his hands. "No, *really* miss her. Her laugh. Her way of knowin' exactly what I need. The way she always makes me feel."

"I miss her too."

He laughs, surprised. "You do?"

"She's always been our glue." I pat his knee. "From the time we were kids."

"I wish I believed you."

"Now." I smile. "If you stop letting Felicity cloud your decisions, we've got a shot."

He groans and hides his face in his hands.

I stand and offer my hand. "You know I'm right."

"Doesn't mean I want to admit it." He takes it and I pull him up.

"Start by showin' up. Fully. We've got new tracks to cut. A shot at touring this summer. A few festivals are sniffin' around."

He perks up. "Seriously?"

"Linus has contacts. Our new songs are better than anything we've done."

His brow furrows. "You really think we can replace her?"

"I know we can."

He looks at me, really looks. "Let's get through the shows we have and low-key look around."

My chest eases. "Yeah?"

"Yeah."

We sit in silence again. Not heavy. Hopeful. Like something cracked open to let something new in.

He glances at me. "So...we're back?"

I grin. "We never left. We forgot who we were."

His slings an arm around my neck. "Let's fuckin' find out."

Seventeen

AVONNA

Nine Months Later

I SIT WITH MY knees pressed together.

My fingers are laced so tight they've gone cold.

Dr. Camille Lane waits for me to speak. She's used to it by now. How I talk in pieces. Like my voice still needs permission.

"I saw something today, Dr. Lane," I manage finally. "I can't stop thinking about it."

"Please call me Camille." Her face stays soft. "Tell me."

"I was seating a couple. At Delgado Cocina, where I work." I try to relay like it's just another story. "They were maybe in their twenties. Not much older than me. He touched the small of her back when she walked through the door. Not in a creepy way. More like he was used to touching her." I

125

breathe through the discomfort. "She smiled when he did it. Like she was safe. His touch meant something good."

Dr. Lane nods. "How did it make you feel?"

"Like I was going to cry," I whisper.

She waits. No questions. Always lets me unspool it first.

"I'm not sure why," I continue. "I've seen a million couples touch each other the same way. It wasn't even sexual. Not really. But it was the look she gave him. So intimate. Familiar. I realized I don't know what it feels like to be touched. It made me sad."

Camille leans forward slightly. "Tell me more about what touch meant in your upbringing."

I hesitate. My mouth tastes metallic, like I've bitten down on something old. I should be used to this, the unraveling of my old way of thinking.

I'm not. It's meticulous, painstaking work.

Ten months ago, when I first sat in her office, I could barely make eye contact. I'd already endured months of religious reprogramming with Megan and her team, but fear still lived in my body.

Camille took things up a notch. Introduced me to somatic therapy. Breath work. Grounding exercises. Taught me through psychoeducation how language can be a tool to reclaim autonomy. I didn't believe her. Not at first. Eventually, through EMDR and narrative work, I was able to tease apart which beliefs belonged to me and what had been forced on me.

The first time she asked me to say the word "pussy" in this room, I whispered it through tears. I grew up believing my pussy was a source of sin. A site of male dominion. I was taught if a man entered me, I belonged to him permanently. Nudity was forbidden. Avoided at all costs.

Even after I left, I changed in the dark. Closed my eyes when I washed myself. Perfected the art of vanishing from my own gaze.

I'm still learning. Still unwinding shame from my skin like barbed wire. Still reminding myself this body belongs to me. I can speak about the past while staying in the present. I don't look away from my history. It's part of me.

"There were rules. A woman couldn't touch a man unless she was married to him. But men could...indicate interest. By handling the women. Wherever..." Her next words feel like blood under my tongue. "The first time I bled, I was thirteen. Mother told me I was ready for the preparation. God was watching me now."

Camille says nothing for a moment before asking gently, "What do you mean, Avonna?"

"It's when men stopped treating us like children and started looking at us like...prospects." I stare at the seam of the couch cushion between us. "They'd have us stand in the chapel after devotion. The men would come in. The Elders, husbands, young male members. They'd touch our faces. Pluck our breasts. See how we responded." My hands fidget. "They wanted to know if we were obedient. Modest. If we knew how to listen. Obey. Sometimes they'd observe us walking or speaking. Sometimes they'd correct us if we didn't do it right."

I glance up. Camille's expression doesn't change. She's listening with her whole body.

"This went on until you were chosen. When I was sixteen, I still hadn't been married, which was unusual. I thought maybe they'd forgotten me, but they hadn't. The Elders were waiting." My voice is smaller now. "I was promised to a man who was sixty-two years old. He already had four wives. None able to bear more children, so I was chosen to be the new breeder."

Dr. Lane doesn't speak, but I can see the grief in her eyes. It's not pity. It's witness.

"When I found out, I planned to escape. I ran the day I was to be married." I recount my story vividly. When I'm done, the silence is heavy but not suffocating. "I was lucky. Nothing happened to me. My only regret is I'll never know what became of my sisters."

"Avonna, what happened to you wasn't nothing." Camille leans in slightly. "You were molested. Brainwashed. You've been shaped by it, conditioned in it. A superior insisting you belong to someone other than yourself is abuse."

I nod, grateful for the confirmation. "I'm scared I'll never be normal."

"There *is* no normal." She smiles. "You survived. Now we continue the work of healing you."

She always makes me believe in myself and the possibility of a future. "I saw what happened to the girls who said no. Or cried too loudly on their wedding nights. They were forced into submission and they changed. Became robots. I didn't want to live if I was dead inside."

Silence folds around us.

"Sometimes I feel guilty." Tears stream down my face. "Maybe escaping and knowing what these women endure is worse. My sisters won't ever know better."

Camille's voice is like soft cloth wrapping around a wound. "You carry what's called survivor's guilt."

My body is wracked with sobs. I can't speak.

"Now," she says carefully, "you're noticing the stirrings of desire for companionship. Love. But you don't trust it."

"No." I shake my head. "I don't know if it's what I want. Or if I deserve it. I see a man and I feel...dirty. Am I ruined?"

"Tell me what you mean."

I shift in the chair. "I think about things a lot. About...sex. About being touched. I'll be folding napkins at the hostess stand and suddenly I'll picture something. A flash. Someone kissing me. My thighs parting. My breasts tingling. I don't know if I actually want to feel things or if I'm fantasizing about stuff I shouldn't be." I breathe shallowly, afraid of my own honesty. "I've never even touched myself. Not really. Not the way I hear my roommates talk about. I tried a couple weeks ago and then felt sick. I cried for an entire day."

Camille doesn't interrupt.

"Part of me thinks, maybe I don't need to figure it out. I can wait until I meet a man, get married and then my husband will show me what to do. Then I remember what marriage means where I came from and I panic. I don't know..."

"What don't you know?" she encourages.

I look at her. "I don't want to be someone's property."

"Good."

"I want to feel safe when someone touches me."

"Yes."

I blink, my throat closing again.

"Sometimes," I choke out, "I think about letting someone see me. *All* of me. Instead of fear, I feel warmth. Hunger. It's faint. But it's there. It makes me afraid."

"Why?"

I stare at the carpet. It reminds me of pressed leaves.

"Avonna?"

I look up at her "Those feelings mean I'm not pure anymore."

"You were never impure, Avonna." Camille's voice is firm. "You were controlled. There's a difference."

"I don't know what to believe."

"Of course you don't." She nods. "You were taught to see your body as made for sin and your thoughts of sex as impure. None of this is your fault."

I don't realize I'm still crying until I feel the heat of the tears rolling down my cheeks.

"I don't know how to move forward," I admit. "Not without shame crawling into my soul."

"You're already wanting," she says. "Imagining touch without hurt or humiliation. Your body is speaking for itself."

I go still.

"I'm scared to ever have sex." I wring my hands until they're sore. "I'm afraid I'll freeze. Or disappear. Or say yes in a weak moment and then want to take it back."

"All of these feelings," Camille assures me, "are common for survivors. We'll take it step by step. You're learning how to trust yourself, and for now, trusting yourself is the only thing you should focus on."

I peer up at her. It's not exactly a breakthrough. But it's something.

A crack in the wall. A small, flickering light under my skin.

I don't know if I'll ever feel normal. I don't even know what normal means.

Maybe I'll settle for safe.

Camille turns to me carefully. She knows I'm basically a cornered little kitten. "You were never allowed to be touched, right?"

"No. Not even as a child." I wince at how many physical interactions I've shied away from out here in the real world. "Hugs were discouraged. I was taught touch was a gateway to sin."

"Even if you didn't initiate?"

"Didn't matter. It meant you'd provoked it."

"So you learned accepting comfort was dangerous." She taps her pen on her chin.

"I remember once, I was five or six. I reached for my mother's hand in a prayer circle. She pulled away so fast it was like I'd burned her." I swallow. "She told me only men touch women, and only in marriage. Everything else leads to wickedness." My voice falters. "I didn't understand. I wanted comfort."

Camille shifts in her seat. "Would you like to be touched now? A hug?"

I flinch—then freeze.

She adds, "Only if it would help."

I don't answer right away. Then I nod.

She gets up and sits beside me. Opens her arms.
I lean in. I'm starving for human touch.
When she holds me, I feel it.
The grief.
Not loud. Not dramatic.
Deep.
Like a well inside me, finally touched by the sun.
Her hands are gentle. Not moving, resting. One on my back. One behind my shoulder. No pressure. No agenda.
I don't know what to do with it.
So I bawl. Silent. Breathless. Like my bones are exhaling for the first time.
"I'm sorry," I whisper.
"You have nothing to apologize for." She pats my shoulder lightly.
When she lets me go, it's measured.
My skin doesn't recoil in shame, which feels like a miracle.
I believe her. A little.

Eighteen

LINUS

Three Months Later

OUR CHEAP HOTEL ROOM reeks of cigarette smoke and old coffee.

The air is still, holding its breath.

As if the walls themselves haven't yet decided whether last night was a win or a funeral.

I sit naked at the edge of the bed, spine aching the way it always does when adrenaline from a show wears off and there's nothin' left but gravity. My phone buzzes again on the nightstand.

Probably Felicity. Or her lawyer.

I don't reach for it. My world is on fire and the madness of last night is the least of my worries.

Across the room, Liam is sprawled out on the couch, one arm slung over his eyes like the light's too much to bear.

He's shirtless, one jean-clad leg is hooked over the back, long and lean and carelessly beautiful. His lips are pursed with tension. He gets this way when he holds in too many things for too long.

I let myself look.

Really look.

God, he's beautiful.

It still hits me sometimes. How this impossible man is mine, if only in the fragile way anything can belong to anyone. I've kissed every inch of his skin. I know every sound he makes when he comes. I know exactly how to touch him when he can't find the words to speak his truth.

Somehow, it's never quite enough. He's slipping away and I don't know what to do.

He stirs under my gaze, exhales. "I feel you starin.'"

"You're my favorite thing to look at."

His mouth curves, lazily. "You're biased."

"Extremely."

He doesn't lift his arm, doesn't open his eyes, but I see the smile twitch again before it fades when he remembers the real world's still out there.

Yesterday, we finally got rid of Felicity.

She self-imploded, dragging the entire band into the blast radius. Padraig finally snapped. Fireball *might* survive. If it does, it'll be a different animal.

One I won't be part of.

As much as I despised Felicity, it wasn't only her we lost last night. It was the illusion Fireball could keep going in its current state. For me, I finally came to terms with the fact Liam and I aren't going to make it.

Not this version of us.

I'm leaving soon. Heading home for Dublin. I don't have a choice. My visa's expiring. Graduation is a breath away. I'll be on a plane back in less than two months' time. No job. No apartment. No plan. Other than I want to continue managing bands. I'm good at it.

Liam hasn't said it, but I know him well. He's been emotionally pulling away in preparation for my departure. The space between us expanding like a fault line.

I know why. He doesn't want to hurt me by making promises he can't keep. He loves me. I love him. I believe this with every ounce of my being.

But, he wants more. So do I.

The worst part is, wanting what seems impossible doesn't make either of us wrong. We're not gay. We can't make it work as a gay couple. We're not straight either, so where does it leave us?

We need a third. A woman. Someone whom we can love and will love both of us. The truth of the matter sits between us like a missing limb.

I want a woman to hold Liam when I can't.

To fuck me while he watches.

I want Liam and I to worship her together and fill her with our seed and make a family, however unconventional this might seem.

We both crave a kind of love that doesn't fucking exist except in fantasy-land.

So, I'm not gonna beg him. It's a sad end to a beautiful love.

Liam moves his arm and opens his eyes. Barely a squint. He studies me for a long moment, trailing his gaze to my thickening cock. Hesitates, deciding whether to speak.

"Are you gonna say it?" he finally asks

"Say what?"

"Goodbye? You're leavin', right?"

I exhale through my nose. "Doesn't matter to you."

"Fuck, Linus." He's furious. "You always go there. Like you've already written me off."

"Not true," I protest. "Did it occur to you I was thinkin' I can't ask you to follow me when I know you won't?"

Silence. It hurts. More than I want to admit.

"Linus..." He grimaces. "You *know* I love you."

I nod. "I do."

"I don't know how to be what you need." He scrubs his face with his hand. "Not without fuckin' it up."

"I don't want perfect. I want real." I lean forward and rest my forearms on my thighs.

His eyes flicker. "We both know real means I can't be only yours and you can't be only mine. We've said it from the beginning."

"Well..." I swallow. "How about we stop pretendin' for a change."

Liam studies me. "Are you serious?"

"Yes." I say it without shame. "I want someone who can love both of us."

He swallows. His fingers twitch where they rest on his stomach. "I want it too, but I don't know how to find it."

"Neither do I." I sigh heavily. "Doesn't mean I'm gonna stop lookin'."

Liam sits up like the weight of it all is dragging behind his shoulders. He looks exhausted. Beautiful. He crosses to the bed and stands in front of me, bare, eyes burning.

"I don't know how to keep you."

I place my hands on his hips and draw him toward me. "Please stop pretendin' we're not already spinnin' toward different skies."

He kneels between my legs. His hands find my thighs. When he rests his forehead against my chest, I wrap my arms around him and hold on like I still believe we can survive this.

Love isn't the problem. It's abundant between us. It's the fear we both carry.

It's always been the knife at our backs.

So we default to sex. Like we always do.

Liam doesn't wait for permission, his mouth demands my cock. The heat of his lips swallows my head and I swear everything goes white at the edges. He sucks in slow, greedy rolls. Tongue dragging along the underside of my shaft, tasting me in long, methodical strokes.

He takes me deep, past the rim of his teeth, and I feel the soft, rough scrape at the base of his throat as he works me the way I love. He hums, a guttural, animal sound vibrating along my cock and into my bones. My hand finds the nape of his neck and I clamp down to anchor myself to him.

Liam sucks me with precision. Throat opening, throat closing, taking me, then releasing me so my tip quivers with each squeeze. Each time his tongue flicks along the thick vein underneath my crown, I see stars burst behind my lids.

His hands aren't idle, either. One clutches his own cock, stroking himself as he works me with his mouth. The other maps the soft hollow where my thigh joins my pelvis, his thumb kneading the warm flesh behind my balls until my breath stutters. Without breaking his rhythm, he descends to the place between my scrotum and my asshole.

He tongues my taint with long, deliberate licks, circling my puckered rim, then dipping inside. A sharp, involuntary exhale turns into a choked wheeze.

Liam loves it when he coaxes this sound from my soul. He works me, sliding his fingers under my balls, pulling them up and nuzzling with his mouth. He sucks one into his cheek, then the other, slurping them both into the hollow and rolling them gently against the roof of his mouth. The sensation is obscene. Exquisite.

Impossibly intimate.

My hips start to buck, betraying me. I wince, trying to carve time out of the pressure building in my gut, but Liam clamps a palm to my sternum and pins me down with his weight.

His eyes are fierce when he looks up at me, pupils blown. "Stay with me."

A command I wish I could obey.

He drags his tongue in wide, velvet strokes, then flicks it sharp at my frenulum until I'm whimpering, fingers digging crescents into his scalp. When he takes me again, he goes deeper than before, pushing until the back of my cock hits his throat and he gags. One sharp, involuntary sound and I can't help but clamp down on his head with guilt and a feral wanting all at once.

Liam swallows my cock down, throat bobbing. His determined motion sends me into a frenzy.

I'm on the edge, lurching toward the cliff, and he answers me—palm wrapping my shaft in a rhythm echoing the bobbing of his throat. His eyes are locked on mine with a wrecked, worshipful look intended to remind me how thoroughly I'm loved.

The sound of his hand on his own cock is wet and urgent. Skin slapping skin, fist jerking himself in time with the way he sucks me, faster now, throat taking and giving, his own breaths hitching. He glances down, watching his hand move then resumes watching me.

The sight of him fucking himself with my cock buried between his lips sends a current through me so hot I taste copper.

"Don't stop," I croak.

His mouth becomes a vise, a temple, a furnace. I feel the knot in my stomach fist and release; it's sudden and total. My orgasm slams into me like a truck: bright white, spreading down my legs, through my hands, making my vision swim.

I howl his name, not a prayer but utter surrender, my cock seizing as ropes of come shoot against the back of his throat. He doesn't flinch. He swallows every drop, leaving me raw. When, at last, he draws back, a strand of spit and come between us snaps like a fragile wire.

He pulls his mouth free with a pop, lips and chin shining with my spunk and he licks his lips clean, eyes half-closed and luminous. For a fraction of a second I watch his Adam's apple flick, his breath hot and ragged against my sweat-slick skin.

My voice breaks, raw and needy. "Liam, please. Fuck, please—"

"Please what?" He looks up at me with wild, hungry eyes, stroking himself languidly. A tease to watch me unravel.

"Fuck me," I beg. The words pour out, shameless, thick with hunger. "I need you to fill me up."

I don't care how I sound.

I don't care how desperate it is.

My whole body's thrumming, open, craving the delicious burn only he can provide.

I lie back on the bed and my thighs fall open without thought, heels digging into the sheets, cock spent and forgotten against my stomach. Nothing matters now except Liam's thick cock buried inside me to the root.

"Liam. Please, I want it. I want you."

He hooks my knees up, wide and trembling.

The blunt head of his cock finds me, unrelenting.

"Then take it," he growls—and pushes in.

Nineteen

LIAM

Two Months Later

THE AIR'S HEAVY WITH uncertainty.

The ghost of last night's bullshit.

Linus is sprawled beneath me, eyes half-open like he needs me to fuck him back into the moment.

I'm the man for the job.

I push into his tight rim. Heat grips me. Swallows me whole. The sound he makes, broken, beautiful, lands somewhere deep in my chest and detonates.

Every inch is a fight between restraint and ruin. I breathe through it, one hand braced beside his head, the other on his hip, holding him still as I drive deeper until our skin's flush. There's no space left to pretend this is anything less than *everything*.

"Look at me," I demand.

When he does, I realize this is truly the end. His eyes glisten with unspilled tears. The sound he emits when I cant my hips is a prayer with its throat cut.

I drive into him so abruptly the bed creaks. My hips roll, find their measure, then pump vigorously. His breath catches every time I push forward. One of his hands slides down between us. He starts to stroke himself and I swear the visual nearly undoes me.

His cock comes alive again, filling before my eyes.

The sound of me fucking him, wet, rhythmic, indecent, fills the small room. His head tips back, mouth open. His heartbeat races under my palm, and he meets every thrust now, desperate, his hand moving faster.

I want to tell him he's beautiful and I love him more than life itself, but the words stay trapped behind my teeth. Instead, I suck on his neck and bite him, anything to leave proof I was here.

His skin burns against mine, damp and trembling.

We're on borrowed time. The clock's ticking down and I'll spend every last second we have together like it's currency. I fuck him like I can fuse us together. Carve us into something permanent with muscle and sweat since I can't do it with words.

Linus is close. I can tell by the way his voice fractures. The way his body arches up to meet me. How his hand moves faster. His ass muscles flex around my cock, gripping, begging, taking.

The sound he makes is half gasp, half sob, the most beautiful goddamn thing I've ever heard. The man's recovery time is unprecedented, he spurts across his stomach, causing me to lose the rhythm entirely.

My thrusts falter and I bury myself in him to the hilt as I erupt, spilling into him with a guttural yelp tearing its way out of my chest. It's not pretty. It's raw and feral. I can't tell if

I'm praying or apologizing. He clings to me through it, fingers digging into my ass, blunt nails catching on my skin.

I feel every beat of our hearts as I collapse over him. The room smells like us now. Sex, salt, loss. My forehead rests against his cheek, his breath is ragged against my lips. For a moment we stay locked together. Listening to the quiet hoping it might give us something to hold on to.

"I don't want it to end like this," I whisper.

His hand slides up my back, soft, shaking. "Neither do I."

I savor his lips as I pull out, hating how the air between us cools too fast. I watch the way he looks at me. Demolished. Still mine, for the moment. I smash my lips against his before I can think better of it.

I've told him the truth. I really *don't* want our relationship to end like this.

Burying my face against his neck, I let the familiar warmth do what it always does.

Distract. Soothe. Convince.

Linus may read my body language better than anyone ever has but he doesn't realize how truly damaged I am. Allowing him to believe we're circling toward a future instead of stalling at the edge of one is wrong.

Cruel.

"This could work." He wipes my cock with a warm washcloth, hope threaded through his words.

I nod into his shoulder, even as I begin the work of closing a door inside myself, inch by careful inch.

My reality is, I chase intensity when times are rough. I default to sex in order to outrun parts of me I don't want to face. Fidelity turns into pressure, then panic, then escape.

Linus deserves a man—or a woman—who doesn't fracture under his love. Someone who doesn't need turmoil to feel normal.

There's no way to have this conversation with my cock in his palm, however, so I stroke his body to memorize every inch. Allow another moment to stretch and deepen and feel real.

For him, it is.

To me, it's goodbye disguised as devotion.

He exhales against my temple, content. Trusting. "You're distracted."

"Nah, baby." I tighten my arms. "I'm here."

It's not a lie. Not exactly.

I give him everything I can in the present tense. I let him believe I'm choosing the possibility of us again.

If I pull away now, he'll ask questions. Offer solutions. Fight for something I already know I won't honor.

So I stay warm. Close. Convincing.

Later, when he sleeps, I lie awake beside him and think about how this is gonna go.

I'll let him go slowly.

Try to make it gentle.

Loving him means knowing when to stop pretending I'm capable of giving him what he deserves. Surviving means choosing restraint over truth, at least for now.

I close my eyes and breathe him in. Commit every part of him to memory.

He thinks we'll try.

I know I'm already letting go.

Twenty

AVONNA

Nine Months Later

Nine months ago, Dr. Camille Lane hugged me for the first time.

Since then, I've allowed her to know every part of me.

We've done so much work, I finally believed I have a body worth reclaiming.

I became comfortable with her. Free with the language of sex. Courageous enough to tell her my biggest worry was my first time. A strange kind of grief followed when I realized virginity was never a virtue, but Camille taught me the concept has been used for centuries to keep women docile.

Untouched, but not whole. Saved, but never safe.

The thought I might have almost lost my virginity to a sixty-two-year-old abuser made my skin crawl. At the same time, I hadn't ever dated and didn't trust myself to choose my first lover wisely.

Camille told me about sex therapy.

A way to bring my body in line with my mind.

Sex wouldn't be for someone else's pleasure. Only for mine. Choice. Safety. Presence. A path to explore without fear. It seemed like a safer way to learn about myself. What I could be capable of.

Now I get to rewrite the story. If I'm going to allow a man to enter my body, I'll make the choice. With someone I trust. In a space I control.

So I said yes.

Together, Camille and I created a phased program with no pressure and no timelines.

Phase one occurred over the course of a few weeks. We did exercises where I'd touch a body part and allow her to touch me there too. Nothing sexual. It was like meeting myself for the first time. Arms. Elbows. Chin. Wrists. Hips. Calves. Feet. Hands.

At night, my homework was to do the same exercises alone without clothes. Beneath the blankets, my palm trembling over bare skin, I did the exercises. It didn't take long before I realized I wouldn't disappear. There was no wrath or hellfire anywhere.

The lesson was, my body's not shameful. Or sinful. It's *mine*.

Phase two ventured into sex education and immersed me even deeper into touch. Camille, essentially, taught me about the birds and the bees. Dispelled myths and horror stories I'd been fed my whole life. Guided me through weeks of learning body parts and how they function.

I studied diagrams of both the female and male body. Using anatomically correct mannequins, she showed me erogenous zones and taught me about reproduction and sex. For homework, I touched myself in the places I'd learned about. Paid attention to what felt good and what didn't.

Each night, I'd allow my hands to explore my skin without apology. Experiment with pressure, speed, combinations. Sometimes I'd cry or panic or not feel anything. Eventually, I was able to trace patterns across my belly. Nipples. Lips. Thighs. Neck.

One night, I grew brave and allowed my fingers to venture between my legs. The heat surprised me. So did the way my hips shifted instinctively. I slid my hand lower and explored my soft, slick folds. Found my clit and caressed. Brushed. Flicked. Circled. *Learned*. I stayed with it and the sensation grew and an energy unlike anything I could have ever imagined crashed over me like a wave too big to duck under.

When it subsided, I didn't feel guilt. I felt...*stillness*.
Deep, sublime, stillness.

I sobbed with joy. Curled into myself. Thanked myself for surviving and being able to give myself an orgasm. By staying with the process, I discovered self-pleasure.

Phase three was about seeing myself. This part was rough, but Camille guided me through the exercises patiently. In the beginning, I stood facing the mirror, still in bra and panties. Only when I felt steady did I watch myself undress. Over the course of many weeks, I was able to stand fully nude and look at myself. Watch myself touch the pleasurable places I'd explored in the dark.

Eventually, I made myself come in front of a mirror. I circled my clit while my free hand pinched my nipple. Aware of the rosiness spreading across my chest. My belly contracting. The exact moment my climax bloomed and my entire body shuddered with gratification.

A few days later, I did the same thing with a vibrator. Buzzing, against my palm. I started with my nipples then moved downward.

Full. Deep. *Perfect*. The moment it touched my clit, I shrieked. Then I watched as I guided it inside.

In the mirror, I saw it all. My hips moving, breasts bouncing, mouth open. When I came, I whispered, *"God."*

It was the first time I knew, with abject certainty, the woman in the mirror is divine.

Phase four was the introduction to Elijah, my sex surrogate counselor. Tall, medium build and boyishly handsome, he entered the room quietly. Never imposing, never assuming.

In the beginning, I sat curled, arms around my ribs, breath shallow. He spoke to me. Asked me questions and over time, my body softened when I became comfortable. At some point, I uncrossed my legs and let my hands fall open in my lap. One day, when he offered his hand, I reached for it. Our fingers twined.

Warmth traveled up my arm and settled low, where my shame used to live.

In later sessions, he touched my forearm, my shoulder, my thigh, always asking first. I learned to breathe through it, to communicate exactly how I felt. Eventually, we embraced and held each other. Elijah won my trust. Made me feel safe. Whole.

Phase five was a callback to phase three, only this time I learned how to be comfortable with nudity in front of Elijah. We undressed standing across from each other, with no fanfare and no words. A candle glowed between us. First, I looked at Elijah. Naked, leaning back on his elbows, legs spread apart. My eyes raked across his body. His chest, nipples, stomach, cock, balls, ass. Then, I assumed the same position and I let him gaze at me. In these sessions, what I used to think of as sin seemed sacred. I cherished the connection.

Phase six was, I suppose, my graduation. It happened over the course of many weekends. I was ready for Elijah to touch me. Steady, unhurried, he glided his hands down my back, tracing muscle, spine, the small dip at my waist. When I rolled over, I covered my chest at first, then let the my hands fall away. His palm rested over my sternum, drifted across my breasts, then lower, to my belly, my thigh, my foot.

The next week, Elijah kissed me. My mouth, the slope of my neck. His lips grazing my earlobe until I shivered. His tongue traced down, unhurried, until he found my nipples, sucking them both until they peaked. I arched toward him without meaning to. His fingers slipped lower, finding me wet, open, ready. He circled my clit with aching patience, until my body shuddered with release. I didn't know it would feel like heaven.

By week three, I couldn't wait to see him again. This time, Elijah's fingers slid through my wetness then pressed inward, curling and stroking upward until a sudden force bloomed behind my pubic bone. Pressure spread like heat through my belly. I didn't recognize the sounds coming out of my mouth when my orgasm built, cresting from my center until I fell apart. My body whispered, *"yes, this is what you were made for."*

Week four was my turn to learn how to give Elijah an orgasm. He grasped his thick cock in his hand and told me to, "Watch everything." I did. Every flex of muscle, the way his hips rose to meet his grip. When he came, it was sudden and hot, spilling across his stomach

I dragged my fingers through his thick cream. Curious, I tasted him. Salty. Primal. He smiled like I'd passed some sacred threshold. Then, he showed me how to stroke him and I discovered exactly how to make his hips buck. When he came again, I realized giving was as pleasurable as receiving.

Week five, we moved into oral. Elijah's mouth hovered over my pussy as his hands parted me gently, then he kissed and licked every inch of my pussy, from my folds to my clit. Nothing compared to the orgasms he gave me by sucking and nibbling on my little nub while his fingers worked the magic spot inside.

When I was able to breathe again, I reached for him. He was hard as steel, watching me with quiet need. I stroked him first, then tentatively took him into my mouth. Patiently, he taught me what he liked with breath and sound, until I found a perfect rhythm. With my permission, he released with a shudder down my throat. I swallowed, stunned. Changed.

Week six is when it all came together, literally and figuratively. With so much preparation under such care and guidance, I was grateful choosing my first time to happen in this setting. I no longer feared sex or felt shameful for wanting it.

Elijah knelt between my thighs, cock smothered in lube, waiting. He pushed the tip in and, once I relaxed, he entered inch by inch. My body welcomed him and he moved. Rhythmic. Precise. The pressure built fast. His cock rubbed my G-spot perfectly while his fingers stroked my clit exactly how I liked. My body convulsed, his name caught in my throat. He followed, coming with a shudder.

The last two weeks with Elijah have been my exquisite undoing. We've spent our weekends in motion, fucking with abandon. He bent me over cushions, took me standing up. I rode his cock. Sideways. Backward. Upside-down. Every which way imaginable.

We fucked in silence, in laughter, in breathless urgency. Every position is a new prayer. Every orgasm, a revelation. I've never been this alive.

There are mirrors on every side of the room now. I watch myself suck him, my body arch as he enters me, the way my skin blushes from arousal. How I look when I come.

Zero shame. No filter. Only the raw truth of embracing my sexuality.

Today, on our last day, he didn't say goodbye like a lover.

He said it like a witness. "You've done it. You know yourself now. Thank you for allowing me to be part of your journey."

Now, as I sit across from Camille to close out my program, I don't hesitate.

"I'm not finished," I tell her. "I can't stop here."

I'm finally courageous enough to tell her about the boys, who have permeated my thoughts for months.

"When I first escaped, there were two men," I recall. "I was hired to play music at a college party and I felt completely out of place. Everyone around me seemed like aliens. Then I saw them. I can't remember much about how they looked, only how it felt to see pure adoration. Love. One had his arm around the other. They moved in sync. Then kissed. I haven't been able to stop thinking about them. Imagining myself between them. Their hands on me."

Camille leans forward. "Congratulations, Avonna. You've come full circle. tapping into your inner desires means you're no longer a victim of your past."

She's right. Owning my truth hasn't marked me for punishment. It makes me feel strong. Certain.

My body belongs to me, I'm not a sinner waiting for judgment. No one will ever convince me otherwise ever again.

Everything cracks open. "Camille, before I go out into the real world, I want to experience two men. At once. I want their hands on every inch of me. Mouths. Eyes. I want to feel filled, stretched, overwhelmed, and still safe. I want to see them touch each other too, and be part of it. I am not ashamed of wanting more. I'm ready to explore it on my terms."

I nearly laugh out loud when I hear myself ask for my deepest desire.

I want to hug myself for the progress I've made. To think, when I started this journey, I couldn't even touch myself let alone ask to be fucked by two men at once.

Desire used to feel like danger.
Now, I'm fully awake to the woman I'm becoming.
Turns out, pleasure is a language I was born fluent in.

Twenty-One

Four Months Later

THE RAIN NEVER REALLY stops in Ireland.

Sometimes it softens to mist, brushing your cheeks like breath, and other times it lashes sideways across the Luas tracks until the whole street gleams silver. Either way, it's constant. Like the ache behind my ribs.

I've been home nearly a year now. You'd think I'd have settled by now, but I still wake up expecting the sound of guitars bleeding through thin walls, or Padraig laughing somewhere down the hall. Or Liam's voice, low and rough with sleep, telling me to come back to bed.

Instead, it's radiators ticking and the sound of the telly.

Dundrum's grand in its own way. My flat sits above a pharmacy, across from the Town Centre. From my balcony,

I can see the glass roof of the shopping complex and the queue for train stretching down the platform. It's all very proper. Good schools, tidy pavements, cafés.

No chaos. No noise. No live music.

Exactly the opposite of what I'm made for.

I drop my bag on the counter and shrug out of my jacket. I've finished another fourteen   hour shift at The Merrion, herding florists, caterers, and entitled brides through a wedding costing more than most people's houses. The ballroom sparkled, the champagne flowed, and every smile felt rehearsed.

My name tag reads Linus O'Donnell, Events Manager. I earn every single penny of my salary.

Not bad for a lad barely out of uni, I suppose. Mum calls it a proper job. My da brags about it to his fellow politicians. The problem is, I can't stop thinking about the smell of beer   soaked wood floors and the thrum of bass under my feet. About doing something with my life I'm actually proud of.

I didn't come back to Ireland because I wanted to. I had no choice. When the clock ran out on my visa, there was no extension left to beg for. No marriage proposal from Liam. I had no choice but to say goodbye.

Oh, what a long, drawn-out, painful goodbye it was.

The night Felicity finally blew the whole thing apart was the end of my era. I'd spent months trying to hold the band together, patching holes in the boat while everyone else drilled new ones. Before I left, I found Arleigh, a raw, talented singer, unbothered by fame. I gave her information to Liam and Padraig, telling them she'd be the one to save them.

They promised to give her a chance, but I was convinced they'd blow her off and Fireball would descend to the bottom of the ocean without me taking the reins. A couple days later Liam texted.

Liam: Arleigh's in. You're always right
about these things, love.

It felt like hope. Maybe we'd continue things long-distance. Then silence.

He's never been in touch again. Hasn't returned any of my calls, texts, or DMs.

I tried a different tactic. I meant it when I said I'd keep managing them from Dublin. I drew up contracts, built spreadsheets, pitched them to a European promoter I knew. Sent it to both Liam and Padraig.

No reply. From either of them.

At first, I made excuses. It's arduous to integrate a new band member. The tour's mad. Wi   Fi's shit. Time zones.

I was lying to myself.

Of course, the masochist inside of me wants to reach out again. Give it one last try to connect. Maybe if I kept the tone light: *How's the tour?* Or encouraging: *I'm proud of you.* Perhaps, something small, human: *I really miss you.*

Then I remember the last thing he said at the airport before I left. *"If you stay, I'll never learn how to stand on my own."*

At the time it sounded noble. Now it feels like a curse.

I still follow every shaky video on YouTube, every tagged photo on socials. Through their posts, I know Fireball now manages themselves. Liam and Padraig run the show, Mitch, their roadie drives, Arleigh sings. They seem to be thriving.

Christ.

Picking up my phone, I pull up the band account and tap on their latest photo dump. Some gig in Atlanta. Liam's delectable. All sweat and sinew, head bowed over his guitar. Padraig's in the back, steady as ever. Arleigh's caught mid   note, arms outstretched, crowd roaring. They look powerful. Immersed. Beautiful.

There's another of the three of them after the set. Arms slung around each other, eyes bright.

Clearly, I'm not needed. The twins have it under control and, truthfully, maybe it's for the best. They can rely on each other, not others, for once.

I tap the screen until it goes dark.

My heart is broken.

Liam was my life. My family. My home. He's living his best life and I'm stuck in a flat smelling of new paint, immersed in a corporate hell which makes my parents proud as punch, but doesn't fit me.

The kettle clicks off behind me. I pour the water even though I don't really want tea, and watch the steam rise.

I lie to myself most days. Tell myself I'm over him. Rationalize his behavior. Our relationship was his first true love, tour adrenaline, lust and sex disguised as something real. Then my mind drifts to the small things. How Liam would rest his forehead against mine before he went on stage to ground himself.

Yeah, the truth fucking destroys me. Liam was my fucking soul and he's doing to me what he always does when he's ripped apart. Burying it. Burying me. He used his bisexuality as an excuse to break up. Claimed he couldn't be faithful.

Now he's probably fucking his way around America to purge himself of our love while I'm still a celibate ghost hovering over Fireball's social feeds, hoping for some small crumb.

I take a sip of the tea. It's gone cold already. Figures. I shut my eyes, lean back against the counter, listen to the sound of car horns honking below.

Glancing down, I see an envelope on the table with The Merrion's crest. Inside, my pay slip. I should feel grateful. My bank account is fat. Aside from rent, I don't spend any money. This job is every hospitality major's dream.

It's not mine. I'm living someone else's life. Every event I manage feels the same. Perfect, hollow, rehearsed. There's no room for creativity. Or mistakes. Or messiness.

I glance at another stack piling on the table. Gig flyers from local pubs and indie venues I'm contemplating scouting on weekends. Wondering if building something for myself will take my mind off of my sorrow.

There's even a name swirling around my head: *Isis Management.*

Isis is the goddess of restoration. If anyone needs restoring, it's me.

I could take everything I learned from working with Niahm's father and from my time with Fireball. Reimagine the bedlam into brilliance. Do it completely my way this time. Maybe in a year or two I'd have a roster. To start, a few Irish acts worth pushing abroad. Once I'm able to make enough to quit the hotel, I'll be able to breathe again, maybe even feel alive.

Until then, my job at The Merrion will fund my company. Keep Mum and Da off my back.

Like clockwork, my phone buzzes.

```
Da. Dinner Sunday? Bring a girl this
time, for God's sake. Your mum's
worried you'll turn into a priest. She
tells me Niahm's single again, maybe
give her a call?
```

I snort under my breath. Typical. They don't know about Liam. About who I am or what I want.

They don't know me. Not really.

My da, John O'Donnell sits at Cabinet meetings and talks about housing policy and national heritage. Molly O'Donnell, my mum, volunteers on school boards and parish committees. Both of them believe faith is strongest when it never bends. My sisters, Bridget and Orla fall into this same line of thinking.

Early on, when I first suspected I was attracted to men, I learned early how to compartmentalize. My personal life had to stay private. Like the time I let a guy blow me on our family holiday. How this infidelity led to my breakup with Niamh.

None of them know about Liam. How I loved him, or how we talked, late into the night, about what it might mean to build a life with a woman we both shared. I don't tell them I'm destroyed inside. Or how lonesome I am.

I suppose I could try. After all, I'm an adult who deserves to live life on my terms and have a family who loves me as I am.

Reality is, I've imagined it a hundred ways. Mum would cry and I'd never know if it was out of worry or disgust. Da would go silent, eyes fixed on the floor. He's old   school, West   Meath born, the type who measures a man's worth in pints and hurling scores.

At this point, why disappoint them for no good reason. There's no one in my life now, so what does it hurt to let them believe I'm too busy for love? Give them hope someday I'll bring home a nice girl from work. Or get back together with Niamh.

For now, I can't fathom someone else in the space where Liam used to be. Until something real materializes, best to stay under the radar.

Outside, the rain turns to mist again. Dundrum Town Centre glows against the dark like a promise of everything ordinary people want. Warmth, security, routine.

I rest my forehead against the glass and watch the lights blur. Picture the twins in their mini   bus somewhere in the States. Padraig probably dozing against the window, headphones on. Liam tapping out a rhythm on his knee, pretending not to think about the people he's lost.

In my bedroom, I pull the blinds down, undress and crawl under the covers. On the dresser, I keep a framed photo of the two of us backstage. Liam's biting my earlobe and I'm smiling cheek to cheek.

Everything good I've ever had is in the picture.

Now he's gone.

I trace the edge of the frame, open my nightstand drawer and shove it to the back. Nestling into my pillows, I listen to the rain hit the window. Hopefully someday, when Isis is real and the name O'Donnell means something in music, I'll call him. Maybe he'll answer and we can laugh about how young and foolish we were.

Maybe we'll find our way back to each other. Find our third and make the family we dreamed about.

Or, maybe not. Either way, I'll keep building. For me.

I close my eyes and concentrate on the rhythm of the rain. Steady, endless, familiar.

For the first time in months, as I drift off to sleep, I give myself permission to move on. Put the past behind me and focus on building the future I want.

The decision feels like prayer and punishment.

I wouldn't trade it for peace.

Twenty-Two

Two Years Later

Mitch's playlist hums through half-blown speakers, some lo-fi mix he swears keeps him awake.

The rest of us are ghosts in motion.

It's been two long years of the same. Long drives, shitty motels, clubs paying in envelopes of damp cash and "great exposure." Hundreds of shows, and my body feels carved out by every one of them.

The mini-bus smells like sweat, old fries, wet leather. The scent of living on the road.

Padraig's asleep beside me, chin to his chest, hair falling forward. It's long now, past his collarbone, dark waves hiding his face. His hoodie's faded and his jeans are torn in the knees. There's a grease stain on his thigh from some van repair he helped Mitch with three days ago.

He hasn't changed his clothes since. Neither have I.

We've been living like animals. Unshaven, unwashed. Chasing something elusive.

Arleigh's got her headphones on, mouthing lyrics to whatever she's listening to. Her voice is the only thing keeping Fireball afloat at this point, and she's at the end of her rope. Mitch keeps one hand on the wheel, the other cradles his third gas-station coffee.

The whirr of the tires fills the silence. My head leans against the window. The glass vibrates against my skull. Outside, the horizon blurs gray-blue, endless. We're two days out from Seattle. We're not headlining our next show, instead we're opening for my brother Connor's band, Less Than Zero at the legendary club The Mission.

The thought of home twists something inside me. We haven't been back since the Felicity debacle.

Padraig stirs beside me. "We still in Ohio?"

"Indiana now, I think."

He rubs a hand over his face, yawning. "Same shit either way. What are you up to?"

"Thinkin'." I shrug.

"Dangerous."

I huff out a laugh. "You'd know."

He stretches his legs. "Cillian texted last night. Says Da's better. Workin' part-time again, even helps Connor on job sites some days. Apparently, he's not like before."

"Connor said the same."

"Yeah." He pauses. "I think he's tryin,' Liam."

I stare out the window. "Tryin' doesn't erase what he did."

Padraig doesn't argue. He never does. Miles of silence spool between us.

I shift in my seat, the memory crawling up before I can stop it. It's always there. The sound of his voice, the look in his eyes, the smell of whiskey and sweat.

"You know what I remember most?" I murmur quietly.

Padraig looks over, wary.

"The sound." My voice barely carries. "The sound my head made when it hit the stairs."

He goes still. Doesn't blink. Doesn't breathe.

"I don't remember the pain," I go on. "Not really. I remember the noise. Like a watermelon splittin' open."

He swallows. "Liam—"

"I also remember your face," I cut in. "You were covered in my blood, and you still tried to make him stop. You shouldn't have had to."

His throat works. "I'd do it again."

"I know."

Silence permeates the van.

Oblivious, Arleigh shifts in the back, lost in her music. Mitch clears his throat and turns the volume up a notch, maybe sensing he shouldn't be privy to this conversation.

Padraig stares at his hands now. "I think about it, too. The sound of you hittin' the floor. The way Seamus cried. How Da walked away without looking back."

My stomach flips.

He keeps going, voice shaking but steady. "He looked right through you. Through both of us. Like we weren't his sons anymore. I swear, Liam, something in me broke. I'll never forgive him for it."

"Aye."

Padraig turns toward me, eyes bright with tears he'll never let fall. "You nearly died. And we never talk about it. We packed up, went to college, focused on the band, and pretended it didn't happen."

"What else were we supposed to do?" My tone's too sharp. I soften it. "Connor did the best he could. We couldn't stay. Da hated me."

"He hated himself."

I scoff. "Generous."

"He did. Still does, probably."

I shake my head. "Doesn't make it easier to see him."

He leans back, watching me. "Are you scared?"

"Of him?"

"Of going home."

I take a long breath. "Yeah."

"Me too," he admits. "But not for the same reason."

I tilt my head.

He hesitates. "You're my brother. I feel like I've spent half my life tryin' to keep you alive. The other half tryin' to convince myself you don't need me to."

My chest squeezes. "Dar—"

"No, let me say it." He runs a hand through his hair, shaking his head. "Every time I look at you, I remember thinkin' you might never open your eyes again. Now, every time you shut down or pull away, it feels like you're still halfway down those stairs."

I look at him. Really look. The dark crescents under his eyes. The weight he's lost. How his hands tremble slightly when he talks.

He's right. I've been slipping for years. Ever since Linus left.

"Sometimes I still hear him," I whisper. "In my head. Callin' me a disgrace. A shame."

Padraig's voice breaks. "You're not."

"Most days I know. But it's in there now permanently, yeah? Part of me will always wonder if loving men and women means I'm broken. Does wantin' too much make me unworthy?"

"You're not." He's adamant

I smile, small and tired. "You're biased."

"Not enough."

For a while, the only sound is the road. A faint snore from Arleigh. Mitch humming under his breath.

Padraig clears his throat. "You think you'll ever tell them the whole truth? About Linus."

"Maybe."

"When?"

"When it doesn't feel like a confession."

He nods understandingly. "He loved you."

"I know."

"You loved him."

"I still do."

Padraig looks out the window. "Then why'd you let him go?"

"I couldn't give him what he deserved. Not out here. Not while I'm still tryin' to prove I deserve to exist."

His brow furrows. "You do exist. You've done more livin' in twenty-five years than most men do in sixty."

I snort. "Yeah, and look where it got me. Broke. Exhausted. Fucked up."

What I don't say is I'm sick of taking scraps of what I want. I keep falling into a trap of fucking whoever's available when I'm horny. The release carries me for a few days until I do it all over again.

It's not enough. Not after what I had with Linus and now Linus is gone. I selfishly ghosted him to save myself from falling apart. I don't deserve him. Probably never did.

Padraig, unaware of this particular inner torment, chuckles. "You're brilliant. And loyal. And the best guitar player I've ever seen."

"Now you're lyin.'"

"Nah." He smiles. "I wouldn't bullshit youse."

We sit in fragile peace for a while.

The van rattles as Mitch swerves around a pothole. Arleigh grumbles, and slumps down on the seat.

I glance at Padraig again. "You think we can do this? Keep going?"

"We don't have a choice. We've given up too much to quit."

"You still miss her?"

He looks away. "Every second."

"I'm sorry."

"Don't be. She made her choice." He shakes his head. "I made mine. I wouldn't trade it if it means bein' with you on stage every night."

His words hit something deep. "You mean it?"

"Always."

I squeeze my eyes shut to stave off tears. "Love you, Dar."

"Love you, Dar."

Outside, the sky lightens. The first gray hints of morning edge along the horizon. I watch the blur of highway signs. "You think the wee ones will be different?"

"Of course. Cillian's twenty now, a proper uni student. Brennan's inventin' some software shit. Seamus still talks about medicine like he's already a doctor."

"Our brothers grew up without us."

Padraig sighs. "We'll make it up to them."

"Yeah?"

"Yeah."

We fall into silence again.

The air in the van feels thicker. Warmed by sunlight bleeding through dirty windows. I close my eyes and let the vibration of the road hum against my spine.

When I speak again, I'm hesitant. "You think Da even remembers what happened?"

"Dunno." He's tentative too. "Hopefully, he remembers enough to hate himself for it."

"Good."

He looks at me. "Would it help if he said sorry?"

"No. It wouldn't change what he did to me. I don't want his apology. I want peace."

"Maybe that's what this trip is for."

"Peace?"

He nods. "Aye. Or something close."

I stare out the window again. For the first time in a long while, I think of home without anger. Mostly, it's a dull ache.

"Please don't tell the others," I ask.

"About what?"

"About this. About how bad it still is. The nightmares. The flashbacks."

He nods. "I know."

"They deserve a good night. A dinner without drama." I fold my arms across my body.

"We'll keep the peace."

I let out a long breath. "One night."

"One night," he echoes.

The van bumps over a crack in the road. The years between us, the scars, the silence. All of it falls away.

We're not rock stars or broken sons or men still learning how to love.

We're two kids again, hoping for the best.

Twenty-Three

AVONNA

The Same Week

I WALK INTO THE room barefoot.

A beautiful space. Warm wood floors, soft, neutral fabrics, a large bed dressed in linen sheets.

There's a mirrored wall on one side of the room. A diffuser sends up tendrils of cedar and rose.

Elijah and Marius are already here. They're barefoot too. Relaxed. Awake. Dressed simply in soft T-shirts and loose pants.

Comfortable.

Intentional.

Camille follows me in to check on the set up. When she's satisfied, before she departs, she places her hand on my shoulder. "Avonna, tonight is the integration you desired.

You've done the internal work. Let your body tell its truth. There is no performance. You are the one in charge."

A breath sticks in my throat. She gestures toward the center of the space.

"Elijah, Marius, approach Avonna with care. Ask. Listen. Let her pace you."

They move.

Elijah steps forward first. He doesn't reach for me, though he and I have had sex in every position imaginable. Tonight is different.

He stands a foot away. "Avonna, may I touch you?"

"Yes." I breathe in.

His hands find my arms. Light. A gentle stroke up from my wrist to shoulder. Like a musician brushing the strings before playing.

Marius comes on my other side. His eyes are locked on mine, intense but not invasive. He waits until I nod. Then his hand settles on the small of my back. He leans forward and kisses my cheek.

I feel myself already pulsing between them.

They undress me together.

No rush. No grabbing.

Elijah pulls my shirt over my head, watching my face the entire time. He cups my breasts in his palms, not to grope, but to caress. Marius kneels and slides my pants down, inch by inch, his fingertips grazing the backs of my thighs as he peels them off.

I stand in only a slip of underwear now. The room is quiet except for our breaths.

Elijah moves behind me, wraps his arms around my middle, chin resting on my shoulder. His chest is warm against my back. I lean into him instinctively.

Marius stands before me, hands on my hips, eyes searching mine. He kisses me deeply.

My heart beats a million times per minute.

"Elijah, may I touch her here?" He brushes the edge of my panties.

"Ask Avonna." Elijah kisses my neck.

Marius turns to me. "Avonna, may I?"

"Yes."

He slides them down intentionally.

I'm naked now, between two clothed men who are fully focused on *me*. They guide me to the bed. Lay me down on the soft sheets. I feel the texture against my back, the air on my skin.

Elijah urges my thighs apart, exposing my soaking pussy. Marius sits behind me and leans back against the headboard. He carefully pulls me up against his chest so he can cradle my upper body.

"You're glistening, may I taste you?" Elijah asks.

"Please." I shiver at the memory of how many times he's made me come this way.

His mouth descends and the wet, sure rhythm of his tongue circles my clit, then narrows in. My hips lift, hands clutching the sheets.

Marius cups my breasts, rolling my nipples between his fingers. He nuzzles my hair. "Gorgeous girl, stay with us. Don't float. Don't leave."

"I'm here." I inhale. "I'm here. *Oh—*"

Elijah slurps everything when I come, like I taste divine.

From there, every transition is purposeful.

"Do you want me inside you?" Elijah looks up from between my thighs. "I've missed fucking you."

"*Yes*. God, yes."

He sheds his clothes and rises over me, naked now. He grips his cock and positions it at my entrance, then he's inside me.

The fullness steals my breath.

Marius cups my breasts as Elijah begins to move. "You look so radiant right now beautiful girl."

"Do you want him too?" Elijah whispers in my ear.

"*Yes.*"

The men nod to each other and we shift. Elijah pulls out and helps me roll to my side as Marius strips. While Marius moves around the bed, Elijah lifts my leg and enters me from behind, his fingers thrumming my clit.

Marius stands in front of me, cock in hand. I reach for him. Guide him to my mouth, take him in. Taste the salt of his skin.

Penetrated. Filled. And yet—*I am not overwhelmed*.

Instinctively, I knew this was what my body was meant for. Between the two of them, I am more *here* than I've ever been. Together, they sync their rhythm. Elijah rubs my clit while pressing against my pubic bone, exactly how I love it.

I detonate around Elijah's cock with Marius deep in my mouth.

After, both men pull out and settle on the bed where I lie between them.

I look in the mirror on the wall, study myself.

My eyes are clear. Bright.

I look *claimed*. Not by them.

By *me*.

I'm more powerful than I've ever been in my life.

They move like we've rehearsed this a hundred times before in our dreams. Elijah shifts slightly, bracing himself behind me. Marius settles between my legs, cupping my face before anything else.

"Tell me if anything changes. If anything feels wrong. We stop, instantly." He kisses me softly.

"I want this," I whisper. "Don't hold back."

Elijah grinds his hardening cock against my ass as Marius drags his crown through the folds of my pussy, using Elijah's release as lubricant. It's intense. He's longer and thicker than Elijah.

"Breathe, Avonna." Elijah holds my thigh up and out to give Marius more space. "Stay with yourself. Relax. You're safe."

I breathe. They wait for me to adjust, bodies sandwiching mine. Not forcing anything. When Marius bottoms out, Elijah squeezes cold lube on my puckered hole. Inserts a finger. Then two.

He's fucked me here before, but this time I'm tense. Tightening around Marius's cock as I await what comes next. Before we go further, Marius and Elijah begin kissing me everywhere. Stroking my body. Holding me open.

Every inch is new. Full.

I feel *everything*.

The burn. The pressure. The overwhelming closeness. I sob, not from pain. From *magnitude*. I'm expanding and then both of them are inside me. Filling me.

They hold me between them like a living altar. Their hands on my hips, my belly, my back. Touching me like they can't believe they're allowed to be here worshipping my body this way.

"Avonna," Elijah breathes against my shoulder. "You're...*unreal*."

Marius gurgles low in his throat. "You're taking us so beautifully."

My hands are in their hair, my breath jagged, my body trembling but steady.

They start to move together.

Marius sucks on my nipples. Elijah murmurs encouragement in my ear.

I break open. The orgasm rolls through me like thunder across a wide plain. My spine arches, my mouth open in a silent scream. They both moan, not just from sensation but from *witnessing* me. Fully alive, surrendered to my own desires, yet fully in control of what I'm giving.

My orgasm doesn't stop. Another wave crashes. Then another. Neither of them rush to finish. They wait for *me*. When they finally let go, Marius first, then Elijah, I don't feel used.

I feel *energized*.
Chosen.
Not a vessel. A *volcano*.

Later, after a few hours of exploring, I'm sitting in Camille's office wrapped in a soft robe. My hair's still damp from the shower. My skin still tingles from sex.

She doesn't open her notebook. "How are you, Avonna?"

"I feel like I knew what I wanted, and I was right. I know myself and am not afraid to go after what makes me happy."

She nods.

"Then the work is complete."

"You're releasing me?"

"I never held you," she says softly. "You needed a place to arrive."

I take a deep breath.

"Go." She takes my hand. "Remember, every encounter in the outside world, you'll meet yourself again and again."`

When I depart, my body is sore and radiant and *mine*.

Twenty-Four

LINUS

Five Months Later

THE MERRION LOBBY ALWAYS smells like old money and lilies.

I nod at Maeve on my way out. Her eyes barely flick away from the clipboard she never puts down.

She doesn't ask where I'm going. Or why I haven't worked a proper shift in weeks. Loyalty and dedication earn a bit of leeway, I guess.

It's tough to drum up any enthusiasm for my day job these days. The arts grant came through and Isis Management has finally became more than a sketch in the margins of my event briefs.

A true entrepreneur would jump in with both feet. I will, I promise myself.

I'm not ready. The truth is, keeping this job stops my parents from asking questions.

They think I'm doing well here. Crisp shirts. White tablecloths. A life filled with structure and respectability.

Neither one could imagine how I find true fulfillment in a low-ceilinged rehearsal space in Temple Bar where I've been coaching Sidewalk Riot, a trio of queer pop-punk buskers through their first showcase. Or the coffee-stained desk in my flat where I spend hours researching tour schedules and Indy labels who actually promote their artists.

I dodge my parents' questions about my love life every week, afraid I'll say too much. They would never accept the truth. How the only thing I think about every time I jerk off is Liam and me fucking our shared female partner every night. The perfect woman whom we love and loves us back.

Would they still send Christmas letters gushing about their perfect son if I told them the truth?

The answer's no. So I stick with I'm too busy focusing on work to commit to anyone right now.

The pub's already loud by the time I arrive. Gear cases are stacked in the corner, half a dozen pint glasses sweat into the old wood. All three members of Sidewalk Riot, none older than twenty, wave me over like I'm some kind of wizard who believes they're magic and knows how to negotiate a lethal contract.

Shay "Fox" Keegan is the lead vocalist and plays rhythm guitar. Finn Gallagher's on bass and backing vocals, Ruairí Hayes is the percussionist who uses all types of surfaces and a synthesizer for samples to fill in the sound.

As I get closer, I hear Finn strumming, trying out a new bridge. Immediately, I focus in. I fucking love when something clicks. When a new sound blooms out of nothing and starts to mean something. Sidewalk Riot, and soon other artists, is why I'm building Isis Management.

A company rooted in possibility. Not merely boys with guitars. Women. Nonbinary artists. Queer, immigrant, neurodiverse voices. Not a mirror of what the industry has always been, but a mosaic of what it *could* become. Maybe one day, I'll be able to manage Fireball again, if they stay together.

Lord knows they need me, even if I haven't heard from them.

It's been years. No calls. No emails. Nothing. But, I still follow Fireball, their tour dates, the gossip. He's earning quite the reputation. Fucking his way across the world like it's all he's worth.

Hell, I get it. I've tried to fuck him out of my life too. Some men, but mostly women. Casual flings in hotel rooms and dark corners of clubs. It's pathetic, but I'm always searching for her. Our Isis. The one who'll stand beside me and Liam. Balance us. Heal us. Allow us to find our way back to each other.

I'm so full of shite it's not even funny, but I can't help how I feel. Deep down, I believe we'll find our way back one day.

If I think about it too much, I'll lose my fucking mind, so I pour myself into what I know. The late nights, the new acts, the festival submissions and visa logistics and grant applications. Every one of them a prayer I say in secret, hoping the universe still listens.

Laughter bursts beside me as someone slams a shot glass to the table. Shay hooks an arm around my shoulder, asking if I heard the bridge change. I nod, smile, give him the exact feedback he needs to believe their thing might work.

We all need something to have faith in.

I slide my phone from my pocket to check the schedule for tonight. The pub light catches the Isis logo on my cracked phone case. Clean lines, black on white, elegant and grounded. A reminder of who I am and what I'm building.

Another band on the roster tonight is one I've had my eye on. GoreGlam are made up of four women, all glitter and rage. The frontwoman is tall with a mohawk and a shredded red slip. She shouts into the mic like she's exorcising the city. The guitarist spits into the dark between songs, grins, and kicks her pedalboard so the next riff comes in jagged. The rhythm section don't have their shit together yet, but they can get better.

I stand near the back, pint in hand, and let the set wash over me. The bass thuds through the floorboards into my chest, a heartbeat bigger than mine. Every time the drummer smashes a cymbal, the crowd shudders forward, bodies slamming together.

It's anarchy. Beautiful, raw, uncurated. What music's supposed to evoke.

A woman behind the bar keeps catching my eye. She's pretty, with a messy knot of black hair and a silver ring through her septum. Ink spirals up her forearms. Blackwork roses, a skeletal bird. She pours drinks like she's in a fight with the tap. When she looks at me, her mouth curves into not exactly a smile, more like a dare.

Between sets, I edge up to order another drink. She leans across the bar, wipes foam from her wrist with the hem of her shirt. "You're here almost every night." Her Dublin accent is rolled in whiskey. "Are you some kind of stalker?"

"Band manager," I correct her. "One of my acts is up next but I'm also scouting."

She glances toward the stage. "They're mad bastards, those girls. In a good way." Her eyes return to me, darker now. "You look like you could use a bit of madness yourself."

Maybe it's the bass still in my bloodstream. Maybe it's the months of restraint. I don't think before saying, "Aye, you're probably right."

Her eyebrows lift. She tosses her bar rag aside, nods toward a narrow door marked STAFF ONLY.

She pushes open a supply closet, yanks me in after her. The door clicks behind us, leaving us amidst shelves of napkins, bottles, and disinfectant. She slams me against the wall, kisses me fiercely enough to bruise.

Her name, when I ask, comes out between breaths. "Karra."

Her mouth tastes like hops. She drags her tongue along my lower lip, bites. I grab her waist, my fingers finding the curve of her hip beneath the thin cotton of her shirt. She's already unbuttoning my jeans. The sound of the pub is muffled now, a thump of bass through the wall.

"Fuck...*mmmmmmm*," she murmurs, when I catch her chin in my hand and kiss down her neck.

Karra strokes my cock. I push her against the shelving, metal rattling.

She laughs, low, dirty. "You needed this."

Without answering, I pull her shirt over her head. No bra. Her nipples are bullets against my palms, I mouth one, then the other, till her head knocks back against the wall.

"Christ, yeah—" Her hips cant forward.

Karra undoes her own jeans, shoves them down revealing black-lace panties, already damp. I hook a finger through, tear them aside. The heat of her against my hand makes something twist inside me, sharp as hunger.

"Condom," she says, breathless.

I've got one in my wallet. She tears the packet with her teeth, rolls it down on me, eyes locked to mine. Then she turns, bracing her hands on the shelf.

I slide in all the way, hips slamming against her arse. The air goes out of both of us.

"Fuck—" she chokes.

I grip her waist and move. The sound of our bodies merging drowns the faint flicker of the fluorescent light above.

Her back arches. She pulls me deeper. I thrust until the shelves shake, until she's sobbing in short, raw bursts "Ah, yes, right there—fuck, yes—"

When I come it's like something tearing loose inside. Months of restraint break open. She slumps forward, laughing breathlessly.

"Now that," she pulls up her pants, "was a bit of madness."

I pull my jeans up, heart still hammering. Out in the pub, GoreGlam starts their next song, a blistering, screaming noise sounding of absolution.

Karra opens the door, light spills in from the hallway. "Go on, manager man. Make more magic."

I step out into the crowd again, mind clear.

I know one thing. I'm done with stolen fucks in storage closets.

Casual sex isn't what I want. I don't have the detachment.

I'm not built for empty.

My body craves something fuller, something I lost.

I won't stop until I find it again.

Twenty-Five

LIAM

Three Months Later

I DON'T TELL PADRAIG where I'm going.

I'm not ashamed.

He knows about my sordid sex life. I fuck plenty of women. Plenty of men. Alone. In pairs. Not always discreetly.

I haven't done the one thing I've always craved.

One of each.

A cock and a cunt all at once.

God, how I've fantasized about it, though. A fever dream I can't wake from.

Tonight, it all changes. I find them on Obsidian, a private, curated platform. It runs more like a virtual sex club than a dating app. Everyone's vetted. Background checked. Health records updated. Video verified. No games. No guesswork.

Johan and Marin are looking for bisexual fun. A hot, fit man to take apart. Raw. No strings, no feelings.

Me.

They're married. Mid-thirties. Profile pic is the two of them. Naked. Confident.

I can't look away. They're exactly who I need to pop my cherry.

It's a goddamn match.

Their house sits above the lake, tucked behind high hedges and slatted cedar.

Marin answers the door barefoot in a black silk robe. It clings to her waist. Her eyes are violet-blue and filled with mischief. She wears her blonde hair coiled on top of her head.

"You're Liam," she beckons.

Not a question, so I don't bother answering. I step inside and she lets me pass.

Jonah waits in the living room. No shirt. Black sweats. His eyes sweep over me, then he nods and motions me forward. Silently, I follow him to their bedroom, Marin is close behind me. When the door shuts behind us, he lifts his hand and points down. "Clothes off."

Kicking off my boots, I strip fast. Shirt. Jeans. Boxer-briefs. I stand naked in front of them, rigid as a hammer handle. Why hide it? I'm well-endowed and I want them to see what they have to work with.

Marin bites her bottom lip.

Jonah walks forward and grabs my cock. "You okay to be restrained?"

I nod.

"Good." He licks along the side of my neck.

I nearly come on the spot.

Together, they guide me to a padded bench in the center of the room. Leather. Metal cuffs built into the sides. I lie flat.

Arms spread. Marin straps my wrists into place, smooth and snug.

Then she drops her robe.

No bra. No panties. Her body's as perfect as I remember from the picture. Succulent tits. Smooth stomach. Pretty pink pussy. She walks toward me, eyes raking over my body like I belong to her.

Dropping to her knees, she spits on my cock. Wraps her fingers around the base possessively and draws me in. She growls as I hit her tongue, and the sound travels straight through my shaft, settling deep in my gut. Every inch of me longs to thrust, but she grips my thigh to hold me still.

My cock twitches, pulsing against the molten heat of her throat. She takes more, inch by inch, until her lips kiss the root and she's essentially swallowed me.

Fuck.

This isn't a blowjob. It's a goddamn revelation. My eyes roll back in my head.

Behind her, Jonah strokes himself watching his wife choke on my dick. His cock is the biggest I've ever seen. Hard. Thick. For the first time in forever, I know I'm exactly where I'm supposed to be.

Jesus. I love being watched like this.

Jonah steps in close and kneels, resting the head of his cock against my lips. I open instantly. His taste hits first. Salt. Musk. Bitterness. He shifts his hips forward. My jaw expands to its limit, forcing me to breathe through my nose.

My cock leaks across my stomach. I'm nowhere and everywhere at once. They're taking me apart.

I'm close. *Too* close.

Suddenly, they both stop. Jonah eases out of my mouth. Marin kisses back up to the head of my cock, then lets it fall from her lips with a smile.

"Bedtime." She unclips one wrist while Jonah frees the other.

I sit up too fast, breath caught somewhere in my chest. Jonah catches my arm, steady but firm. They guide me across the room to the bed dressed in soft black silk. Restraints hang loose from the corners.

I climb on, body humming, nerves shot. Ready for whatever comes next.

Marin straddles me, knees wide against the bed, guiding my cock to her pussy with one hand. She lowers herself until I'm buried in her. Her pussy's grip is so snug I feel every drag, every shift, every little clench.

My hips jack up and she orders, "Don't come. Not yet."

I take a couple of breaths as Marin continues to ride me. Hips rolling but controlled. She leans forward, plants her hands on my chest and grinds down. Pert, brown nipples hover above my mouth.

The mattress dips behind us. Jonah spreads my thighs, his strong hands wrap beneath them and he lifts my ass up onto his lap tilted just so. I feel lube, cold against my rim. His fingers massage and prod. One, then two breach my hole. Twisting enough to make my cock throb inside her.

"Fuck," I whisper. "He's—*fuck*—"

"Don't come," Marin demands.

Her nails dig deeper into my chest, hips grinding in time with his penetrating fingers until he replaces them with his cock. My ass burns with the staggering sensation of him rooting into me while my cock's still stuffed inside of her.

He grunts behind me, breaching inch by inch, until his hips meet my ass, balls slapping against me. I'm split open. Taken.

"*Jesus*—" I choke.

Marin licks her lips. "Let him fuck you with his ginormous cock, honey. He's gonna make you see stars."

Oh, yes he is. I've never felt more wanted. More free.

"*Harder*," Marin demands.

Jonah grips my hips and rams home. The angle's perfect. The thick head of his cock grinds over my prostate. Hot pressure lights my whole body up like a live wire.

I can't hold back a second longer.

Stars? Shit, I'm gonna see the fucking universe.

I'm caught between them, his dick destroying my ass, her pussy gripping my cock. Everything is wet and raw and too much in the best fucking way. It's like someone's ignited a fuse straight to my spine. I can't catch my breath. Can't stay quiet. Pleasure roars through me. It's *insane*. Overstimulating.

Fucking addictive.

Jonah splays my legs out and up, allowing him to go even deeper. The intensity is maddening, my prostate throbs around Jonah's cock and the heat of his thrusts tip me into a place I didn't know I could fall. My orgasm comes out of nowhere.

Fast. Brutal. Blinding.

My entire body seizes. Marin milks my cock through her own orgasm. Jonah slams into my ass, emptying his own load. None of us move at first. I'm shaking. Wrung out. Split open, filled at both ends.

I can't think. Not really. Other than knowing there's no way I can go home yet, I want more.

Jonah pulls out, chest heaving. He wipes a forearm across his mouth then reaches over to a tray set neatly on the nightstand. There's a clean towel. A pack of wet wipes.

Of course there is.

Obviously, this isn't their first time. They're experienced and prepared. Knowing this turns me on more.

Jonah handles it without a word. Cleans himself first. Efficient, no hesitation. Then gently dabs the inside of my thighs. My hole. My cock, cleaning off lube and taint. It's not tenderness. It's something better.

Responsibility. Confidence. Control.

When he finishes, he dives between Marin's legs. She whimpers as he spreads her open with both hands, revealing my come seeping out of her. He lowers his head, lapping at the mess I left behind. She grabs the back of his head with both hands. The slurping, ravenous sounds he makes as he cleans me out of her pussy shoots straight down my spine.

The keening sound I make is much louder than I mean it to be.

Jonah's eyes lock on mine before they flick down to where I'm stroking myself. His cock's also rising again, bobbing against his taut abs. Marin positions herself behind me. Her hand wraps around my cock and it only takes a couple of strokes until I'm rock hard.

"Now, I want both of you." She motions to Jonah.

He nods and lies back against the headboard, cock pointed at the ceiling. Marin straddles him, facing me. He grabs her hips, slides into her with one slow push then tucks his arms under her thighs. Lifts her and eases her back until she's lying against his chest, her legs draped over his.

Jonah meets my gaze over her shoulder and spreads her wider.

"Let's fuck her cunt together," he offers.

He holds her anchored and displayed so I can see everything. Her pussy's stretched around his cock, folds glossy and swollen. Her clit peeks out above where he disappears inside her. She's soaked. Flushed.

It's goddamn beautiful. I'm positive this visual will fuel my spank bank forever.

My cock leaks in anticipation.

She points down. "Put it in there too."

Obediently, I line up my cock. Push in beside him until I bottom out.

Oh my God, this is so fucking tight.

Our cocks skate against each other to fill her wet heat. Every nerve lights up. I'm pretty sure nothing is ever going to compare to this moment when I truly understand what nirvana means.

"Holy fuck," I whisper to no one in particular.

Marin starts coming without us even moving. To keep her in place, Jonah holds her by the elbows, I grip her ass. Jonah thrusts upward into her and I sproing free. Quickly, I guide myself back in and scoot a hair closer so it won't happen again.

This time, Jonah and I find our cadence. We move together. Cock frotting against cock, pressure building. Heat coils low in my spine. Marin's pussy convulses around our cocks as she enters some sort of orgasmic loop. I free one hand so I can rub her clit to amp things up even further.

Her cries turn absolutely frantic and she sprays my entire chest in liquid. She shrieks and shakes, pussy pulsing around both of us. Knowing I've helped her achieve this level of pleasure for her is intoxicating.

"Enough." Jonah lets her arms free. "She's spent."

I slide out of her carefully. Soaked in her juices. Breathe like I've been running uphill for an hour. Marin collapses backward into the arms of her husband. Jonah lifts her off, rolls her to the side gently and kisses her lips.

Then looks at me. "Your turn to fuck me."

For hours afterward, they take the lead. My world shrinks to skin and motion. Bodies merging and shifting in a sexual trance until the clock loses meaning.

This isn't love. Marin and Jonah want what they want. Tonight I'm part of it. I match their pace and let instinct carry me so I can experience as much as they'll allow. Somewhere in the middle of it, something clears inside me.

They're giving me something I need. Proof what I crave is not only possible but permissible.

When it's obvious they're done with me. I don't take it personally, I'm ready to go. I get dressed and they walk me out, locking the door behind me.

No promises, no goodbyes.

Driving home, I grip the wheel. Not to steady myself, to stay grounded in my body.

Tonight was supposed to fulfil a secret fantasy. Turns out, it was a revelation.

I've never felt more like myself.

Has my entire fucking world shifted?

Yes.

I've been used and worshipped. Split and centered.

No label touches it. No name contains it.

I need this.

Permanently.

Twenty-Six

Eighteen Months Later

TONIGHT IS BITTERSWEET.

The end of an era. A new beginning.

I stand outside the patio doors of Delgado Cocina, watching the light shift across the tables. It's wild how different I am from the young girl who started working here years ago wearing baggy trousers and sweatshirts.

Now I prefer form-fitting clothes to display my figure. I'm not uncomfortable, I'm proud to show off my body. I don't have anyone to hide from anymore, including myself.

Out on the patio, laughter rises and spills into the warm air. Strings of paper lanterns extend between trees, glowing pale and soft like moons caught in the branches. Someone's set out the sangria. The scent of roasted tomato and saffron rice floats out from Rafael's kitchen, a scent I've come to associate with care.

The Delgado's didn't know much about me when they hired me at seventeen. They still don't know all the sordid details of my upbringing. Enough to understand why I needed time off for therapy and how to support me if I had a panic attack.

It's not like I don't trust them, I do. After all, even though my references were paper-thin, they gave me a good job. Ana consistently encouraged me without asking too many questions. Each night, Rafael provided me with a to-go box filled with enough food for a few days. Lucas was oblivious, always babbling on and joking. Rosa never coddled me in her own strive for perfection in the restaurant. Marcella, though, she noticed more than she let on.

She's twenty-five, in her first year at a big law firm called Finney Cooper. She made it possible for me to become the woman I am today. Healed. Excited. Thriving. About to leave for a trip I never believed possible.

In addition to some of my favorite customers, my roommates are all here. Wren's spent the better part of the evening making sure the playlist is perfectly calibrated to melancholy, but hopeful. Macie's already slipped into the kitchen twice to hug Ana and steal bites of plantains. Safiya declared the sangria non-alcoholic and therefore unacceptable and started adding tequila from her purse like a rogue priest blessing a punch bowl.

In every corner of this space, I feel it:

Found family.

I've been to hell and back trying to reclaim who I am over the past few years. These are the people I've leaned on. For my livelihood. Friendship. Support. Normalcy.

Marcella stands near the bar, holding a glass of cava. "Avonna, come on up here. I have a few words to say before the night ends."

Blushing, I hide my face behind my hand. Being the center of attention still nudges an old reflex to cower. I'm learning to stay with it.

Not long ago, being the center of attention in a room like this would've hollowed me out. Reclaiming myself hasn't been one single moment or limited to intensive sex therapy. It's been purposeful, layered mind work to help me cope with day-to-day life in the real world.

In a recent session, we explored the reason why I brought the guitar with me the night I ran. It was bulky, obvious. Bound to slow me down when I needed to disappear. I grabbed it anyway, like instinct, and have never let it go.

Retrospectively, somehow I knew I'd need it. First to survive and make money. Now to heal. Recently, music found me again when words alone weren't enough. I started taking voice lessons, then guitar. Played my first set in the corner of a coffee shop, hands trembling, heart loud in my chest.

Each time I return to the mic, it gets a little easier. Songwriting helps me speak from the places I used to keep locked away. Music has become my altar. My voice, my devotion. Singing has become a quiet form of worship. My own kind of prayer. It connects me to something deeper, not outside myself, within.

When I sing the songs I write, I feel present. Honest. Whole. One verse at a time.

I make my way up to stand beside Marcella. Turn and face the small crowd.

"We're here for Avonna Parilla." She raises the glass with her usual eloquent style. "She didn't arrive in a straight line. She took the long way. Came through the fire and has made it look like grace. Our girl has fought to become real, and now it's time for her to spread her wings."

The last line hits something deep in my chest. I breathe through it.

"To Avonna," the crowd echoes and raise their glasses.

"Thank you for coming." I glance around at the crowd. "I'm so grateful for each of you. As nervous as I am about this new adventure, having you in my life makes me feel strong enough to take it."

I take a drink of my cava like I've earned it.

I have.

Later, after a delicious dessert of churros and mango tart, guests begin to depart after laughter, hugs, and photos. I take a moment and duck inside to the restaurant, sitting on a stool near the kitchen door.

Marcella approaches quietly. She hands me a small leather wallet. Gold-foiled with my name on the front. Inside is my passport. A folded note and my boarding pass.

"You're the first person I ever helped," she says. "You'll always be my first client. Thank you for trusting me to know you, Avonna. You'll always be my other sister."

When Marcella was twenty-two and about to enter law school, she took me aside me one day and asked if I had a legal ID. When I told her I'd lost it, she didn't interrogate me. She offered to get me a new one.

I open the passport and look down at the photo. I'm not smiling in it. I didn't know if I was allowed to. The name underneath is clear.

Avonna Parilla.

Marcella clears her throat. "Rosa made me promise to ask. You're going to see her in Barcelona, right?"

"She'd kill me if I didn't, "I laugh."

She smiles. "Good. She misses you."

I miss her, too. Like the rest of the Delgado family, Rosa never made me feel like healing had a deadline. We are the same age but so different, and she let me be me until I wanted to be more. She's been away studying in Spain and visiting her is one of my first stops on the big European adventure.

When I get home, I don't sleep. I unpack and repack about a dozen times. Steam the dress I'll wear on the plane. Check the contents of my backpack. Lay my new passport down on the bed and look at it like it might start speaking.

In a way, it does.

It says: *You were never imaginary. You just had to write yourself in.*

Now, officially, I *am* real.

Marcella helped me legally secure my chosen name.

The legal battle took two years. When I left, I didn't exist My birth, like so many girls in the sect, was considered a "spiritual event," not a civic one.

Through a private investigator, Marcella and I gathered everything we could. It took years. My situation was impossible. There were no records. All I knew was the name I discarded—Aurora. I didn't know my last name. Until I was on the outside, I didn't even know there was such a thing.

I have no birth certificate. No hospital record of birth. No Social Security number. No trace in any state system. There are no records of Master Prophet in Idaho, or the church I grew up in.

I had to obtain a Letter of No Record. Submit Affidavits. A school intake form from the safe house. Scraps of whatever proof I had of my existence. For so long, I wasn't sure we'd succeed.

Now my name is printed in blue ink. A photo. A seal. Proof I belong somewhere.

I won't shrink myself to fit what someone else wants ever again.

With a nice little nest egg saved up, I'm ready to spread my wings. I'm traveling to Europe alone, me and my guitar. My plan is to learn about new cultures, relax and enjoy my life.

Maybe find romance.

I've continued to explore my sexuality. One blaring realization has been therapy sex was about me, but most men aren't. So far, the men I've been with don't ignite me and I won't shrink myself to fit what someone else wants. Or allow myself to be talked over. Treated like a mirror for someone else's insecurities.

I have no reason to settle. Until I meet the right men who I can spend my life with, I'm going on an extended date with myself. One where I'll stare at scenery out of train windows, wander cobblestone streets, taste red wine on my lips at midnight while a city unfolds itself around me.

Tomorrow, I fly to Barcelona. Then Dublin, Paris, London, and wherever else calls.

I don't know who I'll meet or what I'll feel.

Doesn't matter.

I'm not going to Europe to find myself.

I'm going because I already did.

Twenty-Seven

One Month Later

My office is barely bigger than a shoebox.

It's on the second floor above a Chinese takeaway in Temple Bar.

One cracked window, a dodgy door, and a tiny wall-mounted heater rattling like it's chewing rocks.

Still, I love it. I painted the walls myself. Installed cheap shelves which are now filled with demo CDs. Bought some used office furniture and a file cabinet. Use the kettle I brought from home to make coffee like it's a goddamn art form.

My company name's on the door, Isis Management. Black vinyl on the glass, curling slightly at the corners. I stare at it every time I unlock the place. If only to remind myself this is real.

The acts I've signed are pure fire.

Sidewalk Riot, of course. My latest is Peach Harvest, an acoustic trio from Killarney. Two sisters and their cousin. Their honey-warm harmonies and fingerpicked guitars sound like heartbreak at the golden hour.

Their song about their nan dying is known to reduce entire pubs to tears. I've got them booked solid for the next six weeks, circuiting Cork, Kilkenny, Cardiff, Derry, and Belfast. Modest fees, couch-surfing half the way, but they're buzzing.

Then there's GoreGlam, whom I fucking adore. They signed a couple of days after I shagged the bartender in the storage closet at Sidewalk Riot's showcase.

Four loud-mouthed twenty-year-olds from Limerick dressed in leather miniskirts and combat boots shout about rape culture and slut-shaming with such electric rage it makes the hairs on my arms stand up. Their frontwoman, Tasha, is a goddamn thunderstorm.

I managed to bluff my way into a grant panel to get them funded for studio time. It was worth every sleepless night. They're rough as hell, but honest. Exactly the type of artist I dreamed Isis could represent.

Pulling out my phone, I check the time. Peach Harvest is landing in Cardiff today. Tasha sent me a voice note earlier, something about their bassist, Meg, puking on the ferry. I pull out my phone and respond. Then I check my social feeds to see how the bands are trending.

Less Than Zero pops up. I swear to fuck, they have been dominating the charts for years now. I scroll through video snippet after video snippet of their show in Dublin the other night.

I was there.

I'm not sure why I went, curiosity, maybe. The last time I saw them, Fireball was on the bill and Liam still hadn't acknowledged me in public. Even still, Connor was kind to me and LTZ has become such a worldwide phenomenon, I thought it would be inspirational to see how far they've come.

They're raw. Cinematic. Bigger than anything I've ever seen.

Ty's trajectory is insane. His frontman persona is a combination of sex and gasoline. You can tell he's circling the drain, but somehow it makes him magnetic. Like you're watching fire burn a cathedral. You want to look away, but you can't. Connor and drummer Jace have locked in the rhythm section and Zane Rocks, the guitar player, is an absolute musical savant.

Not to detract from their success, but it certainly hasn't hurt them to have the backing of Zane's dad, Carter fucking Pope, iconic guitarist of the 90s band, Limelight. They're super talented and while the industry has embraced them with open arms, I'm convinced their meteoric rise is in large part due to Carter's support.

Not a day goes by when I don't wish Fireball was also enjoying LTZ's notoriety. Liam and Padraig have worked their ass off for a decade, grinding out indie albums and tours. Steadily building up a loyal following. It must be bittersweet for them to watch their brother eclipse their middling success by one-hundred fold in the span of two years.

It's not too late. If someone gave a damn and actually fought for them, they could turn things around. Maybe I'll be the one someday. First, I must continue to cement my own place in this industry, which is exactly what I intend to do.

I've started drafting a mock tour package showcasing my artists using Sidewalk Riot as the headliner. So far, I've confirmed venues across Berlin, Barcelona, and Amsterdam. Peach Harvest and GoreGlam will rotate as openers.

I pick up a flyer from the edge of my desk. GoreGlam's first headline gig in Glasgow. The printer fucked the colors.

Tasha's hair looks salmon instead of red. Doesn't matter, I run my thumb over it like it's gold.

Everything I own is tied up in Isis. I've bet it all on black.

To save money, I traded suburban life in Dundrum for Stoneybatter, like shedding an old skin. Out there, I always felt like I was living the life my parents wanted for me. My own preferences muffled behind double-glazed cronuts and Zara bags.

Now I'm back in the thick of it in a one-bed flat on a lively street in a queer-friendly neighborhood. When I'm I home, I feel like myself again. Not some version dressed up for respectability. I've never been a guy who flinches at mess or truth or late-night music bleeding through floorboards. My place isn't polished. It's practical. Same as me.

My windows might rattle when the bins go out, but on Saturdays I buy fresh bread from a woman who knows my name and coffee from a lad who flirts without apology. The take-out Indian on the corner is the tastiest I've ever had.

One thing hasn't changed, though. I'm still fucking lonely.

Call me obsessed or even delusional, but I'm still stuck on Liam. Nobody else touches me deeply. Not like he did. Even if our relationship was messy and too short and ended with more silence than closure, he made me feel seen. Alive. Like my body had a home.

Goddammit.

Sidewalk Riot is bleeding momentum and I can't waste time on old lovers. I have three tour cities to lock in, a photo reshoot to schedule, and no staff. No buffer. No excuse.

Yet, here I sit, my cock hard as a fucking rock. Heavy with an ache I won't be able to shake until...

I swore I'd stop doing this, but nothing else gets me off anymore. Not porn. Not hookups with men. Or women.

No one compares to Liam, so there's only one thing to do.

I open the folder hidden in my computer files without hesitation. No point pretending I don't need this. The video loads. Fireball in San Diego. Liam is shirtless, dripping in heat and feedback, bending into his guitar like it's someone he wants to shag senseless. Gyrating his hips like he's fucking the music.

Fucking *me*.

Closing my eyes, I picture him undressing in front of me while I unzip my jeans, spit into my palm and wrap my fist around my cock. I imagine him behind me. On top of me.

In me.

His hands roughly grip my hips as he pushes into me and begins to fuck me like we have all the time in the world.

"You're mine tonight," he drawls, pushing deeper until he hits my prostate. *"You feel me, baby?"*

My hand speeds up, hips lifting. I yelp before I mean to. I *can* feel his cock inside me. His rhythm. His weight. The magical way he'd swivel his hips to stimulate me, his fist around my cock. Each of us wheezing with guttural pleasure on our way to nirvana.

The orgasm tears through me. Not quiet. Not controlled. My body convulses, cock spurting hot across my fist and stomach. I grind into my palm, chasing the echo of his voice.

Truth be told, this solo orgasm is better than any hookup I've ever had. Sex with strangers means nothing. Cocks or cunts don't fill the right space inside of me.

Masturbating to Liam isn't some rockstar fantasy. It's muscle memory.

It's *truth*.

Grabbing some tissue from my desk, I clean up my mess without looking down at the come drying on my body. As pleasurable as these sessions are in the moment, afterward shame sits low in my gut.

For fuck's sake, my sex life has been reduced to dependence on a ghost. How do I stop putting energy into a man who probably doesn't even think about me anymore?

One who hasn't touched me in years. I'm not daft. Liam and I are not in the cards.

Wasting precious time isn't an option. One of my grants runs out in six months. Savings might stretch another four if I keep living like a student. At this point, I don't have a backup plan. Don't want one.

I want *this*. Isis Management.

No more bullshit. I'm gonna break Sidewalk Riot. Get GoreGlam's tour finalized. Put Peach Harvest in the studio and release some music. Soon, I might make a behind-the-scenes pitch to get Fireball back to Europe and give Liam a reason to pick up the phone and get some real closure.

Or, maybe I won't on the last one.

Looking down at my cock, soft and flopped over on my thigh, I realize the mess I made is worse than I thought. There's come on my shirt, my waistband, and streaked across my belly nearly up to my nipples.

I strip off the shirt, toss it in my backpack and grab a clean GoreGlam shirt from the merch cabinet. Then I head to the loo. Turn on the warm water and soap up the cloth I use too often for this. I scrub my skin, rinse my face, look in the mirror.

The man looking back already has his borderline obsession tucked away. Buttoned. Neat. Presentable.

Back at the desk, I breathe. Open my calendar. Respond to the label. Confirm the new rehearsal space for Sidewalk Riot. Flag two invoices. The bass player still hasn't answered my texts, but the rest of the day holds. Focus returns not because I want it to, I have to force it.

By seven, I've done enough to justify closing the laptop.

Jacket on. Phone in pocket. Time to scout. Deciding between scoping out a new rock band in the Docklands or an open mic near Wexford Street, I decide on the latter.

The city stretches open as I step into it. Dusk cools everything but the rhythm in my chest. My boots hit pavement like a beat I know by heart. I haven't lost the ear. Haven't lost the hunger. I'm building something I'm proud of.

Sitting at the back bar with a Guinness, I take in my surroundings. The crowd is sparse and so far, the talent isn't anything I'm interested in. I decide to finish my beer and head to the other venue when I catch movement at the small back corner of the stage. Someone new's about to play, might as well listen.

Turning my stool around, I'm not sure what to expect, but it isn't her.

The woman is slight, maybe five-foot-two. Sandy-brown hair falls in waves around her face, sea-glass eyes scan the crowd like she's not sure whether to smile or run. Wearing a plain, slate-blue T-shirt, ripped jeans and no makeup as far as I can tell, there's something compelling about her. Familiar.

She's raw nerves and something...*alive*.

When she steps up to the mic, she tucks a strand of hair behind her ear. There's a shimmer around her, even before she speaks.

"Hi." She glances around nervously. "My name's Avonna. I'm, um...I'm on holiday. Trying a few new things to build my confidence. Thank you for listening."

Huh. American.

Someone whistles, a few cheers ripple through the room.

"I haven't sung in a pub before, but here goes." Avonna adjusts her guitar strap, breathes in, then starts picking a soft, mournful intro.

It takes me a few bars to recognize it. A beautiful old ballad called *The Wind That Shakes the Barley*. Her version is nothing like the traditional. It's richer. Her voice enters like smoke. Ethereal. Each note is soaked in grief and grace, blooming through the pub's clatter like an invocation.

I go still. Hair rises on the back of my neck. My chest constricts in a way I haven't felt since the first time I saw Liam. Avonna's not performing. She's bleeding.

It's fucking beautiful.

My throat works around something I can't name. My heart pounds. My cock, fuck, it's threatening to burst outta my jeans. She's not only gorgeous. It's the truth in her. The fearless surrender. She's naked in this moment, emotionally if not physically, and I want to know her. Want to put my hands in the music and see where it leads.

She finishes on a whisper. The pub doesn't erupt. It holds its breath.

Then applause swells, sudden and thunderous.

She smiles. Small, almost bashful, but I see the glint of it.

Power, barely contained.

I already know. She's the one. The woman I've been waiting for.

For *us*.

My mouth is dry. My heart pounds, a drumbeat of need. I push up from the table before I fully think it through.

I don't care if it's premature or reckless. I have to talk to her.

Hear her voice up close.

Ask if she knows what she did to me.

I've been still for too long.

This finally feels like motion.

Twenty-Eight

LIAM

Five Months Later

DANIEL'S BROILER LOOKS LIKE money fucked a lake house.

White tablecloths crisp as origami, wine glasses polished to a shine, and floor-to-ceiling windows let the lake do all the talking. Everything smells like seared beef, old money, and lemon-butter optimism.

My brother and I don't belong here. Not really.

We walk in anyway.

Padraig and I trail in road-dust , but the host clocks Connor's name and takes us straight to a prominent corner booth. The restaurant's drenched in late-afternoon light, the lake outside glitters like the jewel of the Pacific Northwest it is.

Connor stands when he sees us, pulls us in one by one. He looks clean. Put-together. Sports a designer T-shirt costing more than our monthly tour budget. His arms are leaner and more defined than I remember. Stadium life suits him.

"Youse both look like shit." He slides back into the booth.

"We missed you too," I fire back, slouching next to Padraig. "Nice view. Real subtle."

He smirks. "Treatin' my brothers to something not fried or foil-wrapped."

"Can't argue with linen napkins and cushioned chairs." Padraig glances around. "Haven't been here since we were kids."

The waiter drops off sparkling water without needing to ask. Connor always remembers the little things. Neither of us drink. Not since the incident. Some habits become second nature when you're dedicated to not becoming your father.

We open with small talk. Gear, vans, recording schedules. Upcoming dates.

Connor already knows the most of it. We keep in touch via a three-way group text. An occasional call when service holds. Talking about it in person always lands different.

"Label's small, but they believe in our music." Padraig fills him in on our new plan. "We've got a timeline. Some real promo lined up."

"Koko's cutting vocals this week," I add. "She's sharp. Fast. Has instincts."

Connor tilts his head. "Is she sticking around?"

"Tough to say," I admit. "She's cool. Talented. Tourin' in a van with two broke Irish twins probably isn't high on her vision board."

Padraig adds hopefully, "She's not a diva, though."

"Aye." Connor's lips twitch. "Third singer in how many years?"

"Four." I roll my eyes. "If you count the one gig where the guy tried to fuck the mic stand."

"He was committed," Padraig deadpans.

Connor laughs. "I still think about Felicity sometimes. What a storm."

"Storms pass," I mutter. As far as I'm concerned, the past is in the fucking past. No need to drum it up.

"Yeah, but she left carnage we haven't been able to shake," Padraig sighs.

No one says more. We don't need to.

The waiter returns. Padraig and I order ribeye. Connor gets the salmon. Tons of sides.

"You still have the place in Federal Way?" Connor raises an eyebrow.

He doesn't mean it like a question. He knows. We've talked.

"Yeah," I explain. "Two-bedroom crash pad, cheap as fuck. Van's in the lot. Storage unit two blocks over. Real high glamour, but we need somewhere to live when we're not on the road."

Connor huffs a laugh. "Probably better than most green rooms I've seen."

"Cleaner too." Padraig smirks. "No weird couch stains."

The food arrives and we devour it. It's so fucking good. It almost pisses me off. We've been choking down instant noodles and bar pizza for so long, a proper meal feels like betrayal.

Connor waits until the plates are half-cleared before he goes serious. "I'm not promisin' anything." He folds his hands on the table. "But if the next LTZ album lands the way the label hopes, we'll do a US leg. Then Europe."

I go still. Padraig doesn't blink.

Connor looks between us. "I've already spoken to the guys. We want to bring you with us."

It doesn't hit all at once. It creeps. A weight in my chest. Familiar, hopeful, dangerous.

"You serious?" Padraig's voice is eerily calm. Measured.

Connor nods. "Main support."

"We'd have to find a way to get Koko to say yes." My practical nature kicks in. No point in getting excited about another opportunity likely to be snatched away at the last hour. "She's reluctant to commit to long tours."

Fuck, I'm jaded.

"Well, I'm giving you a heads-up so if you need to, you can find someone new." Connor threads his fingers together. "You've done it before."

"Easier said than done. The girl's got a killer tone." I shrug. "Plus, Koko looks good on stage and has ambition. I'm sure we can convince her."

"She's a fuckin' Siren, even when she's pissed off." Padraig rests his chin in his palm.

Connor smiles. "Well, keep your shit together so we can make this happen."

We fall into a quieter rhythm. Talk setlists, radio play, venue sizes. Padraig and Connor swap notes on lighting rigs and tech crews. I tune in and out, watching the lake through the glass like it might give me a sign.

Padraig nudges me. "Dar, did you hear Connor's question?"

I shake out the cobwebs and glance at him. Tilt my head expectantly.

"You hear from Linus?" Connor repeats, fork paused mid-air.

I go cold. I can't say anything.

Padraig doesn't let it go. "Jesus. You didn't tell him?"

"He messaged again," I admit. "Couple months ago. He started his own management company, has some cool acts."

"And?"

"I didn't answer."

Padraig swears under his breath.

Connor watches us, quiet. "Why? You still have feelin's for him?"

"It's not about my feelin's." I wave him off, uncomfortable. The only person who really knows about my private life is

Padraig and I'm a bit salty about him bringing this up in the first place.

"Then what's it about?" Connor asks.

"He's based in Dublin." I come up with a lame explanation. "We're here, hangin' on by a fucking thread. What am I supposed to say? So glad you're findin' success with other bands?"

"He would manage us again in a fucking heartbeat." Padraig shakes his head. "You could've responded to find out what he wanted."

"He knows we're over," I snap. "We've both made peace with it."

Connor looks at me. "You sure?"

"I'm sure he's better off without *me*," I seethe.

I have an uncanny way of shutting down a conversation. We all resume eating.

A few minutes later Connor tries again, "If the Europe leg happens, you could reconnect."

"Hard pass," I mutter. "I'm not entertainin' a fuckin' reunion tour while I'm still bleedin'."

Padraig grips my wrist. "Might as well bleed with purpose."

I want to punch something. Instead, I drain my water and crunch on a mouthful of ice. Swallow.

"You talk to Stevie?" I turn toward him and smile like the devil.

It's petty. Mean. Retaliation is a bitch.

The silence that follows is different. Heavier.

"How are you holdin' up?" Connor puts on his big-brother hat.

Padraig chews the inside of his cheek. "Nothing I can do to change it."

"You gave up a lot for the band." Connor taps the table with his fingertips.

Padraig glances at me, always leaning into diplomacy despite what an asshole I am. "We both did."

"So." Connor sits back, arms crossed, eyes sharp. "You ever think about comin' home for a family dinner?"

His comment makes me nauseous.

Padraig exhales, pained. "Nah. It's not home for us anymore."

"He's not drinkin.'" Connor leans back. "By all accounts, he's tryin'."

I laugh, sharp and mean. "Oh really? He tried to kill me. Now he's tryin' kale and yoga?"

"No," Connor says. "He's strugglin' to stay alive. So is Ma. So are the boys."

"Clearly, I wouldn't know how to show up without starting a fire," I spit out.

Connor nods patiently. "Then don't bring a match. Come to dinner. See your brothers. Ignore Da if you want."

Padraig looks at me. "We could go to say hi. Eat Ma's stew. What I'd give for a taste of it."

"I'll think about it." I look away.

When the bill comes, Connor lays down his black AMEX without a word. The check disappears like it never existed.

Outside, Lake Washington still shimmers in the background of where our beat-up old van is parked.

Connor throws one arm around each of us. "Let me know when you're done with trackin'. I'll keep you posted about the tour."

Padraig hugs him again. Longer this time. Connor holds on.

Then it's the two of us, staring at the lake like it might tell us who the fuck we are.

"Fuck. Do you still think we've got a shot?" I ask honestly.

Padraig opens the passenger door. "Dunno anymore. I think we've got somethin' worth savin'."

We climb into the vehicle. I start the engine. It turns over like a giant, roaring lion.

As we pull away, I tell myself all of this is still worth it.

Believe it.

Even if only for tonight

Twenty-Nine

Four Months Later

ON MY FIRST TRIP to Europe, I only meant to stop in Dublin for a few days.

I fell in love with the city before I even made it to the Liffey.

It was the Fourth of July, and while Americans shot fireworks across the ocean, I played my first pub gig. Terrified. Energized. Alive.

I stuck to my original plan for a while. Visited London, Paris, Spain, Vienna. With only my guitar and a backpack, I traveled light. Laughed a lot and spent another month in Dublin playing the open mic circuit before my visa ran out.

I went back to the States, gave notice on my apartment and worked two more months of double shifts at Delgado Cocina, and booked a one-way ticket back.

Even while staying in a hostel with creaky bunks and warm tea, it feels like home here. I don't need much. I sing in pubs, slip into trad jams when they'll have me, and busk on Grafton whenever the sky holds.

I'm even brave enough to post it all on YouTube. It's been years since I escaped and no one from my old life has attempted to contact me. With a new name and a new outlook, I'm pretty sure my past is in the past.

Music makes me feel real. Grounded. Free. If I'm gonna make a living at it, I've got to put myself out there. Slowly, I'm building up a following. It's exciting. I finally know what I want to do with my life.

Things are looking up in my love life as well.

Not long after I returned, he came up to me after a pub set off Dame Street. Tall, bearded and handsome with a broad chest and strong arms, Linus O'Donnell handed me a card. *Isis Management*. He asked if I was playing anywhere else and his eyes focused on mine without drifting.

He showed up at my next gig a few nights later. Then again. And again.

Every time I saw him, the pull was stronger. He listened to me like he was memorizing every note. I loved how calm his voice was when he said my name.

Immediately, there was something about him I couldn't shake. He seemed familiar, like I've seen him before in a dream or a different life. I haven't been able to figure out why.

Curiosity has turned into desire. I get wet dreaming about his hands on my hips, pushing my shirt up. My nipples pucker when I remember how he looks at my mouth. I want his weight over me, his breath against my throat, his cock inside me while I shake apart.

Don't get me wrong, I've had a lot of sex in Europe. Fast. Fun. Reckless. Nothing permanent, only something to scratch an itch.

Now I need this.

Him.

Linus is the man for me. I know it with every fiber of my being. He doesn't chase. Or impose. The hunger in his eyes is tempered by patience. Which makes me want him more.

Turns out, I'm ravenous for a man who doesn't rush the unraveling.

Tonight, over candlelight and red wine, between shared bites and confession-shaped silences, he finally asked me back to his flat. I said yes. To now. To *this*.

The second the door clicks shut, I'm on him.

I kiss him like I'm starving. It feels like I've waited a goddamn lifetime for the taste of his mouth. Weeks of him watching me play, his deep eyes marinating in every note like he already knows we're meant to be.

He kisses back with the same hunger. His hands are strong, gripping my waist like he owns it. He spins us and presses me against the wall, and fuck, the way he breathes against my neck...

I'm soaked already. No point pretending I'm not.

"You have no idea," he rasps, dragging his mouth across my jawline, "how many nights I've pictured you like this."

"Say it out loud." I tilt my head, daring him. "Tell me."

His hand slides down, rough palm skimming under my dress, over my bare thigh. "Bent over. Legs shaking. Pussy drippin' down my cock."

Good God. He's a dirty talker. My breath stutters. I grind against him, dress hitched high on my hips now, nothing underneath but heat and want.

"Well, you're in luck. I'm so fucking wet for you," I wheeze. "I've been soaked since dinner."

He growls—*growls*—and drops to his knees in front of me like I'm destined to be worshipped.

Linus pulls my dress up and buries his face between my thighs, tongue sliding through my pussy like he's trying to taste every inch of me. My hand flies to the back of his head, hips rolling against his mouth. He alternates licking me and circling my clit until I'm shaking. Devouring me like he needs it to survive.

"You eat my pussy like you're starving." I bite my knuckle.

"I *do* mean it." His voice is thick with need. "This pussy deserves to be licked and tasted and fucked."

He slides two fingers into me, curling them exactly right, and my knees buckle. I cry out, hips thrusting against his face as he teases my clit and fucks me with his fingers like he's got something to prove. I come fast, and messy, spraying him with my release as my nails dig into his shoulders.

Undaunted, he continues on, licking up every drop like it's his final meal.

When he finally stands, his mouth glistens with me. He kisses me deep, and I taste myself on his tongue.

"Bedroom," I say breathlessly.

He lifts me like I weigh nothing. I wrap my legs around his waist, feel the thick bulge of his cock through his jeans, hot and heavy against my saturated center. I grind against him, shameless.

"You're not gonna last long," I whisper into his ear. "I feel how hard you are."

"Then I'll fuck you again," he says, "and again. Until you forget every other person who's ever touched you."

We hit the bed in a mesh of limbs. Clothes ripped, tossed. His cock springs free and, Jesus fuck, it's thick, long, dripping at the tip. My mouth waters. I want it everywhere.

"Condom," I manage, my breath ragged.

He finds one in his nightstand and sheathes himself in one smooth motion. Spreads me open with his big hands and slides in.

Oh. Fucking. Hell.

Inadvertently, I arch under him. Linus fills me to the hilt, every inch forcing a moan from my lips. He doesn't move at first, allowing me to adapt to his size and girth. His cock is the biggest I've ever experienced and I'm overwhelmed. For a moment, he stays buried, watching me. Like he wants to remember the exact second he claimed me.

"Your pussy," he kisses all over my face, "is perfect."

He starts to thrust. Dragging it out. Making me feel every goddamn ridge, every vein. My cunt grips him like it doesn't want to let go.

"Do you feel me?" he growls. "My cock is yours."

"Yes, I feel every millimeter," I hiss. "You're splitting me open."

Once I've adjusted, he fucks me like a promise. His hands clutch my hips and he pulls me onto his cock with every thrust. I meet him stroke for stroke. He shifts angles, hits my G-spot, and I scream.

"Right there," I beg. "Don't you ever fucking stop."

He doesn't. He pounds into me rough. Relentless. Skin slapping. Sweat slick. His hand slips between us, thumb circling my clit, and I shatter. Loud, raw, pulsing around his cock while he fucks me through it.

"Gonna come," Linus grits. "Where do you want it?"

"Inside me," I cling to him. "Fill the condom. Let me feel it."

He slams into me once, twice, and comes with a sound like an feral animal. His whole body tenses as he spills into the condom. I watch him, eyes squeezed shut, mouth open, and I know I've ruined him.

He's ruined me too.

Linus collapses beside me. We're both drenched in sweat and whatever the fuck passed between us. My heart's still racing. My pussy clenches at the emptiness like it's missing an essential piece.

He pulls me close. "You okay?" he murmurs against my neck.

"Better than okay." I nod, grinning like a woman struck by lightning.

This was something else. Exactly what I've been hoping for. For now, I don't tell him I'm not built for monogamy. Right now, with his memory of his perfect cock inside me and his breath steadying next to mine, he's more than enough.

We lie entwined, heaving, skin still hot to the touch. Linus' hand drifts across my stomach like he's tracing ownership in the grooves of my body. I don't stop him. His fingers find the edge of the blanket and pull it up around us like we need to be cocooned.

Minutes pass. Or hours. I wouldn't know. Time is a meaningless creature when you're this satiated.

"Ice cream?" he rasps, with a glint of mischief, like he already knows the answer.

I blink at him. Then laugh. "You're offering me dessert after sex?"

"Aye." He leans in, teeth grazing my nipple. "I'm offerin' you fuel for round two."

We stumble into the kitchen naked, my thighs glossy with our aftermath and anticipation of what's still coming. The fridge light is too bright. Everything else is dim. Moonlight snakes in through half-closed blinds, catching the curve of his back, the cut of muscle over bone.

Linus looks beautiful in this light. Godly. I can't shake the feeling he's bound to me by heat and something older than memory.

He grabs a pint of mint chip and two spoons. I steal it from him before he can open it, hop up onto the counter, legs spread, spoon in hand.

"Feed me," I smirk.

He does. Spoonful after cold, sweet spoonful. His eyes never leave my mouth.

"You're trouble," he murmurs.

"You like it."

He dips his fingers in the container and, sticky with melting mint, he presses them into my mouth. I suck them unabashedly.

"Mmmmmmm...." Linus sets the pint down, steps between my legs, and kisses me. Hardly gentle, the opposite.

I wrap my legs around his waist. I don't care if we're in the kitchen. I don't care if we fucked like animals ten minutes ago. I need him again. Reaching down, I grip his cock. Run my finger over his slit.

"You're insatiable," he murmurs against my lips.

"Well, I'm not done with you," I breathe. "Clearly, you're not done with me."

His mouth crashes against mine. Cold hands on hot skin and then we're colliding again. He lifts me effortlessly, strong hands under my thighs. My breath catches as he rubs himself against my opening.

"I'm clean," I assure him.

He nods, "Me too."

"I'm on the pill."

"Then I'm all yours."

There's no hesitation this time. No barrier. His bare cock slides into me like my pussy was made to mold around him.

My head falls back as he fills me to the hilt. I swear I feel him in my ribs.

"Fuck, Avonna," he growls. "You're perfect. Warm. Wet. Open for me."

"Don't you dare stop." I grip his shoulders.

"I wasn't plannin' on it." He grinds into me with brutal precision. The fridge rattles behind us. The spoon hits the floor. I can't stop shaking.

He fills me over and over again, all thick heat and pressure. My body welcomes him, no resistance. Raw need. I'm sensitive from the first time but it only makes this second taking more brutal. More real. More fated.

"*Christ...*" He rests his forehead against mine, watching my face twist with ecstasy. "You're grippin' me like you don't wanna let go."

"I don't," I gasp. "I want your cock to live inside me forever. Every inch. Every *fucking* inch."

He pulls out halfway, with the head inside, then he slams in powerfully enough to make my vision blur.

"*Linus.*"

"*Yes.*" He fucks me in steady, devastating strokes. "Say my name while I'm inside you. Let this pussy know who belongs inside it."

"You do," I choke out. "Linus. *Fuck—*"

The friction is devastating. Every time he bottoms out, he hits my G-spot, again and again. He's not human. It's like he knows my body better than I do, like he's been here in other lifetimes, carving this path through me, chasing the same fire.

The kitchen is filled with the slaps of skin, the sound of him sliding in and out of me. Filthy. Perfect. He rocks his pelvis into me, now hitting my clit with a dark, deliberate rhythm. The dual stimulation is unreal. Like two cocks are fucking me at once.

My pussy clamps down so hard he cries out. Good. I want him to lose himself the way I'm unraveling, melting around him like wax.

"You're gonna come for me again." He bites my lower lip. "I feel it. Your sweet little pussy's milkin' me already."

"I want all of it," I shriek, wild, unashamed. "I want you to fill me up. I want to feel you drip out of me."

He slams into me until the edge is right there, coiled and ready, molten and monstrous. When I let go, it's a full-body detonation. My back arches, mouth open in a silent scream as my pussy locks around his cock.

"Fuckfuckfuck—" he chokes, and I feel his cock swell. His whole body tenses, hands bruising my hips as he empties himself into me.

We stay locked together, unwilling to separate, for a long time.

We're not two people anymore.

We are a ritual. A *ruin*. A revelation.

He finally exhales against my neck, kisses my throat, and whispers something sounding a lot like, *"mine."*

I hold on to the moment. The madness.

Fate itself is watching.

Neither of us will ever be the same again.

Thirty

LINUS

One Month Later

THE LIGHT IN MY bedroom is soft.

Honest.

Slanting across the jumbled mess we made last night. My sheets are half-off the bed. Avonna's thigh is thrown over mine.

Our skin still sticky with sweat and sex.

She's not asleep. I can tell by the way her breath holds when I shift. Lately, after sex, she stills. Almost like if she moves the spell will break.

It won't.

Avonna.

Wild, dangerous, honest Avonna.

Except, not quite. There's something weighing her down, like a secret between her teeth.

I have the same pressure in my own chest.

Last night was supposed to burn it out of us. As usual, I woke up needing more.

I slide my hand across her stomach. She shivers. I dip lower. She parts her thighs, breath catching, wet and ready.

Always.

"You didn't get enough either." My lips brush her ear.

She turns to face me, eyes dark, mouth already parted. I slip two fingers into her and her whole body arches.

"Fuck," she cries out. "You're gonna start something."

"I'm gonna finish somethin'."

I move down her body, no hesitation. I eat her like I'm starving. My tongue deep in her pussy, fingers curling up, lapping at her clit like I own it. She writhes, canting and writhing against my mouth, one hand in my hair and the other flat against mattress like she's trying to keep herself grounded.

She's a mess in minutes. Coating my chin. Whispering curses.

When I climb back up, she grabs my cock, strokes. Her thumb smears precum across the tip and I hiss.

"Need you inside me." She bites her lip as she peers into my eyes.

"Turn over."

Her eyes flare and she obeys.

She gets on all fours, ass up, glancing back at me like she knows exactly how good she looks. I guide my cock into her soaked entrance. Her pussy swallows me perfectly.

Avonna half growls, half trills in prayer.

I grab her hips and start to fuck her. The sound of skin on skin mingled together with wetness echoing between us. Her face is buried in the sheets, hands clawing at the mattress.

"Take it," I growl. "Take my cock, Avonna."

"Yes," she warbles. "Fuck me like you mean it."

I snap my hips, driving into her like she's mine. She throws her head back, sweat dripping down her spine. I lean forward, one hand threaded in her hair, the other slapping her ass enough to leave a print.

"Tell me you love my cock."

"I fucking love it," she cries. "Your cock. God, Linus, you fuck me like no one ever has or ever will."

She comes, trembling. I keep going, chasing my own release, and when I let go it's with a guttural shout, buried balls-deep inside her, cock twitching as I fill her for the umpteenth time this month.

We collapse. Her chest against the bed. My body covering hers.

Sweat. Silence. Breath.

I can't let it go any longer. If we're going to make this any more than fucking, we've got to have a conversation.

"You're hiding somethin', baby." I kiss her shoulder. "You can tell me anything. This is a safe place."

She stills for a moment. Then exhales like she's been holding her breath for years.

"Look, this isn't something easy to talk about. I've told you about my extensive therapy." Her voice is hoarse. "I've never shared the details and you have the right to know."

I stay quiet. Let her speak.

"To heal from my past, I needed a special kind of counselor. To teach me how to get rid of the shame. The control they had over my mind and body." She clutches the pillow. "I needed to reclaim sex and I worked with a therapist who specialized in sexual trauma, and a sex surrogate. She provided the counseling. He taught me how to have sex. How to experience pleasure, give it—everything. All of my first sexual experiences were with him and I learned how to feel good in my own body. How to say yes and no without guilt."

She turns onto her side, facing me now. Eyes shining with tears. She's vulnerable, but not afraid.

"It was clinical but loving." Avonna squeezes her eyes shut. "Over the course of nearly a year, I lost all shame and developed skills to express what I want sexually. This might come as a shock to you, but I believe it's my destiny to be loved by two men. Sex. Commitment. Everything. At the end of my therapy, I determined this was a core desire and arranged to explore it with my surrogate and another man. They took me together. In every way possible. Afterward, I felt whole and knew it's what I want for the long-term."

It's all I can do to keep my mouth from dropping. Is this really happening?

I can't believe my gut instinct about her was so spot on.

She pauses. "I realize this might be a shock and Linus, it's not about not enjoying one-on-one. I do. I love it. With you, it's..." She swallows. "It's *everything*. I've fallen head over heels for you. Truthfully, I'm more confused than ever. I could be happy with you."

I'm still speechless, so I wait for her to finish.

"I wanted to tell you." Avonna looks away, almost bashful. "I've never felt safe enough to confide this to a lover. I wasn't sure if you'd be mad or scandalized or...maybe open to exploring this with me."

Fucking hell.

I touch her cheek and turn her face back toward me. "You have no idea how happy I am you felt safe enough to tell me. I'm glad you did."

Then it's my turn to confess what no one in Dublin knows.

"There was a man, back in the States. Liam."

Her eyes widen out of utter intrigue and complete shock.

"We were in uni together. I managed his band, Fireball. He and I loved each other. I truly thought he was my forever, but I had to leave when my visa expired. He...struggled. With himself. With commitment. With us."

I exhale.

"He's bisexual. As am I. Always have been. I've tried to shut it off, push it down. Told myself I needed to find the right woman. Or man." I grasp her hand and bring it to my lips. "Liam and I talked about what it would be like if we could find the right woman, but he didn't believe she existed. Avonna, for the first time, I can stop pretending."

Avonna doesn't say a word. She reaches between us, grips my cock and guides me back into her like I never left.

God, the feel of her. Silken. Molten. Enveloping my shaft like she wants to keep me pulsing inside her forever. There's nothing cleaner, nothing purer than raw truth between bodies.

"No more secrets," I murmur into her neck, thrusting deeper. "Never any lies."

She wraps her legs around my waist, feet clasped around my ass, pulling me deeper. Her words break apart against my mouth. "You're my everything. We can *have* everything."

I see her.

All of her.

An unspoken genuineness behind her eyes. A flicker of hunger beyond this room, this bed and me. I hold her wrists above her head, pinning her.

"Talk to me," I beg.

"I was beginning to think I'd never find someone who'd understand why I wanted two men. Not only during sex. In the quiet too. In the after." What comes out is raw truth. "I don't care if this isn't considered normal, do you?"

Her confession lands like a bell in my ribs. Part of me drifts, briefly, to my parents' kitchen table. To conversations I've rehearsed, but never spoken aloud.

There are entire versions of myself I haven't been able to explain, no matter how carefully I could try to choose my words. Someday, maybe. When there's something solid to discuss. Until then, Avonna and my shared truth would fracture more than it would heal.

First things first.

Liam used to tell me he couldn't commit to one or the other. Said no woman would ever accept a man who wanted both. No man would share. Believed desire like ours was a storm, not a home.

He was wrong. So wrong.

Avonna speaks her truth without shame. With perfect clarity.

"I don't care a bit." I kiss her cheek. Her lips. her throat. "You aren't asking too much. You're fuckin' perfect."

Her eyes close, tears clinging to the edges but refusing to fall.

She isn't broken.

She's prophecy.

So is he.

Two pieces of the same pull. Tugging on me from both sides. Inside my head, I see it clear as sunrise.

Avonna. Me. Liam.

We're three pieces of the same goddamn whole.

I slam back into her, and she cries out, biting her lip to keep from screaming. I know I'm close.

"Let go, baby." I hold her face between my hands. "I want to feel you come around my cock."

She fucking explodes, head thrown back, pussy spasming around me. I follow, chanting her name like a confession.

We collapse in a heap.

She turns, voice hoarse from pleasure and confession. "Did I spoil everything or are we soulmates?"

I meet her gaze. My mouth opens. Closes.

She exhales something between a laugh and a sigh. "It's okay. You can take a moment."

Shaking my head, I smile and my fingers trace lazy, grounding circles on her skin.

"I don't need one. I couldn't have said it better. You don't scare me, baby. You make me braver." I snuggle her under my arm. "I never thought it would be possible. You're goddamn right we're soulmates. I'm so feckin' in love with you, I can barely stand it."

Her hand finds mine. Our fingers knot. Silence settles.

Truth is no longer trying to outrun itself.

"I love you too, Linus O'Donnell. If we found each other..." She pauses. "Then someone else is out there too. Do you think it's him?"

I close my eyes.

Aye.

I see him as clearly as I see her. Dark eyes, callused fingers, a laugh filled with defiance, a heart too scared to stay open. The three of us, bent but not broken, fractured but never alone again.

He's the piece we're missing.

We're not whole yet.

Someday, God willing, we will be.

Thirty-One

LIAM

One Year Later

OUR OLD HOUSE SMELLS like a childhood memory.

Steam from Ma's cooking fogs the windows and clings to the air.

I hover in the foyer, pretending to study some family photos, already itching to bolt.

It's the first family dinner since Da's accident where every chair will be filled. I haven't walked through the front door since I left for school after I was thrown down the stairs. The others continued to live here, Brennan, Seamus, Cillian. Connor, of course, has been on tour but his bedroom is still intact.

My brothers have all maintained some connection to our parents. Padraig and I? We call Ma once a week, or so. Otherwise, we've been ghosts in our own house.

I'm not sure why I agreed to come tonight. I'm expected to sit at a table where he'll be.

The man who almost killed me.

Ma barks at Brennan and Seamus to hurry up and set the table. Ma and Connor bring out platters of food. Roast chickens, mashed potatoes, mounds of vegetables. My stomach's too knotted up to hold anything. Padraig hovers, staying close like he always does when he's afraid I'll start to fray.

On my way to the dining table, I walk through the living room. Not much has changed. The couch still dips where we used to pile on after school. Da's recliner is positioned to the side, the place he passed out most nights after the accident. From here, there's a clear line of site to the stairs, and the landing where I crumpled into a heap.

I close my eyes and feel it again. The shouting. The reek of whiskey. His breath in my face. Slurred hate. Words that still scrape my skin when I let them.

"You're a fucking disgrace."

"Liam." Padraig's voice cuts through the memory. "You good?"

I nod once. He sees through it, but he won't push. Not yet. We move toward the table. I slide into a chair across from Brennan, who's half-focused on his mobile. Seamus, who's fucking twenty years old all of a sudden, to his right.

How did my wee brothers become men?

Connor sits at the head of the table. He's been the man of the house since Da fell apart. It's still difficult for me to comprehend how honorably he handled the burden he never asked for. He was two years younger than Seamus when he gave up everything for us.

Kept me and Padraig safe.

"Cillian!" Ma calls. "Dinner!"

Our middle brother strolls in with a beer in hand. Pops the cap like it's nothing. Something about his casualness rubs me the wrong way. Padraig notices too. His eyes flick to mine. No words pass between us, but the implication is clear.

Pretending this family gathering is normal is a fucking joke.

My entire body tenses when I hear the sound I've dreaded most. A wood cane tapping against the hardwood floors.

I don't lift my eyes. Not yet. I feel him. Each step carved from pain.

"Good evenin', lads," Da mumbles.

Out of an abundance of caution, I keep my gaze fixed on my plate.

Da's chair scrapes. He lowers himself down with a grunt. No one says anything until Ma claps her hands and shovels a spoonful of mashed potatoes onto Seamus's plate.

"Boys, eat," she snaps. "You'll waste away if you don't."

Connor does what he always does. Holds the family together with sheer force of will. Forks clink. Voices try for lightness. My body stays rigid. I chew, but even Ma's home cooking tastes like ash.

The rest of the crew digs in. Cillian takes a slow sip of his beer, watching me and Padraig across the table.

"So," his eyes gleam, "how'd it feel opening for Connor and LTZ? A little humbling?"

Padraig smirks. "If by humblin' you mean sleepin' upright next to a crate of cymbals, then yeah. It was a real groundin' experience."

Connor laughs. "You turned down bus bunks and catered meals."

"We're purists," I say. "Perpetually broke."

Padraig adds, "We prefer limited legroom. Keeps us honest."

"Any proper chaos?" Seamus grins. "Fights? Gear on fire?"

"Nothin' so dramatic." I push my food around on my plate. Bantering with my brothers used to be a sport. Tonight it feels forced and I fucking hate it.

"Oh, don't youse feign modesty. We all know you owned the crowd." Connor shakes his head.

Cillian lifts his beer. "He's right. Fireball didn't look second-tier from my view."

"Thanks." A half smile pulls at Padraig's cheek. "We've been writin' nonstop. Goin' into the studio next month. We'll probably stay in LA a while before Europe."

"How are Koko's vocals?" Connor points his fork at me.

I shrug. "Somethin' new."

After dinner, Ma ropes Padraig into clearing dishes. I get up and wander through the house in a daze. The family room. The hallway. Every step pulls ghosts. I see us as kids, Cillian dancing in his pajamas, Brennan always trying to code something. Seamus tottering after Connor, eyes wide. Me and Padraig huddled in the basement with guitars we could barely afford. Dreaming our way out.

Once the dishes are washed and put away, the entire family crams into the living room. The telly's tuned into some show, background noise no one watches. Seamus curls up under his hoodie. Brennan types without blinking. Cillian's already on his third beer.

Padraig clocks it. So do I. Neither of us say shit. Not our business anymore.

Cane tapping, Da shuffles in. Stops in front of me. "Step out with me a minute, son. On the porch."

The word "son" hits me like a whip. I'm frozen. Unable to move. Padraig shifts beside me, like he's ready to spring if I flinch.

Not happy at being ordered around, I do nothing at first. This man has no sway over me anymore. I stand anyway and, against my better judgment, I follow Da.

It's cold outside. Rain clings to the edges of the rail. The porch light flickers above us, casting a weak halo over the overhang. I stand near the edge, arms crossed, pretending I'm unfazed by the sound of his footsteps behind me.

Mostly, I'm ready to bolt if need be.

Da clears his throat. I brace myself. We haven't spoken one-on-one in years. Not since he shattered every piece of me with one drunken swing.

As he musters up the courage to say whatever it is he called me out here for, I clench my jaw and stare out over the side yard, where Ma's garden used to bloom. The hydrangeas are gone. Dead or dug up. I don't know. Doesn't matter.

Finally when the silence drags on too long, I've had enough. "What d'you want?"

He exhales like he expected me to throw a punch instead of speak.

"Wanted to speak with you. Properly. You and me." His voice is raspier than I remember. Older. Tired.

I say nothing. The wooden slats creak as he shifts behind me.

"You've grown up," he adds quietly. "Yer a man now."

"Jesus Christ. I'm thirty fuckin' years old. Of course I'm a *man*." I face him, arms still folded. "Been one since the day you called me a disgrace, threw me down the stairs and clocked my brother for tryin' to protect me."

His eyes close like I've hit him with a hammer.

Good.

"I don't remember much about—"

"*I do.*" My voice cracks. "I remember *everything.*"

Da lowers himself into the old porch chair with a grunt. "There's no excuse. None. I've not stopped regrettin' it. Every day since."

"You've got a funny way of showin' it. It's been a decade." I shake my head, disgusted. "You didn't just hit me. You made me hate myself for things I can't change."

His hands quiver as he presses them together. "I grew up with different rules. Different beliefs. Doesn't make 'em right."

"No, it doesn't."

We sit in brittle silence. The wind picks up but neither of us moves.

"I was so fuckin' scared." My words taste like blood. "Of you. Of myself. Of what you'd do if you found out I was bisexual. When you did..." I trail off, swallowing the rest.

"I know I don't deserve yer forgiveness, Liam." His voice breaks, brittle and bare. "I devastated our family. Hurt all of you in some way. You the most. The shame eats me alive."

I don't respond. I can't. The pressure I've held inside since I was twenty years old is about to detonate.

"I was meant to protect you," he adds, softer now. "Not become the monster in yer story."

It's the first time I've ever heard him admit what he is. My chest cracks, not open. Enough to cause a dull ache.

Inside, I hear voices. Padraig's mostly. I know my twin's watching me from the window. Probably hasn't taken his eyes off me since I stood up.

Da leans forward. "You don't owe me anything. I needed to take accountability for what I did to youse. Whether you believe it or not, I'm sorry. For everything."

I study his face. The cane beside him. The lines spreading across his forehead. The hollow under his eyes.

He's a shell. Somehow, even with every scar he's carved into me, I want to believe my father means what he says.

"I'm not ready to let you back in," I manage. "I appreciate you makin' the effort."

He nods once, quiet. "I'll keep showin' up."

I hold his gaze for a beat. Then turn and step off the porch, the weight of everything unsaid trailing behind me like smoke.

I don't look back. Padraig can catch up with me later.

It's daunting to believe he's sincere.
Maybe someday he'll convince me.

Thirty-Two

AVONNA

A Year Later

I NEVER GET TIRED of lazy Saturday mornings.

Waking up to the weight of Linus's arm draped over my waist.

His breath warm on my nape.

He always finds me in his sleep. No matter how much we toss and turn, somehow by morning we're fused together. His leg is hooked around mine, cock nudging my thigh.

His entire body knows I belong to him.

I love the drift from dream to touch. How the light filters through the slanted skylight above our bed. My eyes blink open and I glance over at my beautiful man. Full lips puffing out small breaths.

I never knew I could be so happy.

When I shift slightly, his palm instinctively slides over my belly to pull me closer, no words needed. I reach down and wrap my hand around the thick length of him. Drag my fist loosely up and down his shaft until he's twitching with need.

His lips curl into a smile as he wakes up.

"Ah, love," he says sleepily. "You know how to wake a man up, so you do."

"My pussy misses you," I tease.

"Well, we wouldn't want her to go for more than a couple of hours without a visit." He pulls me to him. "Come here."

Linus hooks his arm under my leg to give his cock space to slip inside me. His arms envelop me as he fucks me lazily. Every inch of my skin awakens under his touch. We're one living, breathing body, in no hurry to do anything but remain linked for as long as humanly possible. Eventually, I can't hold back. My orgasm is quiet. Fluttery. He follows a heartbeat later.

He brushes my hair back from my forehead. "God, I love you."

By the time we make it to the kitchen a couple hours later, we're finally showered and dressed. He doesn't complain when I steal his hoodie, which is soft from so many washes. I pad barefoot across the tile while he makes coffee, whistling to himself under his breath.

As he's firing up his laptop at the table, my phone pings. It's a Google alert. My debut single is number seventeen in Germany. Number five in Ireland.

I swallow. "Wow, It's really happening."

I glance over at Linus and cover my mouth with my hand.

"It's *been* happenin'." He leans back in his chair.

We were looking for a long-term rental when we found this house in the Liberties, Dublin's arts district. It's on a quiet lane with a brick front. Ivy climbs the walls and a yellow rose bush blooms wild. Even better, it's only a five-minute walk to his new Isis Management office.

The price felt impossible. Now it's home. My first real home.

The kitchen is light and warm, with creamy cabinets, brass fixtures, and our beloved espresso machine. Most days we leave the back doors open to the tiny garden, where thyme grows in the cracks between stones. The living room has pine floors and a working fireplace. Upstairs, our bedroom window looks out over rooftops.

Our second bedroom has become my practice space where my guitars lean against the wall and I've set up a small desk for songwriting. Most weeks, I play gigs nearby in pubs, cafés, and galleries. It's the perfect setup. I can't believe I'm living my dream.

Almost.

I take a seat across from him at the table, sipping my coffee.

"I never imagined this." I trace the rim of my cup.

He glances over. "Chartin'?"

"No." I grin. "Waking up next to the person I love in our Dublin house drinking too much coffee while he handles my schedule."

Linus chuckles. "I'm proud to be your humble assistant."

"You're my everything," I say, and I mean it. I trust this man with everything.

Not long after we confessed to wanting a third, he asked me to marry him with his heart in his eyes. I said yes without blinking. We filled out the paperwork together, went through the process and, except for Linus's family, have kept it private. Not exactly hidden, but we don't go out of our way to advertise we're married.

Not yet.

Mainly, the wedding was supposed to be practical, even if our commitment has always been real.

In order for me to stay in Ireland, we had to be married. On the flip side, we're in the process of obtaining a US green card for Linus so he can, eventually, expand Isis Management to the States. My dear friend Marcella's immigration colleague is helping us in this regard.

For now, he focuses on his three Irish bands and me. We're not any closer to finding our third, but we've done a great job laying a foundation to make it happen.

Hopefully with the sexy Fireball guitar player.

A few hours later, we're in the living room watching my favorite show, *Strictly Come Dancing*. I don't have a gig tonight and none of Linus's other bands do either. It's a rare night and we're both happy to continue our lazy day.

"I've been thinking about him again." I crawl into his lap and nestle into the crook of his neck.

Linus raises a brow. "Liam?"

"Fireball's playing a bunch of shows with LTZ this summer." I kiss his cheek. "Do you think he'd be open to reconnecting with you?"

"I don't know." He pulls off my shirt and cups my breasts, thrumming my nipples into little bullets. "Let me guess. You're in the mood to play three-way. Wanna tell me again how you fucked two men at the same time?"

I look into his eyes. There's never any jealousy in our role-playing. Only heat. Curiosity. Hunger coiled behind restraint. My fingertip traces the inside of his thigh. Up, across his stomach. His abs twitch beneath the touch.

"It was like being lit from the inside," I whisper into his ear. "Their hands never left me. One kissed my throat while the other sucked my clit. They took their time. I felt everything."

I feel his cock rise against my hip.

"They opened me together. One slid his fingers in first, then the other followed. They made me ready. I was so wet I could hear it. I took both of their cocks. One of them in my pussy, the other in my ass. I was full to the point of breaking. My body didn't know what to hold on to."

I pull down his sweatpants. Stroke him as I speak. "Every thrust made me shatter and reform. They fucked me like I was precious."

He curses softly, shaft twitching in my hand.

"I came all over them. I felt *everything*. My pussy, my ass, my whole body. I didn't feel shame. I felt wanted. Worshipped."

He groans, low in his chest and bucks into my hand.

"You want to be fucked by me and him, don't you?"

"Aye. I think about it all the time." He looks down at my fist. "Fuckin' you while he fucks me. The other way around. Both of us inside your pussy. Or, one of us in your ass the other in your cunt. I want it all."

His cock twitches in my hand.

I smile as I stroke him. "I want all of it too. I'd love to watch Liam fuck you, I can't imagine how wet I'd be."

"Tell me, baby, how did you know?"

I blink. "Know what?"

"You wanted two men? At the same time. Considering your upbringing, I'm curious how it even came up in therapy?"

It's the first time he's asked. Even though his cock is in my fist, I can tell the question isn't about getting off. Well, not directly. He always wants to know me. *All* of me. I love him for it.

"You've never asked me about this."

He slips his hand between us and circles my clit. "I've always wondered."

"It started as a feeling," I recall. "A memory I couldn't stop circling. When I first escaped, I played a college party to earn money. I remember seeing two men in the kitchen. One had his hand on the other's back and I couldn't stop staring. I'd been taught two men loving each other was wrong."

Linus's chest quivers when I rub precum over his crown. He slips his fingers inside my pussy.

"From the living room where I was playing, I watched them in the kitchen across the hall. I remember it vividly. Big farmhouse basin. Old green tile. Fairy lights taped around the window."

His fingers pause inside me.

"They were kissing. Not softly. Like they needed it."

He stares at me now.

"I couldn't look away. One had his hand in the other's hair, holding his face like it meant *everything*."

He closes his eyes. Swallows.

"When I saw them, I knew. What they were doing wasn't sin. It was something holy."

"Avonna," he stammers. "Where were you? What city?"

I tilt my head. "Pullman. A tiny college town in Washington State."

Suddenly, it dawns on me. Linus went to college at a place called Wazzu. As someone who didn't really know what college was, I didn't realize Wazzu was Washington State.

Until right at this moment. Could it be?

No.

The odds would be impossible.

"How long ago?"

I look up to the ceiling to calculate the time. "A little over nine years."

"Baby, I think I was one of the boys." He pulls his fingers out of me. "Liam was the other."

My whole body goes still. Have our lives been fated for longer than I ever imagined?

Linus doesn't blink. "You were there for our first kiss. I didn't give a fuck who saw. Liam had me by the balls."

"Ohmygod." All the air leaves my body. "I was barely sixteen."

"I remember the singer. A hippie chick playin' Justin Timberlake." He kisses my hair. "Looked scared as a rabbit."

I flatten my hand against his chest. His heart is racing under it. "Guilty as charged. Are you as blown away as me right now?"

He nods. The silence and inevitability wraps around us.

"I'm more convinced than before. You should reach out." I stroke the hair at the base of his neck. "Something tells me, he needs us. He belongs with us."

If there's one thing I know about my husband, it's he doesn't love lightly. When he gives his heart, it's for good.

He's *never* stopped loving Liam.

I see it in softness behind his eyes when his name comes up. For all our hopes and dreams about adding a third, part of me felt a tinge of jealousy at the thought of Linus and Liam starting up again.

Until today.

Now I realize, I didn't see them in the kitchen by chance. I was meant to. Their image etched itself into my body before I knew them or had any understanding of my sexuality. It led me through therapy and taught me how to ask for what I desire.

Two men, and not any men.

Liam. Linus.

Not a fantasy. Our future.

One of them is already mine. Fully. Fiercely. Linus has my heart as much as I have his.

Liam's still a question, but something in me already knows. If we can get through to him, the moment he opens himself, all of us are going to fall forever.

I want it. For Linus. For me. The life we've let ourselves imagine.

I take his hand and bring it back to my pussy. "The three of us could be something real."

"I think we already are," he replies, slipping his fingers back inside me.

"Can you imagine? All of us in a house near the sea. Sharing songs, fucking each other. Touring. Raising babies.

"Don't forget, baby, it may not be easy to convince him. He walked away." Linus shifts me in his lap. Guides his cock inside me.. "I've contacted him many times over the years. Now there's so much more on the line."

"Try again," I whisper, rocking against him. "You love him. You always have. I think he still loves you. Maybe he'll love me too."

Linus surges up to meet me, kissing me so deep it cracks something open in my chest.

"I miss him so fuckin' badly some days." His thrusts grow sharper. "But you have to know. You and I are solid. No matter what goes down, we're real."

His fingers slide between us, circling my clit.

"*Nnnnngggggg*." I clutch his shoulders.

"I'm not risking you for stupid mind games," he whispers against my throat.

"Then we'll show him." My breath is ragged. "Not with words. Not at first. With songs. This summer. Let him see what you've built. The music I'm making. Let him decide for himself."

"Then what?" Linus picks me up and sets me on the counter, never leaving my body.

"Then," I wince with pleasure when he slams into me, "hopefully he'll write our next verse."

We come together, his moan buried in my mouth as he spills into me. My head rests on his chest, his palm traces lazy circles over my belly. Through the speakers, my new demo plays. A haunting ballad about how love can heal a painful past.

"You're a fucking star," Linus murmurs.

"I'm *your* star," I breathe. "And, you're mine."

"Forever." He kisses me.

"And *always*." My fingers slide through his hair. "Even if our universe adds one more."

Thirty-Three

Three Months Later

AVONNA DOESN'T TALK ABOUT her newfound celebrity much.

Not in the way other people might.

She believes fame is something peripheral. It floats at the edges of her life like a mirage.

Oh, she's grateful. Humbled. When she performs, I swear the world narrows to a single note. I've never heard anyone harness emotion the way Avonna can. Raw, bleeding, transcendent. Every song sounds like she's shedding her skin right there under the lights. Baring her truth for anyone brave enough to hear it.

At the same time, the spotlight isn't where she wants to be. She'd prefer to disappear into the music and be part of it.

Avonna's first album is bigger than either of us dreamed. It's charting across Ireland, the UK, Australia, and Japan. Her voice slips through speakers like a secret, spreading faster than we can track. Critics call it primal, ethereal, relentless.

What they don't know, is it's her truth.

Every note is a testament to her survival.

No one's heard music like hers before because no one has lived in her shoes.

Invitations started to pile up throughout Europe this summer months ago. Festivals. Support slots. Showcases. Many of which include Fireball on the roster since they're supporting LTZ in stadiums and have the ability to fill in the gaps with other appearances.

Somehow the opportunity feels less like coincidence and more like momentum pulling me and Avonna toward something inevitable.

Liam.

My mind remains blown at the reality Avonna was at the Wazzu party the night Liam and I first kissed in public. How observing our love caused something inside her to shift. The memory of us helped her heal. She carried it forward to become the person she is today

All the way to me.

Now here we are. Married in private. Aligned in public. Everyone knows I manage her. No one but us knows what we want to build behind closed doors. How much I still love Liam. How she plans to get to know him this summer.

If Liam wants us, we'll be ready.

He doesn't realize it yet, but the man already lives in the space between me and Avonna. In the way we sometimes fuck with intention, preparing not for fantasy, but a future we both crave.

Sometimes, I place a plug into her ass while she rides my cock, so we can both imagine what it'll feel like when we're both inside her. Other nights, I'm the one split wide as she works a dildo in and out of me, stroking my cock with her other hand, whispering how wet it makes her thinking about him fucking me in front of her.

We swap roles often. In every position and every combination. Trust is everything. None of what we do is performative. Or a rehearsal. Every orgasm feels like a step closer to our triad being complete.

There's no doubt in my mind when Liam meets Avonna, he'll fall as deeply in love with her as I have. If he still has feelings for me, maybe it'll all happen naturally.

At the same time, selfishly, I have professional designs on Fireball.

The band's momentum picked up when LTZ slated Fireball to tour with them on and off for the better part of this year.

I hope it continues. They deserve more than riding on Connor's nepotistic coattails. As far as I can tell, Fireball has been lurching along without any logical plan ever since their singer Arleigh left.

Without the right infrastructure they're bleeding potential. I see the gaps. Moves they should make but haven't. Headlines they're not grabbing. Lanes they're not owning.

Fireball needs a manager who knows them. Not someone guessing or afraid to push. I've already believed in them. Bled for them. My reputation in the industry is solid. I've had success with many artists. Years ago, I helped build Fireball and I'd like to do it again.

Better. Bigger. Smarter.

Perhaps with Avonna in the mix.

I'm keeping this possibility to myself for now.

Tonight, the queue outside is around the block. Bodies vibrate with pre-show energy. From a distance, the venue looks like any other. High brick walls, rusted signage, a stage barely visible through the open hangar-style doors.

Inside, the air sizzles with raw energy.

I keep my head down as we step in, my hand on the small of Avonna's back. Her hair's pulled back and she wears a hoodie, mainly to keep a low profile. Tonight is the first time I've seen Fireball in person since everything fell apart. It's her first time seeing them at all.

They haven't played Ireland before. Not once in all the years since I left the States. Like most acts on the festival circuit, they supplement the schedule with club and theater gigs in between. LTZ's tour starts in Belfast next week. Avonna and I leave for France the week after. Avonna and Fireball will intersect close to a dozen times over the next couple of months.

Tonight is for her as much as it is for me. A chance to watch from the shadows. A stealth gut check. Are we both all in? Or do we abort the mission?

The lights drop, and the crowd loses their minds. The band walks out without fanfare. Padraig heads straight for the drums. He looks leaner than I remember, but grounded. Koko struts to center stage with practiced ease, long legs, and high confidence. The crowd loves her. She's a professional. Poised.

Liam ambles out. He doesn't rush. Walks like a storm brewing behind calm eyes, carrying the weight of every song he's ever sung. His hair hangs longer now, brushing the collar of his shirt. His shoulders are broader. The way he moves steals my breath.

He stands before the mic and nods to Padraig. They lock in.

The first chord punches through the room. Controlled. A shared breath. I feel it in my ribs. Beside me, Avonna is still. Her eyes are fixed on the stage.

When Liam starts to sing, I feel her fingers thread through mine. His voice cuts through the static of the crowd, low and rough, worn with living. He doesn't perform. He bleeds.

Three songs pass. Neither of us speaks. By the fourth, I feel her shift again.

"He's writing from inside a wound." She cups her mouth to my ear. "His voice echoes off the walls of something broken."

Leave it to Avonna to describe something perfectly.

Her hand traces an arc over the back of mine. "Koko's good. Technically. She hits every note. Her timing is perfect."

I nod once.

"She doesn't live the songs, though."

I glance sideways.

Avonna watches the stage intently. "She's interpreting. Not embodying. There's a distance between her and the lyrics. She sings about pain, but she doesn't seem to feel it."

I follow her gaze. Watch Koko spin, toss her hair, reach for the crowd.

"She's brilliant," Avonna says. "Not a fit for them."

I gulp. The weight of her words settles into the idea I've been thinking about for months.

She leans closer. "They're all in sync. Technically. Something's off, though."

"What is it?"

"Intimacy." She narrows her eyes at the stage. "Trust. She sings at him, not to him."

Avonna doesn't need to elaborate. I feel it too.

When the final song begins, the lights cut low. Liam steps forward, voice raw. The crowd sways, singing with him. His body folds over the chords. The sound swells, thick with emotion.

Avonna's lips part slightly. Her breath catches. I watch her closely.

She holds perfectly still, every line of her body is tuned to the music. The moment the last note fades, she exhales. Closes her eyes and fans her hand back and forth in front of her face.

We slip out before the encore, back through the crowd, out the front door unnoticed. The street is busy but we walk in silence back to the car.

Before we get in, Avonna's hands slide up my chest, eyes shining. "He's even more than I imagined."

"I know."

She sighs dreamily. "I see why you couldn't let go."

I nod.

She cups my face. "We have to be careful. He hides behind charm but there's pain in every movement."

"He's always been this way." I sling my arm around her.

She kisses my cheek. "We'll go slow."

"If we wait too long..." I shake my head.

She finishes, "He'll disappear."

Avonna strokes my chest. "Let's follow through with our plan."

I breathe her in. Her scent. Her strength. Imagine the life we could have with him.

"We have to," she insists.

Leaning down, I kiss her deeply. "We will, love."

The two of us are going to give Liam something he's never had.

Us.

Thirty-Four

One Month Later

LIFE'S PRETTY FUCKIN' GREAT on the other side.

This is the first tour we've ever had with a full crew and a bus driver.

It's fucking luxury and I don't ever want to go back to slummin' it.

The sun's still high when we leave the backstage tent. Hot, heavy air clings to my skin, and my ears are already ringing from the last set we caught.

Germany throws a proper festival. Six stages. Smoke cannons, drone cams, girls in mesh bodysuits and guys covered in glitter and leather. Every ten feet someone hands us a drink or a flyer or a branded condom.

Me and Padraig keep our heads low under baseball hats. No one bothers us. Not yet.

We've played a few of these now, opening for LTZ across Europe, but this one feels bigger. Louder. A little more chaotic.

The best part about it is the downtime. There's no frenzy to pack up, drive to the next town and do it all again. We're able to check out other music, which is how we're spending the next few hours. As we navigate through the crowd, two girls with airbrush tattoos are dancing barefoot next to a line of food trucks.

"It's weird, isn't it?" My stomach growls at the smell of fried onions and garlic. "Still ridin' LTZ's coattails. Openin' for them. Watchin' Connor become a god."

Padraig smiles faintly. "Not weird. Well-deserved."

"Yeah, but still. It's a trip. Feels like yesterday he was hauling drywall to pay our tuition. Now he's datin' fuckin' America's sweetheart." I'm not envious, exactly.

Padraig nods but seems a million miles away. "Ronni's cool."

I glance over at him, walking beside me like he has since we were in diapers. Same gait, same rhythm. Quieter now. Sadder. The lines around his mouth are deeper.

So many years have passed and he's still not over Stevie. When he's in a mood like this, it's best not to push. To be fair, he doesn't push me either.

I'm not over Linus either. I have so many regrets at how I handled things and now it's too late. I'm pretty good at hiding it, though. There's a long trail of people I've hooked up with and discarded. Meaningless fucks leaving me more and more empty with each passing day.

"He's not changed, has he?"

Padraig kicks a pebble. "Not where it counts."

"You heard anything else from Koko?"

My brother frowns. "No, but we both know this is her last run. When we're done with the tour, she'll leave."

God, it pisses me off. We're having the biggest swing of momentum in our career and we'll likely be back to square one.

"New album. Bigger crowds. More money and better tours," I grouse. "She picks now to ditch us? What are we gonna do with no fucking singer?"

"Dar, stop." Padraig chuffs out a snort. "She was never stayin'. We both knew it and we've buried our heads in the sand."

He's right, and while part of me is relieved, the other part is exhausted. It seems like we can never catch a goddamn break.

The music from the nearby stage shifts. Something acoustic, but not soft. Deep. It's a woman's voice. Low, smooth, aching.

Every single one of my hairs stand on end. I turn toward the sound. So does Padraig.

Hers is not the kind of voice you forget. Dusty velvet. Pain polished into pearl. She's not trying to impress anyone, it's more like she's cut herself open to let people see inside.

Without speaking, we change course.

As we approach the stage, she's lit by amber stage lights, barefoot on a patterned rug. Wavy blondish hair, loose around her shoulders. Her fingers wrap the neck of her guitar like she's conjuring the chords rather than playing them.

Her dress clings to her hips, loose and easy, but there's a kind of fire in the way she plays. Controlled. Smoldering. I've never seen anything so innocent and yet dirty at the same time.

"Fuck," Padraig whispers.

I can't speak. Or take my eyes off her. She performs like she's lived in hell and made it a home. No frills. No dancers. The crowd is fully locked in.

The sign on the banner behind her reads: *Avonna*.

I repeat it in my head. *Avonna*.

Padraig and I stand mesmerized throughout the entire set. Every single one of her lyrics cuts through me. Her songs couldn't possibly be about me. Or, me and Linus.

But they *could* be.

I stand with my fists stuffed in my hoodie pockets, trying not to shout my approval. Her voice wraps around me like a prayer and I'm gutted when she lets us know it's her last song. I barely breathe until the final note drops.

When it ends, no one claps at first. Then the entire crowd erupts.

Padraig turns to me, eyes wide. "Who the fuck is she?"

"I don't know."

But we need to.

The two of us meander like common fans toward her merch booth. It's legit. She clearly has a team behind her. Vinyl, shirts, leather-bound lyric books. A video loop plays footage from her earlier sets. Magazine covers. Interviews.

She's not up-and-coming. She's arrived. I'm the one late to this party.

Our artist passes get us behind the barrier to the backstage area without any hassle. There she is, two feet away, smiling politely at VIP festival-goers and a few industry types.

Refreshingly, she hangs back a bit. Unassuming though it's impossible not to see her. Rosy cheeks. Sweat-damp curls. Her wide eyes narrow slightly when they land on me. A flicker of recognition sparks but she's already on to the next.

I'm used to it. Famous without being well-known. In all likelihood she knows Fireball and can't quite place why I look familiar.

Then her eyes flick back to mine, and something goes electric in my chest.

"I feel like I know you," I say before I can stop myself.

She tilts her head, smile widening, but not mockingly. "Do you?"

"Yeah. Sorry. That was—creepy." I glance at Padraig, who probably thinks I'm hitting on her.

"Only a little." She laughs softly, and I'm fucking gone.

Padraig jumps in, always the smoother one. "Your set was incredible. Neither of us are familiar with your work and now you have two more enthusiastic fans."

"Thanks." She extends her hand. "Avonna."

Padraig takes it first, introduces us both. "I'm Padraig. This is Liam. Yeah, we're twins. We play in a band called Fireball."

Avonna's hand fits mine perfectly. Her skin's warm. When she looks at me again, there's something in her gaze. Now I'm certain it's recognition. Also, curiosity?

Heat?

"Liam." Her voice curves around my name like she's tasting it.

I don't let go right away. Neither does she.

"So, twins from Fireball." She finally lets go and mops her brow with a towel. "I saw you in Belfast a few weeks ago. I live in Dublin."

"An American in Dublin." I shoot her my most devastating grin.

She steps closer. Not shy. Not full of herself either. Grounded. Composed.

"You're better live than in videos." She winks.

"Same to you."

This senselessness makes Avonna laugh. Her energy crackles. She's the kind of woman who draws people in whether they want it or not. There's something behind her eyes too. History. Weight.

"You sticking around for our set?" I ask like a schoolboy.

She quirks a brow. "Wasn't planning on it. You inviting me?"

"Aye." I lean in slightly. "Wouldn't be polite not to."

Her gaze doesn't drop. "Then I accept."

We're flirting. I know it. She knows it. I like the way it feels. Easy. Unrushed.

"Your voice…" I start, but the words falter. She waits. I try again. "It knocked me flat. Like you've bled through every lyric."

"Well, sometimes I have."

"You're incredible." I mean it. "The raw stuff's what lasts. Polish washes off."

Her lips part, and I think she's about to say something else. Keep the conversation going. I want her to.

Then I feel it. The back of my neck goes rigid.

Awareness.

A ripple in the air you only get when someone from your past steps into your present.

Linus.

He walks up from behind us and stands next to her.

He hasn't changed. Not really. Obviously, a little older. Full beard. His eyes are the same. So is the way he stands. The tilt of his head, like he's been watching me for years. Same unreadable gaze. His body is leaner now, more refined. Sun-kissed skin under a black shirt fitted like it was tailored to his bones. He looks sharp. Calm.

"Liam." His voice cuts like a memory.

My mouth goes dry. Padraig immediately takes a half step back, giving me space. His eyes flick between us like he knows how monumental this moment is.

I can't speak.

Linus doesn't either. Not right away.

Avonna's gaze bounces between us.

"Linus." She touches his arm.

Neither of us moves.

Padraig speaks before I can. "He used to manage our band."

Linus holds my gaze. "Among other things."

I can't pinpoint how I feel. I sure don't know what I expected if I ever saw him again. Rage? Tears? Something explosive.

Instead, everything stills.

He places his hand on Avonna's shoulder. "I manage Avonna now."

I blink. *What?*

It makes no sense and perfect sense at once.

I look at her. "*Really?* Linus O'Donnell is your manager?"

"Yeah. He's the best." She tilts her head up at him.

"Ah, well, you always had good taste." I direct this to him, trying to play it cool.

Linus's lip twitches. "So does she."

Wait, *what?*

I can't tell if he means her music or something else.

Before I can figure it out, Padraig tugs on my elbow, likely saving me from myself. "Dar, it's getting late. We should check our stage setup."

I nod, not trusting my voice.

"Padraig. Liam." As I take a step back, Avonna touches my forearm. "Thank you both for your kind words. Maybe I'll see you around."

I flick my gaze to Linus before I meet her eyes and hold. "Count on it."

When we walk away, I feel Linus's gaze on my back like heat from a blazing sun.

Shit.

My past has finally caught up with me.

I have no idea what it wants.

Thirty-Five

A Few Weeks Later

THE CATERING TENT IS fast becoming my favorite place on tour.

I love the energy. The clink of utensils on compostable plates. An occasional burst of laughter from a nearby table. Folding chairs scrape against the plywood floors laid down over grass. Crew members and artists move through the buffet line, nodding to each other over steaming trays of roasted vegetables, garlic chicken, and vegan curry.

Beyond the flap is the artist village lined with dressing rooms and green room trailers. A place to disappear if you need to. No one here is trying to stand out.

No matter how famous, everyone belongs.

I should be eating. Instead, I'm staring across the table at Liam McGloughlin.

His fingers curl around a plastic fork, forearm braced on the edge of the table. The scent of cumin and woodsmoke wafts through the air. His eyes are locked on mine, steady and unreadable.

He's intense. Watching me like I've already said something important, even though I haven't uttered a word.

"You were unreal today." He squints like he can see inside my brain. "The way you bare your soul, I have no idea how you do it."

I know I should be used to compliments, especially from the McGloughlin twins, but increasingly Liam's words don't feel casual. They land somewhere low, between my ribs, and unfurl.

He leans back, beanie low, curls escaping the sides. His black tee clings to his pecs, tattoos crisscross over thick, veined forearms. He looks like memory and prophecy at once.

Liam's held Linus's heart for years. We've shaped our bodies and desires around the space he left. Now he's in front of me, flesh and breath, unaware he was never erased.

Only missed. Only waited for.

I tuck a strand of hair behind my ear, trying to will myself to stay in the moment with him.

"You weren't stealth." I take a bite of salad. "I saw you watching."

"You always catch me." He smirks.

It's true. Every time we play the same bill, I find him in the crowd. Face unreadable. Posture tense like a held chord. Scrutinizing me with singular focus, like he wants to memorize my breath patterns.

You caught me first, I think to myself.

He spears a piece of chicken. "You're easy to watch."

"Oh yeah?" I laugh. "So are you."

Our flirtation has been building for weeks. A look. A compliment. The way he always finds a reason to hover near my sound check. I'm not naïve to the effect he has. Liam doesn't throw himself at people. He doesn't charm. He observes. Broods. Draws you in by holding back.

God, does it work.

Linus noticed before I did. How often Liam came up in conversation. How my gaze always drifted toward the stage when he was near. He isn't threatened. He understands. Encourages it. He knows Liam and I forging our own bond is important if we're gonna pull this off.

About a week ago in Paris, Linus had me on all fours, a vibrator pulsing deep in my pussy while he fucked my ass with his cock.

"You think about him when we fuck?"

My wail was the only answer he needed.

He thrusted deeper. "Me too. I see the way he looks at you when he thinks no one's watching. Do you know how hard I get knowing you're spending time together while I'm handling business. I'm not jealous, baby. I'm counting down the days until this is real."

"When it's all of us?" I whispered, pushing back against him.

"Aye." His hand snaked around to stroke my clit. "I want to see you ride him. Want to be buried in your ass while he fills your pussy."

"Yes," I squeezed around him, coming intensely. "I'll give you everything. I want him to see how good you fuck me. I want to watch him fuck you. I want it all."

"He doesn't know it yet, but he's ours." Linus grimaced as he erupted inside me.

Good gravy. I'm soaking wet. So aroused I consider running to the bathroom to make myself come.

Liam stabs another bite, then sets his fork down. His hand slides across the table. Hesitates. Then closes around mine.

It's warm. Rough. Callused.

I don't move as he studies our hands like they're something familiar. My heart races. I bite my lip until it bleeds, pretending I don't want to climb into his lap and ride him until we both forget our own names.

"Can I ask you something?" I say, mainly to distract myself.

He nods, thumb stroking along the inside of my wrist.

"Your lyrics. Do you ever try and go deeper? Beyond the driving, angry energy to access the brutal stuff?"

He watches me now, curiosity edged with something else. "Why?"

"You're good at the nuance. I have to scrape myself raw." I pause. "It's how I process."

"Process what?"

God. Of course. How would Liam know about my past?

"I grew up in a religious sect where girls didn't get to choose anything." I try to keep the confession high-level. "What to wear. What to say. Who to marry. What to believe. Pleasure wasn't ours. Curiosity was punished. Deviation from the norm wasn't...possible."

His expression isn't judgmental. More like protective.

"I escaped when I was sixteen. The day I was supposed to marry a man who could've been my grandfather." I squeeze his fingers. "I'd never kissed anyone. I didn't even know how to touch myself."

Liam's eyes flash, but he doesn't look away. His grip on my hand tightens.

Deciding to confess my innermost secret to Liam feels natural. "I spent two years in therapy unraveling an intense level of shame. Then I went further and learned how to reclaim my body. My pleasure. My voice. Writing is the only way I can name what was stolen and what I took back."

"Avonna. Wow. What you describe is the bravest thing I've ever heard." Liam's eyes glisten. Not quite tears, but deep emotion.

I shake my head and lock my gaze on his. "No. Surviving was instinct. Learning to embrace the things I enjoy during sex was what took courage."

He studies me for a long time. Fascinated. Terrified.

"I went through phases of learning," I continue, deciding to air it all out. "Watching myself. Touching. Allowing someone else to. Giving and receiving pleasure without shame."

His mouth parts slightly.

"It wasn't casual. It was structured. Intentional. The final phase was when I had sex with two men." I tilt my head. "Not for shock. Through a lot of work on myself, I knew what I wanted. Experiencing it first in a therapeutic setting was safe. I know my body inside and out. What feels good. What I need emotionally."

Liam goes very still.

"I don't share this with many people." I lean in closer. "In fact, outside of therapy, you're only the second person who knows. Knowing and accepting myself gave me my life back."

His tongue flicks across his bottom lip. "Jesus."

"You said you didn't know how I write the way I do." I look up to the sky and back to him. "Now you do."

Liam exhales fully, like a wall lowering brick by brick.

"I wish I was as brave." He shakes his head. "I'm holdin' back, Avonna. You can see right through me. I wish I could bleed through my music the way you do."

"You're right on the edge. I think you can if you allow yourself permission."

He snorts. "You think so?"

"Yes."

Liam looks away for a while. Then he stares into my eyes. "Your line, *'They wrote my vows in ash, long before I bled.'*"

My breath catches. "Yeah?"

"It haunts me."

He doesn't let go of my hand. Doesn't look away.

"I don't know why I'm telling you this." His voice dips. Accent thicker now, words heavier. "But it makes me think about my da. He nearly killed me once. Caught me with a guy. Didn't hesitate. Knocked me out cold. My little brothers saw it."

I blink. "Liam..."

"My ma made excuses. Padraig covered the destruction, which made me feel like a loser. Connor packed us off to college like a problem to be solved. Said it was to keep us safe, but it felt like banishment. We've lost years with my brothers, I don't really know them. Oh, and sometimes I wonder if I keep this fuckin' band alive because I love it or I'm afraid to admit defeat. Padraig gave up everything to stay with me and I don't fuckin' deserve it."

The weight of his voice lands in my chest like a stone.

"I've never unloaded so much on a friend." He winces and buries his face in his free hand.

I'm touched. Stunned. "Why me?"

"I don't know." He swallows. "You don't ask me for anything. You listen. There's somethin' about you I click with, you don't make me feel like a burden."

I rub my thumb along his. "You're not."

He stays quiet, but something in his posture loosens.

"I know about you and Linus." I try to keep my voice even. "You don't have to talk about it if you don't want to."

He looks down at our hands.

"I'm not here to fix you, Liam. I'm not here to figure you out or ask you to be anything other than honest." I wait, let it land. "I've spent years learning how to feel safe in my body. I know how heavy it is when you don't."

He exhales. The silence between us isn't tense. It's full.

I continue to run my thumb over his knuckles. "You're allowed to feel. Nothing about you scares me. Do you know what you want?"

He pauses. "Aye. I do."

"Then you should write it."

He looks at me like I'm dangerous. "With you?"

"Sure. If you think it will help."

He nods once. "Yeah. Let's do it."

A beat passes. Then two.

"You're so different from anyone I've ever met," he says finally.

"So are you."

He glances down at his phone. "Shit. I'm runnin' late. Come see our set?"

"Of course."

He doesn't move right away. Our fingers remain laced. We stare into each other's eyes. Filled with everything we haven't said yet, but will.

He squeezes my hand once, then lets go.

It's not a promise.

Or a goodbye.

It's our beginning.

Thirty-Six

LINUS

Two Weeks Later

TODAY IS THE FINAL day of tour.

Avonna and I are done for the summer, heading home to Dublin tomorrow.

This morning she wears nothing but my T-shirt, sipping a lemon spritz on the edge of the bed with her legs folded beneath her. Outside the window, Milan is a frenzy of horns and chaos.

Up here, it's quiet. Golden.

Avonna doesn't talk much before shows. She lets it all come out on stage. All the fire, all the vulnerability. It needs to simmer first, steep in silence, before she burns the world down.

Lately, though, she's lit up in a different way. The glow we have for each other is steady. Over the summer it's widened to include something we both feel coming.

Someone.

"He watched the whole set again." She drags her fingertip along the condensation on her glass. "Same spot, arms crossed, trying to look casual. He doesn't even hide anymore."

I crack a smile. "Liam's never been casual a day in his life."

"No." She looks off into the distance. "He watches me like he's trying to memorize every note. Every word."

She sets her glass down. Comes to sit beside me. I wrap my arms around her and pull her into my lap.

I already know what she's going to say.

"We need to tell him."

Not a question. Or a warning. It's an understanding.

"It started with a few lyric swaps, but it's turned into something wild." She nestles into my neck. "Every time we create it's like a detonation in my chest. I've never felt this kind of creative synchronicity with anyone. We were meant to write together."

I absorb this. I've seen it, too. Their sessions, how they linger afterward. The energy flickering between them, growing louder.

She takes a breath. "It's starting to feel manipulative when he doesn't know about us. Who we are to each other. How much he's been in our plans when we dream about the life we want. He's a fantasy in the bedroom with us nearly every night now. I think he senses it on some deep level, but he hasn't asked."

"He doesn't want the answer," I say.

"Exactly. I'm convinced if he knew I was with you, he'd run." She strokes my cheek. "Not out of spite. Out of guilt. He'd think he'd ruin everything. So, imagine when he finds out we're married."

"We're walkin' a fine line," I admit.

Avonna shifts to straddle me. "He's falling for me, Linus. I know he's attracted. I am too, but this isn't a breathless, infatuated thing. He's...opening. Letting himself be seen. Emotionally. Like he wants someone else other than you and his brother to finally know him."

"It's huge," I murmur into her hair. "Liam's already halfway in, even if he doesn't know what to call it. He's never let anyone see his soft parts but me."

"I know." She caresses the back of my head. "It's why we need to tell him before this goes any further."

I shift her in my lap. "You think he'll stay once he finds out?"

"I don't know," she says honestly. "I'm afraid if he learns the truth later, from someone else..."

"Then it's over before it starts."

She nods. "I've been careful. I haven't lied. But neither of us have told the truth. Emotions are involved now. I don't want to continue without full transparency."

"Neither do I." I trace my thumb over her knuckles. "I've stayed away on purpose so you and he... I've never stopped wanting him. Every time he walks into a room, somethin' in me lights up. My body reacts before my brain catches up. He looks at me, and I feel like I'm nineteen again."

She watches me closely, fascinated.

"We've spoken. Polite, friendly. Nothing more. But it's there. Still bubblin' under the surface. I think he feels it too, but he's keeping a lid on it."

Avonna bites her lip. "I don't want to stand in your way either, Linus. This is supposed to be about all of us."

"You're not, baby," I assure. "I wanted to give you the space to know him on your own. If this has a chance in hell in workin', it has to be three people who want each other completely. Not two pullin' one in."

"I want him too." She rests her cheek against mine. "It's more than attraction."

"Oh, I'm aware. I hear it in the songs the two of you are writin'." I stroke her hair. "Hear it in the way your voices blend. The way he listens to you. It's not casual."

I thread my fingers with hers. "I've been thinkin' about something else. Quite a bit, actually."

Avonna waits. Doesn't force the issue. She knows me well enough to let the words come when they're ready.

"This solo thing…" I glance at her. "You're brilliant. Everyone sees it. You're gaining more and more traction all the time."

A small smile tugs at her lips, but it doesn't reach her eyes.

"You don't love being alone up there," I add carefully. "You never have."

She exhales with relief. "I'm grateful for the opportunity you've given me."

"I know, baby. You're humble. You'd rather disappear into the music, not shoulder the performance too."

She nods, almost imperceptibly.

"My manager brain hasn't shut off since Belfast," I admit. "Watchin' you listen to Fireball. You see things others miss. My God, you understood Liam's lyrics after one chorus. Understood the fracture underneath and how he holds it back."

Her brow furrows. She's listening closely now.

"I heard Koko is leaving."

Avonna's expression softens. "Yes. At the end of these shows. He's spinning, trying to act like he isn't."

"I see it. He doesn't know where to go next. They've clawed their way back and now they're standin' on the edge of something bigger. They need someone who understands the ins and outs. Who can translate Liam and Padraig without breakin' what makes them matter."

Her eyes meet mine. Searching.

"I think you could be their singer," I finally tell her my idea. "The missin' piece."

She draws in a breath. Not surprised. More like she's been waiting to hear it.

"I didn't want to put it in your head before. This whole thing between us and him is delicate." I pause, give her space. "If anything's going to happen with the band, the truth needs to come out. About us. Our marriage. What we want with him. We can't offer him somethin' we haven't defined ourselves."

Avonna squeezes my hand. "Look, it's crossed my mind too. There's a lot of variables. They're based in the US. We live in Ireland. Padraig. I mean, if the three of us are able to work out a relationship, wouldn't it be weird? I guess what I'm saying is, this is delicate. I don't want to force anything."

"God, I love you for being so sensitive." I swallow. "The foundation has to be strong enough to hold all of us."

"When I'm with you, I feel rooted. Known. Loved. When I'm with him—" her voice catches "—I feel sparked. He's waking up something inside me."

I don't flinch. I don't pull back. I feel the same way about him, too.

Liam has always been a current running beneath my skin. Even when he disappeared and I tried to convince myself I was over him. All this time with Avonna, who fills my cup to overflowing. He's still here in the spaces between.

"I want this to work so badly," I admit. "The three of us. Wakin' up together. Creatin' a life together. Fuckin' each other. Comin' home to each other."

"We've got forty-eight hours before we fly home." She pulls my shirt up and over my head.

I know what she's asking.

"I'll reach out," I say. "Ask to see him. Alone."

"Are you ready?"

"No—*yes.*"

Without disentangling herself from me, she grabs my phone and holds it out. "This started as a fantasy. Let's see if it's real."

I take the phone and consider what I'm going to say, then tap in a message and show it to her.

Me: If you're passing through Dublin when you're done with the European tour, maybe let's talk.

"Perfect." She kisses me. Her mouth tastes like citrus and honey and heat.

I hit send, put my phone on the table and savor this moment with her. The life we're building.

I want her. I love her. She's not only choosing me, she's choosing *us*.

"You still give me goosebumps." My mouth brushes her throat.

She smiles, close enough for me to feel it. "Same."

Later, when she rests against me, Avonna asks so quietly I almost miss it, "Will we be okay if he says no?"

I think about it for a second. What we've built and what we stand to lose. Realize my truth.

"Yes," I assure her. "You've always been more than enough. You make me happier than I've ever been."

Her body softens at the words, trust settling deep.

"At the same time, we won't know unless we try," I add. "No matter what comes next, we're solid."

She nods, buries her face into my neck, and pulls me closer.

The rest can wait until morning.

Thirty-Seven

LIAM

Present Day

THE DOOR CLICKS SHUT behind me.

Sealing off the world beyond this room.

The floorboards creak. Once. Twice. I hear nothing else but the sound of my heartbeat collapsing into dust.

When I turn, Linus is there. His eyes graze my body. Up. Down.

My mouth goes dry.

He steps forward. Measured. Controlled. Stops in front of me, eyes locked on mine as he lifts one hand like he's touching a ghost. Fingers trail along my chest. Testing.

Are you real?

I shiver.

His lips crash into mine. No warning. No pause. Teeth. Tongue. Heat.

We don't kiss. We devour. Like no time has passed.

My jacket hits the floor. Then his. He runs his hands all over me, waist, ribs, spine, like he's terrified I'll vanish again.

I stumble forward, grip his hips, and drag him against me, slamming him back against the wall. My cock throbs as it meets his denim-to-denim. Heat-to-heat. The pressure slams through me, too sharp to hide. Too good to stop. His cock skims against mine. Thick. Heavy. Familiar. The friction is maddening.

"*Nnnngghhhh.*" I devour his mouth, rolling my hips, chasing more. I want to crawl inside him. Feel everything all at once. My body remembers him better than my mind ever could.

"You still want this?" My voice cracks, hoarse.

He answers with another rough thrust. "Never stopped."

My breath shatters in my chest. I need this man like air. Every goddamn inch. Every soft word. Every piece I lost when I let him go.

We stumble down the hall to his bedroom like we're starving. Clothes drop behind us, belts clatter to the floor, buttons pop loose, but I don't care. I need to see him. Need him bare.

I shove him onto the bed. He falls back without resistance. Legs splayed. Breath ragged. Cock pinned against his stomach, already leaking.

He's fucking beautiful.

Lean muscle and freckled skin, pink blooming from his throat down to his hips. His chest, with a light dusting of hair trailing down his abs. His thighs are thick, flexing with tension.

His cock—*Jesus*.

Long and thick enough to make my mouth water. I've missed the curve of it, the way it juts from his body, veins bulging under the surface. I kneel between his legs. His hips cant like he can't wait another moment, hands fist the sheets.

"*Liam*," His breath hitches.

I grip the base of his cock, stroke the thick vein with my thumb. His whole body shudders. My tongue follows, licking up his shaft, catching the bead at the tip and savoring the taste. Unable to resist, I swallow his cock. Linus fists my hair tightly. I take him in deep. I want to choke on the pleasure.

Every twitch of his thighs, every broken sound he makes is exalted.

This isn't sex. It's possession. We're carving our names back into each other's bodies.

When Linus shoots down my throat, it's with a guttural cry. He watches me swallow it all, chest rising in sharp pulls as I immediately climb up his body. His cock might be softening and spent on his belly, but the heat between us hasn't cooled.

If anything, it's sharper now, rawer.

I kiss his mouth, messily allowing him to taste his own come on my tongue. He doesn't flinch. Instead, he opens wider.

"We're not done," I promise against his lips.

He shakes his head. "Not even close."

My hand slides down his stomach, teasing. I trail my fingers down between his legs, where he's still sensitive from his orgasm. His hole twitches when I feather my fingers around it. "You want me to fuck you?"

His breath stutters. "Yeah. *Please—*"

His plea strikes me like a match to dry leaves.

Gripping his thighs, I push them up and open wide until his knees are drawn up, exposing everything. His chest rises fast now, pert brown nipples aching for me to taste them. His cock's already trying to wake up again, twitching against his stomach.

Finding a tube in his nightstand, I coat my fingers with lube and press one against his hole. He gasps when I breach him, hips arching.

"You've been dreaming about this?" I curl the tip and stroke.

He keens, "Fuck, yeah. Every time I wank myself."

"Did you come like this?" I add a second finger. "On your back, legs up, imagining it's me inside you?"

"Yes. God, yes—Liam. Keep going. I need more."

I scissor my fingers deliberately to prepare him for my girth. He bites his lower lip and pants like he's on fire from the inside out. I watch every inch of his body react. Cock standing at full attention. Thighs trembling. A wild look in his eyes like he's starving and I'm the only thing in the world worth tasting.

When I pull my fingers out, he whines. I lube my cock up and drive my crown inside.

"Look at me," I demand.

His eyes snap to mine. Glazed. Open.

I push all the way in, breaching tight muscle. He smacks the mattress with his hand as I savor every inch. Reveling in the impossible tightness wrapping around me. Like he's never given this part of himself to anyone else.

"Fuck, you're so—" I grit out.

He shakes under me. "You're the last man I let... Fuck. *Liam*—"

I'm floored. It's impossible to comprehend I'm the only man who's fucked his ass after all these years.

Fighting intense emotion, I bottom out, buried to the hilt. Breathing with him. Allowing his body to adjust.

Leaning down I nibble on his lips. "I've missed this."

"I've missed you." His hands curl around the back of my neck.

I start to move, dragging my cock nearly all the way out and then pushing back in. His legs wrap around my waist, heels digging in to encourage me to pump more rigorously.

I give it to him. Every thrust slams through the years we lost. Every stroke is an apology.

I never stopped wanting you.

I never stopped needing this.

I clutch his hips, pulling him to me, over and over. The sound of our bodies smacking together fills the room. Wet. Loud. Real.

Soon, Linus is feral. Grunting without shame, shaft bouncing and leaking all over his abs. The headboard slams. The mattress creaks. Our breath is a mess of curses and praise and memory. My hips stutter. His name spills from my mouth like a benediction. Then—

I notice him crane his neck toward the corner of the room. Mid thrust, my eyes lift from his face to see what's caught his attention. In the shadow of the lamplight, I'm shocked to see a woman sitting in a chair.

Watching us fuck.

Legs draped over the armrests. Her hand is between her thighs, fingers glistening as she rubs her clit.

"Avonna?" Her name cracks out of me, fragile and broken.

She looks directly at me and shoves her fingers into her cunt. I can't breathe. I can't move. My cock fused inside Linus is more rigid than it's ever been, but my whole body freezes under the confusion about what the fuck is happening.

I'm turned on beyond my wildest imagination.

Linus's hands run down my back, anchoring me.

"Liam, I *love* you."

My heart stutters. We've said this to each other hundreds of times, but hearing him say it now, mid-fuck, destroys me in a way nothing ever has.

"I always have." He stares into my eyes.

I let it land. His words permeate every part of me I've never let anyone touch since him.

Since her...

He's vulnerable in the way only truth can wreck a person. His hands move up to cup my face.

"Linus—"

"No," he says softly. "Let me finish. I need you to know I never stopped. Not once. Not through the silence. Not through all the things I told myself to forget."

My vision blurs. He doesn't look away and won't let me either.

"Do you love me, Liam?"

It isn't a demand. It's a plea. Linus needs to hear me say it aloud.

I nod. "Yeah. I love you. I always have."

He exhales like he has been holding his breath for years. His thumb brushes my lower lip. "Do you trust me?"

"With my life."

His eyes soften. His hand settles on my cheek. "Then trust me when I tell you I'd lay down my life for you. I'd do anything to make sure you have everything you need to be happy. Fulfilled. Whole."

Linus's words hit me like a strike to the ribs. I believe him. Every word. This moment is bigger than I can process.

With Avonna here, he's opened a door I never believed existed.

"Liam." Linus arches under me, his hands clutching my ass "Don't stop. Fuck me. Show her how much you love me."

I thrust again. My vision blurs.

This is madness. Impossible.

Linus's ass pulls me back into the rhythm. Into what we are.

Now she's part of us.

My hands find Linus's hips again, trembling.

I fuck him relentlessly.

For her to see.

For him to feel.

For me to finally believe I'm where I belong.

AVONNA

The Same Night

I'M IN THE CORNER.

This old velvet chair, tucked beyond the edge of the lamp's glow, has never felt more sacred.

I'm naked, thighs spread. One hand buried deep between my legs. The other grips the armrest because if I let go, I'll fly apart.

They're on the bed.

Linus lies open with his knees pulled up, mouth slack. Liam towers over him, thick cock buried to the root, the passion between them so intense, I can feel it in my own throat. Their bodies move like the tide. Urgent. Primal. A rhythm only they understand.

Liam doesn't know I'm watching, but Linus does. He and I don't hide from each other.

We've been planning this reunion for months, but right now, this moment is theirs. A reckoning. Combustion I've only ever dreamed of witnessing.

They're fucking beautiful.

Liam fucks him like he's recouping something he lost. Not rough. Not sweet. Inevitable. Every thrust is deep and full and unforgiving. Linus gives it all back, writhing and chanting Liam's name like a prayer he's never stopped repeating even when it went unanswered.

His blunt fingernails drag down Liam's back. Their bodies meet again. And again. Wet, hot, perfect. The slap of skin on skin. Liam emits guttural howls as he fucks Linus, who grunts with ecstasy each time Liam drives home.

The scent of their sex floods the air. Raw. Masculine. Intoxicating.

My pussy is soaked. Dripping onto the velvet beneath me. My fingers work faster, circling my clit furiously.

God, I want to join them. Feel both their cocks inside me at once.

Hopefully later. For now, I bear witness.

Liam shifts, hips plunging deeper. Linus lets out a sob of pleasure, low, primal, and looks back at me for a nanosecond. Liam's eyes lift and find me too.

My finger freezes on my clit. My pussy is wet and exposed. As Liam stares and confusion sets in, he stays buried deep in Linus.

A shadow passes across his expression. Want. Hunger. Fear?

"Avonna?" he breathes.

The way he says my name cracks something wide open. Need burns throughout my core.

Linus whispers to him, soft words I can't hear. I don't need to. He's soothing Liam. Anchoring him. Explaining I'm here in the room with them because I belong.

All Liam has to do is agree.

When he's finished, Linus turns his head and beckons me. "She's mine. I'm hers. We've been dreaming about you being ours and us being yours."

Liam's body twitches. His face goes impossibly red.

I get up and move toward the bed. "Liam, I told you I wanted to know you, and I do. *All* of you."

Liam's eyes remain fixed on me.

His cock stays buried in Linus.

"I wanted to see him with you like this." I trail my fingers along Linus's face. "And now..." I place my palm against Liam's racing heart. "I want you to see me with him too."

Linus's hand slides down his own chest to stroke himself. Watches Liam's eyes rake over me like he's trying to memorize every inch. I don't look away.

I don't stop touching myself.

"She's beautiful. Perfect. Look at her," Linus rasps.

Liam's gaze falls to my thighs. The glistening arousal between them. My nipples hard as diamonds.

"She wants us." Linus grasps my hand.

Liam doesn't answer. Linus clenches around him again. Enough to make him grunt.

"Come on," Linus hisses, voice shredded with need. "Show her how you fuck me."

My breath catches. I keen, sharp and involuntary, and Liam's eyes lock on mine. Fierce, dark, pulsing with hunger. He begins to move once more. Brutally pounding into Linus. Each thrust punches a sob from my husband, his back arches and his free hand claws at the sheets as he takes every inch like he was made for this.

Up close, I'm mesmerized by them. I can't stop touching myself. My fingers slide over my clit. Hips rolling with every wet circle. Liam watches me unravel, eyes tracking my every movement. Linus wails both of our names now, pleading, half-mad. Liam's cock drives relentlessly.

I rub faster, as the heat coils and I come with a broken squeal, gushing around my fingers, hips jerking as wetness sprays, hot and messy on the sheets and their joined bodies. My whole body shakes with aftershocks nearly as strong as my orgasm.

Liam groans like he felt my orgasm through Linus's spine. He stares at me. Like his brain can't catch up to what his body already knows—I'm real.

This is real.

He's halfway in love with something he doesn't have a name for yet.

Linus keeps hold of my hand throughout. "I want you to watch me fuck her. Hear how she moans when I fill her. See her pretty pussy grip my cock when I'm buried in her."

I look back at him and smile and he tugs me closer. "Come here, baby. Come ride me. Let him see."

Climbing onto the bed, I straddle Linus reverse-cowgirl, facing Liam.

Liam's eyes rake over me like he's starving. He doesn't touch. He drives his cock deeper. I reach between my thighs and wrap my fingers around Linus's shaft and guide him to my entrance.

I sink down and flinch. "Ohh—*fuck*..."

My inner muscles clamp around his cock as I take him all the way to his base. I'm full. Stuffed. I roll my hips and squeeze my pussy around him like I never want to let him go.

"*Ahhhhhhhhh...*" Linus's head lifts. His hands come up immediately, palming my tits. Fingers twisting my nipples the way I love. Liam's hips slam forward into Linus in a sudden, rough thrust, punching a broken yelp out of both of us.

"Fuck—fuck—*yes*." Linus writhes under us. "That's it. That's fuckin' it."

He's savage in the best way. One hand thrums my nipple, the other drops between my legs, fingers finding my clit with practiced ease. Tight, dirty circles make my hips stutter against his cock.

Liam's eyes are locked on where Linus and I are joined. Watching how my pussy swallows him over and over. How the wet sound of us adds to the music in this room with every movement we make.

"Look at her," Linus grits out. "Liam, watch how she fucks me. Hear how she mewls when I touch her."

I can't breathe. I can barely see. We're a knot of bodies Liam inside Linus. Linus inside me.

"She loves me," Linus wails, legs twitching as Liam pounds into him. "I love her. We've never felt whole until now. Not until you."

Liam's mouth opens like he might say something, but it's a rough, guttural growl as he slams forward again, cock driving so deep into Linus I feel it through his Linus' cock inside me. I scream. My whole body shudders.

Linus arches up into me, "I love both of you. I love being split open. I love feelin' your cock in my ass while I fuck her pretty little cunt."

Reaching out, I run my hands up and down Liam's lithe chest, nails digging into muscle, grounding myself in his heat. He doesn't look away. Doesn't blink. His stare pins me in place.

He still hasn't touched me. But he doesn't have to until he's ready.

Linus is at his wit's end. "Ride me, baby. Let him see."

We're close. All of us.

Then Linus reaches back with one shaking arm and grabs Liam's hand, drags it forward across my belly, lower, until

Liam's fingers slide through the slick heat between my thighs, where Linus's cock disappears inside me.

"Feel it," Linus begs. "How wet she is. What you're doing to us."

Liam's breath stutters, but he doesn't pull away. His fingers slide through my folds, stroke over my engorged clit. I bite my lip to keep from coming too soon.

Then he leans in. *Finally*. His mouth finds my nipple. Tongue curling around the peak before dragging his teeth enough to make my vision snap white.

I grind down. Linus bucks up. Liam drives deep.

Everything crashes together.

Liam moans into my breast, rhythm stuttering, thrusts erratic. My clit spasms under his fingers as my pussy milks Linus. Liam pulls back suddenly, his cock slides free from Linus with wet pop. and his hand wraps around himself. One stroke. Two.

He explodes.

"Ahhh—fuuuck—" Thick ropes of come splatter my chest and my belly, dripping between my tits as I ride Linus vigorously.

Linus sobs, "Avonna, I can't hold off anymore. I'm comin'—"

His cock erupts inside me and I feel his whole body lock up beneath me.

It tips me over the edge. I screech as though I'm being exorcised when I come, clit pulsing, pussy gushing, squirting over Linus's cock and Liam's belly with a messy, uncontrollable spray. My body goes electric, spasming around him. Both Liam's and Linus's hands hold me in place, soothing me. Grounding me.

It takes forever to come down.

When I do—

I'm still impaled.

I look back at Linus. Then at Liam.

Who stares at both of us like he can't believe what happened.
Like he never wants to leave this room again.

Thirty-Nine

The Same Night

Our passion is evident all over the sheets twisted beneath us.

The air is thick with the raw scent of sex.

Avonna's draped across my waist, lips parted against my chest, breath shallow but steady. Liam sits facing us at the foot of the bed, spine straight, chest rising like he ran through fire. His cock rests against his stomach, but he doesn't make a move.

He's watching us trepidatiously. I get it. Fucking me and Avonna together is something he probably never fathomed. This isn't some fantasy, but a promise of what we could all have together.

His fingers flex on the mattress as his eyes drink us in, raking over her perfect tits, my half-mast cock still mostly inside her.

She lifts her head, hair falling over one shoulder in damp waves. Here eyes are heavy-lidded but clear. "Don't look at us like you're not allowed to want this."

"Am I?" Liam's throat bobs. "All the time we spent together over the summer and I'm findin' out you're his."

Her voice doesn't shake. "No, you weren't listening to Linus. I'm mine first, then his. I love him. I also want you. *We* want you." Her gaze shifts. Finds me. "We've been married for a while but we've been missing you."

Sliding my hand along Avonna's spine, I kiss to her shoulder. "Baby, if he's okay with it, I want to watch you fuck him."

She nods and licks her lips. Not like I needed to convince her of anything. Her mind was already made up.

I shift to ease out from under her. A soft hiss escapes her lips as I slide free, my cock dragging through the mess between us. Her hand grazes my stomach as I sit up.

I move quietly, crossing to the bathroom. Take my time to let the warm water run and wet a soft towel. She deserves to be cared for. So does he.

When I return, Avonna is resting against the headboard with her thighs parted and glistening. She doesn't flinch when I kneel beside her on the bed. She lifts her hips for me.

Aftercare is her jam. An important part of our sexual ritual. I clean her carefully, wiping gently between her legs where she's puffy and tender. Her cheek melts into my hand when I cradle her face.

I kiss her temple and move next to Liam. Gripping his cock, heavy in my hand, I clean him off. He watches me the entire time, knowing this part matters.

When I'm done, I pull Avonna back against me until her body curves into mine. The damp strands of her hair stick to my chest as I stroke one palm down her belly. Her thighs are spread wide over mine, pliant and open.

Liam watches us. His lips are parted, eyes devouring her like a man starved.

Avonna grasps his cock without shame. Her fingers wrap around his girth, guiding him closer.

"I want to feel you," she purrs. "*All* of you."

He settles over her, like the moment might disappear if he's not careful. One hand anchors her hip, the other caresses her cheek. His eyes meet mine, a silent question in them. I nod once, my hand never leaving her skin, stroking the soft flesh of her inner thigh, brushing over the slick folds of her pussy, already soaked with my come and her desire for him.

I reach down, grip his cock and guide him in. No teasing. No pretending they're not both starving for it.

I watch him breach her entrance. He stops. Looks at me again.

"You're safe here," I assure him.

Liam pulls all the way out and thrusts in quickly. Avonna's whole body constricts.

"Breathe," I murmur into her ear. "Let him in."

Liam angles forward, inch by inch. Her mouth drops open as the sweet mingling of pain and pleasure vibrates through her chest into mine.

I feel it all. Every flutter of her pussy. Every inch of him disappearing inside her.

When he bottoms out, she cries. My cock rises against her back at the sight of such beauty.

Liam's breath is ragged. "Fuck, you're perfect."

"She is." I kiss her temple. "Move, Liam. Let her feel you."

I stroke her hair as they find their rhythm. Liam's salivates with hunger, awe, and something close to reverence. Avonna's stomach flexes and relaxes as he pumps into her.

One hand clutches his shoulder, nails digging in. She reaches for me blindly with her other hand, fingers tangling with mine. I kiss the crown of her head.

This is more than sex. It always was.

Three bodies, three hearts, trying not to splinter from the weight of how much we want to belong to each other.

Her eyes open and find mine. Then Liam's.

He pulls back, then thrusts forward again. A deep, controlled grind. Avonna arches, her head falling back against my shoulder, her body fully offered to him, through me.

"You love this," I whisper against her ear. "You love being fucked like this, don't you?"

"Yes," she whines. "Oh, God, I don't ever want to stop."

The bed rocks beneath us. The air is raw, salty, sweet. Her croons echoes between the walls, mixed with Liam's growls and my whispered praise.

Avonna's back arches and she shatters.

Liam's thrusts falter. He's close.

"Linus," he rasps, barely able to speak.

I gently ease out from under her, kissing her cheek as she collapses back into the pillows, dazed and glowing as Liam continues to fuck her.

"Watch," I tell her.

I kneel behind Liam, my cock aching. He turns his head slightly, already knowing what's coming.

Grabbing the lube, I stroke myself a few times then slide my crown along the curve of his spine. He shudders, opening for me like he always did, his body instinctively angling to give me access.

I guide myself into him, his mouth falling open in a silent cry when I bottom out.

"Jesus," he chokes. "Fuck."

He's still inside her and now I'm inside him.

We're all connected. Again. In a new way.

Avonna watches with heavy-lidded eyes as I start to move.

When I thrust into him, he lurches forward, driving him deeper into her. She exhales and so does he. The rhythm builds. The friction, the pressure, the sound of skin and breath and wet heat.

I reach around Liam's hips and grip the base of his cock, fucking him into Avonna in time with my thrusts. His whole body tenses. He's about to blow and so am I.

Liam's cock twitches in my hand. Avonna rises to meet him, legs trembling, fingers clawing at the sheets. Her eyes find mine.

Raw. Wild. Glowing.

I squeeze the base of him and whisper through my teeth, "Let go."

Liam emits a sound I've never heard, somewhere between a sob and a growl and spills inside her, his whole body seizing. She yells his name, then mine, milking every last drop as my cock erupts deep in Liam's ass.

We fall together.

No borders. No past.

When it's over, I wrap my arms around Liam's chest as he collapses forward onto her, our hearts beating like war drums.

I kiss the back of his neck. Her temple.

This. Us. Now.

I don't know what happens next.

Only in this moment, we are whole.

Forty

LIAM

The Next Day

I SHOULD FEEL GUILT.

Some jagged edge of shame, cutting through the debauchery of what we did.

Or, maybe regret. Cold, rehabilitating remorse creeping in after the high of my orgasm fades, reminding me.

Bliss is a trap.

Except, there's nothing of the sort here.

Only warmth. Acceptance. Peace.

Avonna's curled against me, one leg intertwined with mine. One of her stiff little nipples brushes my ribs. Linus cradles her from the other side, his free hand resting on my thigh.

I can smell her, me, him clinging to our skin, the sheets, and the memories we've made. Radiant. Fucked-out. Glowing.

My body's wrecked. Ass sore from being taken by the only man who's ever made me feel whole. I'm still overstimulated, not from friction or need, but from something deeper. Wanting to do it all again. Never wanting to leave this bed.

This moment.

What's crushing my chest isn't the desire for more sex.

It's the truth settling into my skin.

They planned this.

Not in some manipulative way. Not with games or pressure.

With care. Time. Patience.

Avonna makes a sound, a soft exhale like the final note of a song. Linus murmurs something and kisses her temple. She smiles without opening her eyes.

They're both so at ease. But me?

My head is spinning.

They're fucking *married*?

I think back to those nights back in college when Linus and I lamented about how much we wanted this but didn't believe any woman would consent to share and be shared for the long haul.

Which has proven to be true, in my experience. My first threesome with the married couple might have been life-changing, but in the end, it was merely sex. Nothing long-term. A weekend kink. A vice I've chased over and over throughout the years to find some level of sexual fulfilment.

Avonna, Linus, and me are something else entirely.

Linus is my soulmate. He saw through every mask I wore from the start, calming something in me I didn't know needed soothing with quiet, steady love. When he left, it shattered me. I ghosted him not because I stopped loving him, but because I loved him too much.

Now, I realize he never stopped believing we'd find our way back. He knew we'd find her too. He arranged for me to get to know her over the summer and I've fallen just as hard for her.

She's a voice I can't stop listening to. A body I crave like oxygen. A fellow songwriter who's crept into every part of my brain, one verse at a time until we became friends and grew close.

She told me about her past, how she escaped the puritan religious sect and, through therapy, was able to love and accept herself. Embrace her sexuality without shame.

A concept so foreign to me, I confessed things to her not even Linus is aware of. How even now, despite my da's attempts to make amends, I hear his voice condemning me when I fuck a man. How I flinch when someone touches me like I'm more than a body. How I keep trying to fuck away my depravity and still wake up thinking I've crossed some invisible line careening me into self-hating hell.

Even when it feels like love. *Especially* then.

Love.

Fuck me. Here he is. Here she is. It's madness. *Impossible.*

Lying between them, I realize none of the shameful voices are swirling in my head. All this time apart was one long breath he held, waiting to exhale back into me. Avonna's heart and soul fit me like memory, as if we've known each other in a previous life.

The three of us together are a dream I never let myself believe in.

I want this. I want *them.*

God help me, I do.

Sensing I'm getting too far into my head, Linus threads his fingers through mine. "Shower?"

"Please." Avonna sounds wrecked. Sore. Sated.

Linus lifts her. I slip my arm under her shoulders, steadying her weight. She leans into both of us, arms draped around our necks. We move to the bathroom in sync, the way bodies do when they know each other. He sets her down as I turn on the jets

Linus steps in first, guiding her under the spray. I follow.

Avonna rests her back against his chest, Linus wraps his arms around her middle. My hand finds her shoulder. I lather up a washcloth with body gel and we begin to tend to her. She tilts her face up, eyes closed, letting the water run over her hair.

Linus works shampoo into her scalp, massaging in small circles as I soap her arms, torso, legs. There's nothing rushed in the way we touch her. No hunger. Just attention. She sways between us, breath evening out, shoulders dropping as the tension leaves her body.

"You both make me feel safe." She smiles up at us.

Something in my chest loosens.

Linus kisses her shoulder. I rinse her hair, shielding her eyes with my palm. She leans forward, resting her forehead briefly against my chest. I sense how tired she is. Spent.

It's been an emotional evening for all of us.

When the water shuts off, we wrap her in towels and guide her back to the bedroom. She settles between us on the bed, all of us still damp. Linus sits behind her, arms around her waist. She takes my hand, thumb tracing slow lines across my knuckles.

"We don't want you to run." She peers into my soul. Not asking.

Stating.

Linus reaches for my other hand. "Please let this settle in. We have a lot to catch up on."

I swallow past the thickness in my throat.

"We want you here," she adds. The words surprise me with how steady they sound. "This isn't only about sex."

She squeezes my fingers. I don't pull away, though my primal instinct to flee is kicking into high gear.

"You don't have to decide anything tonight." Linus pulls me toward him. "We're not askin' you to promise us forever—"

"We're asking you to stay for a while and give things a chance," she finishes.

The room grows quiet. I'm not sure how to feel. What to say.

Linus tugs me next to him and Avonna curls into the small space between us. He rests his hand over both of ours. I feel the grounding weight of them and think about how long I've been running from moments like this.

How I've convinced myself closeness always came with a cost.

For the first time since Linus left, I feel complete.

I don't know what comes next. I don't know if I'll be brave enough every day to believe they want me with them.

Tonight, lying warm and held and wanted, I let myself believe I could try.

For now, that's enough.

Forty-One

AVONNA

Two Weeks Later

IT'S TOO QUIET WHEN they're both gone.

It isn't peaceful. It's a void. A bruise inside my chest.

I told myself I'd soak in some me time. Let the silence warm me like a sunbeam. Light incense, brew the ridiculous loose   leaf tea Linus bought at Fallon & Byrne tasting of, "notes of hay smoke and cherry pit." Fold the laundry threatening to avalanche off the bedroom chair.

Give my body a rest from...

Instead, I've been pacing.

Wearing one of Liam's soft black shirts, sleeves too long, hem brushing an inch below my bare pussy. My nipples catch on the fabric every time I breathe. They're sensitive, needy. I'm not even trying to tease myself, but my body doesn't know the difference between want and memory. Every brush of cotton might as well be a mouth.

God, thinking of their mouths on me makes me wet. I've had them both now dozens of times and I'm not sure how I'd live without them.

Linus maps me with his tongue, every pass methodical, every pressure intentional. He listens to the tiny sounds I can't hold back and licks my clit like a ritual.

Liam possesses me. His mouth is pure hunger and heat. He knows exactly how to lick my clit with careful greed. Devouring me with a pressure bordering on too much until it isn't.

Linus touches me with intention. Liam touches me with instinct.

Linus uses two fingers when I'm tender, three when he wants to draw out every tremor, curling them with precision until I'm shaking. Liam fucks me like he needs to feel how deep I can take him, coaxing my body open for something bigger, something powerful, something he knows I'll beg for.

And their cocks—*God*.

I feel myself creaming thinking about them.

Linus glides into me with purpose. The weight of him inside me feels grounding, like he's pinning me to the world. Liam drives into me with fervor, like he's breaking something open I didn't know was closed.

They're so different.

The strangest, most impossible thing is their differences don't compete. My men fill places I didn't know were missing. Linus gives me depth. Liam gives me edge. Linus steadies me. Liam ignites me.

Two sides of the same need. Two tastes of the same hunger.

I pace. My body doesn't know how to choose which memory to yearn for.

It's something deeper than sex. Bone itching. Soul pulling.

They've already given me two orgasms today and I find myself horny as hell with no one to take the edge off.

Linus is at the office attending to some emergency scheduling thing for the office move to Los Angeles. All of the paperwork is in place, thanks to my dear friend, Marcella. He was already zipping up his jacket and cursing traffic before Liam and I finished blinking awake. Kissed us on the temples. Said he'd be "back by dinner, more or less, unless someone dies or sets the fuckin' place on fire."

Liam bolted right afterward. Said he was meeting Padraig and his brother, Connor, who are both passing through town on their way back to Seattle.

I'm sure it's true, but I know his deer-in-the-headlights look now. He smiles too quickly and says he's popping out for a walk, but his phone is already in his hand lit up with Padraig's name. They talk every day, multiple times.

I get it. News about Koko leaving is spreading through the industry.

In between fucking me and Linus, he agonizes about everything Fireball aspires to be and everything it has yet to become. Linus and I pretend it's the only thing he's conflicted about.

Anyway, I'm not in the mood to get myself off, so I decide to distract myself with music for a while. In the studio, my guitar leans against the wall by the spare bed like it's the only other thing in this house with a heartbeat. I pull it into my lap. The body is cool and solid against my skin.

I strum once.

Twice.

The chords come immediately. The melody's there, raw and waiting. I hum as I play and the words fall into place like I've been singing them in my sleep:

They told me not to love the fire

But God, I fed it anyway

Kissed mouths that weren't mine to savor

Let them ruin me, every day.

Now there's ash on all my sheets

Bruises where the halos slipped

I'd still take their holy touch

If they asked me to burn again.

I stop.

Whoa. I like this. A thread of something real. Something I need to follow all the way through. Not subtle. Not even metaphor.

Linus and Liam. Fucking them. Cherishing them. *Loving them.*

I'd take the weight of the three of us every single day. Our complicated history. Untangling old wounds and griefs. The twining of our bodies, hearts and souls.

Being with these two men feels more like home than anything I've ever known.

The front door clicks open.

I hear boots on the floorboards.

Only one pair.

Liam steps into the bedroom doorway, hair damp from the drizzle outside, windblown, cheeks flushed. His coat's open, shirt sticking to his chest. My fingers are still on the strings, the last line lingering in the air.

His gaze lands on me sitting on the floor, legs crossed, wearing only his shirt with my pussy exposed. Something flickers behind his eyes. Lust. Hunger. Tempered with something hesitant. Careful.

"My brothers are on their way back to Seattle. Connor's filming a documentary on the band." His words rush out. "Padraig is hitchin' a ride on the private jet."

I nod. "How is he?"

"Wound up." Liam shrugs out of his coat and slings it over the chair. "Keeps goin' on about how it'll be a nightmare to find someone new. Thinks we'll end up stuck in singer purgatory."

I tilt my head, watching him.

"He's glad I've reconnected with Linus," Liam adds, voice softer. "I told him about the management offer. Thinks we've got half a chance if we sign with Isis."

A smile tugs at my lips. "So, no pressure then."

Liam snorts and smirks.

God, I love it. Stupid how much.

His eyes flick to the guitar I'm cradling. "Did I interrupt? Are you writin'?"

"Trying."

"What about?" He tries to sound casual, but I see how firmly he grips the back of the chair. Like he's bracing.

I answer honestly. "How I feel about what's happening."

His face shifts. Something cracks a little. "Aye?"

I spread my legs wider so he can see exactly how it's affected me.

He shoves the door closed and it clicks shut behind him. Rain clings to his hair as he approaches, moving like he's not sure he should be this close to me without Linus here, but isn't about to resist.

"I half-expected you to go back to the States with your brothers." I blink up at him.

"Didn't feel right." He slides down to sit beside me on the floor.

His eyes are shadowed, but I have to ask, "Did you tell them about what's going on amongst the three of us?"

He shakes his head.

I don't press. It's not my place.

Not yet.

I nod and return to the guitar, strumming the opening chords again, softer this time.

"Play it for me?" he asks after a beat.

"It's only a germ of an idea." I look into his eyes. "Maybe worth finishing, though."

His knees brush mine. He doesn't reach for me. Doesn't need to. The silence isn't awkward. It's thick with everything we've lived the past few days and the hope it will continue indefinitely.

"I know you're still figurin' everything out. I'm not trying to insert myself where I don't belong." He shifts slightly.

"I..." I trail off, choosing my words carefully. "When we were on the road, writing together, it felt natural. The way you and I fit. I feel like I already knew the chords to your voice."

He watches me.

I keep going. "I'm not saying you need new energy. I'm not saying I'm the answer. But if you ever might consider me... I'd be interested."

His gaze drops to my hands. My fingers twitch against the strings.

One hand reaches for his. His thumb brushes mine once. Solid, but tentative.

I set the guitar down next to me. "I'm interested in all of it."

He turns toward me. His lips brush mine before either of us knows who moved first. Soft. A taste. Then again, deeper. He cups my cheek. My fingers curl into his hair as I pull him closer. We kiss like we're discovering the shape of something new.

The two of us.

He pulls his shirt off. My breath catches at the way his body looks in the gray Dublin light. Lean, tattooed. I lift my arms and allow him peel his shirt from me. He kisses my collarbone, then the swell of my breast, then lower, kneeling on the floor before me.

His mouth finds my soaked pussy. He licks a stripe up the center and I gasp, thighs twitching, fingers digging into his waves. "*Nnnh*—Liam..."

He groans against me, tongue circling my clit. "You taste—*fuck*—so sweet." His voice is ragged.

I rock against his mouth, riding the rhythm. His fingers dig into my thighs, holding me steady. His moan vibrates through me.

"F-fuck—I—God—*don't stop*—"

I unravel around him, hips bucking, a soft wail dragged from the center of me. "Aahhh—*yes!*"

He climbs back up, mouth glistening, eyes wide and hungry. I pull him into a kiss, taste myself on his lips. Then I nod.

He understands.

He lines himself up, guides the tip of his cock against my opening then pushes in, filling me inch by inch. My legs wrap around his waist, ankles crossing. He sinks in fully and stills, forehead hovering above mine.

"Feels like I never left," he murmurs.

"You didn't."

He fucks me like he's confessing how he feels with every thrust, every grind of hips. I meet him stroke for stroke, cupping his face, kissing his mouth through it all.

When he comes, he cries out, low and guttural. "Fuck—*Avonna*..."

I follow, tears stinging behind my eyes.

We stay this way, breath slowing. Liam deep inside me, the heat of him nestled between my thighs. His heartbeat steady against my ribs.

The sound of keys startles both of us.

The front door creaks open. Boots. Damp footsteps on the wood.

We don't move.

Linus opens the bedroom door. Hair tousled from the wind, jacket open. His eyes immediately zero in on the two of us on the floor. Liam's cock buried inside me.

His mouth curves. "Huh. Didn't take long."

Liam lets out a soft huff against my throat but doesn't shift. I don't blush. There's nothing shameful here. We're not cheating.

Linus shrugs out of his coat and starts to undress without a word. His shirt hits the floor, belt unbuckled with a clink, trousers peeled away. His cock is purple at the tip. He watches as Liam eases out of me, then helps me up onto my feet.

The three of us cross the hallway to our bedroom and crawl into bed. Liam reclines against the headboard and I settle my back against his chest. He cradles me so I'm facing Linus.

I spread my legs to show him my pussy filled with Liam's come.

"You want my cock too, love?" His Dublin growl radiates low and warm.

"Yes," I breathe.

He guides himself to my entrance, the thick head sliding through everything Liam left behind. He pushes in.

"*Fuuuck*." He grips my hips. "You're full of him..."

My howl is helpless, high and sharp, hips rocking back. Liam kisses my shoulder, my neck. Holds me firmly when Linus starts to fuck me with rolling thrusts, each one deeper than the last.

They're all around me. Liam's chest warm at my back, fingers working my nipples, while Linus drives into me from the front, watching every reaction he wrings from my body.

"God—yes—*please...*"

"You're ours," Liam whispers. "Aren't you?"

"*Yesssssssss,*" I exclaim as Linus slams deeper, rhythm steady, his cock sliding through Liam's come coating my channel. My body shakes at the intensity of the moment and I lose myself in an epic release.

Linus follows, thrusts stuttering as he spills too, thick and hot.

When he collapses, Liam shifts so I'm enveloped between them.

They hold me, fingers brushing mine, mouths soft against my skin. I feel their heat. What they gave. What I took.

I'm home.

This is everything I ever dreamed of.

More.

It's real.

Forty-Two

Four Months later

WE DIDN'T COME TO Los Angeles to start over.

We came to expand.

I'd like to think the three of us are on the brink of building the life we've always wanted.

For now, we're in a rental house in Laurel Canyon. Spanish tile, lemon trees, breeze curling through open windows. Seventies vibes. Not a bad placeholder for permanence.

I've never felt more free. We have lots of space here. For music. For my business. For the shape we're becoming. No need to shrink. No need to hide.

For the most part.

"Look who's back." Avonna crosses toward the kitchen barefoot, hair scraped into a messy knot. Liam trails behind, long hair flowing down his back.

I watch them and immediately want to strip them both and bury myself in their skin. Unfortunately, this moment isn't about sex. It's about everything else.

"So?" I lean against the counter, coffee hot between my palms. "How'd it go with your brother?"

Liam exhales. Runs a hand through his long hair. "Padraig's good. Mara's keepin' him busy."

"Mara?" Avonna frowns as she sits on the cushion below me.

"His new girlfriend. News anchor. Bubbly. I think he likes her. 'Bout time he got laid." Liam's attempts at breezy are always amusing. The man was made for brooding, and he can't exactly hide it.

He's worried about Padraig, it's been this way his whole life as far as I can tell. Most of the time, Liam cares about his twin's happiness more than his own. "What did you talk about?"

Liam's gaze shifts out the window. Says nothing.

Avonna and I trade a look. *Right.*

We know one thing, he didn't mention what's happening with the three of us.

"Liam—" I set my mug down with a loud clack.

"Look." He punches his palm with his fist. "Don't pretend it isn't fuckin' complicated."

I don't argue. He's not wrong. Doesn't mean I'm happy about it.

"He's glad I'm stayin' in LA." Liam slumps into the armchair across from us. "He rented a condo. I told him I was keepin' this place for a while."

Avonna bites her lip. "He didn't ask why?"

"Oh, I don't need to spell things out. He knows why." Liam surprises me. "Look, he's not stupid. I was in Dublin for months. When we agreed to let Linus manage us again, he obviously knew we were fuckin'."

Avonna pulls her knees up. "Does he know about me and Linus? Or me at all?"

"You two have kept your marriage stealth, so no. It's not my place. Obviously, he knows Linus manages you, sweetheart and you're a monster of a writer and your voice can melt a fucking glacier." He pauses. "But, no. I didn't mention the two of you were married and the three of us are, whatever this is."

"Whatever this is?" I can't help but be disappointed at his crass characterization of a relationship I consider sacred.

I know what I want. Avonna knows what she wants. It's a hell of a lot more than fucking.

Avonna gives me a look as if to say, *chill.* Unlike me, she's patient.

"But, you *did* mention Avonna potentially singin' for Fireball?" I continue.

Liam scowls. "I didn't put it to him so bluntly. Fer fuck's sake, Linus. You know how we are. We talk multiple times every fuckin' day. He's aware she and I have been writin' a ton and he sure as shite knows he's not contributed a goddamn creative idea in months. So, the way I approached it was mentioning Avonna should come to practice so he could hear some of the songs we wrote. I've also low-key mentioned how cool it would be if she was interested. I don't want to pressure him. Things are tenuous enough."

I watch him carefully, noting the way he dances around the truth like it's a cliff edge he's not ready to step over.

"To make a long story longer, he's into it," Liam adds, eyes flicking to Avonna. "It's a hell of a leap from where he was when the tour ended and he was talkin' about quittin'."

My stomach knots. I love this band. I know how much it means to Liam, he's given everything to keep moving forward with only middling success. Especially compared to his brother and LTZ. With me back on the case, I plan to take them to the top.

"Okay, great." I soften my tone. "We take things in steps. My only concern is if it goes well and Avonna joins Fireball with me managin' the band, we can't pretend this..." I gesture to the three of us, "doesn't exist."

"I'm not pretendin'." He crosses his arms petulantly.

"You kind of *are*." I furrow my brow. His attitude is so frustrating. "For months we've been livin' together. Wakin' up in each other's arms. You don't see a problem if the person you're closest to on this planet has no fuckin' clue we're in a three-way relationship?"

Liam exhales, rubbing his palm over his mouth. "You haven't been around us for many years, so you don't get it. He's finally somewhat happy. He's got a new girlfriend and seems to finally be over Stevie. I can't drop a bomb right now. A new singer is about all he'll be able to handle."

"Jesus." It guts me how much fear hides behind his defenses. "I know Padraig well. Give him some fuckin' credit."

"Liam, this isn't a fling. Not for any of us." Avonna's delivery is gentler.

His pained expression guts me.

"Aye," My fingers clasp my coffee mug. "This stopped being casual the second we all hooked up in Dublin. What we have is the real thing."

Liam looks at us both, torn. "You think I don't want to shout it from the rooftops? I do. How can I? How the fuck do you think the news is gonna fly?"

I don't answer. Truthfully, I've worried about this too.

"I don't want to lie to him," I land on. "I can't help wantin' to protect your relationship with him. Keepin' him in the dark isn't right."

He tenses and looks away.

"You can't lead him into this blind," I go on, unable to stop. "If we're serious about the three of us, hidin' it from him isn't protectin' him. It's pretendin'. Withholdin' the truth is lyin'."

Liam's gaze snaps to mine. "Oh, is that how you see it?"

"Aye, it's exactly how I see it."

His eyes flare. "What about your truth, Mr. Honesty? Do your parents know you and I were together for three years before you married Avonna? Are they aware I'm back in the picture? Or, do they still believe you're livin' a good Catholic life with the wifey?"

I freeze.

"Surely," he taunts. "You've told them about me fuckin' you while you fuck your wife, right?"

My silence is answer enough.

"Exactly," he says. "Practice what you preach. Committed, my ass."

I grit my teeth. "It isn't the same."

"No?" His voice rises. "You sit here judgin' me for trying to ease my brother into the situation, when you can't even say the words out loud to your own family?"

"I'm not judgin' you." I try to appeal to his common sense. "I'm asking for honesty because of the band. Aye, maybe I'm guilty too. At least I'm willin' to admit it."

His expression softens, but the tension doesn't ease.

"Padraig hasn't changed," I continue. "He'll do anything for you and he deserves the truth. If he's goin' to welcome Avonna into the band and me as your manager, don't you think he should know what he's really signin' up for?"

Liam drops his elbows onto the edge of the kitchen island, staring down at the floor.

"I'm not ashamed of us," he fires back. "I don't understand why you're puttin' me under pressure here."

"He's not stupid, Liam. You think we're gonna hide it? When we're on the road and the three of us share a hotel room?

When the media starts asking questions?" I throw my hands up in the air.

"I don't know what he'll see," he snaps, his head whipping up. "I don't know what he'll feel. I do know I'm not going to drop a bomb unless I'm sure it won't blow up everything we've worked for more than a fuckin' decade."

Avonna, who's watched our discussion with fascination, slides in beside him and cups his face. "From what I can tell, you're worried he'll think you're choosing us over him."

Liam winces. He gives her an almost imperceptible nod.

"I understand you're nervous." She kisses his nose. "At the same time, keeping our relationship in the shadows to make him more comfortable won't work for me if you want me in the band."

He looks at her, shocked. "Avonna, this isn't about hidin' you."

"You already are hiding me. Especially if Padraig knows you're sleeping with Linus." She sits back and crosses her arms. "I sleep with Linus too, do you really think I'm not going to share a room with my husband?"

The air cracks.

I shift forward. "This shouldn't feel like pressure. We're not some experimental phase you get to stash behind band politics. You don't want to tell him you're involved with us for a while, fine. Avonna's right, though. We're not lyin' about our marriage."

"Fuck me." Liam's eyes narrow. "How can you say I'm not an experimental phase?"

"Excuse me?" My jaw drops.

"You two are *married*," he snarls. "You have each other no matter what. Legal. Permanent. If this goes sideways, I'm the one who ends up outside again. If Padraig bails on me, I'll have fuckin' *nothin'*."

My stomach drops. "Liam—"

"You don't get it." His eyes flash. "I'm the odd man out. You wake up every day knowin' you have each other. So yeah, maybe I'm scared to tell Padraig. If this goes to shit, I'll lose my band and the only real relationship I've ever had. *Again*."

"You think we'd let you go?" Avonna recoils.

"I've been let go before. By my own father. Linus left too." Liam buries his face in his hands. "I'm not some naive twenty-year-old playin' house with his boyfriend and girlfriend in college. How does this relationship make sense? How do I fuckin' explain it?"

Fuck. His words hit deeper than I want to admit.

He's not wrong.

Avonna and I were married before we brought Liam into our relationship. We opened our door, our bed, our hearts, but we haven't talked about what this looks like forever. Not with words.

Or paper.

Certainly, not enough to make Liam feel secure. To quiet whatever ghosts still claw at him.

"I'm not goin' anywhere," I promise.

"Neither am I." Avonna moves her hands from his face to grips his hands.

Liam's eyes dart between us, suspicious. "Can you please get off my grill, then? I know Padraig better than both of you, let me handle it. I don't intend to explain myself every fuckin' day."

"You're right." I exhale, the fight releasing in my chest. "We haven't proved our commitment to you yet. You've been carryin' more than a fear of Padraig's reaction. You've have doubt. About us."

He winces. "I *want* to trust this isn't going to vanish if things get messy."

"It won't." Avonna leans her head on his shoulder. "You're not the only one who needs clarity. If I'm gonna be Fireball's singer, I can't do it half-exposed. You know how I grew up and I'm not going to live a life ashamed of who I love. I won't lie. If Padraig asks, I'm telling him the truth. I love Linus. I love you. If you doubted how I feel, now you know."

He swallows.

"Liam, all I ask is for you to stop pretendin' this is about protectin' Padraig." I move to his side and clasp his shoulder. "It's okay to protect yourself. We need to be on the same side to build our perfect future."

Silence.

Finally, Liam nods. "All I ask is we ease into it. No surprise reveals. No chaos."

"Agreed." Avonna tilts her head. "So, what's a realistic timeline?"

"I'll tell him after we jam," he sighs. "Dependin' on how it goes."

We all hold there.

The solution isn't perfect. At least it's a meandering line in the sand.

I guess it's enough. For now.

Silence is a weight I don't want to carry much longer.

The clock is ticking.

Forty-Three

LIAM

Two Weeks Later

THE BEAT-UP REHEARSAL SPACE off Sunset reeks of sweat, weed, and old amps.

There's nothing romantic about it.

Somehow, with the light cutting through the dusty windows and the anticipation of what's to come, I feel like I'm seventeen again. Back when Connor, Padraig, and I dreamt of being in a band together. Before all the shit.

Of course now there's more on the line and a hell of a lot more history.

Avonna adjusts the mic stand while I tune my guitar. She's barefoot, hair piled in a loose knot, wearing a threadbare black tank she always steals from Linus. It slips off one shoulder, exposing her tiny dove tattoo.

Padraig watches her with curiosity, not judgment. He knows her, at least a bit from the festival circuit when we hung out. He knows Linus manages her and we've been writing together.

He still doesn't know...everything.

She nods at him. "Ready when you are."

"Been ready." He spins a stick between his fingers. "Let's hear what you two cooked up."

She shoots me a quick glance, somewhere between *you good?* and *hold on tight.* I step closer to the mic to count us in.

We launch into the first song we finished, *Unbreakable Thread.* Her voice rises. The words tumble out. Clear. Raw. My bridge is urgent, biting.

Padraig's face lifts.

When the last note dies, Padraig exhales. "Uh, that was..." He stops. Looks back and forth between us. "Fuck. Somethin' else."

Avonna grips the mic nervously. "Thanks?"

"In the best way," my twin assures.

I strum my guitar. "We've got a few more."

We tee up the next one called *Reckless Grace.* It's faster, heavier. A chunk of melody, a shout of truth. For the first time in years I see my brother come alive a bit.

Next, we play him my favorite, *Closer to the Flame.* Avonna gets so lost in the emotion, her voice cracks on the chorus. It brings to mind all the nights we've spent writing over these past few months. The unabashed, unquenchable desire.

Three of us tangled like wires.

I'm hard as a fucking rock listening to her.

When it ends, she exhales and I allow the final chord to linger.

Padraig's eyes are wild. "Fuck me." He wipes his face. "I knew you were writin'. I didn't expect this."

"Well." I watch him carefully. "What do you think?"

"I think these songs could save us." He folds his arms. "Truly."

Avonna's face reddens. "Really?"

He shoots her a genuine smile I haven't seen in a while, then he nods at me. "Brilliant."

I glance at Avonna. She peers up at me through the fringe of her hair.

It's validating. She and I know we're creating magic. Life-changing magic. I'm thrilled Padraig feels the same way, even if he hasn't been part of the songwriting process for the first time in Fireball's history.

We run through a few more songs, barely speaking, letting the sound carry. It's the closest thing to communion I've felt in months. Padraig watches in fascination, shaking his head like he can't believe what he's hearing.

When we finish, he leans back, breathless. "Jesus Christ."

"No good?" I flick my sweaty hair out of my face.

He laughs, full-bellied. "Cut the modesty bullshit, you know how good it is."

"Been on a roll." Relief floods through me, masked by a shrug.

He scrubs his chin. "Clearly. I didn't realize how much time you've been spendin' together."

"We kind of found a rhythm. It's been organic." Avonna sits on the edge of an amp.

Orgasmic, too, I think to myself.

"I knew you were talented, but..." He gestures loosely at her. "You've brought somethin' I never even knew was missin'."

I watch him process. He's definitely not upset, it's more like he's connecting the dots. Or trying to.

He misses wildly.

"Wait...are you two going to release these songs as a duo?" he asks cautiously.

"Not exactly." She tucks a stray lock of hair behind her ear. "Liam, Linus, and I have talked about an idea. It's why I'm here tonight."

I shift my weight, on the verge of freaking out. We agreed not to push but Avonna has an uncanny sense of timing. Seems like he's opened the door.

Avonna's keeps her cool. "I know this will sound presumptuous, so I hope you'll hear me out. I've been a solo performer for a few years. Fireball needs a singer. I've never enjoyed being on stage alone, front and center. I don't care about being a star. I care about making music with impact. The chemistry Liam and I have found in our songwriting," she gestures to me, "feels like it should be more."

Padraig's eyes bug out. "You're serious?"

"I don't want to fuck up your dynamic." She touches his arm. "But, I'd love to be considered for your open singer position."

I watch his face closely. He doesn't speak right away. Finally he plops down on the ratty couch. "Fuck me."

Avonna laughs nervously. "Not the reaction I was hoping for."

"No, I mean, we've been stuck. Me, especially. I've been trying to care again. I have no motivation to write. It's been..." He exhales. "Rough. I've been strugglin' with whether I want to keep goin'."

"Dar," I swallow. "You told me you needed to take a break. We've taken a break. I don't want you to hear about you quittin'."

"Truthfully, it's the way I was feelin'." He glances between us. "I didn't think I had it in me to start again with a new singer. But hearin' this? Playin' this?" He shrugs. "It's wakin' me up."

Linus gets up from the chair in the corner he's been sitting in like he's been waiting for a cue.

"I fuckin' knew it." He claps my brother on the shoulder. "Knew you'd feel this way the second I heard the songs."

Padraig rolls his eyes. "Of course you've already heard them."

"Well, yeah. I've got a plan." He claps his hands together.

I smirk. "Don't you always?"

He lays the folder on top of a speaker. "Let's do it right this time. No more van. No more couch surfin'. Full relaunch. EP first, three singles, build the momentum. We tour the States. Then Europe. I've got a bookin' agent ready when you say the word."

Padraig raises a brow. "Oh, and who's payin' for all this?"

"First, invite Avonna in. Then, officially sign with Isis." Linus shrugs. "We'll front the money for you to release them independently, distribute the way LTZ does through a major. This'll leave the three of you with more of the profits. I'm scoutin' for a better publisher and, more importantly, I've got a Grammy campaign strategy. You saw what I did for Sidewalk Riot. Fireball can go bigger. At least three or four of these tracks are song-of-the-year worthy."

Linus glances at me, then Avonna. "What you two are creatin,' it could be the heart of Fireball."

I look down, throat tight. For a second, nobody speaks.

Then Padraig claps his hands like a madman. "Fuck it. Let's do it. I haven't felt the creative flow and I'd love to write with the two of you going forward."

Avonna's breath hitches. Her eyes dart between me and Linus. She raises one shoulder.

I ignore her.

"You sure?" My eyes snap to Padraig and the familiar way he loosens his wrists and tests the bounce of the sticks against his palm before he sits down at his kit.

He smacks his snare. "Aye. I'm in. Firin' on all cylinders." His smile touches her like a blessing. "Avonna, you were the missin' piece."

She moves, instinct more than choice, closing the space between us, like she's done a hundred times since we started this relationship with Linus in Dublin. Her hand brushes mine. No hesitation.

Trust.

Except, I don't meet her halfway. I shift slightly. Enough to avoid her touch. Allow the moment to pass.

To anyone else, it'd look like nothing. But Linus sees. He always sees.

And he *knows*.

Padraig, oblivious, adjusts a cymbal. "Let's run through them, yeah?"

"Okay." Avonna misses nothing and everything all at once. "Count us in, Liam."

I do.

The first chord lands like prophecy. The three of us fall into sync without a word. Her pure voice soars, juxtaposed against my gravely growl. Padraig's kick hits like thunder.

The melody she and I first wrote after fucking each other raw in Dublin was on the edge of something neither of us could name at the time. It's reborn here. Polished under California sun and twisted sheets and everything we've become.

Now with my brother's tasteful percussion, the sound is massive. Unstoppable.

After all the years. The heartbreak. The grind. Sleepless nights in broken vans. Shitty clubs and furious fights and second chances, I feel it in my bones. Fireball is finally complete.

Linus doesn't move from the corner, but I feel the shift in him. Gravity pulling away.

His eyes drop. Not out of anger, but sorrow. He understands the reality of the situation. When he and Avonna confronted me a couple weeks ago, I promised we'd tell Padraig about us when the time is right.

The time *isn't* right. Not now.

The truth is, as much as it's gonna kill me, I've decided to cool things off with the two of them for the time being. Fireball and Padraig are the most important things in my life and nobody comes before my brother.

I'm taking my time to ease him into this new normal. At my pace.

If what I have with Linus and Avonna is real, they'll understand.

She's everything I never knew I needed. Linus has owned my entire heart from the second we met. The three of us together make sense in a way nothing else ever has.

We're a hushed harmony. A perfect balance I never believed I'd find, let alone deserved.

With them, I'm whole.

But Padraig is my beginning. My blood. The one person in my life who's never let me down.

Linus knows me better than anyone. He can tell when I'm pulling away.

Fireball comes first.

Even if I'm risking everything else.

Forty-Four

AVONNA

Seven Months Later

THE ISOLATION BOOTH SWALLOWS me whole.

Glass all around.

My reflection flickers in the studio lights.

I hold the headphones against my ears. The track plays through the microphone, a new arrangement we've been fine-tuning for weeks. It lives in my bones, from the chord progression to the inhale before the beat drops.

I'm supposed to be focused. This is everything we worked for. Months of rehearsals, late-night sets, half-dozen secret shows Linus booked to keep us sharp so we know these songs backward and forward.

He pulled every string to get us into this particular studio for two weeks. Tyson Rainier is available for exactly eight days to elicit an entire album from us. If the reaction of the crowds to our new songs is any indication, all of us know this record will change everything.

Unfortunately, some days, like now, I don't know if I belong.

Liam and Padraig are huddled in the control room with Ty. Padraig's arms are crossed, head tilted. Liam leans forward, watching me through the glass. His mouth is set in a straight line.

He hasn't smiled at me all day. Held my hand. Kissed me.

I miss him.

When I hear my queue, I squeeze my eyes shut and my own voice joins in. Raw. Stripped. I hold the first note too long and my voice breaks. On the second take, I breathe wrong and can't sustain the note. My chest constricts from the pressure.

Not from this recording studio. From the weight of pretending to Padraig, Ty, and the rest of the world Liam and I are merely bandmates.

Other than Linus, no one knows the three of us are building a life behind the scenes. Spending every night entwined in each other's bodies. Holding hands, making dinner together and watching reality TV.

Secrecy was only supposed to be for a little while. Liam tried to pull back. We wouldn't let him, so we acquiesced. Figuring his hesitancy was a temporary blip until Liam felt more ready to tell Padraig the truth.

Weeks have blurred into months. Behind closed doors, we fuck each other in secret. Treat our beautiful love like it's forbidden. Meant to be hidden.

I remember the hours I spent in trauma therapy promising myself I'd never shrink to fit someone else's fear. I vowed I'd never let the weight of another person's judgment make me feel like who I love is something to be ashamed of.

Yet, here I am. Falling into old patterns.

Well, in fairness, Liam's making the choice for all of us. While I admire his sacred dedication to Fireball, it doesn't stop the pain. Linus hasn't pushed the issue further either. Keeping quiet means he doesn't have to explain the three of us to his family.

At least Padraig knows about Linus and I being married. One truth is out in the open, though it's led to other uncomfortable moments. Padraig would never come out and say it, but instinct tells me he believes Liam and Linus have "cheated" on me and I don't know about it.

All of this leaves me torn. Unsettled. Deeply sad. Liam and Linus are the only two men I've ever trusted with my heart. With the need for so much secrecy, I'm beginning to wonder if I made a mistake.

I didn't expect to feel untethered in my relationship.

Linus sits behind Ty, tapping out timing cues and annotating vocal runs. He catches my eye through the glass and gives me the smallest nod. His love is steady. It always has been.

My biggest fear is he and I become a casualty in all of this deceit.

Determined to control what I can, I belt out the bridge again. This time I let it all out. The loneliness. The aching silence. The abject fear my dream is going to come crashing down around me.

When the last note fades, I lower the headphones and stare at the floor. My throat burns.

A moment passes. Then another.

The control room light flashes green. I step into the corridor, legs heavy. Liam meets me at the door.

"You killed it." His hand hovers against my lower back. He holds it there without touching me. I know why. The rest of them are a few feet away.

"Thanks." I want him to wrap me up like he does when we're behind the closed doors of our house. He won't do it, though.

Ty spins his chair. "Great work, Avonna. You've leveled up the whole track."

Padraig grins wide and throws his arms up. "Ah-fuckin'-mazing."

He walks over, not hesitating like the others. His hug is real. Warm. Before we arrived, he was in the booth all morning laying drum stems, yet he looks more alive than any of us.

"Unreal," he murmurs into my hair. "I mean it."

My eyes sting. I don't pull away. I want to bawl. Instead, I press my face to his chest and let his kindness settle in.

When I finally look up, Liam is watching. His expression softens, but he doesn't move. Doesn't touch me. Doesn't acknowledge me except in the smallest of ways. Not in front of his brother.

Linus hands me a bottle of water, gaze fixed on Liam. I can feel the energy between them crackle. Nothing will convince me everyone else doesn't sense it too.

Later, while Ty resets the board and Padraig grabs a snack, I sit beside Liam on the worn studio couch. Linus hovers near the racks, pretending not to listen. I reach for Liam's hand. He lets me take it, but it's more reflex than choice.

"Not being able to touch you in public is becoming intolerable," I whisper.

He shrugs. "There's been a lot to work through."

"You mean with Padraig."

"Aye."

"Seriously? Would it be such a big revelation?" I already know the answer, but I need to hear him say it.

"Look. He loves you. He's happy Linus is managing us. I'm the weak link." Liam pulls his hand free. "He's already lectured me about it."

"He seems happy with Mara. Stevie was a long time ago." I pull my knees up and wrap my arms around them. "He'd want you to live your life."

He peers over. "It goes deeper. I can't throw our relationship in his face. Especially after you told him you and Linus are married. Padraig doesn't want me to screw things up for the band."

Liam's clearly suffering, but this has gone on too long. I can't keep living half a truth. I may not know Padraig the way Linus and Liam do, but I can't believe he'd want Liam to sacrifice his own happiness as penance.

"Your delusional if you think you're hiding everything," I say softly. "It's creating a strange dynamic. He's watching us. Watching you. Wondering if you're fucking Linus behind my back, which isn't fair to any of us. Won't it hurt him more if you continue to lie to him?"

Liam leans back, head against the wall. His throat works like he's swallowing something distasteful.

"He's too polite to ask," I continue. "He won't push you, but I don't think for a minute he doesn't know something's going on. At the very least between you and Linus. It's weird to keep this from him. Really fucking weird."

I wait.

No reaction.

"How about I put this a different way. I'm not willing to hide anymore." I decide to speak from my heart and let the chips fall. "Not from anyone. I'm suffocating, Liam. I don't want to live like this. I'm not some scorned woman. This band isn't Fleetwood fucking Mac."

He balks. It's small, but I see it.

Linus moves closer, settling into the arm of the couch beside me. His hand brushes my neck.

"She's not wrong," he says gently. "It's killin' her. It's killin' me. Can't we rip off the Band-Aid?"

"It's killin' me too." Liam buries his face in his hands. "I don't know what to do. If I fuck this up—"

"We held a commitment ceremony, Liam," I remind him. "It might have been private between the three of us, but we all made a vow. Trust me. The only way you fuck things up is if you let fear win."

Liam sits up. "You make it sound so easy."

"It *is* easy." I cross my arms.

"Fuck me," Linus swears under his breath. "This has to stop. You're already are part of us, Liam. He'll understand."

Linus leans over to kiss him but Liam moves his face away.

A second later, Padraig bounds through the door with a wide grin, arms full of energy drinks. "Anyone thirsty?"

We all sit up straighter.

I shake my head at Padraig. "Thanks, I'm gonna make some hot tea with lemon and honey for my voice."

"Next vocal track's yours." He points to Liam. "You ready?"

Liam nods and enters the vocal booth.

"By the way." Padraig lingers near the couch for a beat. Looks between Linus and me. "You two are solid. Like, rock-solid, yeah?"

My breath catches.

Linus nods once, then puts his arm around me. "We are."

"Good," Padraig addresses Linus, but flicks his eyes to his brother. "Liam needs solid."

I sit frozen, pulse in my throat.

Linus squeezes my shoulder. His touch is warm, but my heart feels cold.

Padraig knows. He's probably always known. He's waiting. Protecting Liam the way Liam protects him.

I watch Liam get settled, headphones in place, head bowed, waiting for the track to start. The beat kicks in. He doesn't look at us. But I hear it. Every single thing he's isn't able to tell his brother comes out through the words he sings, and how he sings them.

His phrasing is breathtaking.
All I can hope is he can conquer his demons soon.
I won't live in the shadows much longer.

Forty-Five

Six Months Later

FIREBALL BLEW THE ROOF off the place.

Less Than Zero is preparing to take the stage in a few minutes.

Connor's bass echoes through the walls. It's part of the act, he always plucks a couple of specific notes to prime the pump.

The crowd of nearly sixty thousand people goes ape-shit.

We're in Seattle at a show benefitting legendary rock club, The Mission. Fireball and Less Than Zero got their start there, so we're happy to help keep them afloat.

The afterglow of Fireball's set clings to my skin along with a bit of leftover adrenaline. Outside the dressing room, the hallway buzzes with post-show static. Bodies moving in half-sync. Crew swapping cables. Security checking passes.

Liam and Padraig's family are gathered in our dressing room. Rory, Liam's da, sits on a folding chair near the far wall. Maureen, his ma, hovers nearby, hand resting on Rory's shoulder. She radiates a quiet command most Irish mothers possess, Brothers Cillian and Brennan are deep in conversation about AI and tour logistics, Seamus hangs back near the door, quiet and observant.

The younger McGloughlin brothers have grown into men. Each of them look at Liam and Padraig like they're gods. Oblivious, Liam, still in the black jeans and T-shirt he wore on stage, stands beside the vanity mirror. Padraig is shirtless and leans against the table beside him, calm in the way he always is after a show.

As usual, they talk in shorthand, an invisible thread running between them. It's strange. Once, I mistook the thread for a rope. Something unbreakable.

Now I view it as more fragile, strained by this past year of Liam's martyr-like sacrifice.

Avonna is curled up on the couch across from me, her body still wobbly from everything she gave during the show. Her color's a little off, too pale under the stage makeup. She hasn't been feeling well but tries to hide it, smiling when Cillian compliments her voice.

It's the first time she's met Liam's family. My first time meeting his da. Instead of being introduced properly, as his life partner, she's been relegated to "Fireball's new singer." As usual, I'm the "manager."

Despite her bravado during our recording sessions, she's hasn't ended things with Liam or left the band. She's pushed through the sadness clawing at her, refusing to falter. Even after she told him what Padraig said that day, Liam's determined to keep things status quo.

Tonight with his family here, however, he keeps himself even more removed from both of us. Other than giving us an occasional smile as his eyes pass over the room.

On the positive side, the show went flawlessly. Studio precision wrapped in live theatrical fire. Avonna brings something special to Fireball. A cohesive energy neither of the twins ever found with their previous singers. Every lyric in the new material carries the tension the three of us all live in.

The story of our love bleeding through sound.

Our girl should be floating. Instead, she looks ready to collapse. I feel the familiar twist more acutely. Want, fear, pride, love, all tied into one impossible knot.

The trouble is, we can't go on like this.

Liam catches my eye. For a heartbeat, neither of us blinks. Then he looks away, muttering something about tuning issues during the encore to Padraig.

Avonna shifts forward to greet Seamus, who crouches before her. He praises her in a careful tone doctors use when they mean well but sense fragility. Her smile wobbles but holds.

Part of me wonders if Liam's family's kindness disarms her. Despite how Liam has portrayed the McGloughlins, the only thing evident here is love and support. Aside from a few dinners at my folks' place when we still lived in Dublin, she certainly has never experienced this before.

"Hell of a show, son." Rory's Irish lilt carries gravel and sincerity. He's never seen Fireball live, for obvious reasons. "You and your brother made me proud."

Liam's reply is half a nod. He shoves his hands into his pockets and looks at the ground. His inability to receive a compliment from his da troubles me more than anything.

Maureen steps in, saving them both. "It was magnificent. You brought the house down, so you did."

Avonna peers over at Liam again, searching for a flicker of warmth. He gives her a small grin before turning back to Padraig. The slight is subtle, invisible to anyone else, but it I see the breath leave her. She hides her pain by reaching for a bottle of water.

"LTZ's gonna have a tough time toppin' our set tonight." Padraig claps Liam's shoulder.

Liam's grin widens. "They can try. They always do."

The twins laugh at the good-natured rivalry they've developed with LTZ. We've all grown close to the band and their crew, having toured together on and off for a couple of years.

Nevertheless, I'm pissed. Mostly at myself for not standing up for myself and Avonna more. I want to shake Liam. Chastise him for failing to clue the fuck in. It'll wait. I'm not about to unravel the whole night, although, I'm pretty sure Liam's picking up my vibe by the tension in his posture, even if he's too careful to let it show.

At the end of the day, this is his family. They're all getting along. Liam suddenly revealing the truth about the three of us could blow the fragile ground the McGloughlin's have traversed to pieces.

Connor's bass hum rumbles through the wall again, followed by Ty's voice testing the mic. The focus in our dressing room begins to shift toward the hallway, where security waits to escort the McGloughlins to their seats. The brothers make their way to the door. Rory shifts in his chair, rubbing his leg, Maureen helps him up and they follow.

When Avonna stands, her knees buckle slightly. No one but me catches it. She laughs under her breath and tries to mask it. I take a step toward her. She shakes her head, subtle, mouthing *later*.

Always fucking later.

Padraig pulls on a fresh T-shirt. "You guys comin'?"

"Yeah, after I check the loadout," I answer.

Liam's half tuned out, eyes focused on their setlist taped to the wall. I get it. He's not comfortable in the presence of his people. He'll do anything to distract himself.

The big-screen monitor in the dressing room flicks on to a view of the stage. The house lights dim for LTZ's set and the crowd roars so loud you can hear it through the corridor. The family departs out the side exit.

"Don't stay in here hidin'," Padraig says to Liam. "Come watch your brother steal the show."

Liam chuckles. "He doesn't need my help."

Padraig laughs, shutting the door behind him.

The sudden quiet feels unusually heavy. Avonna settles back onto the couch, one hand at her temple. Her skin's completely lost its glow. Sweat beads at her hairline, her lips are pale.

"Avonna." I cross the short space between us. "Baby, are you okay?"

"Fine," she says too quickly. "Tired."

"Are you sure? You didn't look right durin' the second chorus." Liam turns, taking in her slumped posture.

Her head lifts, eyes meeting his. "You noticed?"

The question hangs. He hesitates, guilt flashes across his face before he can hide it. "Of course I noticed."

"I'll be okay." She manages a faint smile. "Go watch the show."

He doesn't move. Torn between staying and the pull of being with his family. I see every battle written across his expression, every part of him conditioned to put the everything else before anything us.

Avonna stands again, likely intending to prove her strength, but her body betrays her. The moment she's up, her breath stutters. Knees buckle. The bottle in her hand slips, water splashes the floor. I catch her before she hits the ground.

Liam's there in an instant, panic cracking through his mask. "Avonna. Jesus, what's wrong?"

"Too hot." Her eyes roll slightly, lashes fluttering. "I'll be okay."

Seamus's voice slices through the doorway. "Give her space. Let her breathe."

I set her down on the sofa and Liam's wee brother is at her side in an instant. He's a medical student and immediately takes charge. Calm. Precise.

Liam crouches next to him, concern etched deep in face.

Seamus checks Avonna's pulse with steady fingers. "Her vitals are fine. Probably dehydration, overexertion."

I kneel beside Liam, my hand shakes as it brushes Avonna's cheek.

"She needs rest." Seamus looks between us. "You've all been running yourselves ragged."

Liam nods, eyes glassy. "We'll take care of her."

"See that you do." Seamus's gaze lingers on Linus. "Maybe grab a pregnancy test from the drugstore."

Shocked, I can't help but clear my throat. "Uh, yeah. Okay."

On his way out the door to rejoin the family, Seamus fetches a bottle of electrolyte water and instructs us to make sure she drinks it before we go back to the hotel.

In the background, LTZ's set thunders, a reminder the world outside our small circle keeps spinning. The three of us are left alone in the dressing room with a bomb of an instruction.

The silence closes in around us. Jarring. Expectant.

Avonna sits up, one hand splayed over her stomach. "My period's a few weeks late. I've been blaming stress. Told myself once things slowed down, it would come." Her laugh is thin and painful. "Of course, we never take a break."

I wince and Liam stiffens.

"Could be nothin'," he tries to reassure her.

Her gaze sharpens. "Or it could be *everything*."

"Let's not panic. We'll get a test. Figure it out." He exhales.

She shakes her head. "Sure. Why not? We all know, regardless of the result, you'll bury it like you always do. Like *both* of you do."

The truth cuts through the room and stabs me in the heart.

"Bury it? No. I'm tryin' to protect us," Liam protests, though his words fall flat.

"Who exactly are you protecting?" Avonna's voice cracks and tears pool. "I told you how I felt months ago and you don't seem to care. I've held my tongue because I personally know how rough it is to work though harsh shit. Today, I've come to the end of my rope. I'll not mince words. You're protecting *yourself*. I sure as hell know you're not protecting me."

His hands fall open. "Padraig—"

"Padraig isn't the problem." She holds her hand up. "He's the excuse. I'm calling bullshit."

Liam recoils as if she slapped him.

My head hurts. "She's right. We're both guilty. My parents still think Avonna and I are a normal couple and have no idea about you. How can you feel comfortable goin' all in if I haven't?"

Liam's glare flashes.

"Look, I'm sick of talking about this. I've given you far too much time to work through your issues." Avonna wipes her eyes. "The hourglass has run out. It hit me tonight when Liam ignored me in front of his family and Linus barely touched me." Her beautiful angelic face scrunches with pain. "I'm truly back where I started. I grew up being told love was shame. My body was sin. Silence was virtuous. I trudged through years of therapy to unlearn the lies my parents told me. Yet, here I am, hiding for people who profess to love me. Maybe I'm pregnant. Maybe I'm not. Either way, I didn't work relentlessly on myself for nothing. I refuse to stay in the shadows, let alone force my child to live there."

Liam's face cracks open. "I never *want* to hide you, Avonna."

"You have a funny way of showing it." She gets up and grabs another bottle of Gatorade. "This has been coming to a head for months. Focusing on band stuff has allowed us to bury it for a while. Now we can't. Not anymore."

The air thickens between the three of us.

I try to smooth things over. "I want to take care of you. Our baby. It doesn't matter which one of us is the father—"

"I don't need caretakers," Avonna roars. "I need partners who aren't *ashamed* of me."

"*Goddammit*. I'm not fuckin' ashamed." Liam grips his neck, eyes wet. "When the three of us are together, it's the only time I feel complete."

"Same." I shake my head glumly. "I love both of you so much. You're the most important people in my life, and if my folks can't handle it, then so be it."

Liam is utterly gutted. "I don't know what to do—"

"Stop being a fucking victim." Avonna wrings her hands. "Everyone knows Padraig gave up Stevie. He made his choice years ago and he seems to be happy with Mara. As far as your family is concerned, your dad apologized and you haven't tried to let him know you at all. Your mother and brothers are lovely and do not seem like the type of people who give a shit who you fuck. The truth is, you're a child hiding behind old wounds because it's easier than to be a man and face them."

Liam flinches like she struck him.

I want to step in, ease the edge, but she's right.

Avonna keeps going. "Either get into therapy like you promised or stop letting your warped perceptions of how other people view you control your life. You're so adamant about protecting the band, your brother and your family from the idea of us when we're the ones who love you, would do anything for you. I don't deserve to be treated this way. Stop letting old ghosts decide who you get to love."

Silence folds over us.

Liam drops onto the sofa and stares into space. "You think I don't wake up every day terrified I'll lose you both?"

"Well, congratulations, you're already halfway there." Her eyes close. Tears spill down her cheeks. "Every time you choose silence, every time you let me fade into the background, I slip a little further. I love you both, but love isn't supposed to shrink you. It's supposed to expand."

LTZ materializes on the screen. Liam drags a hand through his hair. I sit on the coffee table in front of her.

Avonna grasps Liam's hand and then takes mine. "It's time for you both to decide who you want to be. If we're a family, then let's be one. If we're not, be honest with me so I can stop pretending this is something precious. If I'm not enough—if our baby isn't enough…"

Her voice cracks on the word "baby."

Liam cups her jaw, thumb brushing away a tear. "You *are* enough. You both are. I need to wise the fuck up."

"Time doesn't stop for anyone." Avonna meets his eyes. "Not for love. Not for fear."

"Tomorrow." He nods, breath shaky. "I'll tell Padraig tomorrow. He'll help me figure out how to tell da."

"I'll book a trip to Dublin when Liam's talking to Padraig."

"You mean it?" Her lips part, a whisper of disbelief.

He nods again. "I won't lose you."

"Me either." I squeeze her fingers.

A fragile sense of relief flickers across her face. "Then let's go to the hotel. I'm peopled out."

I help her to her feet. Liam steadies her other side.

The crowd beyond the walls roars for LTZ's final encore.

We slip out the back of the dressing room, three figures moving through a maze of corridors.

The world outside doesn't know who we are to each other yet.

Tonight, for the first time, it feels like they might.

Forty-Six

LIAM

A Couple Hours Later

S TEAM DISSIPATES FROM THE shower.

I dry off, replaying the night in my mind.

Killer show. My family was proud. Avonna pale and shaking, Seamus urging a pregnancy test. Her fierce insistence she won't be hidden anymore.

All the while, Linus's eyes were on me. Silent. Knowing.

I've been a fucking coward for too long. I love them both and I know I don't deserve either of them.

The mirror fogs. I wipe it clean. My reflection stares back, bare and unguarded.

Enough.

I pull on a T-shirt and joggers. Step back into the bedroom of our hotel suite.

Linus sits on the couch, shoes off, posture folded in on himself. Avonna lies across his lap, knees tucked. She looks smaller than she did an hour ago. Paler. Her eyes lift when I enter.

"Hey," I say.

Linus shifts immediately, making room. "Come here."

I sit on the edge of the couch. Avonna reaches for my hand and holds it tighter than usual. Linus strokes her hair. No one rushes to speak.

"You feelin' any better?" I finally venture.

She nods once, then shakes her head, frustrated with herself. "I'm okay."

I watch her free hand drift to her stomach without her realizing it.

The room is warm. Too warm. Adrenaline still zaps under my skin, but fear has started to edge it out. Sharp and cold. Until tonight, I didn't realize how close I was to losing her.

"You want a shower?" I ask. "Might feel good."

"Yeah." She blinks up at me. "Please."

We don't rush her. Linus helps her stand, arm firm around her back. I grab a towel, turn on the bathroom light, test the water with my wrist before she even asks.

She undresses and steps under the spray. Exhales like she's been holding herself together with string. Steam starts to rise. Linus leans against the vanity, fully dressed. I sit on the closed toilet lid, watching her wash the night's performance down the drain.

"I didn't mean to blow up," she sighs, water running over her shoulders. "The pregnancy thing threw me."

I close my eyes. "You didn't do anythin' wrong."

"Aye." Linus nods. "You told the truth."

I swallow. The seat is cool through my joggers.

"I'm tired," she says as she shampoos her hair. "I hate having to shrink."

The water keeps running. No one interrupts.

"I'm tired of pretending I don't notice when you pull away," she continues. "When you choose silence over love. When you think protecting Padraig means hiding me."

I shift, shoulders tight. "I thought I was buyin' time."

"For what?" She peers at me through the glass.

Neither of us answers right away.

I stand, step closer to her. "I guess I thought if I waited long enough, it would get easier."

"It doesn't." She looks me in the eye. "It just teaches your body you aren't worth being loved."

Her words land like a right hook.

Linus exhales. "I'm not ashamed of us."

"Then stop acting like you are," she says gently. No venom. No theatrics. Just exhaustion.

Linus grabs a washcloth and cleans the stage makeup from her arms and neck like he often does after a show. He doesn't treat her like she's fragile. When she's rinsed off, the two of us wrap her in towels and guide her back into the bed.

I scan the room service menu and order soup, bread, and salads.

She sits cross-legged on the bed, naked, hair damp and curling. She looks smaller now. Younger. The bravado from the stage stripped away.

"So, I'm pretty sure Seamus was on to something. I might be pregnant." She pulls the sheet up around her.

Linus's hand pauses on the duvet. I sit on the edge of the bed, heart thudding in my ears. We glance at each other. Not panicked. Or celebratory. The sobering possibility settles between us.

"I'll run out and get a test." He stands. "There's a drugstore a block away."

"Okay." She pulls her knees up. "Either way, things have to change."

I think about the way my family looked at her tonight. The kindness. The warmth. The unspoken line I refused to cross. How I introduced her to them as a role instead of a truth.

"If you are," I squeeze my eyes shut, "I promise I won't keep doing this halfway."

She reaches for my hand. "I've got to hold you to it, Liam."

"We'll do it together." Linus crosses the room and takes her other hand.

She looks at him. "Will you tell your parents?"

"Aye." He doesn't hesitate.

She turns to me, eyes filling with tears.

"I don't want my child growin' up learning silence from me." I lean forward, press my forehead to hers. "I'm done hidin'."

While Linus runs our important errand, Avonna and I huddle in bed waiting for room service. He's back within ten minutes and the three of us eat. Quiet except for the clink of spoons.

Linus keeps refilling her water. Eventually, she has to use the bathroom and she takes the test in with her. The three of us wait, checking the clock like time might be something we can manage if we watch it closely enough.

None of us are surprised with two pink lines appear, clear as day.

Later, when she's curled into sleep between us, I stay awake, staring at the ceiling.

This baby is a line in the sand for our family.

How are we going to show up for our child?

Linus reaches for my hand in the dark. "You okay?"

"No," I admit. "But I will be."

He squeezes once. Solid. Certain.

Avonna shifts, breath steady now.

Whatever comes next, we don't walk into it alone.

Not anymore.

Forty-Seven

AVONNA

The Next Morning

Liam is between my legs.

His tongue is broad and warm, savoring every drop that spills out of me. He traces through my folds like he's kissing something divine. Like my pussy is sacred, and he'll gladly worship it until the day he dies.

Behind me, Linus shifts. He buries his face in my neck. "Look at her, Liam. She's starvin' for your cock."

He's not wrong. I *am*.

Reaching for Liam's hair, I tug gently, not to stop him. To bring his eyes to mine and ground us.

He looks up. Lips swollen, chin soaked, pupils blown wide with need.

"Come here, baby." I beckon with my finger. "Now."

Liam rises to his knees between my thighs, his cock flushed and straining. He positions himself, and I open for him. Eager and aching. He sinks into me with a contented sigh, angling deep. Once he's fully seated, he stays still. Deep, unmoving. Eyes locked on mine.

"I never get tired of this," he breathes.

"I need you." I kiss him as his hips begin to move, cock stroking me inside while his pelvis brushes my clit. The rhythm is molten. Intimate. Each thrust pulls something deeper from me. I cling to him, nails dragging down his back, thighs trembling as I rock with him.

"Jesus." Behind me, Linus lets out a soft growl. "You two are gonna fuckin' kill me."

I look back at him, over my shoulder. "Join us, baby."

Liam doesn't stop moving inside me, but his gaze shifts too, back to Linus. Something clicks. A new way for us to be joined.

We seamlessly make the adjustment together. I pull Liam in for another kiss, then lean back slightly, one hand still clutching his shoulder as I reach behind me to grip Linus's cock.

Liam follows my lead. He kisses my throat, then leans forward so I can feed him Linus's cock. I stroke his shaft while Liam tongues his balls, hot and hungry, and Linus gasps, his hands fisting in the couch cushions.

"You two—fuck—"

I wrap my lips around the head, and Liam moves to the base, his tongue dragging along the underside as he moans into Linus's skin. The vibration sends a jolt through all of us.

All while Liam drives his cock inside me.

He's deep enough to make my breath hitch. Every roll of his hips pushes heat deeper inside me. Liam's tongue meets mine and we lewdly taste Linus together.

It's so much. Too much. Never enough. We're a single circuit. A closed loop of lust.

Linus's howls grow louder, rougher. His hips cant and buck as we work in tandem, me swallowing the head, Liam dragging his tongue over his balls, sucking gently. "It feels too fuckin' good. I'm gonna fuckin' come."

Liam's hips stutter. "Your pussy is so tight around me. God, I'm not gonna last either—"

"*Noooo*," I stutter. "Neither of you can come. Not yet. I want you both in me."

"Avonna." Liam stops moving. "You nearly passed out last night. You're pregnant. Are you sure?"

"Yes. Help me ride you." I slide my fingers up Liam's chest.

Liam kisses me once. "Yes ma'am."

Repositioning himself, he scoots back into the bed, careful to keep his cock from slipping free. I move with him, until my knees straddle his hips and I lean as far into him as possible.

Linus moves behind me. He grips my hips to guide and steady me.

"Avonna, let me in." Linus exhales against my spine.

"Yes," I beg. "*Please.*"

Liam grips my waist as Linus lines the head of his cock against my entrance. Underneath where Liam is still thick and pulsing inside me.

It's impossible. Unreal.

Except, I'm so wet, so open, so ready I feel my body give. The pressure is staggering. They've both been inside me at the same time before. In my pussy and my ass. Many times.

Never like this.

Linus carefully eases in and my pussy yields around the impossible girth of two cocks frotting against each other inside me. I'm so full I sob, "Oh, *fuck*—"

Except, I'm not just being fucked.

I'm being taken from all sides.

Liam is steady beneath me, Linus is behind me, both of them groaning as they fill me together.

"Gahhhhhhhd," Liam gasps. "I can feel you, against me. Like you're fuckin' me too."

Linus kisses my shoulder, my spine, the back of my neck. *"Aye.* God, yes, squeeze both of us—fuck, baby."

I can't speak. All I can do is feel.

The pressure is unbearable. Beautiful.

They start to move. One thrusts deep while the other pulls back. Then they trade. Back and forth. Timed, deliberate. My body's the axis. My pleasure the orbit.

Liam cups my breasts, thumbs flicking over my nipples. Linus kisses my neck, his hands stroking my belly, reaching down to circle my clit, steady and devastating.

I'm on fire. Tears burn behind my eyes. This time it's not from being ignored. It's from the rightness of the three of us. The completion.

It's about being found.

"I can't—" I sob, voice cracked. "I can't live without either of you."

"I want this forever, baby. I'm goin' to shout it from the rooftops." Liam presses his lips against mine.

Linus drapes over my back to clutch Liam's shoulders. "You're ours. You always were. We won't ever make you feel invisible again."

They thrust together and the jolt of gratification slams through me. Liam's cock surges deeper, Linus's length drags alongside. I feel them everywhere. My pussy is overwhelmed by fullness and friction and love.

My orgasm hits with no warning. A white-hot, all-consuming explosion, ripping through me as my body locks around them, muscles seizing. I scream. I sob. I feel every inch of them.

Liam grips my hips steady. Linus bites my shoulder, barely holding back.

I'm gone. Tears spill from my eyes as they hold me. Kiss my throat. Lick the sweat from my breasts. Murmur broken, reverent things into my skin as I ride out the quake.

"You're a miracle." Liam runs his hands along my thighs.

"You're everything." Linus's hand splays across my belly.

This moment, with both of them inside me, is about me.

I believe them. This isn't some make-up fuck to appease me.

They heard me. Respect me.

I feel divine.

We're one body. One breath. One fire.

It's time everyone knows it.

Forty-Eight

LINUS

The Same Morning

Liam's beneath her.

We are inside her.

Avonna's sprawled over Liam's chest, head resting against his heart. Eyes blissfully closed. She holds us together in the same space. Flesh to flesh.

We've spent the past year fucking her together. Fucking each other. Making love and playing house and hiding in plain sight. Both Liam and I have failed to live our lives authentically. Always finding excuses to keep our love for each other hidden in the shadows.

In the process, we forgot to put the kindest, most beautiful woman in the world first.

She's sick of it. Rightfully so.

Last night everything shifted. She laid herself bare and called us out. Made it clear she won't stay with two scrambling idiots who don't treat her like the goddess she is.

Anchoring her hip with my palm, I slide one hand up her back, tracing her spine with my fingertips. Liam's hands are threaded through her hair. His thumb strokes her cheek. He gazes at her like she might vanish.

We won't let her.

Everything changes now.

I shift slightly, enough to slide deeper into her body against Liam's cock.

"Look at me." I kiss Avonna's ear.

She leans up toward me. Her eyes are half-lidded but clear.

"We love you," I whisper.

Her exhale catches, almost a sob, but she holds it in. As she relaxes back against Liam's chest, her hand finds mine at her hip and she brings it to her belly in between her and Liam. Her skin is soft and warm. His abs are taut and flexed with tension. His arms wrap around us both like he's trying to bring us even closer, if possible.

"I know I've made you feel like a secret," he says into her hair. "Both of you."

I don't interrupt. He needs to say this.

"I told myself it was protection," he goes on. "But you were right to call me out. I'm afraid. My fear is mine, not yours. I haven't put either of you first."

Liam's not the only one to blame here. In fact, I've done the same thing.

Avonna may be my wife, but no one really knows about us. We're never affectionate in public. Our love has always existed behind closed doors.

As for Liam, I've loved him for years and the only time we were open about our relationship was in college. I've never spoken about him to my parents and since I brought him into my relationship with Avonna, we've gone out of our way to hide from everyone, including his twin brother.

Liam kisses her shoulder. "Never again."

"Never again," I repeat and rest my forehead on the back of her neck. "I love you both. Fully. Without apology."

She doesn't speak, but her hand grips mine between her and Liam. She pushes back onto me, her body soft and trusting. Liam brushes her hair from her face, cradles her cheek.

"I thought we should keep our personal and professional parts of our lives separate," I sigh. "I was wrong. I don't want to live in pieces anymore."

Liam looks up at me over her shoulder. For a moment, we both pause there, holding her between us, holding each other in this moment. Neither of us turns away.

We both acutely understand the quiet, aching truth of nearly having waited too long.

I start to move again. Not thrusting, sliding. My chest hovers lightly against her back, let her feel me. My hand slides from her belly to her breast, cupping it gently, thumb circling her nipple. She arches slightly in response, a soft gasp slipping from her lips.

Liam kisses the center of her chest. His hands trail along her thighs, her hips, her waist. We touch her like she's a prayer we never learned properly until now.

I feel her relax between us, the last edge of guardedness dissolving.

"I need this," she whispers as her pussy relaxes, not in climax, but in trust.

Liam lifts his head and kisses her mouth, emitting a sound I've never heard from him before, somewhere between relief and awe. Her hand slides into his hair. I kiss the side of her neck. My hand finds Liam's and I link our fingers together.

We move again, carefully. My hips roll forward, and Liam's lift slightly to meet me. Not hurried or forceful. Enough to remind her we're with her. Choosing her, and each other.

Our cocks glide together inside her, and she whimpers softly. Somehow, we keep the pace languid, not letting the heat override the vow.

"I'm not hidin' anymore," I promise.

Liam kisses her again. "Me either."

"I know." She nods. "I *know*."

Liam kisses her collarbone. His face is vulnerable. Beautiful. I don't think I've ever seen him look like this, destroyed and safe at the same time. She's given us something precious.

Her truth. Her body. Her trust. Her heart.

I thrust again. Her pussy flutters. His cock throbs.

I can tell we're both close now.

My fingers flex as I try to stay in control, but it's slipping. She's pulling it out of me. Out of us both.

"I love you," Liam rasps.

"I love you both," she breathes, her hand reaches back to curl around my neck.

"I'm yours," I say to both of them. "All in. No more hiding."

Liam's cock twitches once and he spills into her, thick and hot, coating my cock as I move against him. Her pussy ripples, milking him, keeping us deep.

She breathes out, faint, aching, and I feel her start to tip over with the certainty of what we're giving her.

Everything.

I thrust once more. The heat builds sharp and sudden. My release takes me before I can prepare for it.

She quivers and cries out with her own climax as I empty into her every ounce of shame, every lie I ever told myself, every moment I kept her in the dark.

After, we hold her.

I bury my face in her neck. "We're not goin' anywhere."

Our new normal envelopes us.
No more shadows.
No more rules.
No more shame.

Forty-Nine

LIAM

Later That Day

I KNOW HOW TO blow things up.

Push people away before they can smell my shame.

Then Linus brought her into my life.

Avonna knows exactly who she is. She names her desires with a steady voice. Goes after what she wants without apology. When she decided on both Linus and me, it's her truth, not a transgression.

I want to fall to my knees for her.

For them.

Instead, I gave them my body but kept my truth locked away. I made myself small again. Starved at the table they set.

Avonna called me on it many times. Made herself vulnerable and told me my silence felt like rejection. Linus gave me space, not punishment. I'm not such which hurt worse.

I'm the problem. My silence. My cowardice. Yet, they're still here. Waiting. Not for perfection. For honesty.

I nearly lost everything tonight, but here we are.

Wet. Clean from the shower. Wrapped in each other on the couch in my hotel suite.

I'm done running.

I press my cheek against Avonna's. She blinks up at me, smiling like she already knows what I'm about to say.

"I want this," I swear solemnly. "You. Him. Us. Our baby. I don't care what anyone else thinks."

She touches my cheek. "Good."

"I feel free." Linus leans in. Kisses the back of my neck. "Whatever the consequences, we're in it together."

I wrap my arm around her from behind and pull Linus against my back. Our bodies are clean and our souls are catching up to the events of the past twelve hours.

It seems so stupid now. How I've deliberately closed myself off to my future. My family.

My family is in this room.

Untraditional. Unorthodox.

Unbreakable.

Avonna's head rests on my chest, one leg draped over mine like she's anchoring herself there. Linus lies along my other side, long and quiet, his fingers tracing absent lines along my forearm. We can hear the low hush of the city outside, distant traffic and the faint rattle of an elevator somewhere down the hall.

We've gone still.

Not awkward. Not tense.

Aware.

"I keep thinking about it." Avonna voice is slightly muffled against my chest. "What it means. It's all hitting me."

Linus's hand pauses. Mine tightens around her shoulder.

"You're pregnant," I marvel.

She nods without lifting her head. "Not in some abstract way. I mean... now. Us. This. The band."

Right.

Shit.

Not fear. Responsibility.

"I want it." There's no hesitation in Linus's voice. "I'm not scared of the work. I'm scared of doin' it wrong."

Avonna meets his eyes. "You won't."

She turns to me. "You okay?"

"Aye." I exhale. "I think so. I just keep runnin' the future in my head. The conversation I can't avoid anymore."

They exactly which one I mean.

"Padraig," Linus says.

"*Padraig*," Avonna echoes.

"I need to tell him right away." I gulp down a wave of panic. "I'm not sure how he'll react."

Linus brushes the hair from my eyes. "He's going to feel pushed aside. Even if he won't admit it."

Avonna sits up enough to look at both of us. "We don't minimize it. Or soften it. We tell him the truth. The entire truth. He loves you, Liam. It's about expanding our lives, not shrinking them."

"He's already at his limit." I rub my face. "Facin' another hiatus or break won't bode well."

"I know." She kisses my forehead. "Hiding will hurt him more."

Avonna reaches for my hand. Then Linus's. Links us together between her palms.

"We don't get to build our family by pretending the people we love won't be affected," she continues. "I know a lot about this and I won't allow our child to grow up dodging honesty."

I stare at the ceiling for a moment, then back at them. "Okay. I'll tell him today. Once we get our day goin'."

"Thank you." Avonna's shoulders drop, relief washing through her like she's been holding herself rigid for days.

We settle back into the couch, quieter now, steadier. "I want to come again." Avonna strokes my chest. "How do you feel about me riding your face while you fuck Linus."

Jesus.

I'll never say no to her.

She shifts and positions herself carefully, one knee on either side of my head, facing Linus. I slide my hands up her thighs, guiding her pussy to my mouth. When I lick her, her whole body shudders.

Linus's thighs brush mine as he straddles me, ass hovering over my cock. He strokes me a few times and guides me to his entrance. His rim is already glossy with lube. Ready.

He lowers himself. I purr into Avonna's pussy as I feel the first inch of my cock press into him. Inch by inch. She rocks against my face. Linus breathes out my name, and we start to move.

I thrust up. He grinds down. She rides my tongue. When Avonna leans over to take Linus's cock in her mouth, we become a single, perfect, writhing, rhythm of need.

The deep, wrecked, sounds we make fill the room until we're all on the verge of earth-shattering orgasms.

Then—a click.

The door. Footsteps.

A voice I know better than my own:

"Dar, wanna get breakfast with the family? Why did you disappear without sayin'—"

Silence.

I freeze.

Avonna stills above me and pulls off Linus with a pop. Linus stops mid-grind.

"Liam?" Padraig's voice tears through the living room.

Sharp. Confused.

Avonna scrambles off me and clutches a pillow to her breasts, giving me a clear line of vision to my twin brother standing in the doorway. My card key in hand.

Staring at the three of us. Mouth open. Eyes wide.

A bag of chips falls from his hand to the ground.

I'm still inside Linus. He and I don't move. We're frozen. Fused.

Only one thought resonates, louder than the blood pounding in my ears.

There's no going back.

Fifty

AVONNA

Four Months Later

Seattle's sky hangs low and heavy as we wind through Capitol Hill.

The streets are glassy from the lingering drizzle. Liam drives with one hand, the other rests over mine on my thigh. Linus sits in the back but leans forward between the front seats, fingers curled around the headrests with enough force to break them.

We're silent as the car creeps toward the McGloughlin house.

I place my palm over the slight curve of my belly beneath my sweater. Four months. We haven't told anyone. Not Padraig. Not Liam's family. Not Linus's either.

This time it's the fear of what we can't yet define. There's no blueprint for raising a child in a trio, considering the circumstances. There's a lot to figure out.

We have a doctor's appointment tomorrow and an ultrasound. We're not sure who our baby's biological father is. Linus doesn't want to find out. Liam agrees. Then they change their mind. Then change it again. I need to know and we've danced around the prenatal tests long enough, but had to finish Fireball's tour in the midst of it all.

The truth is, despite all of us talking a big game, none of us has come to terms with the fact we're actually going to be parents.

My dear friend Marcella's text flashes across the my phone. Something about affidavits and coparenting forms. I silence it. We'll deal with the legal stuff after we get through tomorrow.

It's crazy to believe I used to be the hostess at her family's restaurant and now she's helping us figure out how to legally protect my polygamous family. None of us expected it to be so...challenging. Linus and I are legally married. We both want Liam to be in our marriage with us. Add in triad parenting? We're suddenly juggling guardianship clauses, hospital access forms, power-of-attorney triggers, custody frameworks.

We thought the toughest part would be coming out of hiding. Turns out, no. We also have to protect our chosen life and the parental rights for our baby. There's little precedent and a lot of potential pitfalls.

It's strange how something so tender, so intimate, can start to feel like a grind. We try to remind ourselves every form and every contract is a promise. A safeguard. A modern family. We're in this. All the way.

I glance at Liam. He hasn't slept much. None of us has. Stepping out of the shadows has been wonderful on one hand, disheartening on the other. In Albuquerque, the three of us went out for dinner. We held hands. I kissed my men. Stupid. The hostess's face pinched like she was looking at animals out of their cage. The waitstaff all stared like we were zoo animals.

Microaggressions surround us like minefields. They're triggering for Liam. Which is why coming here tonight to face his family is a huge step and could also be a disaster.

"I forget how green it is here," Linus jests, sensing I'm spinning a bit. "Makes Dublin look like it needs waterin'."

Liam huffs. "Do you have to say it every time we're in Seattle?"

"Still true." Linus grins at me.

It works. I snap out of my broodiness and take in my surroundings. The houses get bigger as we make our way uphill. Stately old queens, with wraparound porches and slanted roofs. Faded trim and fresh flowers. A lot of history.

Up ahead, I spot the one from Liam's photos and feel my stomach flip. He squeezes my knee. Doesn't look at me, doesn't need to.

I've played to thousands. Sung to festival crowds. This is more challenging. I'm vibrating with nerves, even if this is what I want.

"Last chance to fake a flat tire." I try a woeful attempt at humor.

"Nope." Liam raises an eyebrow. "We're doin' this before I change my mind."

Linus clutches the back of his neck. "We didn't have to make it such an event."

"It is one." Liam shakes his head. "I never go home. Not unless Ma begs or Padraig guilts me into showin' up." He looks between us. "I did as I promised. Called her. Told her I was comin' and I was bringin' you both."

A pause.

"I want them to know who I love."

"Well, we love you too." I squeeze his wrist.

The car brakes outside a grand Craftsman. Lights glow in the windows. A porch swing rocks in the breeze. The McGloughlin home is not only where the twins grew up, it's the place of Liam's nightmares.

My eyes flick to Liam. He's pale. I know he's thinking about the night Padraig found us. There's no word for the sound his twin made when he caught the three of us mid-fuck.

It was a full-blown rupture.

I'll never forget the look on Padraig's face when he finally comprehended what he was seeing.

He's never mentioned it to me or Linus since. We've gone about our day-to-day band life like nothing happened. We're gonna have to deal with it at some point, but our schedule has been crazy and we owe it to the fans to keep the train on the tracks.

For now, the three of us keep our relationship private and he doesn't know about the baby growing inside me.

Yet.

Liam parks, turns off the engine. We sit in the quiet tick of cooling metal for a second until he finally speaks. "I don't know what to say."

"You don't need to know." Linus caresses his neck. "You'll know when you see them."

"You mean my da?"

Linus nods. "Yeah."

"I don't want a fight."

"You won't get one." I cup his face. "You're a grown man now. With two partners who'll stand by you no matter what. We can walk out at any time."

Liam exhales and opens his car door. "Right. Let's rip the plaster off."

When we are at the front door, Cillian opens it, and we follow him in. The table is set with a huge platter of corned beef and cabbage is in the middle next to a bowl of mashed potatoes, a loaf of soda bread and small bowl of mustard sauce.

Liam's fingers brush mine. Linus's hand settles at my back, steadying me. The scent is mouthwatering. An unexpected wave of emotion passes through me. This family scene is nothing like the cold scraps and silent tables of my childhood. Here, there are place settings for all of us, as though we'd be missed if the seat were empty.

Maureen appears from the kitchen, apron dusted with flour, arms already outstretched. "Oh, come here, my loves."

She wraps me in a hug and nearly squishes the air from my lungs, then pulls back to cradle my face. "You look thin. Are my boys not feedin' you?"

"Tour life." I giggle nervously at the word "boys," knowing she means Padraig and Liam.

She hugs Linus with equal enthusiasm and turns her attention to Liam like she's trying to stitch him back together. Her hands frame his face, thumbs brush the tired places he can't hide, and I see it clear as breath on glass. She loves her son with a force filling this entire room.

"I'm so glad you're here." She kisses his cheek. "Rory's..." She pauses.

Liam stiffens.

"Upstairs," she finishes.

As if he heard her, Rory appears on the landing and joins as we sit at the table.

Dinner starts with softball questions from Maureen. The flight. The tour. Padraig and Mara. Cillian jumps in with talk about some of the projects he's working on at McGloughlin Construction.

We dig into the corned beef and cabbage. No one says much. It's not exactly tense, more like awkward. Throughout, Rory watches Liam with a careful, almost fragile attention. Not pushing. Waiting.

When plates begin to clear, he speaks. "I'm glad you reached out." His voice carries a weight he has held for years. "This is nice."

Liam nods. "Yeah."

"You're not home often." Rory takes a small breath. "Never on your own."

Liam nods again. "No."

Linus shifts closer to Liam. I slide my hand to Liam's thigh. He weaves his fingers between mine, grounding himself between the two of us.

Rory clears his throat. "I am glad you're here."

"Well, we're here for a reason and I don't know where to begin." Liam puffs out a half laugh.

Maureen grips Rory's arm. A familiar gesture.

"How about this." Liam draws a bracing breath. "I've been hidin' myself from this family and I want you to know who I am."

The room suspends with a hovering stillness.

"I've been in love with Linus since the year after everythin' happened here. We met at Wazzu. He managed Fireball. I was scared to tell any of you..." He pauses. "I didn't think I could ever bring him around our family after. When his visa expired we split. Padraig, obviously, knows all of this."

Linus stays still beside him, eyes low.

Liam continues, "There's more. The reason I cut it off was Linus and I dreamed of findin' a woman who would love both of us but never believed it was possible. We broke up. I didn't think I could be faithful to him. Or anyone. I felt like a loser and was determined to never give my heart away again. Spent years livin' the rockstar life with all of the trappings." He looks directly at his da. "Nothin' was off limits."

I shift in my seat so I can rest my head on his shoulder. I've never been so proud of Liam in my life and I don't care if my affection bothers his parents. He needs me and he has me.

"Linus didn't give up on me. He brought me back into his life a couple years ago." Liam's voice softens. "And he wasn't alone. Avonna and Linus are married. She loved him long before I stepped back into the picture and she also knew Linus still loved me, inexplicable, but true."

Linus chuffs out a laugh. Liam brushes his thumb over my hand.

"They waited for me." He shuts his eyes. "Made space for me. Offered me a home. A partnership. A life where I didn't have to split myself in half to be normal."

He looks at Rory. Direct. Unshielded.

"What did I do to repay them for lovin' me?" Liam's voice breaks. "I hid them from Padraig until recently. From all of youse. From everyone. I was terrified I would drag shame back into this house. I couldn't bear the thought you would see depravity every time you looked at me."

I clamp my hand around his.

Liam breathes in, steadying. "I'm done hidin'. *We're* done hidin'."

He turns to Linus. "You're the bravest, most patient man I know. You never gave up on me." Then his eyes find mine. "You are strength and kindness and make me feel safe in ways I never thought I would." He sits up straighter. "They're my life. Both of them. I love them with every fiber of my bein' and we're startin' a family."

Rory's breath catches. Maureen covers her mouth, eyes filling.

"Avonna is pregnant." Liam brings my hand to his lips and kisses it. "We're not sure which one of us is the biological father. As far as we're concerned, this baby is all of ours. We're workin' with a lawyer to sort out the legalities."

Liam lifts his face toward his parents. "I'm sick of being estranged. So is Padraig. Avonna encouraged me to go into therapy and it's helped. I won't live my life in secret anymore." He meets Rory's stare dead on. "I love them. I choose them. If you can't accept us, now is the time to say it so I don't waste my time here. I'm done being ashamed and I'll protect them from anyone who doesn't support us."

Silence fills the room. A heavy, shifting quiet.

Rory reaches into his pocket. He places a set of keys on the table. The metal clicks against the wood.

"I kept the townhouse for you," he says. "You wouldn't take it before. It can be your home when the four of you are in town."

Liam stares at them, breath trembling in his chest.

"Your mother and I built those townhouses for our children because we knew you all needed a safe place to live. I destroyed my relationships with all of youse." Rory fights back tears. "I don't want forgiveness. None of youse ever owed me forgiveness, especially you, Liam. It doesn't matter if I regret what happened. It happened. I have to face the consequences. You and your family are always welcome in my home, no judgment. I love you and I hope to be part of your life again."

Linus places his hand near Liam's elbow. I feel Liam steady himself between us.

After a long moment, Liam picks up the keys, fingers shaking.

"Thank you," he says quietly. "I'll accept this now, but we still have a lot of work to do."

Rory nods. "I know."

"We're going to the doctor tomorrow." Liam squeezes my hand "Our plan is to be in Seattle as home base until the baby's born."

Maureen's tears slip down her cheeks. Cillian looks at Liam with a mix of pride and pain.

"We will take this at your pace." Rory studies his son's face. "I want to know you. I want to know Linus and Avonna and I want to know the baby. He or she will be our first grandchild."

Tears stream down Liam's face. "Me too."

Linus slides his hand over Liam on top of mine. He looks at both of us with a warmth I feel in my bones.

I know he'll find his way back to his da.

Not tonight.

Not all at once.

At least he'll do it out in the open.

Fifty-One

Two Months Later

AVONNA'S BODY IS PLIANT from everything Liam and I did to relax her.

She rests on her side with a pillow under her belly. Six months along and her movements have grown careful. Her pace is sluggish. Her back is strained. Feet swollen.

Somehow, despite her limited mobility, her voracious sex drive is raging even more out of control.

Tonight she needed our mouths. Our fingers. Our cocks. We gave her everything she asked for, as many times as her body could take. Five orgasms later, she sleeps between us.

Sated. Glow still on her skin.

Liam is passed out behind her, arm draped across her hip. Peaceful. Lighter than I've seen him in years. Telling his parents the truth lifted something in him. He touches us more, smiles every day, sings with a brighter edge.

I wish I felt as relaxed as my loves tonight. I probably should have let myself orgasm.

Instead, my mind was whirling.

We're in Dublin for a few days. Tomorrow is my turn to tell my parents about our relationship. Then we're putting our little flat on the market and moving to the States for good. Life is changing and we're meeting it head on.

None of us planned to be parents. Truth be told, the timing couldn't be worse for Fireball.

Another example of life happening to you when you least expect it.

We probably should have seen it coming. Our sex life is insane. Most days, if I'm honest, we fill Avonna on more than one occasion. It's our rhythm. Devotion to our girl. None of us ever worried about birth control, she's been on the pill for years. Somewhere between time zones and exhaustion, she missed a few and here we are in the craziest situation imaginable.

At our twelve-week scan, the three of us went in expecting one heartbeat. Came out with two. Avonna cried. Liam went pale. I laughed because I didn't know what else to do. We held each other in the hallway outside the clinic while the world kept turning.

Our lawyer gently suggested a DNA test. For protection. Guardianship. Legal clarity. We're doing everything possible to protect our family legally and we don't have the luxury of surprise if we are going to establish parental rights.

The paternity results came in around the time we learned their gender. Two girls. I'm the bio dad of one girl. Liam's the bio dad of the other. It's so rare, the entire office got involved in the test confirmation. Heteropaternal superfecundation, they call it. Two eggs, two sperm, one ovulation window.

The science makes sense, even if the odds are one in a million.

"You're both their fathers." Avonna didn't blink when we found out. "Of course you are."

Restless, I slip out of bed, careful not to wake Liam and Avonna. The flat is dim and cool. I meander into the kitchen, turn on the smallest light, and brace my hands on the counter. My heart races and stomach roils as I think about tomorrow.

My parents love Avonna. They've wanted us to have kids for years and are gonna be shocked to the core when they learn my wife is carrying one of my daughters and one of Liam's. It will be difficult for them to comprehend.

It's my fault they don't know Liam's history with me and how Avonna and I have brought him into our marriage.

With the visit looming, I understand how scared Liam was when he was in the same boat a few weeks ago. I'm afraid of my family's judgement and of losing them. It went well at the McGloughlins. Hopefully the O'Donnell's will be accepting too.

A soft footstep pulls me out of my thoughts.

I turn.

Liam stands in the doorway. Naked. Sleep-warm. His hair messy, cock half-mast, his eyes still heavy with dreams. The sight of him pulls something hot and aching through my chest.

My dick fills. Suddenly, he's the only thing I need.

"Linus," he rasps. "Come back to bed."

"I can't sleep. I'm too wound up." My fist wraps around my hardening cock.

He crosses the room. "What's goin' on?"

"I'm not lookin' forward to tomorrow," I admit. "I've hidden so much. It'll be a lot for them to take in."

He presses his forehead against my shoulder. "They may be freaked out, but it'll be okay."

"I'm scared."

"I know." He kisses my neck. "Come here."

He guides me to the couch and sits. Pulls me into his lap. I straddle him as his hands slide up my back with grounding strokes.

"You always take care of all of us." His tongue brushes mine with deliberate tenderness. My ribs loosen. "Every day. Tonight, let me take care of you."

Liam reaches into the small drawer in the table beside the couch and pulls out the lube we left last time we were here. He works me open, staring into my eyes as he does it. I moan when he slides one finger in, then two, preparing me with practiced care.

"Yes, baby," he whispers. "Relax for me."

When I'm loose, he cups my ass and lifts slightly, then guides me down onto his cock with steady hands, making my breath stutter.

"That's it," he purrs and licks my neck. "Take me in."

I open fully around him and we both groan. He fills me perfectly.

He moves with long, deep thrusts, not hurried, not rough. Each one erasing fear, unraveling worry, reminding me why I've belonged to him since I was twenty. His mouth moves along my neck, down my shoulder. His hands stroke my back.

"You're safe. I love you."

I cling to him as he wraps his hand around my aching cock and jacks me in smooth, firm pulls. Pleasure builds fast. My breath breaks into small sounds I can't hide.

"You're not facin' tomorrow alone. We're goin' together. You and me and Avonna. And our girls," he promises.

I gasp when he twists his hand over my crown.

"Liam..."

He kisses the corner of my mouth. "Come for me."

I shudder and spill over his fist, body shaking. He thrusts deeper and erupts inside me.

After, he wraps his arms around me. Flutters soft kisses along my jaw, thumb stroking the back of my neck.

The apology rises before I can stop it. "I'm sorry for hidin' you. For hidin' us. I let my fear get between us for so long."

"Linus…" His arms surround me instantly.

"I love you so much." My voice shakes but I keep going. "I love you more than I ever said. Havin' you back. Both you and Avonna. It's the life I dreamed about for years and never expected to be my reality."

He brushes his thumb over my cheek. "You're both my dream too."

I breathe in, shaky and relieved.

Held. Loved. Home.

Liam lifts my chin. "We'll tell them tomorrow. Not with fear. With truth."

For the first time since landing in Dublin, I believe him.

Mum opens the door before we knock, warmth blooming across her face.

"There's my girl." She tugs Avonna into a careful hug, hands brushing the curve of her belly. "You're blooming. Let me look at you."

Avonna smiles, one hand on her back. She moves a little slower, glows a little brighter. Mum always adored her. I hope nothing changes once we come clean.

Mum turns to me next. "You look thin."

"Stop." I kiss her cheek and hand her the bouquet of flowers we brought her. "I eat plenty."

Da appears from the hallway with a soft grunt of welcome. "Welcome home."

"Good to be back." He hugs me roughly before looking behind me.

Liam stands patiently.

"Da, this is Liam McGloughlin." I pat him on the shoulder. "We were at uni together. He's in Fireball with Avonna."

Da's brow lifts, curious but not unfriendly. Mum's smile flattens into something unreadable.

Liam offers a calm nod. "Hi, Mrs. O'Donnell. Mr. O'Donnell. Thanks for havin' me."

Mum steps aside. "Not a bother. Come in then."

We sit at the table I grew up around. Mum brings out roast chicken, boiled potatoes, and carrots in butter. She's pulled out the china, even though I told her this wasn't a holiday.

Small talk holds the beginning of the meal together. They ask about the move. About the band. Focus mostly on the twins and Avonna's health. No one asks why Liam's here, it's a friendly conversation filled with a bit of slagging and gossip.

Until I set my fork down and say, "There's something we came here to talk to you about."

The air shifts. The best way to ensure a quiet Irish household is to say you want to have a conversation.

Mum lowers her water glass. Da yawns, looks at me not unkindly.

"I'm not going to dance around it." I take a deep breath. "You both know how much Avonna and I love each other. We've been married a long time now."

They nod, cautious.

I look at Liam. Then back to them.

"What you don't know is Liam and I have a history too. We were together romantically years ago, back in college."

Mum's face doesn't move. Da leans back slightly in his chair, stoic.

"I never stopped loving him," I attempt to explain. "Somehow, we found our way back. Avonna loves Liam too. He loves both of us. So now, our marriage is the three of us."

Mum blinks, confused. "What do you mean?"

"Molly." Avonna's voice is steady. "He means we're in a relationship. All three of us. Liam's part of us now."

There's a silence so deep it drowns the sound of the clock ticking behind me.

"Let me get this straight. You're sayin'—" Mum's voice rises. "You're all *together*?"

"Yes." I nod. "We're all together. In every way."

Mum looks to me, then Avonna, then Liam. "Who's the father of the babies?"

"Well, you aren't going to believe this." I smile at Avonna and Liam. "We're havin' twin girls. One is mine. One is Liam's."

She goes pale.

Da's voice is quiet, deadly. "How long has this been goin' on?"

"Over a year," I admit. "Liam lived with us in Dublin before we all moved to the States. I was afraid to tell you, but none of us wants to lie anymore. We're not askin' for anything. You're goin' to be grandparents, so..."

Mum ignores me and turns her gaze on Avonna. "You're pregnant with two men's babies? You're sharin' your husband? What have you done to my *son*?"

"I love them both." Avonna meets her gaze evenly, not rising to the challenge.

Mum's hands curl around her napkin. "I misjudged you completely. Thought you had more sense."

"*Don't*." I place my hand on her wrist. "Don't put this on her."

"She should've kept you satisfied so you wouldn't give in to some diabolical situation."

My voice sharpens. "Okay. Enough."

"Everyone calm down." Da raises a hand.

Mum turns to me, trembling. "You're my son. My beautiful boy. I thought you'd come home and settle. Not drag us into somethin' unnatural."

"There's nothing unnatural about our love." I take Avonna's hand.

"I don't care what anyone says." Mum shakes her head, trying to rattle the thought loose. "This isn't normal."

Da finally speaks. "How does this even work?"

"Simple. We parent together," I say. "We live together. We love each other."

"You think this is going to last?" Mum snaps. "You think this is forever? What happens when it blows up?"

"It won't."

She gestures to Liam. "What is he? The third wheel? The extra?"

"I love your son." Liam's voice is low but clear. "I love them both."

Mum pushes her chair back. "Well, I hope you all enjoy explainin' this to your children one day. I truly do. I want nothin' to do with youse."

Da exhales. "Molly."

She storms out.

"I need to check on her." Da follows her out.

We leave our plates unfinished. Outside, the Dublin sun is sharp and cold.

Liam walks beside me in silence. Avonna threads her fingers through mine.

It was a disaster.

And a blessing too.

It was truth.

For now, it's all we can give them.

Fifty-Two

LIAM

Seven Months Later

QUINN SPITS HER PACIFIER out again.

I hook it back in place with one hand while shaking her bottle with the other. Sloane sleeps in her bassinet, one tiny fist up near her cheek. She always looks peaceful. Quinn is ready to fight.

Fraternal twins. Same birthday. Different rules entirely.

My spine aches from standing. My eyes burn with a rawness no amount of sleep fixes. I smell old coffee on my shirt and something vaguely sour I'm pretty sure is puke.

Avonna hovers nearby in a pair of sweats she hasn't changed in a few days, hair piled on her head. She scans both girls like she's running surveillance. She taps the baby monitor screen with tense fingers, even though she can see Sloane is breathing fine with her own eyes.

Her doctor calls it postpartum anxiety. She rarely sleeps for more than an hour at a time. Her mind treats everything as a danger she has to ward off before it gets near our babies. We're working out the med levels to get her over the hump. So far, we haven't found the right balance.

"Sloane's color looks off," she mumbles under her breath.

I glance at my sleeping angel. "She's pink and perfect."

"Too pink."

"She's grand, love."

I see her swallow down a wave of fear. She's a fortress. A tired, overworked fortress with a dented gate and no drawbridge.

"Why hasn't Linus called?" Avonna chews on her thumbnail.

"He texted." I show her my phone. "Things are runnin' late."

He's with Peach Harvest in Zurich. One of his longtime clients hit the top of the charts all over the world this year. The show is a big deal and a huge opportunity for Isis. Not to mention a massive paycheck.

Avonna and I are on full-time parent duty with infants, which means Fireball isn't touring and neither of us has steady income anymore. Linus has to keep us afloat, even if work takes him farther away from us.

He's making a monumental sacrifice, missing these first months with our daughters. Avonna and I should be writing, it was the plan up until the reality of having two babies knocked us over the head with a two-by-four.

Fireball is on shaky ground. Padraig is off galivanting with Mara somewhere. He's been distant since the girls were born and I don't blame him. The band was finally gaining traction and now we've been out of the game for nearly a year. He suggested we take an official break and reconvene in a few months to decide if we want to go on.

I refused. I can't let him quit. As far as I'm concerned, the situation is temporary and the band will figure out a long-term solution soon.

A soft knock lands on the door.

Avonna lifts her chin on high alert. "Check first before you open the door."

I peek through the window. It's my parents.

"They're here." I glance back at her.

"Oh, good." Avonna nods. "Remember they need to sanitize before touching anything."

She's calm but rigidly diligent. I love the hell out of her but the hypervigilance is tough to deal with. It's like her easygoing personality has been replaced with a mini-dictator germaphobe.

I open the door. Ma has two giant bags of diapers. Da's carrying enough food to feed a rugby team.

"We brought dinner. They'll be plenty left for tomorrow." Ma cups my cheek on her way in.

Da shakes his head at me. "Yer eyes are half-closed, lad. Yer wrecked."

"Aye. You're right." I'm too tired to pretend.

Ma and Da wash their hands and coat them in sanitizer without a reminder.

Ma heads straight for Sloane and peers down at her. "There she is. Our little sleepin' angel."

"I'll take Quinn." Da sets a hand on my shoulder. "Sit for a minute."

Quinn's tiny fingers grip my shirt like she'll never let me go. I pry them loose and hand her over. Da takes her like he's done it a thousand times, which he probably has at this point. She relaxes into him and her body softens instead of stiffens. A tiny sigh escapes her tiny lips.

I swear to fuck, something hot pricks behind my eyes. Fatherhood has made me emotional. Nostalgic. Mostly, the scene triggers a memory of when I was little.

Da taught all of us construction from a young age. One day, Da was showing Padraig and me how to hammer nails into a practice board. As usual, I started smashing away and crushed my thumb and bawled my fucking eyes out. He swept me and my twin up and carried us inside. Set Padraig down at the kitchen table and held my hand under cold water.

I distinctly remember how he kissed my thumb to make it better. When I stopped crying, he promised I'd be alright and gave us both ice cream.

So many memories like this have come back since the girls were born. Things I'd shoved down so deep I thought they were gone. Before Da's accident and the worst of the drinking. When rage came in waves I never understood.

I didn't always hate him. I loved him. He adored me. It ended abruptly and his downfall affected me in horrific ways. I'd buried all the good stuff. Until recently, I didn't know how to access anything but the trauma.

In therapy, many of the techniques were similar to those Avonna used. Even though I've stopped going regularly, she's helped me immensely, reminding me how the body stores pain like a knot you didn't know you'd tied and healing isn't about rewinding, it's about reclaiming.

When I breathe with her and live in truth. I feel it. The missing piece. Safety I never had. It was all right in front of me and I teetered on self-destruction for years. I refused to allow myself any happiness. Punished myself for no reason.

"Liam?

I snap back to focus.

"Where's Linus today?" Da cups Quinn's head and sways back and forth.

"Switzerland." I lean back on the sofa. "He'll be home Tuesday."

Da nods. His voice lowers. "How you holdin' up?"

"Depends on the day." My laugh is short and broken. "Lately, I've wondered how the fuck I ended up jugglin' burp cloths and bottles instead of gear and busses."

Ma overhears and smiles. "Some dreams change shape, love."

"Rory." Avonna pops up. "Watch Quinn's head. Support her neck."

Da's already doing it but he makes a show of appeasing her. "Aye, thanks for the reminder, love," he trills in his Belfast lilt.

Sloane stirs so I pick her up and settle back onto the couch, arms full of tiny weight and huge responsibility. I swear, every moment feels like a new universe I'm terrified to fuck up.

"Padraig's pissed." I nuzzle Sloane's hair. "He's used to me drivin' relentlessly and I can't even fathom it. We've got to get an album out, though, and we haven't written a song in months. The studio date on the calendar is getting closer and I won't be ready."

Truth be told, we could've stayed in LA. In many ways, it would have been easier. Linus's business is mostly there and he'd be with us a lot more often. During therapy, the three of us decided healing the relationship with my own family was a priority. With the babies on the way, the three of us decided as a family it was important to face my past head on. Be around my brothers. Spend time with Ma.

Sit across from my Da and say words I never thought would come out of my mouth. *I love you. I want to try.*

So we made Seattle home. Temporarily. For our girls and our long-term future.

Padraig and I haven't talked much since the girls were born. Every time I try to explain why I'm here, he changes the subject. Says I'm wasting time trying to fix things that can't be fixed. He doesn't understand. I'm learning what it means to stay and do the important work.

Da lowers himself beside me. "So push it back. Pick it up when you can."

"What if we never get there again?" I lean back on the couch, still amazed I'm able to have a heart-to-heart with the father I avoided for nearly twenty years. "Fireball's makin' some money. Not enough to support five of us. Forget songwritin', I haven't picked up my guitar in weeks. Linus has put everythin' he has into Isis and we're relyin' on him to pay the bills. If we didn't have this townhouse, my family would be in real trouble. It's tough right now. He's missin' out on so much. Avonna's anxiety is through the roof. I don't have the bandwidth to do anythin' but get through the day."

Da studies me thoughtfully. "Welcome to fatherhood."

"It's fuckin' panic," I admit. "Every second of every day."

He watches Quinn nestle into his chest. "Aye. And you wouldn't change a thing. The love you have for them is indescribable."

"Yeah."

"You'd burn the world for them." He kisses her head. "Even if it means you lose parts of yourself along the way."

"*Yeah.*"

He shifts Quinn slightly as she squirms. "Try not to stress. You won't lose the music, Liam. Or Padraig."

Sloane lets out a tiny coo. She looks and acts so much like Linus. Calm. Content. Quinn looks and acts like me. Wide eyes. Fierce lungs. A tiny warrior already fighting the world for space.

Fraternal. Different. Ours. It doesn't matter Quinn's my biological daughter and Sloane shares Linus's DNA. Not to me. Or them. They're pieces of the three of us. I'll protect Sloane's soft peace and Quinn's wild fire until the day I die.

Avonna touches my shoulder and holds up the ear thermometer. "Should we double-check Sloane's temperature?"

"You can, love, but she's warm from sleep." I take her hand and squeeze. "It might read high."

She hands it to me. "I'd like to check."

"Okay." I do as she asks and show her the result when it beeps. "Normal."

Avonna exhales with relief. Scans Quinn again. She's not checking for errors. She's checking for safety. Her mind plays out every possible threat she survived growing up. Every danger she learned to expect. Every harm that could potentially happen.

"It's terrifying how much I love them." She drapes her arm around my neck to stroke her daughter's head. "Thank you for not making me feel crazy. I know I'm a pain in the ass."

"You're not, baby." I thread my fingers through hers.

"I didn't think love could feel this big." She looks at my da. "Like my heart is glass."

"Yer a good mother." He smiles.

Avonna's eyes shine with tears. She looks away fast, embarrassed by emotion she can't cage.

"Let us watch them while the two of you take a break and eat." Ma sets two plates on the counter. "Both of you sit."

Avonna and I eat. Across the room, I watch Da coo at the girls and my chest twists.

A year ago my nights were noise and neon, hotel walls shaking, bodies and sweat and adrenaline. Music first. Chaos second. Everything else a far-off third. I lived in my own head and everyone else learned to keep up or fall behind.

Now the loudest thing in my life is a baby's cry.

Linus, Avonna, and I never planned to be parents, at least this early in our commitment to each other. We've spent over a year convinced the only consequence of love was pleasure. Turns out the universe had other ideas and now we're responsible for tiny humans.

I want this. I do.

Even when the learning curve hits like a brick wall every day. Freedom traded for bottles and burp cloths. Sex turned into schedules and survival. No room for luxuries like sleep or sanity.

My guitar case still sits in the corner, clasped shut like a secret I'm not ready to reopen. Some days I look at it and feel a flicker. The music's inside me, waiting to break free. Other days, I don't remember it's there.

I lift the fork to my mouth and chew. Take in my surroundings. Enjoy a meal I didn't microwave.

I'm here. I'm breathing. Present in the moment. Being here for my family.

With my family.

For the first time in my adult life, I'm not disappearing.

Fifty-Three

AVONNA

One Year Later

THE MORNING IS PURE chaos.

Quinn barrels across the living room on wobbling legs, shrieking with triumph like she owns the earth she walks on.

Sloane sits on the floor beside the couch, turning a wooden block over in her hand with quiet concentration.

Fire and water. One wild, one still. Fraternal twins in every possible way. They mirror their father's respective personalities.

I lower myself onto the rug beside Sloane, knees cracking in protest. Their birth was rough on my body and mind. Some days I feels like a house someone forgot to finish building. Out of the corner of my eye, I notice Quinn making a beeline for the bookshelf. Liam swoops in before she can climb it, planting her on his hip. He kisses her cheek until she squeals, catching my eye over her shoulder.

He smiles with relief. I'm not freaking out like I would have done a year ago.

Postpartum anxiety consumed me for months after they were born. My brain conjured up danger at every weird noise. Every creak of the house. I checked their breathing religiously. Melted down if they slept longer than expected.

Pregnancy drummed up a lot of old emotions. Then, suddenly, I was in charge of two small lives in the midst of shaking off shadows of my past. I kept guard over them the way no one ever kept guard over me, afraid my childhood might slip through the cracks and touch them.

Liam and I have been each other's rocks. As I helped him navigate his relationship with Rory, he contacted my old therapist for a referral. The right drug cocktail helped. The fog has thinned. My hormones leveled out. I'm able to be present with my babies without shaking from unfounded terror.

I breathe easier now and love being a mother more than I ever dreamed possible. The mess. Their weight against my chest. Every sticky kiss.

My body on the other hand? Not so much. My curves are different. Softer. Squishier. I'm heavy in places I never expected. I can't seem to be bothered with any sort of fitness routine.

Liam assures me he loves the way I look. Linus, when he's home, still adores me like a religion he invented. While I'm happy they're both still attracted to me, it's time for me to get ready to step back into the spotlight. Even if the thought of leaving my daughters is unfathomable.

The guilt sits low and constant, wanting to be home with our girls instead of getting back to work. Liam's chomping at the bit to be on stage again. Spends hours working on music in our makeshift recording studio after the girls are asleep. Traveled with Padraig last month to an award show and came back raring to go.

I can't fault him for getting back into the groove. Over the past year since the twins were born, he's been incredible. Hands-on, steady, shoulder to shoulder with me every sleepless night. We've been together for every bottle, every fever, every first. The rhythm of our days is shaped around their needs, their laughter, their cries.

It's changed us.

We're a true triad now. Linus and I had our years alone, Linus and Liam had theirs. Now, Liam and I have sealed our side of the triangle.

Today, Linus is coming home in time for the twins' first birthday. We're so ready to have him back.

He opens the front door and lets his suitcase fall against the wall with a soft thud. The sound of his voice sends Sloane squealing across the room. Quinn freezes mid-squack, eyes wide with recognition. He's already on the rug before I can stand, scooping them both into his lap, covering their cheeks in kisses until they're shrieking with laughter.

Then he turns to me. Pulls me close until our foreheads touch, his breath warm against my skin. The second his hands find my waist, I feel his relief at him being home.

Also, something deeper. Hungrier.

Liam stoops down and kisses him, like he's grounding all of us.

"We missed you." He nuzzles his beard.

Linus's hand finds the small of his back. "I felt it. Every minute."

He misses us more than he lets on. I see it in the way his messages get longer the later it gets, when the hotel curtains are drawn. He longs for our quiet intimacy, laughter in the kitchen, sex in person instead of watching me and Liam fuck to get him off.

Life now is far from the steadiness of when the three of us did everything together.

The thing is, Isis Management exploded. Every artist he signs turns to gold. He's building an empire, and it's beautiful to watch. On the down side, Linus knows the Delta first class lounge menu by heart. Remembers which flight attendants will sneak him biscuits and what airports have the best espresso.

He sends us videos from green rooms and side-stage corridors, eyes tired, promising, "Next month will be quieter."

It never is.

He tries. God, he tries. Overcorrects with too many gifts for the girls. Never misses a FaceTime call with them. Puts way too much pressure on himself.

Linus is always afraid of not being enough, even when he's already everything.

Every time he comes home to us, his whole body radiates with tension. Urgency. A need to re-anchor. He's wired. Overstimulated. Rather than rest and have some downtime with his daughters, he wants to immediately integrate into our routine.

We try to keep him involved, but he always feels disconnected from raising his kids. Our sex life. Liam's reunion with his family. All of the day-to-day activities.

To cope, we've been seeing a relationship therapist to navigate this stage of our life. It's like everything else. We hit a wall, then build a door. Slam into another, then build stairs. We're learning by bruises and patience. Find tools to communicate before and after fights. Make commitments not to gang up on each other. Hold space for each other's insecurities and fears.

We're inventing the rules. There's no manual for a life built by three hearts.

Today, we're meeting with a colleague of my family friend, Marcella Delgado, who helped LTZ guitarist, Zane Rocks' fiancée gain full custody of her daughter in a bitter dispute and specializes in complicated family structures.

We're finalizing all of the paperwork to legally protect each of our parental rights with the girls and with each other.

Decidedly the least sexy part of our relationship.

Realizing it's time to go, I stand up. Linus watches me struggle to my feet and frowns. I shoot him a look before he can say anything. "I'm fine."

"You're tired," he observes helpfully.

"We're *all* tired," I retort.

Liam hugs me from behind. "Quinn woke us at three, Sloane at five. We're more than tired. We're spiritually defeated."

Hearing him joke about it means he's over the grumpiness. Linus's presence has a funny way of helping him in this regard.

"You two take the girls, I've got to change." I head to the bedroom to find something presentable to wear. My jeans fit again, but not comfortably. My hips look fuller. My stomach isn't flat. My thighs touch in new places. I try to repeat the mantra *"your body is beautiful, a map of everything you've survived."*

If I'm ever going to be on stage again, I need to be strong. Grounded. Able to stand in front of a mic without feeling like the floor will swallow me whole.

Liam comes up behind me as I fasten my necklace. He places his hands on my waist, warm and steady. His cheek rests against the top of my head.

"What are you thinkin'?" he asks.

I meet his eyes in the mirror. "I'll be glad to get this paperwork done."

"Aye." He slips his arms around me. "I'll go change the girls. I wanted to check on you."

I lean up and kiss him. Liam's so thoughtful and supportive. He's grown so much. Fatherhood rewired him overnight but

I know he misses the road. He's ready. So is Linus. I'm the hold-up.

One day we'll find balance again. I believe it more today than I did a year ago.

Linus comes in next. "Marcella texted. She's ready whenever we arrive."

He meets my gaze in the mirror. A flicker of nerves. He maintains he doesn't care about ceremonies or paperwork or symbolic gestures, but he does. Ever since the fallout with his family, we're all he's got.

On the way to the firm, Quinn babbles in her seat and Sloane kicks her feet in happy silence. Marcella waits for us in the lobby like she can sense the chaos approaching.

Her smile is warm. Confident. "You five ready?"

I swallow. "Ready enough."

Marcella leads us into her conference room like she's done dozens of times before. Today, there's something quieter in her step. Not cautious. Intentional. She knows what this meeting means to us.

Our future is about to be formalized.

Skylar Morgan, seated at the head of the table, gives us a welcoming nod. "I've reviewed the drafts and we're in excellent shape." She sets stacks of documents in front of us. "Today is about clarity and next steps."

Liam, Linus, and I take our seats, leaving the girls in their car seats. The platinum Claddagh rings on our fingers glint under the overhead lights, proof of the choice we made back in Dublin. The day after Linus's family fractured, we went to a little shop off the River Liffey and bought symbols of our own making.

Love. Loyalty. Commitment.

"Everything's been incorporated," Skylar continues. "The shared ownership of your Seattle home, which you can mirror on for any other properties you buy. Your healthcare directives and power of attorney. The coparenting agreement, guardianship instructions, and the trust language surrounding your daughters."

Linus takes my hand. I squeeze gently.

Skylar scrolls through her notes. "Let's talk public-facing details. Your relationship is private. You don't owe anyone an explanation. At the same time, you're not anonymous. Fireball is known. Your audience is growing. Linus, as their manager, and Avonna and Liam, as rising artists in your own right, you'll need to agree how you want to be seen."

"You don't have to label yourselves." Marcella glances at us. "It'd be good to be on the same page about how public you'll be. Joint interviews? Social media? Tours? Awards shows?"

Liam leans forward. "We're not hidin'. We're not making any announcements."

I nod. "If people notice the rings, fine. If they ask, we'll handle it. We're not pitching a documentary."

"Good." Skylar smiles faintly. "Lead with boundaries, not defensiveness."

Linus clears his throat. "My bigger concern is band logistics. If things go sideways, like if someone uses our relationship to question Avonna's role in Fireball, or my role managin' them, I need protections in place."

"We've included conflict-of-interest language, non-retaliation clauses, and a contingency if Fireball ever wants to restructure leadership." Marcella is already ahead of him. "You're covered."

Liam's jaw sets. "Not gonna happen."

"I know," Linus says quietly. "If it does, we'll be ready."

Marcella folds her hands. "There's one last item to confirm."

I look up.

"Parenting," she says. "If anything happens to Avonna. Or to either of you."

I exhale. "We already decided. They're *our* daughters. Both of them. In every way."

"The paperwork reflects your wishes." Skylar nods. "Contractual paternity for both fathers. Cross-adoption finalized before their second birthday. No ambiguity."

Liam looks at me. Then at Linus. "They deserve to grow up never questionin' how loved they are."

"They will." Linus slides his hand across the table to take Liam's hands.

Skylar closes the folder. "Well, we're finished. The rest is signatures and notaries."

"Congratulations." Marcella looks at each of us in turn. "You've finished the tricky part. You've chosen each other. The rest is structure."

We convene in her office with our signed documents, a parenting plan, and a trust protecting everything we've built.

Sloane crawls toward Linus and lifts her arms for him with a quiet chirp. He picks her up, kisses her forehead, and she melts against his shoulder. Quinn tries to scale Liam's leg with wild determination before he scoops her up, laughing softly as she claws at his shirt.

Marcella watches all of us with a steady gaze. "You three have already built the love part. I envy you, Avonna."

I look at my daughters. One serene. One fierce.

One from each man I love.

Nature wrote our story before we even knew there would be a chapter like this.

Fifty-Four

One Year Later

THE REALTOR IS WAITING at the gate when we pull up.

Avonna clocks it first, narrowing her eyes at me from the passenger seat.

"This was supposed to be a drive." She places her hand on my thigh. "A *scenic* drive."

Liam snorts from the backseat. "He's way too quiet for it to be a scenic anythin'."

I say nothing and turn off the ignition.

Quinn kicks her heels against the car seat, humming tunelessly. Sloane's head lolls as she nibbles on string cheese, crumbs from the oat bar I gave her scattered in her lap.

"I mean," Avonna stares at the sleek black gate, "there's literally a woman in a blazer waving us in."

"Could be a coincidence," I offer.

Liam laughs under his breath. "You scheduled a tour of a house? Devious bastard."

"Aye." I shrug and open the door. "We're here, aren't we?"

Avonna unbuckles her seatbelt, scoops Quinn out of her car seat and kisses the top of her head. "If we're moving to LA, I swear to God, you're cooking every meal for a month."

"We'll DoorDash." I raise an eyebrow. "Unless you want to be poisoned."

"True," she replies, sweetly.

Liam climbs out with Sloane, who immediately starts wiggling toward the grass like her tiny sneakers have minds of their own.

The gate slides open and the realtor steps forward, all smiles. "Hi, Mr. O'Donnell. Welcome. You must be Avonna and Liam. So glad to meet you."

Avonna gives me a look over Quinn's shoulder. "So this *was* scheduled."

"You caught me." I hold up my hands.

The property rises behind her. A terraced, sun-soaked mid-century with glass walls and a wide wraparound deck. Olive trees flank the sides. There's a peek of a pool behind a safety fence. And below, in the distance, the city sprawls like a painting.

"This is 3132 Oriole." The realtor guides us toward the house. "Completely remodeled last year. Five beds, four baths, recording studio space, nanny quarters with a separate entrance. Fully gated, quiet street."

Avonna walks beside me, Quinn perched on her hip. "Not very subtle."

"I wasn't aimin' for subtle." I wrap my arm around her. "I was aimin' for home."

Inside, the open layout is filled with warm wood and natural light. Utterly gorgeous, even more so in real life than the website pictures. I feel calm the second we step in. The kitchen is cozy but modern, already stocked with toddler-proof drawers and a breakfast nook perfect for finger paints and plastic bowls of yogurt.

Liam trails behind, Sloane balanced across his shoulder, her face sticky with fruit leather. He stops at the sliding doors leading to the deck. "Jesus. The yard's massive."

There's a play area already set up. Mulch. A small slide. Room to run.

Quinn points. "Mine."

"Yours, huh?" Liam grins, setting Sloane down so she can toddle after her sister. "A bold stance for a two-year-old."

Avonna drifts toward the open living room, soaking it all in. She runs her hand along a sun-warmed beam and closes her eyes.

"I want to say I'm surprised," she comments without turning. "I'm not. You've been talking around this for months."

"We need a base in LA." I don't contradict her. "You both know it."

Liam leans against the frame of the doorway. "We have one in Seattle, all bought and paid for."

"A townhouse we've outgrown," I counter. "We've been on tour more than not for the past several months. The opportunity for Fireball is here in LA. The producers of *The Kerry Line* want you to be part of the PR push for the show. *From the Ashes* as the official theme for what might be the most anticipated Netflix release in years isn't something we can miss."

I let it hang.

"Fireball is chartin' across platforms we've never touched. There are interviews lined up. Endorsement deals for Avonna, you and Padraig are already rollin' in. We're going to be recordin' at Ty's in a few months. Do you really want to drag the girls back and forth every week?"

Liam stares out toward the yard. Doesn't answer.

"The Kerry Line is going to change everything," I add. "You saw the numbers. *From the Ashes* is still climbin'. It's Fireball's biggest hit by a mile."

"I know." He glances back at me.

"This place, or one like it if you don't like this one," I gesture around us, "allows us say yes to what's next without blowin' up the girls' routine once they're in school."

"We've already hired Shannon for the tour." Avonna refers to the middle-aged nanny we hired a couple months ago. "She's based in LA too. Ready to go full-time if we move. This is a perfect setup. Detached living space, pool, office for Linus, studio out back. It works beautifully."

Liam scrubs his scruff. "My parents are gonna be sad."

"You're not cuttin' them off," I say, steady. "You've come a long way these last two years. Rebuilt the relationship. They're not going anywhere."

Liam watches Sloane toddle toward him, her chubby fists punching the air. "I know. It's not them I'm worried about."

I wait. Let him get there.

"It's Padraig." He snatches Sloane up. "He's impossible to read lately."

"He's definitely been quieter." I pluck Quinn and settle her against my shoulder.

"When he's tryin' to convince himself something's a good idea, he deflects important conversations." Liam pauses. "Mara, for instance. I get she's excited about being pregnant. She's also romanticizin' bein' on the road with us."

"She still wants to come on tour?" Avonna raises her eyebrows.

Liam huffs out a breath. "She essentially declared as much to Padraig. Apparently, she wants to 'nest backstage' and write about it for some lifestyle site. She already ordered a custom tour jacket. Black satin. Gold thread. 'Road Wife' embroidered across the back."

I bark a laugh. "Please tell me it has rhinestones."

"On the collar." He shakes his head grimly. "And shoulder studs. She showed me a picture the other day."

I choke back bile. "I threw up in my mouth a little."

Avonna snorts from a few feet away. "Please keep her away from our wardrobe trailer."

"It's not about the jacket. Or the baby." Liam's smile fades. "I think he's goin' through the motions."

"Shit." I smooth Quinn's hair as she sleepily nestles into the crook of my neck.

He shrugs. "Well, if he's anythin' like I was, he's scared he's not ready."

"Or…"

Liam laughs nervously as the three of us move outside to the play area. "I'm more scared he's realizin' he'd rather quit the band. We've taken so much time off already."

"I know how he feels." I set Quinn down and Sloane follows her to the swing set. Sloane falls in the mulch and Quinn sits beside her like it's a performance piece. "I've missed so much of their day-to-day lives. Somethin' needs to change."

He meets my eyes. "So let's buy this place so you can stop missin' it."

Avonna slides her hand into mine, fingers squeeze. "I love this house. It can be home base for all of us. Then you'll be closer to your brother. I think you need some time to reconnect."

Liam looks between us, then at the girls.

"They're almost two." He bites his lip. "How the fuck?"

"We blinked." I kiss Avonna's temple.

A silence settles amongst us. Not heavy. Full.

"You think this place can hold all of it?" Liam asks.

"It think it already does." Avonna takes his hand.

He nods once. Then again.

Liam takes her hand and pulls me in with his other arm. "Let's do it."

"I'll go find the realtor." I head for the back door.

"Ask if a waffle maker's included," Liam calls after me.

From the sawdust, Sloane yells, "*WAFFLE!*"

We all laugh.

For the first time in a long time, we're setting down roots.

Maybe the building phase is over.

We're already here.

Fifty-Five

LIAM

Two Months Later

AVONNA IS THE MOST magnetic person in the room.

She stands near the edge of the private dining space, laughing softly with someone from Atlantic, a glass of sparkling water cupped in both hands. The emerald satin dress clings to her hips and thighs, skimming the curve of her belly, celebrating the softness she hasn't rushed to lose. Her hair falls loose over one shoulder, glossy and wild.

She looks powerful. Grounded. Alive.

I'm in a black suit I've owned for a decade, tailored enough to feel intentional. No tie. Open collar. The kind of clean I save for nights like this. Padraig lounges next to me, sipping club soda, hair tied back, boots scuffed to hell. His black jacket's a little more rock than red carpet, but he wears it like armor.

The Isis Management Grammys pre-party is in full swing. Linus never does anything halfway, but there's something especially intentional about tonight. No blown-up logos, no bloated guest list. Seventy-five people packed into the private dining room at Fleming's downtown. The carpet is low-lit, the wine is flowing, servers circulate with trays of steak and salmon, and the conversation crackles with names I recognize from playlists on Spotify.

No one's performing. No one's pitching. It's the biggest award show in music. Tonight is about presence.

Fireball hasn't toured in two years. Tonight is Linus's way of saying we're back without saying a word.

He's gorgeous, across the room in a dark suit, crisp and sharp, working the crowd. The LTZ guys are posted near the back, talking to a few nominees. Connor catches my eye and tips his glass. I nod. We haven't had time to catch up in ages.

My focus has been on Avonna. On the girls. On getting through the sleepless nights and early mornings and fragile hours in between.

Padraig's girlfriend Mara sits down next to him. She's a pretty girl. Wearing some shimmery bronze number.

A server passes with a tray of drinks and she politely declines the offer stating, loud enough for everyone to hear, "I can't. We're pregnant."

Padraig smirks and shrugs like it's no big deal. "Figured we'd make the announcement while everyone's dressed up."

"Congratulations." Avonna joins us.

Mara beams. "Thanks. We haven't told many people. We wanted to wait."

I nod tensely. "Right."

"I'm going to go out on tour with you guys." Mara claps. "I'm so excited."

There it is. My pulse thuds.

Avonna shifts closer to me. "Wow, a whole tour?"

"Yeah. We've talked about it a lot. Mara wants to see the whole thing. Experience it." He looks at me pointedly. "I figure if your family's all gonna be there, so should mine."

I feel the thrum of pressure under my ribs. Avonna and I stepped back for a while. We needed to. Babies. Healing. Everything. But Fireball's ready. I'm ready. Goddammit. Padraig.

You had to knock her up now?

Padraig grins at me, like he knows what I'm thinking. "Don't worry. I've got earplugs. I never want to walk in on the three of you fuckin' again."

"Seriously?" Mara frowns slightly.

Padraig winks at her. "It's a runnin' joke now. I survived."

This is the first I've heard of it being a joke.

"I'm happy for you," I manage. It's not a lie. It's not the truth, either.

He shrugs. "Wasn't planned. But I'm not mad. We'll figure it out."

"Besides." Mara smiles wider. "We'd love to meet the twins."

My face freezes. "You've had over a year."

Padraig tenses but says nothing.

Avonna touches my arm. Light. Reassuring. I hate I need it. Hate the distance between me and my twin.

We don't say more. We don't need to. We've had too many years of this. Building the dream, letting it fall apart, chasing it again. This time, it was supposed to be different. Clean. Rebuilt from scratch. Avonna's the future. The music is coming fast and deep, like something we can't outrun.

We were supposed to finally be Fireball again. Another day. Another road bump.

Avonna drapes her shawl across her shoulders and gives us a look. "It's time."

"We should go." Linus appears beside us, checking his phone. "The cart's outside. They're expectin' you on the carpet in ten."

He meets Avonna's eyes, then mine. His expression is smooth, unreadable.

Mara takes Padraig's arm. Linus offers her a polite smile. "Come with me. Let Fireball have their moment."

She hesitates. Doesn't make a scene but you can't help but notice the flicker of irritation.

Not my problem.

Avonna steps between me and Padraig, looping one arm through mine and the other through my brother's with a smile that doesn't quite meet her eyes.

Linus nods toward the exit. "Let's do this."

The golf cart waits at the curb. Bright lights pulse beyond the barricade. Flashbulbs. Voices. Media lines.

Fireball's first public step forward.

We haven't released the album yet. We haven't even booked the full tour.

Tonight, we show up.

Avonna. Padraig. Me.

The future might still be tangled, but the spotlight is ours. And it's time.

Her heels hit the floor with a soft thud.

Avonna's dress is halfway unzipped, her hair wild. The scent of perfume lingers on her skin. She's spent from the party. Hours of smiling. Attention she still doesn't quite love.

I close the door behind us, lean back against it. My chest is tight. Not in a panicked way. In the way it gets when I'm too full of something I don't know how to name.

Gratitude. Desire. Awe.

Linus sets a bottle of water on the nightstand. He's already undone his tie, sleeves rolled up. His eyes find mine across the room. Then slide to her.

"Look at you." He rakes his eyes over her body.

She turns, the green satin hugging every curve, a slit revealing the soft swell of her thigh. No shapewear. No pretense. Only her. Real, lush, glowing.

My mouth goes dry.

"We haven't been alone in months." She looks around in wonder. "Really alone."

I cross the room and kiss her before I answer. Her lips are warm, her breath sweet. When I pull away, her eyes are glassy.

"I miss the girls, but this is nice." I stroke her cheek.

She nods. "It is. Thank God for your parents looking after them."

Linus steps behind her, slides his fingers beneath the dress. Peels it down like he's unwrapping something sacred. When it pools at her feet, she stands there in nothing but the necklace we gave her when the girls were born.

"You're the most beautiful thing I've ever seen," he says.

Her chest rises.

Linus kisses her shoulder. I kneel in front of her, kiss the inside of her thigh. She threads one hand through my hair, the other reaches blindly for Liam.

The bed behind us is already turned down. She crawls onto it without a word, sprawled across the sheets.

Linus undresses, eyes never leaving her. I follow.

We take our time.

My lips trace the faint stretch marks along her hips. Linus kisses the curve of her breast, then her throat. Her hands reach for both of us, pulling us in.

"Let me taste you," I whisper.

She opens her legs for me. I lower my mouth to her while Linus strokes her nipples until she cries out. Her body rises to meet me. She's soaked. Sweet. Ready.

"I need to be filled," she breathes. "Please. Both of you."

Linus meets my eyes. There's no hesitation.

He spreads her open to watch me slide inside her. She moans, wraps her arms around my neck. Linus moves behind her, strokes her spine as he lines up his cock with her ass.

"Tell me you want this," he says.

"I *need* it."

Her body accepts him and we begin to move in rhythm. One after the other. Her name in both our mouths. She shatters between us. Her nails rake my back. Her cries echo in my throat. We keep at it, until I can't hold back. I grip her hips and spill. Linus follows with a growl, pulsing inside her as he kisses the back of her neck.

When we're done, we collapse on either side of her. She's boneless. Glowing. Her thighs still sticky with all we gave her.

No one speaks for a while.

She turns her face into the pillow.

"I love you both so much," she says sleepily.

We say it back.

Later, when she's asleep, I think about how far we've come. What it took to get here.

Two babies sleeping in Seattle. A band finally ready to rise again.

Tonight, the three of us together where we belong.

I close my eyes.

Wherever they are, I am home.

Fifty-Six

Eleven Months Later

FIVE MONTHS INTO THE move, the house finally feels lived-in.

Sunlight streaks through the kitchen in the mornings.

Sloane and Quinn chase each other barefoot across the tile. Our shoes pile near the door. Linus's favorite coffee mug lives on the windowsill.

We're finally in our forever home.

Only, we haven't been here much.

For the past ten days, we've been buried in the studio with Ty and Connor, chasing the same lightning we caught on the last album three years ago.

Tyson Rainier is one of the most-sought-after producers in the business now, but he's back with us, hoping to help us strike gold again. Our previous collaboration sparked

Fireball's last resurgence, right before everything paused when I got pregnant.

Then, unexpectedly, *From the Ashes* exploded as the theme for Netflix's hit show, *The Kerry Line,* and our appearance at the Grammys turned heads. Linus's solid guidance has the industry paying attention again. People want to believe in us. We all know this is probably our last shot.

The pressure is high.

This record has to hit.

Most nights, we crawl into bed still in our clothes, too wiped to do more than grab a couple of hours of sleep. No kissing. No cuddling. No sex. There's nothing left to give each other at the end of the day. Liam and I are pouring it all into the music.

Linus is holding us together with paperclips and strings.

Maureen flew down to help the nanny while we work. I thank her every day, even when the guilt gnaws at my ribs. We leave before the twins wake. Come home long after they've gone down. We're able to keep this pace because we only have a few more days before Ty times out.

The clock's ticking. We have to finish what we started.

The record is good. Better than good. It's wild, sharp, and tender. Guts and glass. It sounds like all of us, pulling in different directions, trying to make something real.

It should feel like a miracle, but there's something out of reach.

Liam's unraveling. He won't say it, but I see it in the small things. The way he won't meet my gaze when he misses a harmony. The way he lingers in the booth after a bad take, as if the silence will punish him more brutally than anyone else. The way his body flinches when Padraig barks a correction from the control booth.

Linus sees it too. He doesn't push. He stays steady, as always. He's able to calm Liam when he needs it most. During breaks, he checks in. Re-centers us. Keeps the center from cracking.

We're an unbreakable unit. Linus, Liam, and me. Onstage and off. The rhythm is instinct now. The way we move. The way we reach for one another when things fray.

Unfortunately, Padraig's the fray.

The dynamic has shifted from the twins being the inner circle of Fireball. Since day one of this recording session, Padraig's cut through every moment with sharp edges. Loud. Moody. Unpredictable. He slams doors. Rewrites fills mid-song. Pulls apart arrangements he loved the day before.

"I don't know where I fit anymore," Padraig confessed last night, pushing his takeout container aside as if he'd lost his appetite for more than food. We were crowded around the table with Connor, Ty, and his wife Zoey, the conversation drifting between logistics and half-made plans. "You three talk about your family and I'm standing on the outside tryin' to figure out where my life went sideways."

The room went quiet.

Not awkward.

Heavy.

Liam stared at his hands like he was counting old scars.

Padraig kept going, voice uneven now. "You've got this...unit. A direction. A house. I'm stuck living a life I don't know if I want."

No one interrupted him.

His personal life is in tatters. Padraig isn't cruel. He's drowning.

Instead of asking for help, he keeps circling a wound Liam has always worried about. His anger and hurt when Liam kept his life secret. The moment he realized the three of us were a unit he wasn't part of.

Liam absorbs it all like penance. He continues to believe he owes his brother every inch of himself. Every compromise.

Every silence. He thinks holding the band together means letting Padraig take pieces out of him without protest.

He's wrong.

Every time Padraig pushes, Liam retreats further inside himself. Shrinks. Carries the weight alone. Linus and I see it happening in real time, the fault lines spreading between the twins like cracks in a foundation.

If we don't find a way to bring Padraig back into the fold, the band won't survive.

The brothers might not either.

I glance over to where Padraig's adjusting something on the kit he's already tuned twice.

"Hey." I walk over and touch his shoulder. "How are you holding up?"

He tightens the hi-hat like it's a ticking bomb. "No sleep."

"Is Mara okay?"

He sighs heavily. "Hard to know. She's always restin'."

"I was thinking." I crouch down. "I'm happy to keep her company one of these days. Maybe give you and Liam time to spend together."

Padraig finally looks at me. "Her mum's there. She's got it covered."

"I know." I tilt my head. "I just thought…"

"I'm fine," he cuts in. "There's no need to try and patch things up with me and my brother. It'll work itself out at some point."

I wait a beat. "You're carrying a lot."

"Well, Avonna." He exhales through his nose, short and sharp. "We all are."

"True."

He swallows. "Let's get through this fucking session so I can get home."

Padraig grabs his sticks and heads into the control room. Liam waits in the booth, headphones on, eyes forward.

The track rolls. He belts it out. Gritty, raw, full of fire.

Silence.

Padraig taps on the mic, loud enough for everyone to hear. "Jesus, Dar. You're still rushin' the bridge."

Liam yanks off his headphones. "You fucking wanna sing it then?"

"Maybe I should."

"Okay, kids. Walk it off." Ty stands, already tired of this.

Liam's gone out the side exit before the echo of Ty's voice fades.

Padraig stays, polishing a cymbal with a smirk on his face.

Connor goes after Liam.

Linus crouches beside me. "They can't keep doin' this."

I lean into him. "He's unraveling."

"Aye. I see it."

"He thinks he has to fix everything." I glance out the door Liam departed from. "Padraig's resentment, this album, our future, us."

"He's scared." Linus kisses my temple. "Wants to prove his choices were worth it."

"They are."

"I know."

We sit in silence for a while. Connor and Liam return about ten minutes later. Liam heads into the booth, slides on his headphones, and closes his eyes.

Ty hits record.

What comes through the speakers isn't clean. It's guttural, aching, alive.

Liam doesn't perform the lyrics, he confesses them. Every note scraped from somewhere deep, where pain meets purpose.

Padraig doesn't move. His hand drops from his knee. His gaze stays locked on the glass.

Linus slides his fingers into mine.

When Liam finishes, the entire room is electrified.

Ty exhales. "We've got it. Perfection."

No one speaks. Even Padraig.
What lives between us is bruised, but breathing.
We're going to survive.

Fifty-Seven

LIAM

Five Months Later

CONNOR LOOKS EXHAUSTED WHEN his face appears on screen.

He's sitting on the couch at Padraig's townhouse in Seattle.

My twin moved back to our home town after we recorded the album.

It feels like the beginning of the end of Fireball.

My laptop's balanced on the edge of our home office, sunlight slants across the floor behind me. Connor looks older than he did a week ago. Padraig's not fully on screen. I hear his voice before I see him, saying something muffled to someone in the background.

He finally drops into the chair beside Connor. Doesn't look at me.

Linus, Avonna, and I have seen the news. Vague headlines. The "unforeseen circumstances." No one's saying what happened, which means it was bad. Linus has heard some things through the grapevine, but I've learned to believe nothing unless it comes straight from the source.

Connor wastes no time. "I can't get into the details, but LTZ is clearin' up our obligations through the rest of the year."

He looks between us. I can't believe what I'm hearing.

"I spoke to management this morning. They're going to offer Fireball every single one of our festival slots in Europe. All of them. Some of them at prime times."

My heart punches against my ribs. I lean back like it's Christmas morning. "Holy fuck. Those are the biggest stages—"

"I know," Padraig cuts in. His voice is calm, too calm. I know him well enough to hear the catch under it. Something's already wrong.

Connor studies him. "You've earned this. Don't waste the opportunity."

I nod automatically, already spinning out logistics in my mind. I cannot wait to tell Avonna and Linus. This is huge. Album rollout, media schedule, visas, promo. Could be our biggest break yet. The Netflix theme song gave us a second wind, the buzz on our new album is fire.

A tour would seal it.

Padraig's eyes are somewhere else. Not here. Not with us.

Connor and I dive into dates, rough routing, the crew we'd need to bring. I'm talking fast, fueled by adrenaline and possibility. We've waited years for this kind of break.

Padraig doesn't seem to be paying attention. Then he leans forward. "You're gonna have to find a fill-in drummer."

"What?" I freeze.

He doesn't flinch. "I can't do it. If you want Fireball to take the festivals, get someone else behind the kit. I'm not leavin' for three months."

The words hit me like a slap.

"You'd walk away? From everythin' we've been building?" My voice goes sharp. "We have a fuckin' *album* coming out."

"I'm sayin' figure it out without me." His tone rises. "I'm tired of puttin' my personal life last. Why should I?"

I shoot a look at Connor, begging him to jump in.

"Fine," I grind out. "Bring your family. We can make it work."

Connor nods. "It could. You'd have your own space on the bus."

Padraig shuts it down. "No."

I try to soften. Urgency still bleeding through. "We need you, Padraig."

He shakes his head. "You don't. Not for this. The three of you've got your groove. A fill-in could handle the festivals."

Anger flares. "Fuck this." I direct my attention to Connor. "Talk some sense into our brother before he walks away from the biggest tour we've ever been offered. A chance to make stupid money for a change."

I slam the laptop shut. If I don't, I'm going to say something I can't take back. Afterward, I can't stop pacing. My brother's voice still rings in my ears. *You're gonna have to find a fill-in drummer. I can't do it.*

I tried to keep my cool. Offered solutions. Compromises. But he shut it all down. Flat. Like none of it mattered.

Fuck.

I toss the laptop on the couch and run a hand through my hair. The sun's dipping low behind the hills, painting the edges of our backyard in rose-gold light. Still, I can't find peace. Not with this weight in my chest. Stepping onto the balcony of our LA house, I watch the skyline blur beneath me. For once, the house is quiet. Linus and Avonna took the girls to the park.

I grip the railing and breathe.

This was supposed to be the chapter where we all rise. Everything was finally lining up. The album is strong. The label's backing us. We're finally making real money. Enough to have help. Enough to tour smart.

Now Padraig wants to walk.

I should have known. There's a new light in him I haven't seen in years. I wonder if he'll tell me someday. Wouldn't blame him if he didn't, after my own failures.

I can't believe how far apart we are. I miss him.

I stare out at the sunset, a thousand versions of a future spinning through my mind. Every one of them missing the one person I thought would be beside me until the end.

I'm not angry. I'm sad.

There's no Fireball without him and I'm not ready for it to end.

The front door clicks open, and I hear the thud of small shoes on hardwood.

"Da-da!" Quinn barrels around the corner, curls wild from the car seat. I scoop her up as Sloane rushes in after her.

Linus follows, carrying their bags and looking exhausted but happy. "We're home."

"They were angels. Mostly." Avonna kisses my cheek.

We settle into our evening rhythm. Linus reheats the pasta from the night before. I cut strawberries for dessert. Avonna pours water into their little unicorn cups. It's chaos. Squeals, spilled sauce, bouncing feet. I love every minute.

While the girls devour their dinner, I recount the call. Every word.

"He said no?" Linus frowns.

"For now." I lift my gaze. "I don't think he will forever."

Avonna's already nodding. "He's scared. Maybe he needs to see what's possible."

"We could fly up for a McGloughlin dinner," Linus suggests. "Bring the girls. Make it a weekend."

"Show him what the tour could look like if he's ready. Not a pitch. Just...a window," Avonna adds.

"I want him back," I admit. "I miss him."

Avonna reaches for my hand. "Then we go."

Later, after baths and bedtime stories, the girls are finally down. Sloane's foot dangles over the side of the toddler bed. Quinn's already kicked her blanket off. I pull it up gently, smoothing curls from her cheek before slipping out.

Our bedroom glows in the soft light of the moon filtering through gauzy curtains. The windows are cracked open, letting in a whisper of wind. The custom bed, California King dimensions, specially built extra wide, is a cloud of linen and pillows.

Linus is already half-sprawled across the center, shirt off, in his boxer briefs. Avonna's in nothing but one of my old tees, the hem riding up her thighs, exposing her perfect pink pussy.

I hover at the edge, watching the two of them. My anchors, my chaos, my home. Tonight, I want everything.

"I need you both." I strip off my clothes as I step closer.

Avonna's breath catches, eyes going molten. Linus rises to his knees, divesting his briefs with calm precision. His cock bounces against his belly, the visual makes my own twitch with anticipation.

After pulling off her shirt, Avonna plucks her nipple with one hand and spreads her legs. Beckons me. I practically dive on top of her. Her hand slips between us to grip my cock.

Linus moves behind me, lips brushing my shoulder. "You ready?"

"Always," I whisper, voice already breaking.

Avonna guides me into her, groaning as her heat wraps around me. Linus breaches my ass with his fingers coated with lube. I rock forward into Avonna as he begins to open me, his mouth at my neck, his voice in my ear. "Let us spoil you."

"Yes," I breathe. "Do it."

We fuck with reverence. With need. Knowing whatever waits beyond this room, we'll face it together.

Avonna's breath hitches as she calls my name. Linus buries himself deeper, growling low against my neck. We break together, all nerves and want and devotion.

When it's over, we stay where we are. Skin to skin. Breathing in sync.

Outside, the world demands more than it ever gives back.

The band. The spotlight. The weight of everything we can't control.

Here, there's no audience. No agenda.

Only us.

The quiet, burning certainty we'll always have each other.

Three Days Later

MAUREEN GREETS US WITH the kind of warm authority only a mother of six can summon.

Apron on, she opens the door like we've been expected for hours.

Even if dinner's still finishing and the house is packed with family.

Sloane and Quinn hesitate at the threshold, wide-eyed. At nearly three, they don't remember much from when we lived in Seattle, and the sheer size of the McGloughlin clan takes a moment to absorb.

Liam steps in behind me, easing the door closed with one hand while his other settles at my waist. It's grounding, familiar. Avonna lingers a beat on the porch, taking it all in.

Her hair catches the sunlight, sunglasses perched casually on her head.

She doesn't flinch at the noise, the motion, the overlapping voices. She's steady. Comfortable in herself. The woman we married is fully present in this life the five of us built. Her softness, her power.

All worn without apology.

Inside, the house brims with noise and heat. Cillian emerges from the living room and greets Liam with a clap on the back before crouching to offer Quinn and Sloane each a high five. Connor's already in the kitchen setting out a tray of soda bread. Ronni follows with one of their twins on her hip, laughing at something Brennan says as he slips past with a stack of plates. Rory's deep in conversation with Seamus.

Sloane darts in first, Quinn on her heels. They pause like they always do, reading the room before charging ahead. Cillian waves them toward the living room, where a pile of toys waits near the fireplace.

Connor's twins are tucked into a playpen, wide-eyed and sticky-fingered, making garbled sounds at each other as Connor's wife, Ronni shakes a jingle giraffe above their heads. Next to them, Rafferty bounces on Padraig's lap, chubby fists gripping his dad's hoodie while Mara sits quietly beside him.

Liam freezes beside me. Then he swears under his breath.

"Oh *shit*." His eyes widen.

I follow his line of sight. Stevie Hayes stands near the back of the room, half-turned toward her sister, Joni. She has longer hair. Sharper edges. Same presence.

Avonna looks between us, confused but calm. "What?"

"Whoa." Liam doesn't take his eyes off her. "Stevie."

"Wait, *the* Stevie?" Avonna looks over.

"The one." I glance at Linus.

Liam exhales, disbelieving. "Wow. Not on my bingo card today."

"Oh," he says. "Fuck."

Avonna's brow furrows. "What now?"

"Our mom's are best friends, I didn't realize she would be here today" He rubs the back of his neck.

The room feels smaller suddenly. Louder. The familiar chaos cushions the edges.

Liam huffs a short, stunned laugh. "Jesus. Padraig didn't mention any of this?"

"Padraig doesn't mention anything lately until it's already happenin'," I remind him.

Avonna doesn't speak. She's watching closely, reading the moment instead of reacting to it. She doesn't know Stevie. Only knows the history through what Liam and I have told her about.

Liam straightens when Stevie finally turns to see the three of us. Her face changes instantly. Surprise. Recognition. Something softer underneath.

She crosses to us. "Linus, God. It's been a long time."

"Too long." I offer my hand, and she pulls me into a hug instead. Her scent is all memory. Summer nights and wafts of lilac.

She turns to Liam, who's unreadable. "Hi, old friend."

"Hey, Stevie." He rakes a hand through his hair. "This is Avonna Parilla. Avonna, Stevie Hayes."

Avonna's smile is immediate. "Nice to meet you. I've heard..." she glances at me, then Liam, "so much about you."

Stevie grins. "Same here. Sounds like you've got your hands full with these two."

"Wouldn't have it any other way." Avonna chuckles.

They exchange a short hug. Brief, natural. When they step back, there's an unspoken understanding between them.

Padraig motions for Stevie to join him from across the room. The minute she's out of earshot, Liam mutters, "Deja fucking vu. No wonder he was bein' a little bitch about going on tour."

"Do you think they're together?" Avonna stares after them, eyebrows raised.

I glance between them both. "Dunno. You saw it, right? The way he looked at her?"

"Aye," Liam scoffs. "The man dragged me for being secretive. Meanwhile he's probably fuckin' his ex and keepin' it on the down low?"

I lean against the wall, still processing. "He probably thought we'd all flip."

"I'm not flippin'." Avonna smooths her hand over Liam's back. "I think it's kind of sweet."

Liam gives her a look. "Sweet? It's going to make this tour even more of a circus."

"Everything with this band is a circus," I remind him.

Dinner is loud. Comforting. A flurry of half-eaten rolls, toddlers begging for dessert, and familial chaos. Evenings at the McGloughlins are often bittersweet for me because of the situation with my own family. I miss them.

Next to me, Liam leans into Avonna's side, stealing a bite of mashed potatoes from her plate. Across from us, Padraig pretends to follow the conversation Seamus and Connor are having about the upcoming football season. Cillian's telling Brennan some long-winded story, half-yelled over the kids all making dramatic sound effects and giggling like lunatics.

I can't keep track of it all. Don't need to.

When Maureen stands and grabs a bunch of dishes, Avonna nudges me under the table.

"Go help," she mouths, nodding toward the kitchen where Maureen's already disappeared.

I kiss her temple and rise.

"Aye. I'll do the dishes." I grab what I can from our end of the table.

When I nudge the door open to the kitchen, Maureen looks up at me with a knowing smile.

"Thought you might offer." She nods her head toward the dish towel. "Come on, then."

The kitchen is warm with steam and the low hiss of water running into the basin. I set the bowls beside her and start scraping plates while she rinses and stacks.

For a while, we move in rhythm, her washing, me drying. The window overlooking the back yard fogs slightly from the heat.

After a few minutes, Maureen speaks. "Any change with your parents?"

I keep my eyes on the plate in my hands. "No."

"They haven't asked about the girls?"

"No." I pause. "They haven't asked about any of us."

She nods and passes me another plate. "Ah."

I dry in silence. She and I have never had this conversation before.

"The last time we saw them, Avonna was pregnant." I turn to her. "Now, we send letters. Photos. So they know our girls are healthy and loved. Keep things positive."

She lets out a soft sound, not pity or disapproval. More like presence.

"Instead of a response, Mum sent a clipping from some Catholic newspaper. Highlighted the bit about eternal damnation." I shake my head. "Said she'd failed me."

Maureen's hands still in the water, then she dries them, sets the towel aside, and turns to face me.

"You're a good man, Linus. A beautiful father. A loyal partner."

"They don't see it."

She doesn't flinch. "They never looked."

I grip the edge of the sink, steadying myself.

"They're missin' everything." Maureen shakes her head.

I nod once, I can't speak.

"We didn't raise you," she peers over at me, "but you're ours now. You, Avonna, Liam, the girls. We love you all."

My eyes sting. I mop the towel on my face. "Thanks, Ma."

"You don't have to pretend here." She squeezes my arm.

I nod again. Unable to react.

"I know it's not the same," she continues. "I know a part of you still wants their approval. Remember, you've built something stronger than they ever dreamed."

I think of the rings we wear. The quiet promise we made to raise our daughters in a home filled with truth. "We have."

"You're doin' it." She pats my hand. "Now. Help me with the puddin'."

I manage a smile. "Aye. Anything for your trifle."

She rolls her eyes, but the softness in her face makes me melt.

Whatever they called my relationship. Sin, shame, wrong, I call it family.

No matter what we've lost, we have each other.

This loud, complicated, stunning mess.

Fifty-Nine

LINUS

Two Months Later

SEVENTY THOUSAND BODIES ARE jammed together in an open field.

The roar of the crowd builds until it's a living thing.

The stage is electric as the intro crashes in. Liam's guitar wails to my left. I prowl to the front edge of the stage, hair whipping, My voice is sharp and clean, cutting through the chaos.

The cordless mic is warm in my hand. My lungs sting. My thighs burn. I give them *everything*.

Fireball's resurgence is unprecedented. Our album, *Wild Honey* exploded. Two singles at the top of the charts, a third one climbing. Viral on TikTok. Most played Spotify song this year.

We've been on the covers of *Rolling Stone, Variety.* Billboard named me the "future of feminist rock." NPR ran a headline: *The Voice That Doesn't Apologize. Vogue* called.

Vogue.

Right now the media seems to only focus on me. I don't love the attention. Fireball is the three of us.

Always us.

Padraig masterfully anchors the backline. Liam stalks the stage beside me, guitar slung low, lost in the music like it's the only language he speaks. Linus watches side stage, flanked by security, headset on, lips pressed tight like he's running a command center. I catch him mouthing the lyrics, eyes flicking between me and Liam.

He grounds me.

I'm not the first Fireball singer. I'll never replace the ones who came before me. I know what I bring, though. I'm the third side of the triangle and this moment is mine. We've played every rung of the ladder. Dingy clubs, borrowed gear, no soundcheck, no sleep.

We've earned this.

Every song folds into the next. The setlist is a blur, but my body remembers. I move effortlessly. The songs live in me now, deeper than muscle memory.

The stage rumbles under my boots, bass and kick drum shaking the risers. My heart beats in rhythm with the crowd, sweat sliding down my spine. When I launch into the first chorus of our final song, flags rise over the crowd. Pint cups lift.

Liam catches my eye, gives me a lopsided grin, sweat soaked and radiant. Behind me, Padraig hits the cymbals like he's trying to split the sky. In front of us, the field is a living thing. Arms raised. Voices rising. The shimmer of color and light. I never thought I'd feel this free. Never thought I'd step into something that felt so much like home.

The crowd knows every word to *Tír na nÓg*. When I hold the mic to the sky, they roar it so loud it rattles my spine. We hit the final note like it owes us something. I raise both arms. The roar doubles. The crowd chants our name.

Fireball. Fireball. Fireball.

We've never sounded better.

A crew member waves us toward the tunnel beneath the stage. I'm drenched, my eyeliner feels smudged, adrenaline still coursing. Liam hooks an arm around my shoulder as we move. "Flawless."

"Thanks, baby." I kiss his cheek and he's already off, fingers twitching like he's still playing.

Linus runs up behind me. "A lot of media today. Girls are fine. They're with the nanny in the hotel room."

I nod, the tension in my shoulders easing. Being on the road with our daughters is chaos, but I wouldn't have it any other way. They nap in soundproofed bunks on the bus. Eat lunch on yoga mats backstage with mini guitars in their hands. They think this is normal.

For now, I face the media tent. Sit in front of a branded backdrop with about fifty mikes in front of me to answer any question lobbed my way.

Reviews. Streaming numbers. The European leg selling out in record time. Filling in for LTZ. Upcoming US Tour. The new album pushing old albums to chart. I give them everything they want. A few smart quips. A few knowing smiles. Keep the momentum light, intentional. Polished.

Predictably, the questions shift.

"What's it like being a new kind of frontwoman in rock?" one woman asks. "You're a mother, you're a writer, you're headlining festivals across Europe. Some are calling you the feminist voice of the genre."

This one gets to me. "I'm flattered by the label, but I didn't ask for it. I try to speak from where I've been. There's power in the voice you reclaim for yourself."

They nod, eat it up.

Another voice cuts in. British. A bit snooty. "Speaking of reclaiming, you've alluded to your upbringing in other interviews. The restrictive religious environment. Purity culture. You escaped it, obviously."

"Avonna," he glances at his notebook like it's a legal document, "there are rumors circulating about your personal life. Specifically about your relationship with your guitarist and your manager. Are the rumors true?"

The tent goes still.

Liam and Padraig are in Press Line B, but Linus is at the edge of the tent watching me. His eyes flash, lock on the man. The rest of the media watches me.

No one so much as blinks.

"Would you care to comment?" he adds. "There are some who find it hypocritical. You left a high-control belief system only to enter a nontraditional polygamous arrangement, arguably mirroring the environment you fled. It raises questions, don't you think? About consent. Power. Influence."

The question lands like a slap. It's calculated.

Designed to go viral.

My entire body stiffens. This is the moment. One we've known was coming. We haven't exactly hidden our life, but we've never invited the world into it either. Not publicly. Not loudly.

Immediately, I picture my beautiful girls. Rumors spread faster than facts. If I don't handle this carefully, their lives become the headline.

I sit up straighter. The air in the tent stills.

"I don't comment on gossip." I keep my voice cool. "Especially when it's crafted to provoke more than enlighten."

The reporter opens his mouth like he's going to argue, but I cut him off with a look.

"My story isn't a cautionary tale. It's a reclamation. Everything I've built, I've chosen. I spent the first part of my life following rules made to control me. I will not spend the rest of it justifying the freedom I fought for."

I let this settle. Hang in the air.

Then, softer, but no less direct. "I'm raising daughters, so this is important. I didn't leave one cage to build another. No one in my life controls me. Every choice I make is mine."

Behind the cluster of cameras, I see Linus step forward. Not intervening. Present. Steady.

I draw a breath. Hold my line. "If that unsettles anyone, it's between them and their own reflection."

The tour publicist jumps in fast. "Okay, folks, That's all for today."

I'm already on my feet when the crowd of reporters shifts, questions still bubbling, My daughters are waiting. My partners, too.

Let the media write their stories.

We're living ours.

Linus's hand finds mine as we cut across the gravel path toward the performer village, heads ducked, energy spent. The crowd still roars somewhere past the barricades, another band taking the stage, but I'm already thinking about juice boxes and bedtime stories. Our girls are with our nanny, Shannon and Maureen, back at the hotel, probably begging for more bubble bath.

Linus squeezes my fingers. "Handled that well."

I raise a brow. "You mean the part where the reporter called me a brainwashed slut in different words?"

He doesn't flinch. "Still proud of you."

I give him a small smile and lean into his shoulder.

Our dressing room sits at the end of a cluster. Not a trailer this time, a proper suite with a table full of food listed on our rider, couches draped in soft throws, iced towels ready to go. Most of the bands have cleared out by now, so there's not a lot of activity, except for the getting-to-be-too-familiar raised voices.

Linus frowns. "Jesus, how do they still have eardrums?"

We laugh, the kind of bone-weary sound coming from too many days on the road. He holds the door open for me. Inside, Liam and Padraig stand toe to toe, the air around them practically crackling.

"You think this is what we worked for?" Padraig snaps. "So we could be the goddamn punchline at the end of some clickbait article?"

Liam fires back, "They asked you one fuckin' question. You didn't have to explode."

"Didn't I? You weren't the one who had to explain to some guy why our band's legacy might get reduced to a poly sex scandal!"

Linus steps in quickly. "What's goin' on?"

Both turn toward us. Padraig looks broken. Not from the set, we all are, from something heavier. Deeper.

Linus crosses to the fridge, pulls out a bottle of water, tosses it to Padraig. "If it's any consolation, Avonna got the same line of questionin'. You're not alone."

"For fuck's sake," Padraig scoffs. "Easy to say when you've got your family out here. Your girls." His eyes flit to mine, then Liam's. "I've got my own life. You think I want to see my face on TikTok next to some slow-mo footage of Liam lickin' your neck durin' the bridge?"

Liam's face clouds. "It happened once and was spontaneous. Don't make it sound like Linus, Avonna, and I are fuckin' under the goddamn lights."

"I'm not judgin' you." Padraig plops into a chair. "I'm angry at the way our story gets hijacked. We started this band in the literal basement. I hate how twenty years of blood and sweat can be overshadowed by one headline. We didn't build Fireball for our legacy to be reduced to this."

The silence hangs heavy.

"Me either." Linus folds his arms.

Padraig's eyes narrow. *"Don't. Make. Excuses."*

"I'm not." He holds his hand up in surrender. "Don't you twist this into somethin' it isn't."

Padraig exhales, shoulders slumping. "Fuck."

"We get it." I sit next to him. "The curiosity factor sucks."

Liam sinks into the couch across from us, dragging his hands through his hair. "No one's goin' to think we're a gimmick unless we act like one. We've been through hell and back. People love this record. The reviews are insane. Our work is payin' off and we've seen it with LTZ, when you have more money, more problems. More success, more trolls."

"Yeah." Padraig relaxes. "True."

"They keep calling it a rebirth." Linus snorts. "Which is ironic as hell."

All the fight leaves Padraig's body. He stands and heads toward the door. "I'm sick of bein' defensive. I've given so much to this band. Don't you ever wonder, what's the payoff? I'm exhausted and need to get back to the hotel. Text me what the plan is for tomorrow."

Then he's gone.

Across from me, Liam slumps over, elbows on his knees. Linus lowers himself beside me. We sit in gravity Padraig left behind.

"He's still spiralin'," Liam speaks after a while. Not with anger. With guilt. "I push him without thinkin'. We're grown men, for fuck's sake, and both of us still tryin' to take care of each other first."

"You're twins, babe. It isn't the wrong instinct," I try to soothe him. "You want to keep space for him, as you should."

Linus leans back and pulls me into his side. "We all know what this is about. Liam, we've been here before. He's behavin' exactly the same way as he did in college."

No one says her name. We don't have to. It's written in every line of Padraig's face when he speaks about her. Evident by how fast he retreats the moment she calls.

Liam buries his face in his hands, then looks back up. "I want him to be happy."

"Same as all of us." Linus strokes my shoulder.

I glance between them. "I understand the fight or flight. I'm guessin' he's trying to find any reason to quit so he can write a different endin'."

"Aye." Liam drags a hand through his hair. "We've made our fair share of messes."

"Sure, but we're still here." Linus squeezes his eyes shut.

There's a long pause. Not uncomfortable. Honest.

"Do you think he's gonna be okay?" I direct my question to Liam.

He nods. "Yeah. He's stronger than he gives himself credit for."

"Even when he pushes us away, we've got him," Linus adds. "I'll do my best to make sure we can accommodate him, whatever it takes."

We sit for a beat longer. The three of us, breathing in the quiet, surrounded by gear cases, discarded water bottles, and the echo of fifty thousand voices still reverberating outside.

"Come on." Liam rises. "Let's get back to our girls."

Linus stands and offers his hand, pulling me to my feet.

Whatever the world wants to say about our love, our band, our history.

We won't go through it alone.

Like always, we face it together.

Sixty

LIAM

Eighteen Months Later

Eighteen months later, the whirlwind hasn't stopped.
Fireball's worldwide now.

We were in South America in the spring. Europe again in the summer. Australia last winter. Released another album, cut in stolen weeks between tours, recorded half in LA, half wherever we could find a studio while on tour.

This record is our masterpiece. Not louder. Not shinier. Deeper. Critics call it the kind of music people play alone at night.

Padraig's still here. Pounding the kit. Grumbling. Showing up, which matters more than anything.

We learned a bit from Connor's mistakes. Shorter runs. Real breaks. Home when we can be home. LTZ burned itself to ash once. I won't let Fireball do the same.

At the same time, we're riding a high most bands never achieve. A second wind no one saw coming, including ourselves. We have Linus to thank. Fireball's legacy is no longer a footnote.

My family's been loud lately. Rory turned sixty. He's fully sober. Still trying. Ma's religious about her Sunday family dinners, we're all expected to attend if we're in town. Connor's a TV star now, starring in Ronni's new sitcom. Cillian's blowing up his own life in creative ways. Brennan's disappeared into code and investors. Seamus thinks he can save the world with a scalpel.

Everyone's moving. Everyone's struggling. No one gets out completely clean.

As for my own family, Linus, Avonna, the girls and I are at home in LA for a bit.

The sliding glass doors are open in the living room. Sun leaks across the floor, filtered through the olive trees, warming the wide-planked hardwood. Sloane and Quinn's toys are scattered around like breadcrumbs leading us back to real life.

It should feel peaceful, but the air is heavy.

Avonna hasn't gotten off the couch. She's curled beneath a blanket, one hand tucked under her cheek, the other resting on her belly. Our pregnancy was only nine weeks along, but we'd heard the heartbeat the day before. Talked about names. Laughed about whether Sloane and Quinn would be better as big sisters or stagehands.

Then, five days ago, she started bleeding.

A nurse stood stiff in the corner of the ER room while the doctor delivered the clinical term, Unviable spontaneous abortion, with the ease of someone who'd said it too many times.

Avonna went silent. Linus gripped her hand. I couldn't find my breath. She didn't react until we were released the next morning.

Today, she's in our living room, barely moving, except to accept the tea Linus keeps refilling, or to glance toward the girls when they come running in, unaware they're not going to be big sisters. We haven't told them anything. They're still too young.

Linus sits on the floor beside the couch, one arm propped on the cushion near her waist, gently tracing shapes on her hip through the knit of her leggings. His other hand holds a printout of the preliminary findings from the private investigator. He glances up at me when I join them, his eyes shadowed with the same grief I feel.

All of us wanted this baby. Unfortunately, Avonna's miscarriage isn't the only tragedy we're dealing with.

A few months ago we returned home from tour to find an unsigned letter taped to our security gate. Handwritten. Quoting Bible verses equating our family to sin. Warning Avonna to repent before she damned her children. Threatening her sisters.

Since then it's been relentless. They knew our schedule inside and out. Dozens of the same letters, scripted in a distinctive scroll, found their way to Avonna. Mailed to venues. Delivered via clueless production assistants. Left at hotels under fake names. One was slipped under her dressing room door. Another left in a bouquet at a meet and greet. A few days ago, a letter was mailed to the girls' preschool.

Each one increasingly menacing and scary.

Sliding behind her on the couch, I wrap my arms around her chest, knees bracketing her hips. I tug her back against me and pull the blanket up around us both. I kiss her head. "How are you feelin', my love?"

"Destroyed." She shakes her head. "I'm sad about the baby and keep thinking about the letters."

Yeah. Me too.

My stomach lurches when I remember what some of them said:

Every filthy act stains your soul. He sees them all.

Your body is a grave, not a cradle.

No child should be born into your sickness.

You will know loss until you return to the fold.

Hell does not forget. It prepares a room for you.

Avonna doesn't know about the barrage we received the day we lost the baby. Voice messages. A package sent to Linus's office. A delivery driver intercepted by our beefed-up security.

We know where you are. No matter how far you run, the righteous will find you.

Your sins have a scent. We are trained to track it.

You cannot hide from His justice. Or ours.

The reckoning begins soon. Prepare your daughters.

The last one chilled me to the bone.

I wanted to burn them all. Linus refused. He's doing everything possible to protect our family. We're locked down with even more security measures. Two more bodyguards have been hired to discreetly shadow each of our girls. There are new mail and technological protocols. He also hired the best investigator in the state, who worked fast.

Yesterday he traced all of it back to her old sect. Same phrases. Same scripture. Same bile dressed up as righteousness. Lawyers are circling. Authorities are involved. Hopefully arrests are imminent.

"You need anythin'?" I murmur into her hair.

She turns her head slightly, looking toward the window. The light catches the curve of her cheekbone, illuminating the dark circles under her eyes.

"Do you think it's my fault?" Her voice is barely a whisper.

I squeeze her instantly. "*No.*"

"Of course not." Linus leans up and caresses her cheek.

She swallows. "I keep remembering things. From when I was little. Warnings. About purity and punishment. About women who disobey."

"Baby, no. The world doesn't work that way. You've had years of therapy tellin' you otherwise," I remind her.

Avonna looks up at me, her eyes wet. "Of course I *know* it's not my fault. Now you see how I was raised. I'm terrified for my sisters, but there's not a thing I can do. It's horrific."

"Aye." Linus kisses her ankle. "You were raised to be quiet."

I lean closer. "But, you're not."

"You were taught to obey." He kisses the arch of her foot.

"You don't," I add. "You question. You lead."

She gives a small nod. Wipes her eyes with the back of her hand.

"I *know* it's bullshit," she whispers. "I have to fight the voice telling me this happened because I wanted too much."

I pull her closer. "No. Those fuckers are trying to take your joy. Your power. We aren't gonna let them."

"You scare them," Linus agrees. "You left. You're loved fiercely by both of us. They're pissed you didn't crawl back. They're trying to get under your skin with your sisters. Don't let them."

I kiss the top of her head. "They hate how the world embraces you. Our fans support us. We're authentically ourselves, and nobody can touch us."

She blinks, but is unable to stop the tears from falling. "I'm so *sad*."

"We are all are." Linus wells up. "We wanted our baby."

Her lips tremble. "I still do."

I rest my forehead against hers. "We're gonna be sad for a while. Meanwhile, nothing they say matters or has any influence on the outcome. You're not what they call you. You're a fucking beacon."

Linus slides his hand up her thigh to interlock with mine and hers. "You show women what's possible."

She breathes in, ragged. Squeezes our fingers together.

We hold her for a long time.

Avonna's told us before, over the years, what her childhood was like. The things they preached. How she was punished. It wasn't until reading those letters and seeing it laid bare Linus and I were able to finally understand the weight she walked away from.

It makes everything she is now much more extraordinary.

Our wife had the strength to escape. The will to rebuild. The audacity to want love on her own terms.

She didn't break.
She became.
We'll build the family we dream of.
No one will define what love looks like inside these walls.

Sixty-One

Eighteen Months Later

FIREBALL IS STILL BURNING brightly.

Though it's been years now, the headlines still say resurgence.

The awards say something stronger. Multiple Grammys. Songwriting accolades. Crowds we once dreamed of now showing up early and staying late, singing every word back to us.

The new record cuts deeper than anything we've ever made. Cleaner. Smoother. Honest. Music built for long drives. Sitting alone with your thoughts. Critics call it mature.

I call it earned.

We tour, but carefully. Short US runs. Select European festivals. The money is excellent, steady enough to make choices instead of sacrifices.

Padraig's still in, but on his own terms. Present, professional, no longer mentally bound to the band the way he once was. The band began as twin brothers and now is centered on Liam and Avonna, the creative gravity shifting without announcement.

Success creates space to ask challenging questions. Should Fireball continue in its current shape, defined by history and loyalty? Or will the next chapter belong to something new. Built from the ground up without dragging the past along.

No decisions yet.

Only awareness. Futures can change.

Liam carries it deeper than he ever lets on.

I see it after shows, when the stage goes dark and he lingers at the edge, staring as if something important might still be waiting there. Offers keep landing in his inbox. Fashion houses asking him to front campaigns. Luxury brands dangling endorsements. Stylists pitching covers and spreads. He's done a few. Smiles for the camera. Wears the clothes. Takes the check.

The spotlight isn't what he thought it would be.

He talks about the future now without mentioning songs or tours. His thoughts drift toward home. Toward the girls. Toward mornings instead of soundchecks. He wants to build something lasting, something quiet enough to breathe inside. The attention follows him everywhere, but it never fills the space music once did.

When Avonna and I reach for him, he holds us longer now, grounding himself in the weight of us, in the warmth of what we've built.

The three of us have grown into an impenetrable unit in ways I always hoped. Not only lovers. Parents. Protectors.

Sloane and Quinn move through our lives with a steadiness born from routine and vigilance. Shannon is a steady presence. A private tutor comes to the house now, guiding them through kindergarten and into first grade. Their safety is our first priority.

Always.

The threats directed at Avonna changed everything.

Federal agents speak in measured tones and long timelines. Rumors circle about the sect losing its grip. Investigations widening. Doors finally closing.

None of it moves fast enough to ease Avonna's fears, so we build walls where we can. Choose privacy. Control.

Avonna takes the weight with grace I still don't fully understand.

Her voice carries across worldwide stages in so many forms. Strong and unflinching, impossible to ignore.

NPR invites her back again and again, not for promotion, but conversation. Journalists clamor to interview her about art, motherhood, faith rebuilt on her own terms. *Vogue* photographed her barefoot in linen, a woman who refuses polish for permission. Late-night hosts stop joking when she answers, realizing she isn't there to charm. She's there to tell the truth.

Podcasts line up. Women-run panels. Creative collectives. She sits across from activists and other artists who recognize something familiar in her eyes. Survival. Clarity. Refusal. Her words travel faster than Fireball's songs now, shared in memes and reels and handwritten quotes taped to mirrors and notebooks.

Wherever Fireball plays, the crowds lean in. When she sings, it feels personal. Not performance. Confession. Communion. Women cry openly. Men stand still, stunned. The songs land somewhere deeper than sound, in places people forgot existed.

The world wants to name her. Icon. Survivor. Feminist anthem. Spiritual rebellion. They circle closer to the three of us, curious about the men she chose. Hungry to define what we are, to label the shape of our family and turn it into something digestible.

We don't indulge. Not to hide.

To live. Our lives belong to us.

Love. Family.

It hasn't been easy to get back here. The harassment from the sect nearly broke Avonna. Nearly broke all of us.

Scripture bent into weapons. Promises of punishment wrapped in prophecy. Fear followed her everywhere, into dressing rooms, onto planes, into bed at night. We lived on edge for months before the trail led back to her former sect.

Federal investigators stepped in. Procedures began. Interviews. Paperwork. Long silences between updates. Nothing moves quickly when institutions protect themselves.

The damage didn't wait.

Stress does things to a body. To a heart. To hope. We lost three pregnancies in the span of a year. Each loss carved something out of her. Out of us. She blamed herself, even when logic told her otherwise.

Liam and I watched helplessly when she'd flinch at sudden noises. Cringed at the way her hands shook when unfamiliar mail arrived. We talked about stopping. Protecting what we already have. Hunkering down with the family we've been lucky enough to build.

Then she'd sit at the piano again. Late. Quiet. Fingers trembling, voice cracking open, grief pouring into melody. She never said she wanted to keep trying. She didn't have to.

We knew.

She wasn't finished dreaming.

As for me, Isis Management is thriving. I salvaged the profitable parts of Niamh's father's firm after it collapsed and let the rest fall away. LTZ signed with us this year. It's been a strange kind of full circle.

With my stellar roster of managers, mostly I mentor careers instead of chasing mine. Every night I come home to Liam, Avonna, Sloane, and Quinn. When Fireball tours, so do I. Otherwise, I have staff to cover the rest.

One part of my life has never settled. My family back home. I've kept them looped in as best I could. It's a goddamn void. Photos sent into silence. Updates on the girls met with nothing. Invitations to Fireball shows in Europe go unanswered.

I've tried. Never stopped.

Now, everything's fractured.

My father died three days ago.

A massive coronary. Sudden. Final. I didn't hear it from Mum, a cousin called instead already assuming I knew.

I didn't.

Liam and Avonna immediately offered to come with me without hesitation, but I couldn't add to everything else going on. I already knew they weren't welcome. My mother made it clear years ago.

I'm on my own.

The plane cuts through cloud and drops low over the water. Dublin Bay comes into focus, slate and steel and familiar in a way my body recognizes before my mind does.

I missed the wake. By hours, not days, but it might as well have been a lifetime. Irish rituals happened without me. Stories shared. Pints raised. Doors closed.

Instead, I arrive for the service.

St. Patrick's is full but hushed, quiet built from obligation rather than grief. I slip into a back pew. My sisters sit together near the front, shoulders angled inward, a unit I'm no longer part of. My brother keeps his gaze fixed ahead, hands clasped as if prayer might excuse him from acknowledging me.

Mum wears black like armor. Veil pinned just so. Spine straight. She doesn't look back once. Probably would be shocked to see me here.

I walk forward when it's time. Kneel beside the coffin. The wood is smooth under my palm, polished to a shine my Da would've appreciated. I press my hand there anyway, grounding myself in the weight of him, of what's finished. I whisper goodbye under my breath. No one hears but me.

At the graveside, the wind cuts sharp. Soil thuds hollow as it hits the casket. I stand apart from the family cluster, close enough to be seen, far enough to be separate. A cousin nods. An aunt touches my arm briefly, then pulls away, as if contact might be contagious.

I wonder, standing there, if my da would've wanted me present. If pride would've outweighed disappointment. If his love for me could've survived the truth of who I am. Rather than reframing my sexual preferences as a choice.

There's no answer waiting, now or ever.

When it's over, people drift toward the gates in loose groups. I overhear someone mention lunch. A reservation at a local restaurant. My sisters and brother load into a car with Mum. No one looks in my direction or invites me.

Mum pauses before she gets in. Hands folded, gaze fixed somewhere past me. For a second, I think she might make eye contact.

She doesn't.

Afterward, I walk.

Past the hotel where I worked after college. Past the first cramped office where Isis Management existed in name only. Past the flat Avonna and I bought, where we seduced Liam and never looked back. Past clubs where my bands played to little pubs and restaurants that made up my life back then.

Each place holds a version of me I needed to experience. None of them fit anymore.

Dublin doesn't judge. It simply remembers.

By the time I turn back toward the hotel, my legs ache and my breath comes easier. Grief permeates my body, but it's no longer sharp. I did what I came to do. Showed up. Was present where it mattered.

I can live with the effort I made. When I leave, I won't carry regret with me.

Even if no one else wanted me there, I showed up anyway.

For him.

Two days later, I go back. My mother opens the door and steps aside. Not an invitation. Not a refusal. An obligation fulfilled.

The house feels smaller than I remember. Narrower. As if grief has closed all the walls in. We stand in the hall. Coats still on. Neither of us moves to sit.

"I wanted to say goodbye," I tell her. "To him."

She nods once. "So you did."

"And..." I hold up my hand, " to you."

"Well, then, there's nothin' more left to say." Her mouth presses thin. "You've chosen a path."

"I've chosen to be true to myself." I shake my head in frustration.

She turns then, and really looks at me. Not with anger. With something colder. Resolution.

"Linus. I can't accept your life," she states plain and final. "I won't pretend I can."

The words land heavy, clean. No cruelty in them. No softness either.

"I didn't come to ask you to pretend," I reply. "I came to tell you I'm happy."

"Happiness isn't always proof of being right." Her hands fold in front of her.

"I'm not askin' to be right."

Silence draws out between us, deep and unbridgeable.

"You're my son," she says at last. "But I've already mourned your loss."

Wow. There it is. The truth I came for.

"I won't ask you to change," she continues. "I won't change myself."

"I understand."

She steps aside and opens the door.

"Take care of yourself." She looks straight ahead. Not unkind. Not loving. A farewell.

I hesitate at the threshold, waiting for something else. Anything.

Nothing comes.

Outside, the air bites cold. I don't look back. In her world, the son she raised no longer exists.

In mine, I am alive. Loved. Building something real.

I walk away carrying both truths. Her God is unforgiving. My God allowed my beautiful Avonna to escape a sadistic religious cult. Placed her in the very room where Liam and I fell in love. Years later brought her here to Dublin to mend my broken heart and, as fate would have it, bring Liam back into my—our—lives.

I'll take my God every day of the week.

I know I'll never see my mother again. She's not my family.

In the car on my way to the airport, I text Liam.

Headed home.

He responds immediately.

We'll be here.

The plane lifts again. Los Angeles waits. My family waits.

Fireball still burns.

It may not be the closure I want, but at least I'm not split between who I was and who I am.

I know where I belong.

I'll be there soon.

Sixty-Two

Two Months Later

OUR HOUSE GOES QUIET at night up here in the Hollywood Hills.

Cool air slips through the bedroom window, stirring the curtains.

The soft whisper of cotton when I shift on the bed reminds me I'm here, present in my body, no longer braced for impact.

Four miscarriages. Each loss sending me into despair while under the constant fear of threat and vigilance. Then, a few days after Linus came home from Dublin, the news broke. Arrests. Mighty Prophet. Brother Gideon. My parents. The Elders. Names I hadn't spoken aloud in years finally spoken by someone else.

Something inside me loosened. For the first time in a long while, I felt safe enough to try again.

All three of us have been tested. No issues. Strong counts. Healthy eggs. There's nothing standing in the way now so we began tracking. Not with panic. With intention. Quiet check-ins, shared calendars, conversations of hope instead of pressure.

Tonight, the timing is right. The test strip on the bathroom counter confirmed it hours ago, two faint lines settling into certainty. I didn't rush to show them. I sat with it first, breathing, letting my body recognize readiness instead of fear.

Padraig says our last Fireball show is coming on New Year's Eve, a clean line between chapters. I believe him. This time, his threats to quit feels different. He wants a different life.

Linus, Liam, and I also want to move forward together with our girls with less tension and stress in our day-to-day lives.

I rest my hands over my stomach and let myself imagine a life joining ours, rounding out the family we've built with care and resilience. Whatever comes next, we'll meet it together, steady and open, ready for a new beginning

A new baby.

Already I know tonight's different. My body feels primed. Low in my belly, I'm ripe and electric.

Liam's mouth finds me first. Tongue sliding through the slippery heat between my thighs. His hands spread my legs wider, thumbs kneading gently into the creases where my hip meets pelvis.

Liam groans softly as he licks me. "You taste different."

"Let's make a baby, love." Linus shifts beside me.

The bed creaks under his weight. I feel his knees slide up beside mine, the warmth of his chest against my back. One hand curls around my breast, thumb flicking my nipple. The other slides between us, fingers dipping where Liam's mouth already works.

He finds my clit. Swirls his finger around it.

"Stay open." He kisses along my neck.

Liam French kisses my pussy with his tongue, lips sealed around my clit like he's drinking me. Linus pinches my nipple with one hand, fingers my clit with the other in tandem with Liam's tongue.

My thighs shake. My back arches. I try to breathe but there's no room left.

"Now," Linus says.

I come with my head thrown back, mouth wide, the sound torn from somewhere deeper than I know. Liam holds my hips down. Linus grips my chest like he's anchoring me to the bed. I chant their names in prayer, every nerve lit.

Liam kisses me. Linus joins. Their mouths are warm, and when they kiss each other across me, my entire body becomes pliant.

I reach for Liam's cock. It's thick in my palm, veins standing out on his shaft like it's straining to be inside me. Linus watches, propped up on one elbow, eyes shadowed with hunger. His legs are parted, cock flush against his belly. He shifts in a fluid, deliberate motion and rolls between Liam's thighs. Leans in, mouth open, and swallows Liam's cock to the root.

Liam chokes on a breath, hips wrenching up. One hand flies to Linus's hair, gripping, but not stopping him. Linus takes him deeper, I watch his lips sliding up and down Liam's shaft, cheeks hollowing. Sinful. His tongue flicks under the head with practiced precision, and Liam's body arches into it.

Then Liam slides down, flipping them easily, and suddenly his mouth is on Linus's cock. Both of them, naked and sprawled, mouths full of each other.

They know this is my favorite act. My private heaven. Their mouths full of each other right in front of me.

My body prepares like it knows what's coming. Arousal floods through me. My womb softens, opens. Purposefully.

Fertility. Fire.

I yearn to be filled by both of them in the wake of their devotion.

Liam pulls off first. "She's already tremblin'."

Linus smirks, lips still wet. "Tell us when you can't take it anymore, Avonna. Until then, we'll keep goin'."

"*Now*. Please. I want you both."

Liam leans back against the headboard, and I climb into his lap, straddling him in reverse. His cock is hard, hot, waiting. I lower onto him, gasping as he fills me perfectly, inch by inch, until I'm seated fully.

"*Mmmmmmm*." His hands slide up to my waist. "God, you feel so good. You're so fuckin' wet, baby."

I begin to move in leisurely, rolling circles. Every grind sending sparks through my spine. Liam's hands run up my stomach, find my breasts and tease my nipples between his fingers. He's not merely letting me ride him. He's preparing me.

He shifts, arms sliding under my knees, lifting my legs and spreading them wide and high so my hips tilt back. I recline against his chest, thighs open. On full display for Linus. I can barely speak. The pleasure's too sharp. Too deep.

"You're so fuckin' beautiful," he breathes against my ear. "Let him see how ready you are."

Linus's eyes lock on the way I'm spread around Liam's cock. "Let me in, love. I want to feel both of us inside you. I need it."

"Come here," I whisper.

He kneels between our spread legs, strokes himself once, then moves closer. Liam holds me steady as Linus guides the head of his cock above where Liam's buried, and I whimper. With one cant of his hips, Linus's cock slides easily into me too. My body opens. Full. Trembling.

I bask in the overwhelming rightness of being taken by them.

"Fuck," Linus moans. "You're soakin' us."

Their cocks frot together inside me, filling my pussy to its limit. I gasp, one hand flying to Linus's chest for balance.

"Oh my God—"

"You feel everythin', don't you?" Liam whispers into my neck, hips shifting. "So full. So fuckin' good."

"I love you," I breathe. "I love both of you. Don't stop."

They move together. Liam slides his hands to my hips and thrusts up. Linus presses my thighs back and drives forward. I become the center of a rhythm designed only for me.

Liam gasps. "Every time I think I've felt everything with you, you show me more."

"You're mine. You're his." Linus's voice breaks. "You're fuckin' ours."

Their rhythm builds, perfectly synced. Liam thrusts up as Linus slams forward. I'm suspended between them, every inch of me is touched, filled, adored. Liam's fingers slide to my clit, rub with purpose. Linus sucks on my nipples as I start to fall apart.

My orgasm hits like a lightning strike. I scream, loud and unfiltered, my pussy soaking their cocks, my body shaking with every wave.

Their thrusts turn erratic. Liam grips my hips, slams up deep, and spills inside me. Linus isn't far behind, his cock floods me too.

We stay locked, breathing, shaking, a single body made of three hearts pounding. Liam kisses the side of my neck. Linus strokes my thigh. Then, gently, they ease back.

"We want to keep every drop in you." Liam keeps me steady as their cocks slide from me, glazed with our mingled release. I whimper, already missing the connection.

Liam lifts me, easing me onto the bed, tilting my hips with pillows. Linus adds more beneath my back, my head, arranging me like something precious.

I know we've made our baby tonight. None of us say it aloud. We feel it.

Liam leans in first. His lips meet mine, full of breath and love. His hand cups my jaw as if I might drift away. Linus kisses me next, gentle but deep, tasting me. Then they kiss each other, eyes closed, mouths hungry.

We're all tied here.

Their hands begin to roam, not possessive, not rushed. Linus strokes my belly with both palms, watching my face, then the small curve of my hip. His fingertips slide along my ribs, my sides, down the outsides of my thighs like he's memorizing every line.

Liam brushes hair from my face, then traces the hollow of my collarbone, the dip between my breasts. He cups them, soft, reverent, then kisses each one, lips warm and open.

"You're so beautiful like this," Liam whispers. "Overflowin' with us."

Linus kisses the inside of my knee. "We love you so much, Avonna."

Tears burn behind my eyes. I reach up, cradle both their faces. "I've never felt more loved."

Linus cups my knee and spreads it wider to see me better.

"Look at her," Liam murmurs. "Drippin'."

"She's full," Linus adds. "We're gonna keep every drop."

Liam's fingertips trace the wet curve of my lower lips, barely brushing. Linus leans in and kisses my hip and moves down my inner thigh. He doesn't kiss my pussy. He breathes against it, warm, close, teasing. Liam's finger slides to my pulsing clit with enough pressure to make me squirm. His other hand spreads my outer lips, letting more of their come seep into view.

"Don't let it fall," he whispers. "Take it back in, baby."

Linus watches my face. His mouth hovers over my breast. "Come for us again. Pull us deeper."

Liam circles faster. The pressure builds. My pussy spasms when my orgasm hits. My body convulses to take every last drop deeper.

I arch into it, flooded and adored.

Linus's mouth latches on to my nipple as my climax rolls on. They stay with me. Watching. Touching. Loving me through every aftershock until I go soft beneath them.

Utterly satiated.

Liam shifts first, settling on my left side. He curves toward me, one arm sliding beneath my neck to cradle my head. His thigh drapes across my hip, anchoring me without crowding. His lips brush my temple, and I melt against him.

Linus follows, moving to my right, chest close to mine. He props himself on an elbow for a moment, long enough to kiss the edge of my mouth. Then he lowers onto his side, facing in, his hand resting on my stomach.

I'm sandwiched from both sides. Their chests warm against me, legs entwined with mine. My hips are still lifted by the soft stack of pillows beneath me, letting me stay open, letting nothing escape.

Liam's hand splays across my waist. He finds Linus's hand on my belly. Their fingers brush. Then intertwine.

Over me.

They lean across my chest, mouths meeting above my heart. There's no rush. Only the shared breath of men who've done everything they came here to do.

Liam hums against Linus's lips. Linus smiles into the kiss.

They kiss me next. Liam to my cheek. Linus to my collarbone. Then my lips, one after the other, until I don't know which kiss is which anymore.

Their hands drift.

One palm cups my breast. The other strokes the soft skin above my thigh. They don't grope. They don't tease. They touch as if memorizing everything we've done.

Liam's hand curls under my ribs. Linus's arm wraps under my waist. Their legs cross gently through mine, staying close. Their fingers remain linked above my stomach.

I am full. I am theirs.

Being loved like this is not punishment.

Never shame.

This is the holiest thing any of us have ever known.

Sixty-Three

LIAM

New Year's Eve

The arena breathes like it's alive.

Weighty.

Pressure pools under my boots. Climbs the risers. Settles into muscle and bone.

Climate Pledge Arena holds its breath with us, twenty thousand people leaning forward, waiting for ignition. New Year's Eve sharpens everything. Endings feel closer tonight.

Beginnings louder.

Fireball is opening for LTZ. Our last fucking show.

The room feels seismic. Two forces sharing a single night, we may be playing first but there's no hierarchy anymore.

Backstage teems with movement. Techs shouting counts. Guitars being tuned in standby. Drum cases stacked shoulder high. I roll my neck once, feel sweat already forming. Padraig stands a few feet away, sticks loose in his hands, wrists easy.

No pacing. No edge. His stillness unsettles me more than nerves ever could.

"You ready?" I ask warily.

He looks up and smiles. Calm. Certain. "Aye."

Linus stands off to the side with Avonna, not directing or watching screens tonight. He's soaking in the moment too. Sloane and Quinn have their headphones on. Avonna kisses them both and adjusts her in-ears and meets my gaze.

No hype. No pep talk. "You good?"

"As long as you are."

She nods once. No need for more words, she understands how emotional this is for me.

We climb the stairs to the side stage. The lights drop. Our intro sound detonates and the sponsoring radio announcer thunders into the mike, "Ladies and Gentlemen hometown heroes, *Firrrrrrrrebaaaaaallllllll!!!"*

We step into it and the roar slams through my chest, rattles my ribs, buzzes my teeth. Avonna moves straight to the lip of the stage and the crowd surges forward in response. Her voice slices clean through everything, strong and unflinching.

I hit the opening chord.

Padraig locks in behind me, every hit lands with purpose. No waste. No hesitation.

The first song lifts and the room moves. Irish flags wave somewhere beyond the lights. Hands rise and fall in time. Sweat runs into my eyes. My fingers burn on the strings.

I don't slow down for a fucking second.

Between songs, breath ragged, I glance back. Padraig grins, already counting the next entry.

We tear through the middle of the set. It's going by too fast. I feel twenty years collapsing inward. Small clubs with sticky floors. Vans rattling through rain. Missed birthdays. Fights screamed and swallowed. Reconciliations built on sound instead of words. Every sacrifice a thread beneath the notes.

Avonna sings and the crowd follows. Cheering. Listening. *Receiving.*

During a quick interlude, I lean toward Padraig. "Still good?"

He laughs. Loud. Free. "Never better."

Something shifts then. Not fear.

Recognition.

He isn't bracing. He isn't clinging. He's present in a way I haven't seen onstage since our college years.

By the time we reach the final few songs, my body vibrates with exhaustion and release. Avonna closes her eyes and opens the last song softer than expected. Forty thousand people quiet at once. I feel the pause ripple outward, a held breath shared by strangers, friends, and family alike.

The chorus hits and the crowd gives it back to us. Every word. Every note.

Padraig lifts his sticks high on the last beat.

Silence.

Then the noise breaks open.

We stand shoulder to shoulder, arms hooked, out of breath. Avonna laughs through tears. I scan the seats, see families blurred together, faces lifted, voices gone raw from shouting us back into existence.

Padraig steps forward and bows. No speech. No signal.

He doesn't need one.

Backstage crashes in again. Shouts. Hands. Movement. LTZ's opening bass rattles the walls. Someone shoves a bottle of water at me. I don't drink.

Padraig doesn't bother changing. He makes a beeline toward the elevator.

I follow.

Cold air slips through the crack and cuts across my sweat-soaked shirt. He grips the metal rail with both hands, shoulders rising and falling as he breathes. The noise from inside the stadium vibrates through the concrete.

"So…" I kick the ground.

"So," he answers.

For a moment neither of us moves. The space between us holds twenty years of noise and motion and stubborn loyalty. Vans breaking down in the rain. Gear hauled up back stairwells. Nights spent sleeping upright so amps wouldn't freeze. Arguments shouted, swallowed, forgiven without ever being named.

"This is really it?" I fight back tears.

He nods. "Aye. This is it."

The words settle heavy. Final. I feel them in my chest, squeezing everything we built together into dust.

"I don't know how to do this without you." My voice cracks, despite myself.

He turns then, meeting my eyes, steady and calm. "You do. You have your own family now and you'll do it differently."

"You sure you won't regret this?" I toe the ground.

"Nah." He shakes his head once. No hesitation. "I won't regret choosing my life."

I think about all the times he chose my life instead of his. Tours taken when he should have stayed home. Chances passed because the band came first. Years spent holding the rhythm steady so I could chase the music with him.

"There's nothin' left to argue about," I say, more to myself than him.

"No," he agrees. "There isn't."

I step closer. "I love you, Dar."

"Ah, Dar." He exhales, eyes softening. "I know. I love you too."

It lands deeper than any crowd ever could.

We stand there a few seconds longer, breath fogging between us. He looks lighter now.

Unburdened. I hate him and love him for it in equal measure.

I step forward without thinking. He does too.

We collide chest to chest, arms locking, the way we always have when words run out. I feel his breath hitch before he steadies. My hand grips the back of his T-shirt, fingers curling into fabric worn thin from years of travel and use.

Padraig and I are two bodies who learned each other before we learned anything else. I think about Padraig as a kid, hands too big for his first sticks, eyes locked on me during every practice. How many times he saved us without asking for credit. How many times he carried the weight so I could stay out front.

Same bones. Same stubborn heart. Same rhythm carried since the womb.

He pats my back twice, firm and familiar. I do the same. No lingering. No spectacle.

Twin love, clean and undeniable.

Then he steps back, already pulling away toward whatever comes next.

When I turn back, Avonna waits near the wing, eyes bright with everything she refuses to hide. Linus stands beside her, hands loose at his sides, watching me with the quiet understanding he always carries.

"He's done." I fight bursting into tears.

Linus wraps his arm around me. "I know. You're gonna be okay, my love."

"We're here, baby." Avonna grasps my hand. Her grip is firm, grounding. "We're always here."

I squeeze back. "Yeah, I know."

Inside, LTZ shakes the building on its comeback show. The sound rolls through the walls and into my bones. Fireworks prime somewhere overhead at the Space Needle. The timing of the countdown echoes faintly from the floor seats.

Voices rise together and then a new year is upon us.

The three of us stand at the side of the stage and seal a brand new year with a kiss. A promise of the future.

Fireball doesn't end here.

It changes shape.

For the first time, I don't chase the noise to drown the pain. I let it move through me instead. Every note from the stage behind us carries history, loss, love, stubborn hope.

I let the music say goodbye in a way words never could.

Epilogue – Eight Months Later

THE CONTRACTION HITS BEFORE she finishes sitting.

Avonna freezes halfway down, one hand gripping the back cushion, the other braced beneath her belly. I see the shift in her eyes before she makes a sound.

Focus pulls inward. Breath narrows.

"Oh," she says softly.

Then again, louder, "*Oh.*"

I look up from the kitchen table where Sloane and I are coloring a thank-you card for the neighbor. Linus sits on the floor with Quinn, folding the last of the baby clothes into neat piles.

My chair scrapes back. "Another contraction?"

"Yeah." Avonna nods, breathing through it. "Not practice."

Linus rises immediately. "You sure?"

"I've been timing them since morning." She manages a smile through the wave. "This one had teeth."

Sloane and Quinn spring up together, identical reactions from shared instincts.

"Is he coming?" Sloane asks.

"Sure seems like it, my loves," Avonna answers calmly. "Are you excited?"

Quinn spins once. "Yay! We're having a brother."

"Today." Sloane claps before wrapping her arms around Avonna's waist, reaching as far as she can. "Can I help pack?"

I gently guide her back. "Everything's ready. Remember?"

"Oh right." She bounces up and down. "I forgot for a second."

Linus hands Avonna a bottle of water and steps in behind her, arms around her shoulders, palm settling over her belly. She leans into him without hesitation. I see her body register safety.

"We waited a long time for you, little man." He pats her belly lightly. "Let's get to the hospital."

"I was starting to think I'd be pregnant forever." Avonna laughs, breathless but smiling.

I wink, a subtle nod to Avonna's extreme sexual appetite when she's pregnant. "We'd keep you pregnant forever if you'd let us."

Oblivious, Quinn raises her hand, solemn. "Can we be there when he's born?"

"Not in the room." Avonna smooths her hair. "You two get first turns when we're home."

Both girls nod, solemnly. Six years old and already fluent in love.

Linus's phone buzzes. He glances at it. "Doula's on her way. Hospital's ready."

Another contraction rolls through Avonna, stronger. Her fingers curl into my sleeve.

"I'm ready." She winces.

Before we leave, Linus makes sure Sloane and Quinn are already curled under their blankets. The nanny sits on the couch with a mug of tea, promising updates and pictures and no midnight surprises unless we ask for them.

Avonna pauses in the foyer, one hand resting on the doorframe, about to say something else.

I wrap an arm around her shoulders. "They're good."

She nods, nuzzles her face briefly into my chest, then straightens.

"Okay. Let's go."

Outside, the night is cool and clear. I guide her into the back seat, Linus gets in beside her. I take the wheel, heart pounding in a steady rhythm. Not panic.

Focus.

The city slides past in streaks of light. Red. Green. Gold. Every stoplight drags. Every turn feels sharper than necessary. I drive slower than instinct demands, faster than comfort allows.

"You okay?" I ask repeatedly.

Patiently she nods in reply each time.

Linus murmurs counts under his breath, grounding her through the waves. I keep my eyes on the road. Hands on the wheel. Knuckles white as snow.

Memory creeps in uninvited. Hospital corridors. Doctors choosing words carefully. Silence after ultrasounds. Avonna staring at walls instead of me. After the first loss, she cried for weeks. The second, she went quiet. By the third, she wanted to stop. Last time, she folded inward for a day and came back different.

More determined. We made this baby with more focus and purpose than anything else we've done with our lives.

At the hospital entrance, everything brightens. Clean. Efficient. Familiar in a way I never wanted to learn. Linus opens Avonna's door. Another contraction hits as her feet touch the pavement. She grips my arm.

"We've got you." I cover her hand with mine.

"I know."

Inside, time fractures. Names checked. Bracelets snapped on. Shoes swapped. The doula arrives breathless and smiling, sliding into place without fuss. We move into the room as if rehearsed.

Contractions build. Rise. Break. Rise again.

Avonna grips my forearm during one wave, Linus's hand locks with hers during the next. We rotate instinctively. No discussion. Instinct and presence.

Avonna rests her forehead against my shoulder. "I'm not scared," she says quietly. "I want him healthy."

I close my eyes. "He will be."

On a deep level, I believe it. Not because certainty exists. Because faith does.

Another wave crashes. She gasps. I count with her. Linus mirrors the rhythm. Sweat beads along her hairline. Determination intensifies her gaze.

"You're incredible," Linus encourages.

She laughs weakly. "I'm doing what millions of women have done for centuries."

"Yes, but none of them had our son," I remind her.

Time slows to a standstill. Contracts. Expands again. When the moment finally arrives, the room sharpens into focus. Sound drops away except for her breathing. Her hands clamp on to ours.

"Here we go" she whispers.

"Here we go," Linus and I repeat.

With one final, brutal push, he arrives. Wet. Red. Loud. His cry splits the room open.

I laugh and sob at once. Linus buries his face into Avonna's hair. She cries openly now, relief and disbelief all at once. They place him on her chest. Small. Perfect. Furious about being here.

I rest my hand on our son's back. Warm. Solid. Undeniably real. The weight of him settles into me. Every fear drops away. Every waiting room fades.

Later, when the room settles and our son sleeps against Avonna's chest, Linus lifts his phone and angles the screen toward us. Sloane's face fills it first, hair sticking up, eyes bright despite the late hour. Quinn squeezes in beside her, blanket clutched under her chin.

"Is he here?" Sloane whispers.

"He's here," Avonna answers softly. "Sleeping. I love you, my darling girls."

They grin so wide it hurts.

"Tomorrow," Linus tells them. "You'll meet him tomorrow."

Quinn nods, solemn. "Okay. Night, baby brother."

Linus steps back and watches me.

"Go." He nods toward the bassinet. I hesitate, then lift my son carefully, feeling his small weight shift against my chest. He quiets almost immediately, breath evening out.

Linus watches, eyes shining. "You okay?"

"I am now."

Avonna catches my free hand. "Look at you, boy-daddy."

"Look at us." I smile through tears.

The nurse adjusts the lights. The world narrows to this room.

This moment. Not loud. Not frantic.

Held.

I kiss my son's head. "Welcome, Lennon McGloughlin."

He squirms, fists punching at nothing.

My son through and through.

Everything else can wait.

Thank you for reading Hushed Harmony.
If this story stayed with you, I would be so grateful if you left a review. A few honest words help more than you know and mean everything to me as an author.

And if you want more, I've left something extra for you.

Behind the Scenes

Hi loves—

If you're reading this, it means you've walked with me all the way to the end of the McGloughlin Brothers and the *Charming Irish* series. I don't take this lightly. Truly.

This world lived with me for years, through chapters and dialogue written late at night, outlines scribbled in margins, conversations I kept having with these characters long after I closed my laptop.

Letting them go feels a little like leaving family behind, which feels fitting given who the McGloughlins have always been.

Thank you for trusting me with every book. For staying when the story got messy. For leaning in when the choices weren't easy or tidy or familiar. For loving these men, and the people who loved them, as fiercely as I did.

Hushed Harmony matters to me in a way that's hard to put into a neat sentence. I've loved MMF romance for years, yet one thing I kept noticing as a reader was how often the structure existed without the psychology. The heat was there. The fantasy was there.

What was missing, at least for me, was the why. Why this configuration works. Why it isn't simply sex multiplied by three, but love complicated, stretched, tested, and when done right, deepened.

I didn't want a triad where one relationship mattered more than the others. I wanted to honor the reality an MMF relationship isn't one love story. It's four.

Him and him.

Him and her.

Her and him.

Then the fragile, electric thing they build together as three.

Each bond needed oxygen.

Each connection needed agency, desire, fear, consent, and choice.

I wanted to sit inside the discomfort, jealousy, insecurity, power shifts, old wounds, and let the characters wrestle with them instead of smoothing them over.

Love doesn't become less complex when more people enter the equation. It becomes more honest or it breaks. Exploring how it holds, how it stretches without snapping, felt important.

Following each character's journey into shared space mattered because no one arrives whole. They arrive with history. With longing. With damage. Watching them learn how to love without erasing themselves, without demanding someone else disappear, became the heart of this book for me.

Not shock. Not novelty. The intimacy of choosing each other again and again, even when easier paths existed.

Ending the McGloughlin saga here felt right. Their stories always centered on loyalty, family, survival, and love refusing to fit inside expectation. Closing this chapter with *Hushed Harmony* feels less like an ending and more like a deep exhale. Earned. Intentional. Complete.

From the bottom of my heart, thank you for reading. Thank you for trusting me to take risks. Thank you for loving unconventional romance alongside me.

While this door closes, more waits ahead.

The *Hearts Without Borders* series continues, with the next book arriving this spring. A brand new rockstar romance novellas series also launches later this year, bringing shorter, intense, emotionally immersive stories rooted in music, desire, and connection.

At long last, Carter will receive his full-length book. His story waited patiently, brewing and churning and percolating in true Seattle fashion.

Once you step inside, the reason becomes clear.

Thank you for being here.
Thank you for every page turned.

I can't wait to share what comes next.

With so much love,

Kaylene

Maureen McGloughlin's Sherry Trifle

My signature holiday showstopper!
Bold, boozy, and breathtaking in a glass bowl.

INGREDIENTS

FOR THE CAKE & FRUIT BASE:
- 1 (18 OZ) BOX YELLOW OR VANILLA CAKE MIX (PREPARED AS DIRECTED ON BOX)
- 2 LARGE BOXES (6 OZ EACH) CRANBERRY OR RASPBERRY GELATIN
- 4 CUPS BOILING WATER (OR PER BOX INSTRUCTIONS)
- FRESH RASPBERRIES
- FRESH BLUEBERRIES
- POMEGRANATE ARILS
- 1–2 JARS OR CANS MANDARIN ORANGES (PEELED AND WELL-DRAINED)

FOR THE CUSTARD:
- 21 EGG YOLKS
- 1½ CUPS GRANULATED SUGAR
- 1 FULL 750ML BOTTLE DRY SHERRY

FOR THE WHIPPED CUSTARD TOPPING:
- 2 CUPS HEAVY WHIPPING CREAM
- 2 TABLESPOONS CONFECTIONERS' SUGAR
- RESERVED ⅓ OF THE COOLED CUSTARD (FROM ABOVE)

FOR GARNISH:
- RESERVED FRESH RASPBERRIES, BLUEBERRIES, POMEGRANATE ARILS, AND MANDARIN SLICES
- FRESH MINT LEAVES

INSTRUCTIONS:

STEP 1: BAKE THE CAKE
PREHEAT OVEN TO 350°F.
PREPARE THE CAKE MIX ACCORDING TO PACKAGE DIRECTIONS.
BAKE IN A 13X9-INCH PAN UNTIL GOLDEN AND A TOOTHPICK COMES OUT CLEAN.
COOL 10 MINUTES IN THE PAN, THEN TURN ONTO A WIRE RACK AND LET COOL COMPLETELY.
CUT INTO 1½-INCH CUBES.
STEP 2: ASSEMBLE THE FRUIT & CAKE BASE
IN A CLEAR GLASS TRIFLE BOWL, BEGIN LAYERING:

1. ADD A LAYER OF CAKE CUBES ACROSS THE BOTTOM.
2. TOP WITH A GENEROUS MIX OF FRESH RASPBERRIES, BLUEBERRIES, POMEGRANATE ARILS, AND DRAINED MANDARIN SLICES—ARRANGED DECORATIVELY SO THE COLORS SHOW THROUGH THE GLASS.
3. REPEAT LAYERS UNTIL THE BOWL IS ABOUT 2 INCHES FROM THE TOP, ENDING WITH FRUIT.

IN A SEPARATE BOWL, DISSOLVE 2 BOXES OF GELATIN IN 4 CUPS BOILING WATER, STIRRING UNTIL FULLY DISSOLVED.
LET SIT FOR 5 MINUTES TO COOL SLIGHTLY, THEN SLOWLY POUR JUST ENOUGH GELATIN OVER THE TOP LAYER TO SATURATE THE CAKE AND FRUIT—THE GELATIN SHOULD SOAK THROUGH THE TOP AND BEGIN TO SETTLE INTO THE LOWER LAYERS, BUT NOT FLOOD THE BOWL.
REFRIGERATE THE ASSEMBLED BASE UNTIL FULLY SET, AT LEAST 4–6 HOURS, PREFERABLY OVERNIGHT.
STEP 3: MAKE THE SHERRY CUSTARD
WHILE THE BASE SETS, PREPARE THE CUSTARD.
IN THE TOP OF A DOUBLE BOILER, COMBINE:

- 21 EGG YOLKS
- 1½ CUPS GRANULATED SUGAR
- ENTIRE 750ML BOTTLE OF DRY SHERRY

SET OVER GENTLY SIMMERING WATER.
WHISK CONSTANTLY AND VIGOROUSLY FOR 10–12 MINUTES UNTIL THE CUSTARD THICKENS TO A RICH, VELVETY CONSISTENCY (LIKE WARM PUDDING).
DO NOT STOP WHISKING OR ALLOW IT TO CURDLE.
REMOVE FROM HEAT AND ALLOW TO COOL COMPLETELY.

INSTRUCTIONS:

STEP 4: MAKE THE WHIPPED CUSTARD TOPPING
IN A CHILLED BOWL, BEAT:
- 2 CUPS HEAVY CREAM
- 2 TABLESPOONS CONFECTIONERS' SUGAR

WHIP TO SOFT PEAKS.
FOLD IN ABOUT ⅓ OF THE COOLED CUSTARD TO CREATE A RICH, SHERRY-FLAVORED WHIPPED TOPPING.
STEP 5: FINISH THE TRIFLE
- ONCE THE GELATIN BASE IS FULLY SET, GENTLY SPREAD THE REMAINING ⅔ OF THE CUSTARD OVER THE TOP. SMOOTH INTO AN EVEN, THICK LAYER.
- SPOON THE CUSTARD-INFUSED WHIPPED CREAM OVER THE CUSTARD, SMOOTHING IT FLUSH WITH THE TOP EDGE OF THE TRIFLE BOWL. THE TOP SHOULD BE LEVEL, FULL, AND CLOUD-LIKE.

STEP 6: GARNISH
USE YOUR RESERVED FRUIT AND MINT LEAVES TO DECORATE THE TOP IN A FESTIVE PATTERN—CLUSTER RASPBERRIES AND MANDARINS INTO FLOWER SHAPES, DOT WITH BLUEBERRIES OR POMEGRANATE ARILS, AND TUCK MINT LEAVES AROUND THE EDGES FOR A FRESH, HOLIDAY FLOURISH.
TO SERVE
CHILL UNTIL SERVING. SCOOP CAREFULLY TO PRESERVE LAYERS.

This dessert serves a crowd and steals the spotlight every single time.

Acknowledgments

Cover/Graphic Designer: Regina Wamba
Editor: Grace Bradley Editing, LLC
Formatting: Willow Yanarella
PR: Dani Sanchez, Wildfire Marketing
Literary Agent: Stephanie Phillips, SBR Media
Website Maven: Sherri Kiarsis, Ruby Moon Designs
My Right Hand: Willow Yanarella
Can't forget about Anna Theurer, not only one of my PAs, she has been with me since the beginning.
A special thank you the Kaylene's Backstage Krew!

you always wanted for me. Your belief steadies me. Your love holds everything I build. None of this exists without you.

I'd also like to dedicate this series to the people who support me in my business life: my assistants and staff. All of you show up when hours run short and push me to lead better. You help inspire me to maintain a public presence even on days when staying inside in my jammies seems far more appealing. You make ambition sustainable and creativity possible.

All of you have made me better, as a human, businesswoman, and author.

For my part, I'll keep doing the work and hopefully keep raising the bar by telling stories with heart.

With endless gratitude and love,

Kaylene

KAYLENE WINTER IS A best-selling author of steamy, contemporary romance.

Each character-driven novel is filled with snappy dialogue, pop-culture references and enough steam to make you fan yourself. Kaylene weaves authenticity, emotion and angst into a turbulent rollercoaster ride of love, passion and soul-searing romance always ending with a delicious HEA.

Kaylene lives in Seattle with her amazing Irish husband and her Pomsky, Phalen. She loves creating art of all kinds.

Other Titles